COUN

BOOK ONE

THE
THOUSAND SCARS

MICHAEL R .BAKER

NORDLAND
www.nordlandpublishing.com

Copyright

This books is dedicated to my family, my friends and especially to V for putting up with my annoying habits as a writer.

CONTENTS

ACKNOWLEDGMENTS

This has been a wonderful (and frustrating) journey, and I would like to express my gratitude to the many people who gave their support through the first part of my quest to bring the world of the Counterbalance into reality.

First of all, I thank Michael Kobernus and all those at Nordland Publishing for taking me under their wing and believing in me. Thank you, for everything.

I thank my family and friends for staying with me and allowing me to pursue my dreams, all those who helped proofread this book, and my support team for keeping me going.

Most of all I thank Vicky for standing with me throughout.

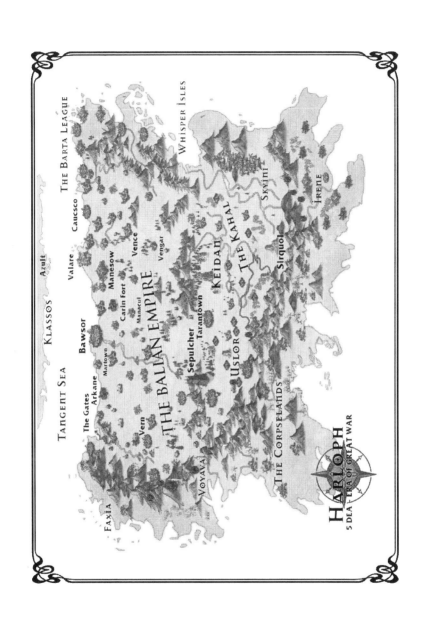

Cabal

There is no choice. With the darkest of my people's creations, I will end this abomination.

~ Pharos Animar

Bane Aldmer shivered as he glared up at the angular glyphs of ancient Valian carved into the marble wall of the burial vault. *A relic of a dead race,* he thought. Tall, fair-skinned and handsome, he was First General of the Balian Empire, a position that held much prestige. He looked around the table at his allies, those he could trust. They were few enough. *Will they support the plan?* The eight men pulled their cloaks closed, unconsciously moving closer together. *Is it cold, or fear?*

Breaking his gaze from the other councilors, Aldmer surveyed the scroll laid out flat on the sarcophagus, each corner held down a small stone. The map was truly exquisite work, by the hand of the cartographer, Marcus Dragen. He was dead now. *But so are we all, unless we do what is necessary.*

"Where is he, Aldmer?" Carris Montague snarled in his gravel voice. Tall and brutish, the copper-haired master of law glared at Aldmer through red-rimmed eyes. "We don't have time for delays."

"Patience, Carris," Hardenne Nomar interjected soothingly. "Trust his word." Hardenne, a tall, slim man, greying in the temples, his eyes still kind even after all he had seen, placed a calming hand on Montague's scarred forearm.

Carris scowled and snatched his arm away. "I do." Carris gave Aldmer the barest of nods, his way of apologizing. "I just don't like this place," he muttered, glancing around the crypt. "Why do we need to meet here?"

"So we aren't overheard by others," Aldmer said.

Their chosen meeting place was in the catacombs below the temple of the Octane in Bawsor, but it suited them; only members of the elusive Pharos Order were allowed access into this section of the tunnels, where the great priests of the Sepulcher were buried. *An odd place for advisors to the greatest kingdom in Harloph*, Aldmer thought.

The chamber was wide and low ceilinged, an ancient tomb marked with the faith of the Octane. *Our eight-bodied savior*, Aldmer thought, his handsome face twisted as his lip curled into a snarl. Aldmer had never felt any loyalty towards the gods. Making their priests' final resting place the site of the secret council meetings amused him.

Lanterns kept the chamber well-lit in contrast to the dark tunnels they had traversed to reach the chamber.

Hardenne rapped a knuckle against the cold stone slab they had repurposed as a table. He was Aldmer's oldest friend and Aldmer instinctively knew that he would be the hardest to convince. And if that was not enough, Aldmer was well aware that Carris had his own misgivings about Hardenne, but friendship still counted for something.

"I hope this doesn't take long," muttered Long Brandon, pulling his cloak tighter. He glanced towards the chamber entrance. "My wife's bedridden with fever. I need to get back."

"It'll be over soon," Aldmer said confidently. "Then you can go to her. But the fate of the empire depends on this meeting, Brandon. Sacrifices need to be made."

Brandon's narrow face displayed his obvious displeasure, but he reluctantly bowed his head in acknowledgement. A voice crept from the shadows then, to Aldmer's trepidation and relief. *At last, he is here.*

"It's good to see you, Aldmer, and your council. Welcome to my temple." The voice was weary, feeble and old. A man limped arthritically into view from one of the doorways. He was draped in a black shawl as worn and frayed as he was, with a distinct hunch to his shoulders. Several of the council muttered, others taking a step away from the old man. Aldmer ignored their looks and walked over to greet the newcomer.

"No need to apologize, Raphael. We're here at your pleasure."

Raphael bowed his head. "Indeed you are." He crossed to the map, and extended a withered hand, one bony finger tracing the line of a river.

One by one, the council gathered in closer, except Petere and Pierad Cordon, the two brothers from Bawsor. The elder and stronger of the two, Petere's shrewd green eyes narrowed at Raphael with mistrust.

"What's he doing here?"

"Mind your courtesies, Petere," Carris growled.

"Fuck you. Why is a priest of the Order here, Aldmer? Explain! The Order is always interfering in our affairs," Petere spat out, his chin jutting.

"Raphael is the head of the Order's operations here in Bawsor," Aldmer reminded him coolly. "Second only to Hinari himself. You'd do well not to sully his name."

"That still doesn't explain why he's here," Petere muttered, slightly deflated.

The old man leaned forward, his bloodshot eyes fixed on his challenger. "I'm here to help you fight this war," Raphael said, his voice like dry sand. "Need I remind you, that the Dominion was responsible for the murder of Empress Adriena? May the gods forgive them, for I surely won't. They must pay for their savagery. Now war is on our doorstep, and we need to act fast."

Petere didn't reply, but at the mention of the Empress he looked away, unable to meet the old man's gaze. With a heavy sigh and a shrug, he joined the other men around the map. They made for a strange council. Aldmer might have smiled at the sight of them, but the mention of the Empress took that away.

Adriena had been their queen, his ruler. She was beloved. Her slaughter at the hands of Dominion assassins was the catalyst for the war. Aldmer frowned, unwilling to dwell on what could not be changed. "We have a lot to get through," he said, "and time isn't on our side." He examined the map, the continent of Harloph and the Empire stretched from the Tangent Sea in the north to the southern shorelines of its sister continent Klassos, where the much larger Selpvian Dominion ruled. The south of the map was far less detailed, down from the Order-held lands of Kahal, then the western oracle steppes of Voyava, and the mountains of the old Valian fortress, the forbidden city of Sirquol. The hair on Aldmer's neck prickled as he looked at Sirquol, remembering the tales. But that was not important now. First things first, they needed to discuss the recent setbacks.

"We've all heard the news from Klassos, I trust?" He addressed the group at large. There was a murmur of reluctant assent.

"Aye," muttered Carris. "The news has brought chaos to Bawsor. I had to hang several men when a mob panicked and tried to storm the Temple."

"The last of our forces in Klassos were defeated. The remnants have fled back across the Tangent," the mousy Pierad moaned, the youngest in their group at twenty-two. "The Dominion will surely invade!"

"Brother, keep your wits about you," Petere said harshly. "This war isn't over yet."

Standing to the right of Petere, the huge Mitori slammed his hand on the stone table. His thick Faxaen accent could not mask his anger and frustration at the news. "We should never have mounted another offensive. The High Council should have listened to us!"

Aldmer regarded the big man through narrowed eyes. He needed Mitori, and his skill with a blade, but his habit of stating the obvious was grueling. Aldmer cleared his throat.

"It is grave tidings. All our allies in Klassos have been defeated, or have conceded to the Dominion. The Tangent Sea is all that protects us. Our fleet must hold them."

The navy had already taken severe losses in the five years since the Empress had been killed. But the Council had taken measures. Two hundred warships from the major houses had joined the remains of the royal fleet in patrolling the wide channel.

"We cannot stop the Dominion crossing the Tangent," Augustin Temzinar mused, the Keeper of Ships for the capital. "Their naval strength is triple ours. They could engage our entire fleet in equal strength, and still have ships enough to land elsewhere."

If only we could have taken Azult. It was the prominent harbor in Klassos. But with their reduced strength, attacking the formidably defended port now would be suicide. Aldmer took a deep breath. "There is too much at risk now, and squandering the Empire's fleet in such a risky attack would likely doom us all." He paused. "I fear we can't stop the Dominion invasion from sea, but we'll make them fight for every inch on land."

"If it comes to it, we can defeat them on our own ground, surely?" Pierad waved at the map, gesturing towards the capital city, where the map-maker had inked its name in red: Bawsor. "The capital has never been taken by force," he finished proudly.

Many were unconvinced by his bravado. Strong walls and a defendable location made it well protected, but would it stand against a protracted siege, where supply lines could be cut at any time? Of course, the invaders had to reach the capital, where a naval landing would be nearly impossible. Only by land could they logistically do it.

"The survivors should make it back to the capital in a few days, if the winds are good," Hardenne said.

"Even with the survivors, and our levies," Brandon grunted, "how many then?"

"About one hundred thousand, maybe twenty more," Carris replied.

"What about the Order? They have men. Surely they will fight too," Pierad said.

Petere snickered dryly. "The Order. They lack the belly to fight."

Mitori chortled thickly along with him, his deep voice booming. "Even if they number forty thousand, how much have they really proved to us?"

Raphael turned his gaze from one man to another, his face carefully neutral.

Aldmer brooded. *The Order has a strong military force, but are they strong enough to face what's coming?* He kept silent. He'd never cared much for the Order's whims himself. But his concern steeped further than their fanaticism. Petere wasn't wrong though. They haven't proven themselves in battle for a long time. Their leader, Hinari Amos, had done a great deal in his long life to improve the Order's archaic forces, and although they were well equipped and superbly trained, their tactics were ancient.

"What of the Barta League?" Petere said. "I know they declared neutrality, but the Dominion won't show weakness. They don't have the strength to stop them should they attack. They've been sending requests for reinforcements for weeks."

"We heard from Valare four days ago," Carris replied. "Lazarus has united with the rest of the League. They've unified their fleets to patrol their shores. We'll know if the Dominion approach."

"Lazarus is an old man. Aldmer's fingertips caressed the worn parchment of the map as he spoke. "It's a hard task for him."

"He defended Valare when it was besieged by House Duston for over a year," Carris reminded him. "He's not useless." Mitori snorted and Aldmer silenced him with a sharp glance.

"Even so, they can only muster eleven thousand men at best, with Valare's forces totaling half of that," Pierad pointed down at the eastern side of Harloph to where the Barta League was clustered in several black blots on the parchment. "That won't be enough to hold off the Dominion's assault, should they attack."

"Would they even land on their shores?" Hardenne asked. "The League has no quarrel with Klassos."

"I would. Attack the weak link," Carris replied.

Pierad whispered something to his brother. Petere rounded on him at once. "No, brother. We will not discuss anything with that traitor."

"What's he saying?" Aldmer asked, his cold voice breaking over them all. Pierad looked down, his cheeks flushed.

"He's suggesting we should re-negotiate with Mercer Duston," Petere snapped. "Like hell we should. That bastard turned on the Empire and killed thousands. You wouldn't understand brother; you were too young back then."

Pierad tried to reason. "Yes, he's scum, and an exile, but the Dominion is clearly the greater threat. Besides, Mercer's break from the Empire was over fifteen years ago. You said it yourself, Aldmer. We need more men. Mercer has an experienced force at his command. He gained strong encampments in the east during his exile, and he's rebuilt ties with the League. He could be useful."

"No," Aldmer said shortly. "We will not talk to traitors of the Empire." He exuded authority, but inside, a battle raged. *We need all the men we can get. Maybe we'll need to call for help from those we hate.* Even so, he mentally shuddered at the thought of having to potentially join forces with Mercer Duston. The siege of Valare had lasted for nearly a year before the forces of the Empire united to crush him. Rather than face justice, Mercer had fled east with his surviving sons. *Adriena, our sweet matriarch. You should have burned him alive.*

The discussion revolved around defense of the Empire, including troop strength, patrols, and enemy movement. The situation was dire. Every man knew it.

It's time. Aldmer turned to Raphael, who had been listening intently to every word. "Well, Raphael," he said calmly. "You said you may have a solution which will change this war. You know what we face. It is time you proved your words. Tell them what you told me."

"As you wish, Aldmer." Raphael looked up. Despite his age, his alert gaze took in all around him. "There is a way. It is costly, but the need is great. The Empire's salvation is not through the living, but rather the dead."

There was a stunned silence at his words.

"You mean necromancy," Pierad said, his face twisting in disgust.

Hardenne stepped back from the table, too surprised to speak. Aldmer met his accusatory look, unflinching.

"Not quite." Raphael's eyes glittered. The room filled with the men's mutterings, some of whom were outraged, but most regarded the priest with curiosity.

"Necromancy? But I thought it were impossible," grunted Mitori, while Long Brandon raised a bushy eyebrow.

Aldmer said nothing. *Necromancy.* Virtually all sense and knowledge of magic in the world, or their corner of it, had been lost with the fall of the Valians, but there were still some rare incidents here and there throughout the centuries. The Pharos Order, descendants of Valia, had enforced a ban on all magical arts throughout the Empire and the rest of the continent, since before their mutual alliance at the Empire's birth. Aldmer had a stark memory of his early days in the teaching schools of the Order, where elderly scholars lectured the students on the dangers of the art, and the grim underworld which lay beneath them. The realm of the damned, they called it. *And now, they're beckoning for us again, if we believe the stories.*

"You're suggesting we turn to sorcery to fight this war?" Hardenne's cracked lips made a thin hard line.

"To an extent." Raphael replied. "My kin has purged much of the knowledge of such arts, but some remain. What I am proposing is one of the darkest, forbidden arts known to our Order. The last rites of the Old Masters themselves." He hesitated a moment, looking around at them all. "The Counterbalance is necromancy of the highest level. Much has been deduced from its existence, but its origin comes from the creation of this plane. You're all familiar with the legends, I trust?"

Aldmer had learned a great deal in his time with Raphael. Even though he first heard of dark tales a few years ago, it was still imprinted on his soul. He shuddered. The others nodded solemnly.

"Your kind's been interfering in everyone's lives for centuries!" Temzinar spat. "Why would one of the Order be convincing us to use the same arts that they've been purging?"

Aldmer raised a pointed finger to the man, and was about to retort when he was interrupted.

"No," Petere pointed at Raphael. "Sorry, my lord, but Temzinar speaks true. I'd like to know why."

Raphael's reply came silky and cold. "I'm not like my associates within the Order," he said. "They're afraid of the past. You can scarcely blame them. My kin are the living descendants of Valia. They used sorcery and it ended in their destruction. But it is our only means of winning this war. That's why I approached Aldmer."

"You brought me the scroll, Raphael?" Aldmer asked him.

The old man reached inside his robes and retrieved a worn and ancient parchment. Wordlessly, he handed it to Aldmer, who unrolled it with stiff fingers.

Hardenne leaned forward to get a better look, his eyes furrowing at the strange symbols on the papyrus.

"What is this?" he asked.

"Secrets of the old world," Aldmer said quietly. Hardenne made a noise of disgust. Looking around his council members, Aldmer could see that Petere and Temzinar felt the same. *You know his teachings now*, Aldmer thought. *You can read it again.* He lifted up a silent finger to his lips as he continued, his lips wordlessly moving as he traced the symbols upon the scroll.

"Well?" Carris whispered. "What is it? Tell us."

"You can read that?" The Faxaen asked, slack-jawed.

Aldmer shook his head as he gazed down at his own hands, almost as though he were seeing them for the first time. Instead, he addressed Raphael. "Tell us. How'd you get your hands on this?"

"It's been inside our vaults for centuries, Lord Aldmer." Raphael replied. It's only an excerpt, however. The only true version lies within the Keidan,"

As one, the council shivered at the mention of that unholy place. The light in the chamber took that opportunity to flicker, making the moment more ominous still. They all knew of the Keidan, far south in the Kahal steppes. The stronghold lay in shadow, its very existence seldom admitted. Even the native Kahal tribes had only fear and mistrust for the great underground citadel. Its black towers, the only part visible above ground, were thought to have been scorched by sorcery.

"Very well," Aldmer said, almost to himself. He looked to Raphael. "I already know what must be done to perform this ritual. If it's successful, it will turn the tide of the war in our favor." Aldmer gestured. "Raphael, tell them how it is to be done."

Raphael smiled. "What I am about to tell you is forbidden knowledge, punishable by death by my foolish brothers. But since the future of the Empire is at stake . . ."

And so he told them. When he finished, Hardenne stumbled and nearly fell. Aldmer reached out a hand to support him. The battle-hardened Temzinar, a man that had killed more men than Aldmer could count, was pale, his mouth hanging open in horror.

"You mean for us to commit mass murder?" Petere asked, in strangled tones. "You're suggesting we slaughter untold thousands of our own, maybe millions! How can we support this?"

"Are you saying," Pierad shuddered, his face a grey pallor. "That this abomination was used to create our world?"

Several men were clearly upset at the prospect, but others took a more pragmatic view, and nodded reluctant approval at the proposition. Aldmer pushed his concerns away, all the niggling questions about the lore. *Do we even know the truth?* It made no difference.

"That is what the elders believe," Raphael replied simply. "It's a weapon of power beyond the comprehension of any mind, but yes. Some say it was the final weapon wielded by the Old Masters, in order to break the prison of the Messeahs, and enable the opening of a rift from their realm into the world we call home today. The pinnacle of creation itself. Imagine that." His voice tailed off, his eyes watery.

Messeahs. The old stories of the sentinels guarding the shadowlands. The demons of the underworld. Aldmer could recite those childhood tales even now.

Shaking his head furiously, Pierad stumbled away from the table as though in a daze.

"And nobody else has attempted to use it?" The voice belonged to Carris, full of wonder and longing.

"Who would?" Raphael spoke softly. "It's a lost relic known only to those who have extensively studied the lore, and much of that died in Sirquol, along with the Valians. Very few even know about it, let alone are able to perform the ritual. Oh, there have been attempts of course. But those days are long gone. But you have the strength, Bane Aldmer." He placed a hand upon Aldmer's own. "It is a weapon of terrible power, but we have need of it."

Nobody spoke for a moment. Aldmer squared his shoulders, his back straight. He took in the gaze of each man there, one by one.

"Men. What say you?" Aldmer said finally.

"What of the high council, Aldmer?" Carris spoke up, his harsh voice cutting through them all. "They will not listen to this, we all know it. Their hearts are too grey."

"Then we will cut them out," Aldmer replied with icy coolness. He caught Hardenne's eye. His oldest friend looked dismayed.

"Is there no other option?" Pierad asked sharply. "This is going to create unimaginable suffering."

"Unless we can find a way to mobilize an army to defeat the Dominion before they invade, then I'm afraid not," Aldmer replied. "This is my home, gentlemen. I have lived here since the day I was born. I will not let it fall. Remember the Empress, slaughtered before our eyes by Dominion's knives. No, I will not stand by and watch our homes be destroyed."

"But to invoke such a weapon," Hardenne said, "We're talking about the deaths of so many." His face screwed up in anguish. "Is it even worth it?"

"Of course it's worth it," Carris snapped angrily. "This is the Empire's very survival we're talking about."

"This is war," Temzinar grunted. "We're facing that reality at any rate. But I don't know." Shaking his head, Temzinar looked to their leader. "Do I have some time to think it over? It's not a decision to take lightly."

Aldmer's eyes narrowed, but he nodded. *I still have use for you.* He and Raphael had discussed Temzinar at length. "Very well. What about you?" He said, addressing Pierad. The younger man looked conflicted, until his brother whispered in his ear. Pierad gulped, and the two embraced.

"I guess we have no choice. May the gods forgive us for what we're about to do." Pierad looked around, then shot a glare at Raphael. "You'd better not be playing us false, old man."

Raphael said nothing. The others nodded, but some looked uneasy. Petere in particular seemed sickened. Like Temzinar, he asked for more time.

Finally, Aldmer turned to Hardenne. "What say you, my friend?" *I know your answer.*

Hardenne took a long time to speak. "I don't know. It is a lot to ask. May I too, have time to think it over?" It was a blatant lie. His answer was written on his face.

Aldmer nodded his consent. *What have I become?*

"Very well. Gentlemen, it has been a long evening, and we have much to do. We meet tomorrow with the High Council." He turned to Raphael. "Thank you, greatly," he said softly. "We will meet again soon."

Raphael bowed his head. "I am here to serve." His gaze passed over them all, lingering on Hardenne, Temzinar and Petere. Then he clapped his hands and a young child carrying a torch entered the chamber.

"Go with the boy, and he'll show you the way to the surface," Raphael said, nodding to Hardenne. Hardenne took the lead, Temzinar and Petere following. As he passed Aldmer, he bowed his head, unable to meet Aldmer's eyes.

They made their way down twisting passages, the small child sure in his steps. Aldmer watched them go, surprised at the lack of remorse in his heart. *It is for the best*, he thought. There could be no division. Either they stood united against the enemy, or they would fall.

"How old are you, child?" Hardenne asked the boy. His voice was loud in the stifled silence of the tunnels. The young boy turned around only briefly. He could not have been more than six.

"Old enough to serve," he replied in a gentle voice. His eyes were a piercing blue, two chips of ice. "This way now."

Further and further they stepped through dark corridors until they reached a doorway so small that Hardenne needed to stoop to pass through. Temzinar and Petere followed just behind.

Hardenne struggled with the knowledge of what Aldmer had requested. *We cannot allow such sorcery!* Behind him, footsteps echoed from the stone walls as if a larger group were following. When he looked round, all Hardenne saw were the other council members.

"Are you well?" the boy asked, making him jump.

"Yes . . . of course." Hardenne's mouth was very dry.

Slowly, he entered the small chamber. Inside was another sarcophagus, this one very small.

"Go to it," the boy said to Hardenne, nodding to the stone casket.

Hardenne approached the center of the chamber reluctantly, his feet dragging. He could not deny he was afraid. It occurred to him how cold it had become, biting deep through his clothes. Temzinar and Petere followed, shivering. Hardenne took a last look at the young boy's face. Clenching his jaw, he examined the rough surface of the sarcophagus. There were marks carved into the stone. *What am I supposed to be seeing here?*

The markings did not make any sense to him. And yet, there was something familiar. A lump rose in his throat. This was history, the very blood of their ancestors. It was painful, almost cruel, yet he found it beautiful nonetheless. But something didn't add up. Suddenly, the door behind them slammed shut.

"Why are we here?" Petere demanded, reaching for his sword.

"To ensure the end. Or rather, the true end," the child replied. "We cannot have non-believers."

The voice was high and cold. With alarm, Hardenne turned, nearly falling backwards in shock as he saw that they were surrounded by men carrying naked steel, their faces obscured by hoods, bodies draped in black robes.

"What are you doing?" Hardenne demanded. He reached for the hilt of his blade, but his fingers were clumsy. He was never any good with a sword.

The child's eyes twinkled. "You don't need to fear, child," the boy whispered.

Petere ripped his sword from its scabbard. "What is the meaning of this!" He raised his weapon, only to let out a roar of pain as one of the hooded figures wordlessly slashed at his throat with a bare hand. Petere dropped his sword with a deafening clang, clutching at himself. Hardenne looked on in horror as blood, black in the muted light, pumped from a gash in Petere's neck. His eyes were wide in shock, then slowly started to close as he slumped to the ground. Nobody moved, but the look on the boy's face had changed. There was something almost predatory there now. This drove Hardenne into action. He took two steps and seized Temzinar's arm.

"Captain!" He hissed, pulling on his sleeve. "What are-" Temzinar wrenched his arm away with such violence that Hardenne was sent sprawling to the ground.

"What's wrong with you?" Hardenne demanded, his voice rising. As he scrambled to his feet, Temzinar collapsed to the ground; his powerful legs crumpling and shaking beneath him. A horrific stench filled Hardenne's nostrils, pungent and cloying. *It stinks of death*. The smell was overpowering but something else was filling his lungs. It was cold and paralyzing, slowing his movements. He looked to Temzinar, only to recoil in disgust; there was only a gaping hole where once there had been a face, all tissue and bone having crumpled, dissolved. With a great, painful heave of his stomach, Hardenne vomited onto the ground, chunks of his last meal splattering already soiled clothes. He screamed hoarsely, eyes wide. He reached for his blade, but his fingers meet only an empty scabbard.

Hardenne twisted and groped for his sword. It was his only chance, the blade was his life. Righteous anger burst through his veins, strengthening him. As the cloaked figures closed in, Hardenne lunged for the boy. The child did not move as Hardenne thrust, the razor sharp steel hitting its mark, biting deep into the boy's chest until the blade slid out of his back. No blood welled from the wound.

"This will not do." The boy's voice again, cool and faint, barely above a whisper. He looked completely unperturbed by Hardenne's attack. "We are granting you a kinder fate. Yield to us, child, and you will serve a greater cause."

The words broke through into Hardenne's consciousness. He stood, the feeling of weakness in his veins extinguished by a burst of fury. His friends. They had killed them!

"What are you?" Hardenne pleaded, as his voice wavered and broke. A sudden burst of pain tore through his left calf and he collapsed to the ground. He screamed against the white-hot agony.

"We are only servants, child. We see that the duty is done." The boy approached him, holding out a gentle hand. Hardenne thrashed around, half blind. Temzinar's faceless corpse lay on the ground two feet away. The stench in the chamber was overpowering, shit and the metallic scent of blood. Hardenne couldn't move, his eyes fixed upon the child standing over him. Emotionless blue orbs stared into his own. Hardenne shied away, suddenly focused upon a curious symbol burned into the child's neck. Through the fog clouding his brain, recognition began to penetrate his senses. He knew that symbol. An assassin's refuge whose name was soaked in blood. His fingers grasped thin air, helpless.

"What?" Hardenne lacked the strength to say anything else. *The Keidan. What are they doing in the capital?*

"Easy, child." The boy smiled, raising his hand. "Look behind you, and you shall know the truth." Hardenne did not trust in this, but slowly began to crane his neck, every inch torture. However, his gaze had barely shifted from the child's face when a hiss made his blood run cold. It was a foreign thing, alien. The sound paralyzed him. Cold filled his lungs. The hiss pounded through him, the sound in his head. It was inside of him! He shut his eyes tightly. He did not care what they did. He would not look.

"See, human, and embrace your fate." A voice rasped, cold and thick with an odd accent, but Hardenne understood. It sounded like ice cracking and it demanded obedience. Hardenne felt his eyelids pulled open. He blinked automatically. There was smoke and gleaming grey eyes. He stared into the darkness, into the eyes. He could see something there, a force he recognized, something primal. It was hatred. Hardenne screamed.

Eye of the Tide

Malharbor used to be beautiful. The sky burned violet from the fires of my kin. Now the air is poison and only decayed ruins remain.

~ Pharos Animar

War will reach us soon. The white haired patriarch of Valare, Lazarus Oltor, sat at his wide, oak desk, his already wrinkled brow furrowing. He glanced up to the window. Outside lay the city, blanketed in a dense cloud of fog. It was quiet, sounds muffled, the normal hustle and bustle subdued. Even Lancil, his pet falcon, was not his usual vocal self.

Footsteps rang out on the marble floor. Piez Vertigen entered the Atrium. He stopped before Lazarus' desk, bowing low, his eyes puffy and grey. *He's tired.* They all were.

"Morning, my Jaal." The youthful man's perfunctory smile did not reach his eyes.

Lazarus grimaced. The formal title of Valarian leadership still sat queer, even after twenty years. "Please, there's no need to call me that."

Piez chuckled. "Just force of habit, Lazarus. Apologies . . . my Jaal." His shrewd eyes gleamed and this time the smile was real.

Piez Vertigen was young for a chancellor. His father Samuel had died during the siege when he was just a baby, and Lazarus had become something of a surrogate father to the boy. He was a good man, and intelligent. *Just like his father.* Although Lazarus was

20

the supreme leader of Valare, most of the day-to-day business of running the city was down to Piez. That suited Lazarus. *Valare belongs to him, not me.*

"I've recruited another two hundred men into the Keep Guard," Piez said.

"Good. They can join Cassel for training drills. It's essential we hold the port."

Piez shivered, looking pointedly at the open windows. Lazarus' chambers were cold, but he didn't feel it, in spite his old age. "I apologize for the chill." he added. "Should I call for a fire?"

Piez shrugged. "No need. I won't take up much of your time." He glanced over the table where Lazarus was sitting. It was littered with old letters, maps, and details on the city's defenses.

"Anything from across the Tangent?" Lazarus asked, as he did every day. Instantly, Piez's face darkened.

"Not today. We've kept a lookout across sea. I sent out the few warships we have left, though I fear they won't see much in these conditions." He grimaced. "The Dominion has already broken the lines and attempted invasion. The Empire's forces cannot hold the tide much longer."

We know that. Lazarus looked out of the window. *Damn this mist.* There was a melancholy to this unnatural fog, blowing in from the Tangent. The last he'd heard from the Empire was that they had withdrawn most of their men from Klassos to their borders, to prepare for the invasion they knew was coming. On the horizon, plumes of smoke still rose from the ruins of slums near the bay, testament to the most recent attack. A small force had bypassed the guards and their naval watch, only a few days earlier. They had beaten it back, but it had sent fear into the hearts of his people. It was little more than a probe, intended to instill terror. *It mustn't happen again.* On Valare's walls stood spearmen, archers and scorpions, ready to protect the city. The Dominion was going to attack again, but when?

"Any word back from Bawsor?"

"None." Piez's hands clenched into fists at his side. "They still think protecting their coastline is a higher priority than our borders. Valare has a great strategic position in Harloph. They know this. But do they do anything?" He slammed his hand down on the hard oak of the table in frustration. "No. Instead of the Legion, they send us Order fanatics, and expect us to thank them."

Lazarus bristled at that. *Fanatics who have no business being here.* As part of their defensive agreement, the Order had sent men to the city. For almost a month they had been here, lording it up like they owned the place. They were arrogant, demanded too much, and scoffed at the faith of Valare's population, mostly following the old Octane gods. *And they keep making new demands.* He looked to the letter he had been writing. He had to address that, and soon. *When will they realize that they will never have him?* Even so, he needed these men. The assault by the Dominion had shaken the city, and an extra five hundred swords did much to bolster resolve. But what good would they be if the Dominion attacked again? The Order's military had much to answer for.

A servant approached. She was dressed in a simple white dress, her long black hair tied back. She held out a note. Lazarus took it.

"What about the League? About their armies?" he asked, unfolding the parchment.

"Onslong and Garro have mobilized, but the rest haven't responded," Piez replied, his eyes flicking to the messenger.

I should send reinforcements, but we've enough trouble. If he were a Dominion commander, he would move against Valare. He looked down at the note the girl had given him. *Not again.* Another demand from the Order's lapdog, Sil Naso. Even though Lazarus had left them decades ago, he maintained peaceful relations with the Order. And they'd repaid that peace with insolence. With no need or desire to read the message, he crumpled the parchment and threw it on the table.

"Very well," he addressed the girl kindly. "I shall see them in my solar. Bring me breakfast. I'm going to need it if I'm to deal with these fools."

The girl nodded and hurried off.

"They've started already?" Piez clucked his tongue in sympathy.

"Yes," Lazarus said shortly. "They can wait."

The girl returned shortly with a tray containing various titbits. She placed it on the table then left. Lazarus picked at it, eating sparsely while he studied reports.

It was an hour later when he finally graced the unwanted visitors with his presence. Three men were admitted into the chamber. Their clothing clearly marked them as members of the Order; blood red robes embroidered with a black and silver sigil.

Lazarus scowled. *Thank the Gods I got away from all that.* He stared at the argent sigil on one of the man' chest: Two falcons entwined. A pretty symbol, but one of slavery. There was silence, except for the sudden shrill cry of his falcon from his cage. Lancil's beady eye was fixed upon the unwelcome arrivals. *You're an excellent judge of character, my friend.* None of them looked happy from being made to wait. Lazarus suppressed a smile.

He recognized Sil Naso immediately. He had known him for years, and although courteous enough, Lazarus had grown very tired of the man's constant visits, bleating with the voice of Hinari, head of the Order. It was a shame the old man was still in power. Powerful and wise in his youth, Hinari was greatly weakened from war and age, and long past any use to the world, Lazarus believed. He still demanded respect from his subjects, who treated him as a god. Sil clearly thought he should be afforded the same respect.

Lazarus examined them with distaste and growing anger. *When will they realize they have no power here? At least Sil tries to exact some control over his garrison.* He turned his gaze to the two other commanders of the Order's garrison. Sil was amiable at the best of times, but his two fellow commanders were both arrogant and foul tempered. He could feel the glares of them both upon him as they came closer.

Lazarus let the silence extend uncomfortably, until at last Sil cleared his throat.

"Jaal Lazarus." He bowed his head deeply, but with a twisted smirk on his face. "It's an honor to see you again. I thank you for your hospitality in allowing us to defend Valare against the challenge of the northern infidels." He was a tall man, handsome and strong, his long copper hair tied back in a ponytail. He carried an oversized tanto blade by his side, a sign of his status.

At least Sil shows courtesy even if he mocks. The men on either side of Sil displayed far less regard, the shorter of the two regarding Lazarus with open contempt. He watched them warily. He had made no friends within the Order since his departure. While Sil at least attempted conciliation, Loch and Quinn were entirely different. Lazarus knew their families by name, and knew that both had lost men in the south to Tyir, when his friend had used necromancy to defeat the Order.

Sil began again, his voice unctuous. "I apologize for dragging you so early from your rest."

Barely two minutes, and they already anger me.

"Why are you here, Sil? Speak quickly, and go back to your duties. I'm a busy man." Lazarus leaned on the edge of his table, his fingers clasped together tightly. He was an old man, shorter than the men of the Order, but they cowed like sheep.

Sil cleared his throat. "Hinari asks, once again, for you to hand over Tyir of Irene to the Order, to reclaim the justice stolen from us. We have been patient with you, but he has flaunted his freedom long enough. And so have you, for protecting him. It's been years. Let him go."

And there it was again. How many times must Hinari be told? Tyir will find this amusing. Where was he anyway? Lazarus glanced coolly into Sil's eyes. "No."

The commander strained to achieve a cold, sycophantic smile. "Lazarus, please think about this. You have denied us justice for a very long time. Hinari is growing impatient with you, my Jaal. He knows you who freed Tyir. It's been twenty years, and he wants his head. Hinari was merciful enough to pardon you,"—he glanced at both his comrades—"although many within the Order wanted you dead."

"Aye, me, for one." The man to Sil's left stepped forward. His bald head was covered with scars and voice grated with undisguised hatred. "You betrayed the Order, Lazarus. If not for the mercy of Hinari you would be dead in a ditch with your balls hacked off. You know what we do to traitors."

"That's good to know, Loch." Lazarus was used to discourtesy from the Order. "When are you going to get it into your thick skulls? Tyir is not yours to take. He is under our protection, and free of your laws. You have no authority here."

"You forget that Hinari is your leader too, Lazarus." Sil's face flushed red beneath his beaten olive skin. "You share the same blood, and you swore the same oath we all swore. Just because you deserted does not release you from service. When you swear to the Order, you obey for life."

"I swore, Sil. I will not deny that. But I am an old man now. An old man of Valare." The debate was wearing thin on him. "My time serving the Order is long past."

"But what right did you have to set him free?" Loch's eyes were bulging as he spat the words out. "His fate was in our hands."

"I have right enough, Loch." There was a bite of savage impatience to Lazarus' tone now. *These fools weren't there to see the truth.* His hand caressed an old book, flipping it open with rather more force than necessary. Dust flew everywhere. He felt a surge of triumph as the men of the Order recoiled from his rage. "As the Jaal of Valare, it is my duty to protect all the city's assets. Tyir is valued here, more than I can say for the likes of you."

It was the truth, or at least part of it. Tyir was guilty as sin. It was mere chance that Lazarus had passed by his cell, where he was awaiting execution.

"Valued?" Loch whispered, his shocked reproaches ringing through the hall. "He tortured countless victims and experimented on their corpses!" His hand reached for his sword "He murdered hundreds of our kind during the Kahal civil war. Not only that, but he's responsible for more murder of our kin down there. Only a month ago we found his vile servants raiding one of our banks. Dozens of the Order were killed!"

Lazarus blinked. He didn't know that. "What of it?"

"What of it?" Loch repeated incredulously. How can you protect a monster like him? He has flouted our laws, studying knowledge forbidden by the Order, and he has violated nature with his vile necromancy. Do you not realize what he's done? We almost lost everything because of creatures like him!"

We? Lazarus nearly smiled at that. Loch was young, early twenties and green as a sapling, but he acted like a master of the arcane, of the knowledge of the great Pharos himself. Pharos, the hero who had saved them all from the horrors of the Chaos. That sad chapter turned Harloph into a corpse. *And now the might of Klassos bears down upon us, to sweep away the canker.* It was a disturbing thought.

"You speak as though you think you understand. I would say nothing more on that subject, before you embarrass yourself, my boy." Lazarus stood, his slender, bony fingers clasped into a fist in front of him. They fell silent.

"This is exactly why I left," he said. "How can you evolve, when regulation is all you know? You say that we should shelter ourselves from the terrors of world, and just forget our history. I say why not explore the past, where we can learn from it, and better our own lives? That's why the Order is doomed. Why should the world convene to your laws?" He felt his voice rising with fury, but he could no longer stop himself.

"You call yourselves peacekeepers? You try to persecute men like Tyir for his crimes, when you are all guilty of greater atrocities." Lazarus paused, anger burning inside him. He didn't need to remind them of their crimes. *I know what you bastards do to those you call unclean.* "You wish to condemn Tyir when you're no better than him."

27

"Such arrogance!" Loch's mouth twisted into a murderous frown as he pulled his sword halfway out of its scabbard.

Sil stepped forward immediately, wrenching him back. "Enough," he hissed. "We need to be diplomatic! We cannot fight while the Dominion threatens."

The guards at the door had dropped into combat stance, their spears lowered, ready to charge. Just one command and Lazarus could condemn the lot of them to their deaths. But it wouldn't be without cost.

The Order would not tolerate such an act. Hinari would never forgive the murder of his own. *They would deserve it, but even so. . . Tempting though it may be, I need them to help hold Valare.* Lazarus glanced at Quinn, who as yet remained silent. Tall and imposing, he was less vocal then Loch, but more dangerous by far. *He will snap sooner or later.* Once again, Commander Sil made the first attempt at diplomacy.

"Listen, Lazarus. I hold you in high regard, and I have only the deepest apologies for my comrade's behaviour." Sil shot Loch a furious glance. "But it is my duty, as it is yours, to ensure that Tyir is brought safely into our custody."

"You're a weak piece of shit, Sil." Loch's associate shoved his commander aside, glaring at Lazarus. His sword rasped as he freed it.

"Quinn, you fool!" Sil snarled at him, but his demands fell on deaf ears. Quinn sneered into Lazarus' face.

"If you refuse to hand him over freely Lazarus, then we shall have to take things into our own hands."

Lazarus laughed. "Oh, do tell. What will you do?" He stared Quinn down, unblinking. "By the way, baring naked steel in Valare is a high offense. Put it down, my dear fellow. The guards in the room will skewer you faster than you can blink."

He was not afraid, but his demand fell on deaf ears. Loch pointed the tip of his sword towards Lazarus' heart.

"We have five hundred men inside your walls, Lazarus," Loch said. "Hinari is not to be denied. If we must use force to retrieve him, then we shall."

The tension broke; Lazarus fighting the urge to laugh. *Now this is getting interesting.* "You're clearly more stupid than I thought. Tyir must be important to Hinari, to sacrifice so many men to have him. You're weakened as it is, thanks to your infighting. We are fighting a war against an enemy strong enough to destroy us all, and you fixate on a retired necromancer?" That was a lie too.

Sil regarded him coldly. "It seems to me that diplomacy is a waste of time." His mouth twisted hard. "I was wrong about you, Lazarus. But if you are unwilling to negotiate, then we will have no alternative. Maybe Quinn has the right of it."

"Strange." The whisper snaked into the room, coming from the shadows. The effect was immediate. Sil and his men stiffened, reaching for weapons as the new arrival continued speaking. "The guards of Valare number at least five thousand, not counting our forces on either side of the city. Your odds do not seem good. Such a fuss. But then again, you seem to be under the impression that I can be taken."

Lazarus could not resist smiling this time, his mood lifted in an instant. He just couldn't help himself.

"You." Quinn's face twisted with hate as Tyir of Irene glided softly into the room. He was draped in black, his cloak flowing over his tall frame. His eyes dark with mischief, the fugitive regarded the men of the Order from a pale and pockmarked face, covered with scars from his long and brutal past. He was old, almost as old as Lazarus himself, but his presence radiated power and demanded respect.

Quinn started forward, but halted just short of Tyir's reach. Sil readied his own blade as he stepped up beside him, but whether to stop Quinn or aid him, Lazarus didn't know.

"You have the nerve to show your face?" Quinn snarled at Tyir, spit flying from his mouth. "There are many who want you dead. The great Hinari for one, and all the Order's strength alongside him."

"No surprise. He has been after me for a very long time," Tyir replied coolly, his milky-white eyes staring into Quinn's. He stepped gracefully, seeming to glide across the floor to stand in front of Lazarus, facing his enemies. "I guess I don't blame him. I did kill many of your kind. I remember them all, though I recall some with more detail than others. Your uncle, for instance, Loch. He screamed like a little girl as I cut out his lungs. All for study, of course. I recall some from your house too, Quinn, during the Kahal's civil war."

Loch and Quinn growled in fury, but Sil held them back. His face had blanched grey at Tyir's sheer lack of remorse. "You realize how much your liege has sacrificed to protect you?" Sil said, taking a step towards Tyir, his shoulders firm and steady before the hated necromancer. His face however, gave him away; beads of sweat shone across his olive skin, and his hands trembled so violently that he could barely grip his sword. "Lazarus has forsaken the protection of the Order, his own family, all to rescue your murderous hide. Think of the damage you've inflicted upon him, upon everyone you touched with the filth that you willingly infected yourself with."

"Oh, that's not the cause of his desertion, trust me. If even a shred of that accusation was true, I would go with you and accept see my fate," Tyir smiled thinly. "The truth would destroy you."

Lazarus seethed at Sil's words. *Those fools, thinking I left due to some kind of sorcery.*

"You think I hoodwinked him?" Tyir went on, voice smooth as silk. "He left you of his own accord, and whatever you may bleat about sacrifice, it means nothing to him. Vilify me all you want, but don't darken his name."

Sil's henchmen bristled. They spread themselves further out, flanking Tyir on both sides.

"Is that a threat?" Loch's saggy eyes bulged as he screeched at Tyir, whose smile grew even colder.

"I'm sure you're smart enough to figure it out."

"This has gone on long enough! You will come with us to await your trial, which is more than the likes of you deserve," Sil addressed him through gritted teeth.

Lazarus shook his head, no longer smiling. Although he enjoyed seeing the Order provoked, he needed to tread carefully. *This could get dangerous.*

"You're still under the delusion that I'm going to come quietly, Sil." Tyir gently reiterated. "I have no intention of going with you. That is a death sentence, and frankly, I like living. But if you want me dead, then fight me, man to man. Single combat."

"Don't tempt me." Loch snarled, spitting upon the ground as he raised his blade.

"You're no man, but a monster amongst demons," Quinn said. He too, pointed the tip of his sword directly at Tyir's heart. "You slaughtered thousands of the Order with your sickening arts. You are a mercenary and a brigand."

"I did. I am. What are you going to do about it?" Tyir's mouth curled into a sneer.

"Mind yourself, Loch." Lazarus warned him casually. "I won't tolerate the use of force against my people."

Loch gaped, opening and closing his mouth like a trout. Sil looked on as his portly red face blanched, the color draining.

The door swung open forcefully, and several red robed men strode in, their spears held ready for battle.

The Order. How did they get through? "What is this?" Lazarus said furiously. His own guards rallied, facing them. Spears on both sides were held ready to kill.

"Quinn, what's this? I gave you no such orders!" Sil protested, but his fellow officer ignored him.

"Pathetic," Quinn sneered, throwing a withering look at his superior before turning to Tyir. "Tyir of Irene." Quinn's voice shook. "You are charged with murder and violation of the laws of the Order. You will come with us immediately back to the Sepulcher to await justice. Refuse and my men will take you by force. We of the blood of Pharos never march alone." He puffed out his chest arrogantly. "Five hundred of our kin are inside the city walls, and at our word they will kill. Across the Empire, there are many calling for your blood, and won't hesitate to help us if it comes to it."

Tyir chuckled. "Five hundred men, you say? All you'll achieve is spilling your own blood. Take a step back, and look at yourselves. You'd threaten Lazarus to gain vengeance against me?"

He shook his head. "Even the false Pharos would balk at your actions. Are you men or cowards who would violate safe conduct within your ally's hall?" Tyir's voice lowered to a gentle hiss. "Like it or not, we must not weaken against the Dominion. They'll invade any day now. Though if they do, I hope they slaughter you like the pigs you are."

"You dare blaspheme?" Loch's voice rose shrilly, his eyes brimming anger.

"Pharos is the only true god!" One of the Order shouted, raising the butt of his spear and slamming it onto the floor.

"True god?" Tyir's eyes sparkled with malice, his grin widening into a threatening leer. "There are no gods, you pathetic fool."

"I've heard enough." Quinn turned to the men behind him who had just arrived. "Take him!"

They turned to look at each other, and Lazarus could see uncertainty and fear in their faces. They were equal in number to Lazarus' own men, but Tyir's presence clearly unnerved them. *Try it, and you'll all die*, Lazarus warned them silently.

"Commander Sil gives the orders, Sir," one of them said.

"Do it!" Quinn's eyes bulged. They glanced at each other uneasily. One took a nervous step forwards, then another.

Tyir's eyes burned red, exuding a cold, bitter aura. The Order soldiers froze. "I cannot allow my friend to be threatened by your venomous words. So be it. If you are foolish enough to fight me, then you will face my judgement." He raised his hands.

"Tyir, no!" Lazarus shouted. He had to stop this, now. *If Tyir kills them my relationship with the Order will be jeopardized. I can't risk it.* "We should not fight amongst ourselves. There is a common enemy who will destroy us all." With a swish of his robes, he made to shield Tyir.

"Enough!" Sil roared, his booming voice bringing his men to an instant halt. Even Quinn stopped, his sword outstretched towards Tyir. "We are guests in

Valare, and this has gone on long enough. This isn't the way. Stand down."

"You would let the traitor go?" Quinn whispered. "You fucking bastard. Only a snake would do such."

"We did not come here to spill blood!" Sil roared, so loud that Quinn took a step back. "Do you want to get us all killed? Because you would have succeeded if you took another step. You would have had that overly inflated head of yours on a spike. Look to the doorway."

Still with an arrogant smirk on his thin lips, Quinn turned, sword still in hand. His sneer sagged at the sight of six white cloaked Valarian Guards, their arrival unnoticed, led by the portly Tai Cassel, Commander of Arms. His usually jolly face was contorted with barely contained fury. Six powerful Pyran bows pointed at the Order. With a scared look at Quinn and Sil, the Order soldiers lowered their spears.

"That is why I am commander, and you are my subordinate, Quinn," Sil said coldly. "You are a good servant of Pharos, but your recklessness would doom us all. Unless you think you can live with an arrow in your back?"

Quinn glared, before finally backing down, throwing his sword to the ground with a deafening clatter. "He'll still die."

Lazarus had heard enough. "I suggest you take yourselves out of my sight immediately, Sil." His heart was racing, every word laced with ill repressed fury, as the reality of it hit home.

"You've disturbed me long enough. Not only that, but you threatened the lives of my guards. Get out of my city. Leave someone else in charge of your men. And tell Hinari this. Any attempt to take Tyir, by force or otherwise, and I'll withdraw all support from the Sepulcher."

The Order's men exchanged looks of horror. Even though he had left the Order years ago, he still extended a hand of friendship with them. His threat meant that not only would he sever that important link, but he could then use it against them, supporting their enemies. The Order didn't lack for those. It was a bluff, but the Order didn't know that.

"You can't!" Loch exclaimed, eyes opening wide. "You wouldn't? You need us, like you said. The Dominion threatens us all."

Oh, now he tries logic. That door had long closed.

"Get. Out." Lazarus hissed.

The men of the Order glanced at each other. Finally, they caved.

"Very well," Sil said, keeping his eyes fixed upon Tyir the whole time. "The demands still stand, my Jaal. Tyir is a wanted man, and will suffer justice sooner than you wish to believe, Pharos will make sure of that. But until then, we depart. Men, withdraw."

Most hurried out without question and undisguised relief. Loch and Quinn were the last.

"Take your sword with you Quinn," Lazarus said. "And if you threaten any of my own again, you'll pay for it in blood. Your blood." This time, he was not bluffing.

Quinn's eyes narrowed, but he was too cowardly to take the bait. Retrieving his discarded blade, he stalked out, his face blazing red. Loch paused at the doorway, turning to face Tyir.

"You won't be in their protection forever," he sneered. "You should prepare yourself for the block."

"I look forward to it," Tyir replied coolly, turning his back upon the door as it slammed shut, causing the falcon to screech and beat its wings against his cage in agitation.

"Quiet, Lancil," Lazarus said. He reached his bony fingers through the cage to stroke the bird's feathers, calming him. *A great start to the day.* He felt exhausted. Cassel glared at the closed door, weapon still drawn.

"Shall I escort them from the city, Lazarus?" He asked. "We haven't seen the last of them, I fear."

"No, they're nothing if not predictable. They will do their duty."

Tyir stepped closer to the cage and the falcon squawked, eager for attention.

"Thank you, my Jaal," Tyir said. "The Octane guide you." He bowed his head deeply, but the smile was mocking.

"Didn't take you for a praying man, Tyir."

"They will learn, in due course, how meaningless their false faith is." Tyir raised a pale hand, turning it so they could all see. His hand was crisscrossed with countless scars. "One day, everyone will understand. I don't want innocent blood spilled for my cause."

"Innocent?" Cassel snorted. "No worse than what you have done, right?" His watery blue eyes were full of discontent. "And I'd keep your blasphemy to yourself, if I were you."

"Don't take Tyir's words too much to heart, my dear friend," Lazarus said, still stroking Lancil's crown. "He is not a pious man."

Cassel lowered his bow, his jaw clenched. "That was a close call. But what if this escalates? We can't have the Order rising against us in our own city."

"They won't. They're not stupid."

Lazarus opened the cage, and the falcon hopped out, landing on its master's outstretched finger. It screeched and chirped, nipping affectionately.

36

"Hinari will have no choice but to comply with my wishes," he said.

"I doubt that, my friend," Tyir laughed. "He hasn't stopped hounding you, and it's been twenty years."

Cassel shuddered, his double chin wobbling. "The Order will balk at such a threat. What if they take it as a declaration of war? We have enough problems as it is, with the Dominion mounting attacks every day. If they decide to strike from inside the city with their garrison here . . ." He broke off.

Lazarus felt a stab of pity for him. Cassel was a warrior, made for battle. He had fought with the legions of the Empire for years before coming to serve in Valare. And though he had gotten soft in the body, his mind was as sharp as the blade he carried. But Cassel was a double-edged sword. Ever a pious man and a follower of the Octane faith, conflict with the Order was his worst nightmare.

The Dominion frightens him, Lazarus thought solemnly. *But the Order's faith scares him more. Its existence is a challenge to his own beliefs.*

"You don't need to worry, my dear Cassel," Tyir said. "The Order won't like it, but Hinari values Lazarus more than the great Order families can ever dream. He'll bleed before he turns on him."

Lancil took off from Lazarus' hand, flying silently around the chamber before swooping in close to Tyir's head. He eyed the bird and chuckled.

"I've always liked animals," he said, his voice lowering into a gentle whisper. "I prefer them to humans. They don't backstab, lie or kill for fun. Everything they do is for survival. Strange, how an inferior species can teach us how to live." He held out his arm, and Lancil landed, gripping with sharp claws. Tyir stroked the falcon's breast with his fingers.

Lazarus sat back down behind his desk with a grimace. "Now that unpleasant business is taken care of, to the matters at hand. Cassel, how goes the training?"

"The men will be ready. Two thousand patrol the borders outside Valare, and we've staked and ditched the area. Should there be any landing from the enemy, they will give them hell. But our scholars are angry. They want to go back to work." Looking relieved that Lazarus had changed the subject, Cassel reached within the depths of his tunic and pulled out a parchment, handing it to Lazarus.

"Damn them," Lazarus took the letter. "They know they can't." *Unfortunate*. Every year until the outbreak of war, he would send a selection of students across the sea into the great ruins of Kan Azult, where they spent their months assisting in the excavation of the site. But then the war came, marooning their work. While some of the students had taken up the task of serving in the militia, others turned to drink and gambling. It was a shame to see good people fall from grace. He could have sent them elsewhere of course, to another site, but with the war, that was impossible. Research and dreams had to be put aside. At least for now.

"Sir?" Cassel's voice brought him out of his reverie.

"I'm sorry," Lazarus said. "Go on, please."

"Penor also wants a pay increase to bring in the rest of his company into the walls. The 'blood price,' he called it." The corners of his mouth twitched, threatening a sarcastic smile as he nodded to the note in Lazarus' hand. "Three hundred gold pieces, he asks. It is only fair I say. A third of the forces on the eastern bank are his men."

Lazarus looked down at his breakfast and pushed it away, his appetite long fled. Penor was the bigger issue, the ferocious and headstrong leader of the Mer Hammers. Sellswords. But they needed more men. Penor was able, but greedy, quick to demand.

"He drives a hard bargain. Very well," Lazarus grimaced. War swallows up gold more than greed itself. Even so, it would still be a worthy investment to keep the man appeased; Penor was a hardened killer, and unlike the Order, listened to reason. "Penor will get his blood money. They can join those on the Iriat Wall. See to it that they have the extra coin."

"It will be done." Cassel stood at attention, stern and proud.

"Good," Lazarus was heartened.

Tyir hobbled forward. "Lazarus, if you have a moment, there is an important matter I need to discuss."

"What is it, friend?"

"Well," Tyir began, frowning. He turned away, unable to look Lazarus in the eye.

"I received a message not two days ago, from Bawsor. Bane Aldmer has called on me to meet him. He requests assistance."

"Aldmer?" Lazarus said, his eyes opening wide. "What did he want?"

"They want my art to assist them in the war, no doubt."

"And your response?" Lazarus asked, already knowing the answer. *He has no love for the Empire, nor does he care for them.* Lazarus knew quite a lot of this Bane Aldmer. He was dangerous, unpredictable and a military genius, who had rapidly risen through the ranks in the Empire and had been responsible for many of the early victories. Even so, he had heard very dark stories of the man, and his harsh ideal of justice. A respectable war leader, but not a man of peace.

Lazarus disliked the man and his new regime, and trusted them even less.

"You know my answer." Tyir replied caustically. "Their whims are not my concern, nor is their war. What does concern me is their timing. They had no interest in me at all, until now. Of course, most of my history is far from their borders. The Order's hatred for me at least has some good merit; I fought many of them during the Kahal war of independence. I tortured and experimented on those I took captive, for research. But the Empire I stayed clear of. So why now?" His brows furrowed. "I like it not."

"They know your reputation. They want you to fight in a war they're losing," Lazarus said carefully.

"Which beggars the question. Why ask for my help? They know what I am." Tyir's eyes were full of doubt. He looked up at Lazarus. "Why do they need necromancy?"

Cassel shuddered. Lazarus could think of no answer to that.

"You have powers they need?" Cassel suggested. "They've heard of your deeds, of course. They're nothing short of legendary."

For a fleeting moment, a smile crossed Tyir's thin blue lips. "Oh my, Cassel. That was almost a compliment. Have you had a change of heart? Perhaps I could have the honor of you joining me for drinks at the Roaring Lion when this mess is over?"

Cassel flushed an ugly purple and turned away. "Fuck off, you unholy bastard."

Tyir's smile faltered. "If they truly know what I am, then they'd know that it's folly. My power to raise the dead is temperamental at best. It's a hard road, the path I've followed. Fifty odd years, and I'm still learning new things, and even now, success is chancy."

"I wouldn't say that," Lazarus began. "You've achieved more than any man alive today. You saved-"

Tyir cut him off with a pointed glance at Cassel, and Lazarus clammed up at once.

"You flatter me, but I speak true. What do they want with the art? It won't help them." Tyir mused. "How desperate are they?"

"The Dominion murdered Adriena in cold blood, remember?" Cassel cut in sharply, shooting Lazarus a curious frown. "They'll fight to the death if need be." His fingers clenched around the blade by his side. "So, yes, they're desperate. And I don't blame them."

Lazarus was about to speak when something banged into him; Cassel. An explosion outside had rocked the building, filling the chamber with dust. Ears ringing, Lazarus pushed Cassel away and climbed to his feet. He was dizzy, the blast still echoing in his ears. Cassel appeared stunned, but Tyir rushed to his side, gripping his arm in support. Screams filtered through his damaged ears, the voices of the dying.

Cassel shook his head, getting his senses back. He staggered to the window.

My people! A cold, horrific dread filled Lazarus. "Cassel! What's happening out there?" Lazarus demanded, his eyes squinting against the hot dust. Cassel turned slowly, a look of horror on his face.

"Dragons."

What? Then Lazarus understood. "The Dominion."

At that moment, Piez hurtled into the hall, followed by a dozen guards. All carried horn longbows.

"I'm sorry, my Jaal." He fell to his knees. "This is all my fault. I didn't realize it was the enemy! There's hundreds of them, pontoons moving into the bay. They're attacking." He was babbling, his eyes wide, pupils black pinpoints.

"Are you alright, Lazarus?" One of the guards shouted, hurrying to him. Lazarus recognized the fearsome growl and thick rainbow-colored cape billowing behind the man.

"I'm fine, Penor," Lazarus panted. He looked around; his men were alert and ready.

"Cassel, go to the Iriat Wall and rally every able-bodied man to battle." He moved to the window, looking out at the bay. Through the haze of flame and smoke now filling the air, it was impossible to see anything approaching from the sea. "Piez, alert the Valarian Guard and evacuate the civilians from the city."

Piez hadn't moved. "I saw them." He was whispering hoarsely, hands wrapped tightly around his knees. "I saw their fleet from the tower. It's the Dominion. They're attacking here, and it's my fault!"

Two of the men knelt down and gently picked him up.

"Take him to safety." Penor commanded. "May the Octane give you peace, young Piez," he soothed, clutching the crying man's shoulder consolingly as they departed.

"Your men better be ready for battle, Penor," Lazarus said.

Penor strode away. "Of course they are, old man." Lazarus heard the grizzled veteran scoff.

"And someone alert the fucking Empire!" Lazarus turned away. His jaw clenched and grey, Cassel nodded, drawing his sword as he ran out.

Tyir remained rooted to the spot. "Lazarus. Let me fight."

Lazarus turned around. "No."

Tyir's eyes narrowed. "You need me. I care about these people too, you know. I was a warrior before anything else. Let me fight, and I shall bring my power upon them."

Lazarus marched over to him and grasped his shoulders firmly. "I cannot risk your life. Go down into the vaults with the civilians, and wait. If the Dominion knew you to be here, then they'd use everything at their disposal to destroy you, and us. I need you to approach the High Council when this assault is repelled!"

"But I want to fight!" Tyir demanded, his usually calm eyes blazing. "Let me help!"

"That's an order!" Lazarus hurled at him. The screams outside grew louder, as did the sound of crackling flames. "Please," Lazarus croaked. "I can't have you in danger too!"

Tyir stared at Lazarus with such intensity it was impossible for him to look away. "As you wish," he said, deflating. "And what will you do?"

Lazarus blinked hard, his eyesight was still hazy. In his mind, his suit of white plate armor shone. He hadn't worn it since Mercer and the final battle which liberated the city from the traitors. Unease tingled inside him for a moment. *Could I truly do it? Do I have the strength to see this out?* Then it was gone, replaced by a surge of courage. Of course he could. *This is my home. I defended it against injustice and brutality once. I must do so again.*

He still knew how to use a sword, even after all these years. He had saved Tyir once with his skills.

"I will lead." The image of Mercer Duston's host, camped outside his city, swam before his eyes. The pain and suffering. And now the Dominion. No more. He would protect Valare, or die.

Red Tide

*I have seen many wonders during
my travels, but nothing prepared me
for the Pillars of Daractus.*

~ Marcus Dragen

The noise in the street was deafening. Tyrone Cessil kept a tight grip on his sword, eyes wide as he took in the chaos. A gritty mixture of fear and determination had taken hold, churning his gut. He had been woken with a jolt by Valarian guards storming in, screaming about invaders. It took a few moments for him and the rest of his dormitory to realize what was happening, but duty took hold. Something was on fire. The air was thick with smoke and dust, people coughing and choking for air as they scrambled in their panic, the fighting men rushing to the docks.

The Dominion. They're finally here, Tyrone thought as he pushed through the crowds.

"Tyrone!" That was old Herber the cobbler, him and his young son. They were struggling on the edge of the fleeing civilians, as armed soldiers pushed in the opposite direction.

"Get to safety. I have to join the defense!" Tyrone shouted back. He heard a feeble "The Octane praise you, Tyrone," as he charged into the hysterical mob.

Tyrone had grown up in fear of the Selpvian Dominion. The Empire's strength was unparalleled on their side of the sea, but it quaked under the shadow from across the Tangent. As the war went against

44

them, Valare been placed on high alert. All traffic in and out of the port had been monitored, even boats from their allies in the Barta League, and the city guard had been quadrupled in size. It seemed impossible that an enemy ship had been able to sail close enough to launch an assault upon the city, yet they were here. Now it was up to the city defenders.

This is where we throw them back. If only he had his helm.

The crowd around him jostled and pushed for escape. He took a shortcut around Mud Square, following a detachment of archers as they sprinted through one of the smaller alleyways and down a flight of steps. He kept a hand on the pommel of his sword at all times. The smoke from the harbor was thicker and darker now. Smoke always comes before fire, and with it, death, his quartermaster Cassel told him once.

Someone shouted in a foreign tongue, and he was thrown off guard as hands grabbed him roughly and pulled him to the cobblestones. It was pandemonium, the crowd in the street broke in all directions as men attacked, masked and armed. *The Dominion.* Tyrone spat out a mouthful of blood as his knee hit the cobblestones hard, but he refused to shut his eyes; his fighting instincts taking over. He turned as one of the assailants launched himself on top of him in silence, only his eyes visible through the grey cloth covering his face. The Dominion soldiers wore bright colors and light, flowing cloaks.

Tyrone struggled to fight off his attacker, who slashed clumsily at his throat. There was a dull thud and his assailant convulsed before falling limp against him. Tyrone gritted his teeth as he rolled the corpse off, an arrow shaft deep inside the man's back. He drew his sword to take on the next attacker, who was aggressively forcing back a Valarian spearman, jabbing forward with his pointed needle. So engrossed in his personal battle, the Dominion soldier fell with a scream as Tyrone found a gap between his light ringed mail. His blade found its mark, punching deep into his flesh. They weren't very well trained from the looks of it, but in close-quarter brawls, that might not matter. Tyrone didn't stop to check if he was dead or not. He rushed onto the next, and the next, but the stairs ahead of him were swarming with men, foe and friend alike. Suddenly he slipped, crashing to his knee again. This time the pain was excruciating. He deliberately did not look down to see what had felled him.

"Tyrone!" His heart leapt as he turned to the edge of the stairs on his left flank; Oman and Jermaine were there, along with more of his fellow scholars, mostly teenage boys. They were his friends, those he had studied with for years.

Holding his large pavise shield aloft over his head, Jeramine sprinted the short distance to him as the men clashed, pulling Tyrone so forcefully to his feet that he nearly stumbled again. Dominion soldiers tried to attack, but arrows whistled through the air from the defenders' bows, and nobody got close. Bodies covered the ground like autumn leaves.

"Come on, with me," Jeramine bellowed, but the din was so loud that Tyrone could barely make out his words. He was dragged, not at all kindly past the wall into the relative safety of one of the primary parapets. They were safe, for a moment at least.

"Nearly ripped my fucking arm off, Jeramine," Tyrone muttered, rubbing at his shoulder, wincing. "Thanks." The huge lad barely heard him.

"You alright?" Jeramine shouted in reply, wiping soot and blood from his face. Tyrone nodded and looked round at the others. They had cobbled together whatever armor and weapons they could muster, their faces marked by fear.

"There's too many!" One boy said, his sword limp by his side. Tyrone didn't know his name. They heard a crash, and then the whistle of more arrows.

Jermaine turned on the boy. "Shut the fuck up with your crying, you spineless cretin. We have to protect the city! If we don't, those Dominion bastards will destroy it!"

Tyrone felt a pang of sympathy for the boy; he was trussed up hastily in a light grey tunic, the boiled leather cuirass only half-on. *Poor lad. He never expected to have to wear it.* Most of them had some training at arms, but none had actually expected to have to fight. Jermaine grabbed him by the shoulder, thrusting something into his hands.

"Found it, knew you'd need it," He grunted. Tyrone stared in surprise. *My helm.* The gift from Cassel for his twentieth birthday. The steel was polished, the leather unmarked. Tyrone clamped it over his head. He felt safer already. But instantly that feeling was replaced with the knowledge that he was not safe. None of them were.

"We need to get up onto the Iriat Wall!" Tyrone shouted to them. The fear in his voice had died, replaced with anger. His brush with death had sharpened his nerves and he would die to protect the city and its people. *Valare is my home.* Not Vern, which was merely his birthplace. This was his true home.

Oman hurried to him. "You're injured, Ty!" His roundish, sweaty face was red and shiny, the tip of his spear dripped scarlet. Tyrone shrugged off his concerns. He had taken a blade to the shoulder, but had hardly noticed it during the fighting. Tyrone glanced at his left shoulder; the wound was barely a scratch. It stung, but only slightly.

"It's nothing, don't worry about it! How did they get here anyway?" His bottle-green cloak was spattered with blood and dirt.

"The Dominion attacked the port with a fucking dragon! I haven't seen anything like it!" Oman's owlish eyes were wide with terror.

A dragon? Tyrone had no words for that. The fact Oman swore was almost as disturbing. Oman never swore; he was almost as pious as a maiden of the Octane. The whistling of arrows in the air grew louder. *We can't stay here.* "How many?" He demanded.

"Fucking hundreds!" Jeramine pushed Tyrone out of the way as he pushed to the front, holding his huge axe in one beefy fist. "Follow me to the Wall! We'll join the defense there."

"Come on!" Oman reached out a hand and was pulled along one of the recruits in front of Tyrone, causing him to stumble. The younger boys were shaking, some making pleas to the Octane as they hurried along the pathway.

They're right to be frightened. He couldn't blame them. This was the first real taste of war for most of them. Tyrone may not have physically fought in a fight to the death, but he had trained for years. That was his priority, when his prospects had dwindled on him. He knew though, that no amount of sparring with a friendly face, or even a hostile one, could compare when fighting for real, against an enemy who wanted you dead.

Grunting, they ascended the top end of the steps, reaching the parapet of the Iriat Wall. Valarian longbowmen were already assembled, shooting arrows down upon the chaos. One of the commanders turned and saw them. Though his face was masked by a cracked helmet, they could see fear in his eyes. Behind the line of archers, catapult crews loaded flaming boulders.

"Pick up bows and man the wall!" The commander was blunt and quick, pointing to the large stack of bows propped on a rack. "We need them so fucking full of arrows they can't move an inch. NOW GO!" He marched away, barking orders hoarsely down the line.

Wordlessly, they hurried to the rack of bows, made of yew. Tyrone picked one that looked the right draw weight. He grabbed a bundle of arrows, rushing to a spare spot on the wall, looking out below. He was no expert with the bow, but he was confident enough, and at this distance with so many targets, he could hardly miss. His heart thudded as he pulled back on the string, taking aim at the scene unfolding below. Someone nearby whimpered, then began to pray.

Fifty feet beneath him was a sea of smoke and heaving bodies. The port buildings burned and thick plumes filled the sky. A crowd of men streamed from a great ship, wrestling through the debris. Towering above them stood what could only be the Dragon. A vessel so huge that it was unable to fit within the mouth of the port, instead blocking entry to the harbor. From its yawning mouth, dozens of little pontoon rafts were approaching the shore, packed with Dominion troops.

"Loose, loose!" Tyrone let fly his arrow. There was little need to aim. The arrow storm was thick and fast, the whistling of the goose feathers loud. The enemy down below shot back, but the wall's height protected them, and enemy bowmen were quickly targeted. The great yew longbows of the Valare defenders were exacting a toll, but more of the enemy kept coming. Through the smoke, Tyrone could see the great ship was pulling back, and smaller boats were streaming in.

"Nock! Draw!" came the order repeatedly, the command like a pendulum. Tyrone pulled back the arrow as far as it would go, his fingers stinging now.

"Loose!" Again and again, Tyrone loosed alongside the archers as they maintained a barrage of arrows on the crowd below, but he was beginning to tire, clenching his jaw to overcome the pain in his aching shoulder. The archers among them on the ramparts were slowing too, he realized. The smoke from fires below were clouding their vision, and he couldn't stop coughing. Several of the defenders had fallen now, hit by enemy arrows and lay dead or dying on the stone. Nobody noticed.

Every inch of Tyrone's body was in pain, but he couldn't stop. He lost himself in the work. Draw, loose. Again and again. He was only mildly aware of Oman and Jeramine beside him. One more arrow, then the next, then the next, until his fingers were chafed raw, but every blister and drop of blood was another dead Dominion soldier and he cherished them.

He was running low on arrows and the enemy was still coming. How many were there? This was no skirmish, Tyrone knew. This was the real thing. Something was going to break, one way or the other.

"I need a force to hold them at the culvert!" Someone shouted. The voice was strangely familiar. A loud, putrid screech drowned out the rest of the man's command, Tyrone's heart leaping to his throat. *What in the hells was that?* It was a chilling, blood-curdling scream that tore through their souls. Footsteps thundered beneath him. There were screams from the wall too, grown men shrieking like banshees.

"What was that?" Jeramine choked out in fear and awe. Then Tyrone saw the claws and he hurled himself at his friend.

"Down!" He screamed as a spiked tail crashed into the wall. Stone shattered, raining shards of rock upon them. Tyrone was stunned. He pulled himself onto his knees and looked about in a daze. Somehow he was no longer on the wall. He had fallen. The stench of something unholy assaulted him, and he looked up, straight into the eyes of the creature. A lizard, every sane man's nightmare. It was thirty feet long, its forearms flexing enormous muscles as it tore men to pieces, it's scaled hide rippling like black armor. Arrow shafts jutted out of its flesh, but the attacks did nothing to slow it. Around its neck was an iron collar. Tyrone staggered to his feet, and the great yellow eyes stared down, yet somehow the creature did not appear to notice him.

"Weyvern!" Someone shouted.

Tyrone tried to move, but he was numb, cold with shock. The creature was beyond anything he had ever seen in his life. The monster opened its jaws, revealing rows of jagged teeth. Then it reared back on its hind legs.

Somebody pulled his arm; Oman, ashen-faced. There were nasty welts and cuts all over Oman's face, but he was alive.

"We have to get out of here!" Tyrone shouted, even as he was being pulled away. Oman made no reply. *Does he not know?* Fear gripped his heart.

They had taken a couple of stumbling steps when the air became cold. A stinking, crippling cold, bleaching out the stench of the smoke, seeping through his robes and the warmth of his blood, choking him. Men on both sides of the battle shuddered, some convulsing. Tyrone felt his chest contract, and he almost fell.

Oman had pulled him to safety behind a patch of rubble, part of the wall that had collapsed when the weyvern had landed upon it. It served to shelter them. Just a few paces away, men fought in close combat.

"The weyvern's blind! Kill it! It must not breathe again!" Someone shouted behind, and Tyrone was dimly aware of guards rushing in with spears and swords, bellowing war cries, anything to drive the beast back. Tyrone felt a tugging on his tunic. He looked down to see Oman pulling aside the blood soaked garment.

"What are you doing?" He stammered, as his friend bit down deeply on his own arm, piercing the wrist. Tyrone swore as he tried to pull away. Blood ran from Oman's mouth.

"Shut up, I need to concentrate!" Oman said thickly, grasping Tyrone's shoulder. The pain made him scream. The blood from his shoulder flowed freely, and it was all he could do not to vomit.

Tyrone tried to stand but Oman's grip on him was strong. Realization dawned. He knew the stories some told of the tribesmen to the south, where Oman was from.

"It will . . ."

"I said shut up!" Oman pushed his wrist into Tyrone's mouth. He gagged at the taste of blood. However, he could feel his body getting lighter, his shoulder clicking into place and the pain easing.

Tyrone smiled, closing his eyes in relief. That was his mistake. *What are you doing?* When he opened them again it was too late. Two men, draped in thick auburn cloaks of leather and satin moved purposefully towards them. They faces were covered, their eyes dark. Tyrone felt his friend's hand leave his body, and

52

the pain returned leaving him powerless, helpless. He writhed on the ground, watching the inevitable.

Oman moved faster than he had ever seen him. Grasping part of a longbow that had snapped, he wheeled it around in an arc as he dodged the edged steel from one of the assailants.

He turned, spinning on his heel, dodging another thrust, then he plunged the point of the broken bow into one man, the thick wooden tip slamming deep into his unprotected chest. Like a marionette with the strings cut, he slumped to the ground motionless. Then Oman reached forward and tugged the foreign broadsword out of the dying man's grasp, wielding it around and catching the second attacker across the stomach as he swept in to take advantage of Oman's blind side.

The man on the ground stirred, getting to his feet. Tyrone forced himself onto his knees, his eyes spying a fallen spearhead just a hands reach away from him. With a murderous screech from his mouth, Tyrone threw himself forwards. His knees hit the ground painfully, but his fingers found their goal; the deadly point from a polearm. He turned, swinging it with all of his might. It caught the attacker behind the knees, and Tyrone winced as he felt the steel slice through tendons and muscle. The enemy soldier cried out, and Oman finished him off with a quick slash across his throat.

Tyrone staggered upright, his wounded shoulder now pain free. At that moment he knew what his friend had done.

"You alright?" Oman asked. Tyrone nodded.

"Where's Jeramine?"

Oman didn't reply, only nodding towards their fellow defenders. A chill filled Tyrone. Steeling himself, he clutched the broken polearm like a dagger.

I have to keep fighting. Jeramine had to wait. Bracing themselves, the two charged back into the fray. His helm was lost, but no matter.

The weyvern was still screeching in the distance, its song blistering the air. As Tyrone fought, he felt the bloodlust return. Somehow he held a sword in his hand, the spearhead still in the other. Together they weaved a deadly dance that claimed anyone who came into reach. He grinned wildly, his which teeth red with blood. His own, his enemies. It did not matter. This was what he was meant for and it exhilarated him.

Dodging a wild swing from a crazed axman, Tyrone drove the steel point of his polearm into the man's throat as his sword intersected with the axe. Blood spurted, some splashing his face.

"Pull back!" Someone shouted. He could feel rough fingers pulling at him and he moved back, weapons held ready.

A volley of arrows from above hit home, and several men fell. Tyrone readied himself for the inevitable, but felt himself being dragged away.

"I said, Pull back!"

Then something with the force of a sledgehammer hit him and everything went hazy.

"Get up boy."

He knew that voice. Gentle fingers pulled his eyelids open. Tyrone slowly focused, and the concerned gaze of his beloved master of arms, Tai Cassel, swam into view.

"Cassel?" Tyrone muttered. His tongue felt heavy, slow in his mouth.

"Can you still fight?" the old man had a deep cut to the side of his stubbled cheek. It would leave a scar, the kind that some women found attractive. He grabbed Tyrone by the arms, pulling him up as easily as if he were a baby.

It was Cassel alright; his chest was like a keg of ale, made more prominent by his heavy breast plate. Tyrone rose to his feet, looking round in a daze. They were in the armory courtyard, where they held training drills. The place was a ruin, the buildings derelict and worn. But now the yard was packed with wounded men and women. Children hurried, carrying buckets of water, while armed men rushed back and forth, checking on the injured. Grey-robed women of all ages attended to the wounded, a mixture of trained septons of the Octane and a couple wearing tattered scarlet robes of the Pharos Order.

"I can still fight," Tyrone replied shakily. *Not like I have any choice in the matter.* Cassel had that quality of making you do his bidding, whether or not you wanted to. His leg was throbbing painfully, and he was having trouble standing straight. "There's a weyvern," he warned.

"I know, Tyrone. We've just fought off another two." Cassel's voice was grim, strained. His face, usually so fierce, was pale and grey. "Where the fuck are the bowmen! I need some archers!" His bellow took Tyrone aback. "Talk to me! I need some fucking archers!" Cassel's thunder bawled over the parapet. "Any time now would be nice!"

"Here," shouted a man.

"And here!"

"Get in front and rain hell upon them, and get the Lanberts to make a spear-wall in the Cloudmor District!" Cassel ordered. The archers rushed to their tasks. "And you lot skulking with the wounded, ready those bloody bows and get up to the wall. We've trapped them on the Iriat pathway, but we have another force scaling the Northern Wall behind the bay. We can't let them pass! Anyone who shirks will have me to deal with."

A scarred faced veteran shook his head, saying almost matter of factly, "We don't have enough men to hold both the wall and the bay. They have more ships inbound."

"We've been fighting for hours!" Someone groaned faintly, then another voice; "They're sending more barges up the harbor! We have to beat them back there!" Somewhere close, someone began to sing in a quavering voice.

"May the Octane save us, may the Octane guide us."

A hard-faced officer turned on the singer. "Any more pious bleating from you, and I'm going to shove that spear so far up your arse you'll be really praying for the gods!" The singing stopped, followed by strained cheering. It died just as quickly. Tyrone made for the archery racks, but Cassel shook his head.

"You've done enough, lad. Get back. Archers to the wall!" Cassel roared. A score of bowmen hurried forward. "How they were able to sneak up on the city like this, I have no idea . . ." He tailed off, his fist clenched to his side.

"Oman said something about them moving a dragon ship into the harbor under the cover of the fog." Tyrone remembered, shaking his dead. He drew his sword anyway.

"Yes, but that doesn't explain why it wasn't fucking seen!" Cassel's nostrils flared like a bull as he turned to face him. "How did we miss it?"

Another screech from below, the Northern wall. *Weyvern*. That sent the weaker souls scurrying like rodents, some sobbing. However, twice as many rushed to the outer wall facing the sea, their bows drawn back while others brandished swords and axes waiting for the attackers to come into range.

56

"You lot! Get back there! You run, you'll be dishonoring your fucking souls forever!" Cassel roared at them. Some turned back, but just as many continued.

Fear is spilling more than blood. Tyrone made his decision. "Give me a bow!" He seized Cassel's arm. "You're going to need every man on the walls."

Cassel stared at him stonily for a moment. Then he nodded and growled, "Fine! Don't fuck up."

A crowd of archers hurried to the opposite wall and Cassel joined them. Limping, Tyrone picked a bow from the rack and hurried to his place by the Northern wall, down by the cliff face.

Over eighty feet tall, the wall brooded over the shoreline. Tyrone took a position on top of the wall. He had a clear view of the ground below, a death trap of rocks and slippery moss, the hill too steep to climb. It was a formidable obstacle for any force to breach, suicidal. Yet the forces of the Dominion kept coming, grappling up the slope in their dozens. Their progress was slow, but they were many, and Valare was few.

The air on the wall turned freezing, the chill flooding his lungs. He coughed and held his breath. *Don't breathe that in, no matter what.* This siege bow had a heavy draw. It was far more powerful than any other bow Tyrone had used before. *At this distance every arrow will makes its mark*, he thought. But that weyvern was another story. Taking a shaft from one of the many baskets set up across the battlements, he notched it. Munitions they had in plenty.

The weyvern was clawing its way up the cliff, it's huge talons raking the rock, closer and closer. Soon it would reach the wall itself. It was forty feet thick stone at the base, but did the builders take into account foulness such as this?

Dominion men surged forward to fill the gap where the defenders had caved. There was a banshee scream, and the entire wall lurched. Tyrone waited, choosing his target. And then he saw the blazing gaze of a single, dilated eye. Drawing back the bow, he let loose and the arrow flew true.

Yes! The defenders roared in triumph as the creature fell; Tyrone's arrow had found its mark. The men below yelled and scattered as the weyvern landed heavily on the beach, crushing several soldiers as they tried to get out of its way. Behind it however, the legions were advancing, while others dragged large shields from pontoons onto the land, protecting themselves from the deadly sting of arrows raining down. A large number of them had landed now, a swarm of attackers.

Through the smoke, Tyrone could make out the outline of another boat in the water, not far off the shoreline. Rowboats, which meant only one thing. Squinting through the gloom, he could make out advancing galleys. How many were out there, he did not know. First a few, then dozens. Tyrone knew then the horrible truth. *The dragonboat was just a poke at our defenses.* The Dominion was out there. It was a full invasion fleet, thousands of men ready. It was the real thing.

"Rain hell on them, lads!" Boiling oil was brought up in great, steaming vats. "Fight them, send them back!" roared Cassel, appearing by Tyrone's side. His whiskered face turned white.

"There's thousands of them!" Someone cried. More were coming up the beach beneath them.

"It matters not," Cassel said. "We hold them back, no matter the odds! Do they scare us, warriors of Valare? Are they superior to us, the golden spear of the Barta League? Are you afraid?"

"No!" screamed the defenders, afraid. There was a whoosh as the vats were unleashed, and searing heat fanned Tyrone's face. He wiped his brow with his free hand.

"Damn right. Let's show the Selpvian Dominion what true power really is!" Cassel howled, in full battle fury. "Now fight, you cunts!" A boulder crashed high over his head, shattering into the ground twenty feet behind him.

"Fuck their siege ships and everything they stand for," he snarled, his eyes a horror. Hands grabbed at the top of the wall.

Tyrone moved fast, his sword hacking through flesh and bone. But as soon as one man fell another took his place, then another. Before they knew it, brightly colored cloaks were flashing before their eyes, and Tyrone found himself beset on both sides by men brandishing sabers wet with blood. More poured over the wall, and the few holding the front line had to withdraw back to the reserves. Tyrone followed, stabbing the unarmored pursuer in the armpit as he fell back. As the other man followed hacking away like a butcher, a Valarian soldier plunged his spear into him. With a great roar, the two battle lines clashed.

The bright midday sun bore down upon them all, the heat baking Tyrone in his armor. Sweat drenched his beet-red face as he recovered his balance. He pulled his sword out of another enemy fighter, but the defenders were pushed back further and further from the wall, as more and more of the Dominion clambered onto the battlements.

"We have to retreat!" Someone said. Then Cassel's warhorn sounded and all hell broke loose. Stumbling and turning, Tyrone was swept up in the stampede of Valarians pulling back, the invaders in hot pursuit. He could barely see a thing, his head bursting with pain.

After what seemed like an eternity of running, Tyrone found himself standing below the stone archway leading to the market district. Now, it was a graveyard, strewn with debris and rubble, broken carts and bodies. The smell of blood and smoke was thick. They kept running.

The marketplace led to Cheapside, the most vulnerable section of the city, in spite of efforts to reinforce the defenses. A formation of Valarian defenders blocked the path; their shields locked tight in a phalanx formation, bowmen waiting behind the wall of pikes. Even so, there were far more of the enemy.

Tyrone and his company rushed to join them. The Caroste Gate was the main entrance onto the beach, used by sailors from the coast to bring their daily trade into the city. Tyrone knew that if the Dominion took it, the fight would be over.

"Ty!" A choked voice bleated. Somebody stirred on the ground not far away. Taking short, painful breaths, Tyrone made his way through the carnage to reach the prone figure and the man hunching over him.

"Jeramine!" He threw himself onto the ground beside his friend. Jeramine's face blanched as he clutched his leg. Oman was tending to him, his large eyes wide.

"What happened?" Tyrone demanded.

Oman wordlessly removed part of the bloodied cloth covering Jeramine's thigh; a glint of white bone poked through an oozing wound, congealed blood surrounding the gash in his leg.

"Can you help me carry him?" Oman asked. His fingers busied with Jeramine's mangled leg. "I can't manage him on my own," he stammered, blinking rapidly. "They attacked here. We pushed back, but they're returning." He coughed violently, raising a swollen, bruised hand to brush the sweat from his face. "I don't know where the others are."

Bile rose to the back of Tyrone's mouth, but before he could reply, a dreadful gong rang through the air. All the shouting and encouragement died in an instant. Then the heavy beat of great drums began, growing louder. Tyrone looked up and saw a flurry of movement above their heads; on the parapet overlooking the marketplace, the archers were firing again. A dark skinned man clad in black plate armor moved to the front of the lines, bellowing so loud his voice could be heard even above the dreadful sound of war drums.

"This is where we hold them!" He bellowed. It was Penor, the sellsword.

"Get out of here, both of you," Tyrone muttered to Oman; he forced himself onto his feet.

"We can't leave you," Jeramine gasped faintly, reaching up, but Tyrone pushed his hands back. "Give me a blade," the giant lad protested. "I'll swing at the foreign cunts from here."

Tyrone shook his head. He drew his sword and joined the secondary line of Valarian defenders: the spears up front and the swordsmen and archers in the second column. As he took his position, he caught a glimpse of a tightly packed formation of men at the road junction ahead. In the gleam of the sun, the light reflecting off their red armor was dazzling, and Tyrone had to shut his visor over his eyes to block it out. As they entered the marketplace, Tyrone recognized them.

"It's the Guardian of the Porte," someone whispered next to Tyrone, awestruck.

"They've taken the north of the city!" Another muttered, green with fear.

"The elite of Klassos. We're finished."

"And we'll throw them back. They're only men!" Said another voice, weary with age. But at his words, Tyrone felt a wave of hope rise amongst the men. He knew that voice. Turning his head he saw Lazarus. He stood beside Penor, his white armor pale as winter's snow. He held an oval shield in one hand and a longsword in the other.

I will fight with you, Lazarus. But even as Tyrone braced himself for battle amongst the defenders, galvanized by the presence of their beloved leader, the Guardian of the Porte were closing the gap; great plumes of red feathers in of their steel helmets, the sheen of their fully clad bodies; thick mail and plate, vibrant crimson. They carried long spears and shields which protected their whole body.

They were the elite of the Dominion's vast armies, brought forward as a battering ram to break the enemy lines before hordes of horsemen and savage beasts finished the job. Above him, the archers upon the walls and from open windows in the houses shot volleys of arrows. Lazarus advanced, and the shield wall moved forward, spears out. And yet . . . something odd was happening. The bodies on the ground were stirring. Tyrone couldn't believe his eyes. *How can the dead move?*

The entire marketplace seemed to writhe and shake, the ground coming to life. The invaders stopped, startled by the phenomenon. They shouted in a foreign tongue, then retreated.

"What's happening?" Tyrone said, as Lazarus looked up at the parapet behind them. He thought he could see him mouth a word. The guardians were fleeing now. Fallen soldiers rose up all around them. Some of the corpses, with legs hacked off, crawled across the ground, fallen foe and ally alike, their movements slow and jerky.

"The Paladin!" Tyrone heard somebody cry out, in what almost seemed like triumph. The hardened guardians were backpedaling as more of the dead clambered painfully to their feet as though forcibly awoken from their slumber. *They're going to break.* That was the signal they were hoping for.

"Penor, sound the attack!" Lazarus roared.

A warhorn bellowed and the front line of Valarians charged into the mass of rising dead, straight at the now fleeing Dominion forces. Tyrone made to follow when he heard Oman's voice calling faintly.

"He's losing too much blood! Ty, please help me!"

Tyrone doubled back, darting in and around a dozen conscripts as they followed the front line into battle, catching up with Oman. He had Jeramine on his feet, an arm around his shoulder as he struggled to support him. Jeramine's eyes were wide and staring to the heavens, oblivious to the carnage around them. His face was a death mask.

"Can you heal him?" Tyrone hurried to lend support, heaving an arm over his shoulder, sending a streak of pain through his back. Gritting his teeth against the strain, he helped Oman drag Jeramine out of the marketplace into a side alley. Smoke billowed in the distance, far north-west. The high walls of the surrounding buildings muffled some of the din from the battle. Oman didn't speak.

"Can you heal him? Like you did with me?" Tyrone urged.

Oman shook his head violently. He was bleeding too, a cut down one side of his face.

"Not for something this bad," he whimpered. A tear streaking his cheek, carving a path through dirt and grime. "We have to get him somewhere safe, get him to the hospital."

Tyrone hesitated, powerless. "Come on. Let's get him out of the city, out of harm's way," he said. There had to be some kind of help. Maybe the little villages to the south.

Nodding, his eyes screwed up to stop the flow of tears, Oman obeyed, and the two together began to carry Jeramine through the narrow street. It was exhausting work, for Jeramine was larger than their combined size and weight, but with nobody trying to kill them, it was easier than fighting. Finally they got him out onto the Soldmer Road. The gate ahead was choked with people. But as they stepped out into the road, the fleeing civilians roared in horror and dismay.

What's going on now? Tyrone wondered. His grip of Jeramine tightened, and he seized Oman's hand to prevent him getting swept along with them. He could hear rapidly moving footsteps. Turning his head, he saw a disheveled member of the Keep guard sprinting towards them. His heart leapt to his mouth when he saw the look in his eyes; hysterical fear and despair etched in every line of his weathered face.

"What you fools waiting for!" He bellowed, wheezing as he came to a halt. "We have to get out the city; it's over, we've lost!"

"What?" Oman demanded, his reply coming out as a mere squeak.

"They're hurling Kyrm fire into the city!" The man snarled, his anger at Oman's hesitance breaking before his own distress.

Kyrm fire? A lead weight dropped into Tyrone's stomach. Kyrm fire was the darkest of arts. Liquid flame so potent, it burned through skin, bone, metal and stone alike.

"Hurry up! Leave that lad, he's finished!" A soldier barked at them.

No. Tyrone grabbed hold of Oman and together they began to haul Jeramine through the crowds towards the gate leading out of the city; buffeted left and right as others rushed past them in their haste to escape. More than once someone collided into Tyrone as they passed, and he nearly stumbled, but kept his footing. To fall now was a death sentence. All around them, fully grown men with blood on their clothes and swords cried, everyone shoving each other to escape the coming hell.

Screaming guards helped them escape, pushing them, hurrying them along. When the throng grew too thick, they lifted children over the heads of the pressing mass, passing them forward to others, who helped. Some of the crowd cleared as they reached the gate. He was pulled away from Oman, and try as he might he could not go back. He could hear Oman's desperate pleas.

"Help me get him through; he's hardly moving, please!"

As Tyrone struggled against the human tide, his eyes caught something high in the air hurtling down towards him; he opened his mouth to scream, but no sound came. Instinct took over, and Tyrone tried to run.

A black, oily ball the size of a horse crashed into the cobblestones in an eruption of flame, igniting the air around them. People screamed as flesh melted, the air so hot it burned the lungs of any who breathed. Terror pounding through him, Tyrone reached out a desperate, futile hand, his gaze fixed upon Oman and Jeramine; their bodies were covered in a yellow, molten goo. Even before his eyes, Tyrone could see their features bubbling, smoke rising. He closed his eyes.

Someone had hold of his arms then, dragging him upright. Screaming, he fought to free himself, but it was no use and he stumbled away, joining the exodus of fleeing, terrified and bloodied men, women and children. The city was doomed.

Turning his head, Tyrone looked back in shock as more of the terrifying firebombs struck the city, each one sending a ripple of fire into the air, followed by great plumes of thick, black smoke.

He stumbled upon the ancient stone path leading away from the city, grief overwhelming him. In the far distance, half obscured by the hill overlooking the sea, Tyrone could make out the immensity of the invasion. There were hundreds of Dominion warships. The northern horde had come.

A Reluctant Pact

Justice is the same for a man as vengeance,
but those who call it justice lie to themselves for
their brutality.

~ King Alver II

The horses were skittish, stamping and snorting nervously. Their masters did what they could to calm them, holding them to a short rein, patting their necks. The early-afternoon air was thick with fear and silence, mixed with smoke from the village smoldering in the distance.

Nazir Cessil watched the trials, tingling with unease. *This is not right.* Everywhere around him, destruction ruled over common sense. The elders of the village had refused to let in the Balian legions, which had mustered to fight the invading Selpvian army. Whether it was fear or exhaustion of war, Nazir didn't know. The rebel's corpses now littered the roadside in their hundreds. *We should be exacting the toll on the invaders, not our own people.*

A crowd watched silently as prisoners were brought single file to climb three steps to the execution platform, lining up behind a block of stained, dark wood. There were six in total; four men, an elderly woman and a young boy, perhaps eight years of age. All were bloodied and bruised.

Facing them, the forces of the Balian Empire awaited, grey-bearded veterans and green lads alike, all wearing equally grim expressions. They made an odd crowd; the elite, heavily armored volunteers of the legion, trained and brilliantly disciplined, along with the ragged House levies, carrying pikes, swords, axes and bows of varying quality. Two columns of heavy horse, ready to ride out at any time, flanked the yard. The executioner mounted the platform, a leather hood over his head, with only eye slits revealing the man beneath. The condemned stared ahead, their listless gaze taking in nothing. *Their minds have shut down*, Nazir thought. He watched the scene unfolding with distaste. *Since when did the Empire execute children?*

Two guards forced the first of the condemned to his knees. Clearly a man of noble birth, he was a bearded hulk of a man with a bloodied face and hands tied behind his back. Thrown roughly onto the plain wooden planking by the guards, he continued to struggle. The bear of a man struggled against his chains, roaring and sobbing, not out of fear, Nazir realized, but with anger. He did not go quietly, spitting and hurling abuse at those dragging him.

He didn't look like a traitor to Nazir. But then, what did a traitor look like?

Bane Aldmer climbed the steps. His eyes lacked any pity as he examined the prisoners.

That is not a man of mercy. Aldmer was an odd one, Nazir reflected. Before the war, he was a skilled soldier, but of little name. Now, he held the power of an emperor. He certainly fitted the image of Bale's leader however. Six foot tall, young and strong, Aldmer was a formidable choice, even though Nazir did not wholly agree with the decision.

"You all stand accused of treason," Aldmer said. His voice loud enough to carry across the crowd.

He doesn't use their names, probably doesn't even know them. Their deaths mean nothing to him. Nazir knew Aldmer's tone all too well, and understood it. He used it when dispensing justice as head of House Cessil.

Aldmer continued, the words they knew would come. "Your punishment is death by beheading."

The belligerent giant raised his face for them all to see. His right eye was a ruin, a gaping chasm of blood and pus, torn out by Aldmer's men.

"My name is Harold," he called out through thick, bloodied lips. The child next to him began to sob dryly. A shudder went through Nazir, not for the first time.

"Your name does not matter any longer, traitor." Aldmer's hooked nose looked down on them all. "You are lucky not to be boiled alive for your crimes." Aldmer turned to the executioner. It was Carris, one of his men. "Do your duty." A cold, fast command.

Harold cursed at them all, screaming obscenities. The crowd became noisy, fury at the rebels uniting their voices. Nazir looked away, barely hearing as justice fell upon the prisoner's neck. His right hand Adane Nesseton stood by his side. The two exchanged a look. Adane's lip curled.

"Kill the rest." Aldmer declared.

There was a pause. "Even the child?" Carris' voice was rough through his hood. Nazir was pleased to hear it. Some objection at least.

"Aye. Unfortunate, but traitor's spawn will grow to be traitors themselves." His eyes fell upon the crying boy. "I'm sorry, child. But this has to be done." He said shortly, before walking away.

Nazir had heard enough. "We're done here," he said to Adane. Nobody stopped them. Their backs turned, Nazir heard a whimper, then the thud of an axe. Cold anger stole over him.

"That was poorly done," Adane whispered, his face hard. "Traitor's spawn, he calls them! Madness and stupidity."

Too true. Their march east to fight the invaders took them out of Crown lands into the vast grasslands of the Adnis, recruiting as they went from the surrounding villages sworn to the Empire. However, many of the commoners resisted conscription.

"Your lords offer us nuthin. Why should we fight for you?" The stubborn baron of Castle Una demanded from the safety of his castle wall. They weren't the first to feel Aldmer's wrath. All those who refused to hand over their men and boys for war had their assets stripped, and in many cases were threatened with the removal of protection from the capital. Dark threats, and most of the villages bowed to Bawsor; it was suicide to refuse protection from the Legion with an enemy as formidable as the Dominion on their doorstep. The worst cases saw bloody fighting, and all those who physically resisted were exterminated.

"Only the start." Nazir replied. "This is a war we're fighting, brother." The last few weeks had been a daze since they received news of Valare's fall, and the Dominion invasion of the Empire. It had been a blur as they struggled to respond.

"Even so, a child beheaded in plain sight of the army? That is not justice, nor is it inspiring." Adane went on as they passed the Imperial tents, before reaching their own camp. A makeshift town had grown up overnight as the army paused, allowing the great baggage train to catch up.

This place used to be beautiful, Nazir reflected sadly. That had changed as the Empire called its banners to arms. The countryside was now a wasteland of men and women, churned mud and shit. Everywhere, men were training, drilling lines of ragged spearmen, or archers lined up shooting at targets. They were the levies called up in their thousands to defend their homeland. Few had any real experience of battle. Only the hardened legions with their heavy shields and chainmail had seen much fighting. What the levies lacked in experience they made up for in passion, knowing they were defending their homes.

"Aldmer is a hard man, but he hates the Dominion." Shaking his head, Nazir was relieved to reach his own tent; the largest of the array of pavilions that surrounded his own. It had been sparsely lavished at his bequest. They were greeted at the doorway by Nazir's guardsmen.

"Leave us," He ordered, and they departed. He removed his boots and slumped into a chair. Tiredness washed over his body like a wave. He was sick. Sick of Aldmer, sick of the council, sick of this forsaken war.

"We cannot remain here much longer." He needed a drink. Nazir nodded to a flagon of wine. Adane took the hint, pouring two glasses. The two sat in silence for a while.

"No, we cannot," he agreed. "We have ten thousand camped here, not to mention the refugees fleeing the Dominion. We'll have to march east soon."

Nazir sipped solemnly. He had brought an immense supply wagon with him when he called his banners, but the combined host was draining them fast. Four thousand hastily raised foot soldiers were from his own lands, some well-equipped hunters and rangers, and of course the essential cavalry, hundreds of mounted lances and bows. Many had come prepared, but some of the marching bands didn't, and the villages paid the price. Crops and barrels of preserved food had been stripped from the villages. They moved across the land like a plague of locusts, leaving hunger in their wake. *Soon we will only have roaches to eat with our rats.* At least they had a unified army. In total, nearly thirty thousand levies marched alongside the legions.

"I will send for more supplies from Vern before we march." Nazir drank deeply. "We should have used our fleet to harry the invasion as they crossed." The anger of that still rankled. Valare was the strongest city in the Barta League, a trading acropolis with impregnable walls. No. They were thought to be impregnable. Even Mercer Duston had failed in his attempt to storm the city, and he had nearly twenty thousand at his back. *How could it fall?* They needed the city. Only a month before the attack, Nazir had pleaded with Aldmer to let him use his fleet to patrol Valare's waters, but had been overruled.

"The war council." Nazir growled. He kicked at a chair, sending it crashing. The frustration of it all made him want to strangle somebody. "Adriena would have listened." Things had indeed become darker since her death, first being the war, which was now on their doorstep. *Was it all worth it?* The rallying of the troops, marching for justice. That had worked, at least in the beginning. Then the might of Selpvia stirred, and the tables had turned.

Adane turned away. "We'll get vengeance for her, I swear it. The Dominion will pay."

But with what? They sat in silence for a moment, listening to the sound of the camp outside, loud men's voices going back and forth, women chattering as they brought water and snatches of drunken singing.

"Maybe Randyll was right about attacking Azult at the beginning of the war." Adane finally spoke up, his gentle eyes ablaze. "It might have avoided this mess."

There are many things we should have done, Nazir thought. "It would have been impossible to reach, let alone besiege," he said. Azult, the formidable port of Klassos. It had ten thousand men dedicated to protecting the ancient city day and night. No. It would have been impossible. Randyll had always been hot-headed, arrogant. But Nazir sympathized with his argument, remembering his words at the council meeting.

"The Dominion needs its ports to mobilize its war machine if it's going to attack us," Randyll had said ferociously, trying to persuade the war council. However, the more able Lance Ironheart had quashed those dreams on the spot.

Maybe if we had tried, we wouldn't be in this hell now, Nazir thought glumly.

"I haven't seen Lance in a while, come to think of it." Nazir would have liked to see the man. He was one of the few able men in the Empire that he trusted. "I thought he'd be with us."

"Lance." Adane's tone was grim. "He's gone, my lord. As soon as he heard of the catastrophes at Yang Point, he laid into Aldmer's regime. Resigned from the council on the spot. Nobody's seen him since. Aldmer was livid."

"What?" Nazir shot to his feet, seething. "Why have I only been told this now?" The young ambassador had been a frequent part of the council for years, and Nazir had nothing but admiration for the man. Adreina had high praise for him. "Why did he leave?"

"I forget sometimes how much time you spend at sea, my friend," Adane laughed sourly. "He called the council fools and that our barbarism would be repaid." His eyes darted back and forth. "It gets worse."

"Worse?"

"Aldmer placed a price on his head for desertion. Sent men to his estate and everything."

Nazir was surprised to see a mocking smile on his right hand man's lips.

"Lance has always been a slippery customer, and it's said he now has an army of his own. Some jumped-up mercenary company, I hear. Wherever they are, I hope they're far away from this hellhole." His smile curdled. "They torched his home you know. Burned it to the fucking ground. It's said he held his dead sister in his arms before he fled south. There's been some nasty rumors about what Aldmer ordered done to her."

Nazir was stunned, sickened. Bile rose to his throat, and it took all his willpower not to retch. "She was barely a woman grown," he said softly. He put down his flagon. *If only I had gotten to Lance first.* He could have protected him and all his family.

Later that evening, Nazir had barely stirred from a restless stupor when he was someone called his name.

"What?" he grunted out.

Adane was there, a grimace on his lips. He was already dressed, sword on his hip.

"I thought I gave orders not to be disturbed?" Nazir said. Adane had the grace to look abashed.

"This cannot wait. Our sire, Bane Aldmer, has called a war council." The dry sarcasm in his voice told plainly how he felt addressing their ruler by that title.

"So much for sleep," Nazir chuckled dryly, but the humor wasn't there. Even so, it was good of Aldmer to make preparations. The enemy was drawing nearer. He got out of bed and grimaced as he stretched. He had no choice but to attend. "Adane, wait outside for me while I dress." Adane nodded and departed the tent.

74

Nazir breathed in the cool air as he left his quarters. The sky was still dark blue, faint stars painted across the heavens. He had decided on simple, comfortable garb. A woolen tunic, with a light sheepskin cloak wrapped around his shoulders. It was usually his custom to dress elaborately, but he was in no mood for it today.

"Where they holding the meeting this time?" He asked.

"At Arban's great wheelhouse, back of the Imperial camp." Adane replied, as the two walked over to where some of Nazir's banner lords were sparring, surrounded by onlookers and camp followers.

At least they're taking this seriously. Third Sword Temar had ordered drilling five times a day, and his levies were, for the most part, co-operating. Nazir was proud of them. Most were veterans from patrolling their lands against the fierce Faxaen clans. *But are they ready for the true enemy?* Nazir hoped they would not have to find out. The clansmen of Faxia were deadly fighters, and life-long enemies of the Empire, but they weren't exactly disciplined. The Dominion was another danger entirely.

The smell of meat from the cook fires filled the air, making Nazir's mouth water as he passed. But it was baked bread he craved most, washed down with ale. That would have to wait.

Trust Mance to flaunt his wealth. Nazir smiled. Fifty feet long, the giant wheelhouse was drawn by three dozen horses. It was a lavish luxury, even if Arban Mance was too frail to sit a horse. Riding for hours on end had its flaws, mainly in the form of painful saddle sores. Nazir was no novice to horses but still found the bane of riding long distances uncomfortable.

"That man has more money than sense," Nazir quipped, reaching the stables. Two burly grooms held their steeds. He felt a little calmer as he climbed onto Jasper's back, his favorite grey stallion.

"He does indeed," Adane laughed back, as the two set off for the wheelhouse, a mile away. This was what he was born to do, as he pushed his stallion faster, urging it on. It felt like freedom, something he hadn't felt in a long time. They rode past endless tents, where peasants and hardened legions alike were bivouacked together, sparring and bonding. It was good to see the Empire in unity, something that didn't happen too often. They passed freeriders, camp followers, servants and refugees, survivors of the fighting east. Most sat around campfires, scrounging for food. A couple begged to their nobles as Nazir and Adane rode past.

Nazir felt a pang of sympathy for them, but there was little he could do. He had enough trouble feeding his own levies, let alone catering to the freefolk. Finally, they made it to the wheelhouse in all its splendor, great curtains of red silk and satins drawn back. Dismounting, they passed the reins to a couple of boys. As they reached the doorway, they were flanked by six men of the Bessian Guard, looking splendid encased head to toe in their iron-clad armor. Aldmer's men. Nazir couldn't help but cast them a disapproving glare, thinking of Lance.

"I'll stay here," Adane offered, casting an uneasy eye at the guards. Clapping him on the shoulder, Nazir entered the wheelhouse.

Hells, even the Order are here. The room was crowded and bustling with angry voices. The heads of the other three houses were present as was customary at these council meetings; the elderly Arban Mance, his spindly fingers flexing angrily upon the table as he sat beside his eldest son, the fiery warrior Carr. There was the sharp-tongued matriarch of House Bael, in Valerie, and of course the two brothers of House Thendil. Arban Mance had been his father's friend when Nazir was only a boy, and was his favorite. Carr gave him a curt nod, a prickly lad of nineteen.

Aldmer beckoned. He gestured at a spare seat next to Mance. Opposite Aldmer and his cronies, at the far end of the table were the men of the Pharos Order, standing like sentinels behind their masters. He didn't know their names, but the man in the middle was unmistakable. Cloaked in blood red robes, his face lost amid wrinkles and battle scars, was Hinari Amos.

He's finally got off his arse at the Sepulcher, Nazir thought.

"You arrived sooner than I expected, Nazir. Excellent." Aldmer had changed from the black robes he was wearing when he had given the execution order, replacing them with great flowing robes of thick blue silk.

My, they look just like the Emperor's, Nazir thought, a slight frown creasing his brow. Still, Aldmer was his leader now, and he shook the man's hand. Aldmer's grip was firm and he smiled kindly at Nazir, though it conspicuously failed to reach his eyes. "Please, sit. It's good to see you."

Nazir took his seat next to Arban Mance, who nodded feebly. The leaders greeted him courteously as he sat, Randyll and Gilbert actually getting from their seats and vigorously shaking his hand. Carris Montague cleared his throat, rising alongside Aldmer.

"Before we move on, first things first. Nazir, the Dominion are marching towards Manesow. We would like your input for the deployments."

It took a long time. All of them started speaking at once, giving their opinion. Nazir let it slide over him, but snippets kept him in focus. Manesow. At least Aldmer hadn't been idle. They currently had sixteen thousand men at the old Valian fortress, fortifying it against the enemy's projected march. *Manesow is where it ends.* The citadel was the obvious place for them to mount a defense. It was well fortified, and the mountains around the Iris river commanded the view for leagues. A vital point of the Empire; they all knew it. It was one hundred miles from Valare, and forty from their current position. If it fell, the Dominion's army had full reign over the Empire's lands, and the rich cities of the western Empire could be attacked. Even the Order was committed; Hinari had pledged fifteen thousand to Manesow.

A couple of Bael men made scathing noises, but thankfully nobody said anything. Nazir was thankful. The amount of support their eternal allies had given the Empire during the war had been exceptional, and tens of thousands gave their lives for the Empire over the five years.

The conversation quickly turned to espionage and their lack thereof in Klassos. *We need to address that too.* With the loss of their holdings in Klassos, their spy network had collapsed with it. In just five short years they had lost centuries of gain.

"Can't we employ the Whisperers?" Randyll grunted. "They could give us the information we need in Klassos."

"Are you mad?" His brother scoffed. "They charge a ridiculous price. And they're strange. They worry me." That matter was quickly dropped. As the talk continued, Nazir felt a growing resentment amongst the council. *No. It's anger. What was going on?* Finally, his confusion was answered.

"He's late." Arban Mance grunted from his corner. "He'd better arrive soon."

"And I still say he can die like the turncloak cunt he is," Randyll spat from his seat. "That traitorous bastard has some nerve running back to us after what he did." Randyll Thendil was a short, angry man, pale and squat. Over his right eye, he wore a fading black patch, a "gift" a sailor had given him when he tried to rob him.

"You will hold your tongue, Randyll, if you'd be so kind," Aldmer silenced him at once. "You have a right to your own opinion, but I won't stand for bickering. It is vital that this goes ahead. I like it no more than you do, but the truth of it is that we need him, and his army."

Randyll fell silent, glowering.

"Who are we waiting for?" Nazir had lost patience.

"Mercer Duston." Gilbert curled his hands into fists. That was most unlike him. The exact opposite of Randyll. The news of it hit home slowly.

"Mercer's coming here?" Nazir said slowly. His eyes swept the council. Every face held the same look, mistrust and fury. "No." He looked at Aldmer. "You cannot mean it." There was an uncomfortable silence. "You want them to ally with us?"

"That is what they want." Carris answered for him, his brutish face grey, his jaw clenched. "Mercer contacted me after the fall of Valare, regarding matters of an alliance. I deemed it prudent to hear him out. Of course, there are misgivings from our fellow members."

"And for good reason!" Randyll's fist slammed onto the table. "Mercer betrayed the Empire and attacked the Barta League. He violated our laws. Thousands in Valare died during his siege. It took nearly two years to defeat him, and you're asking us to simply open our arms and suck his cock?"

"The situation is more serious then you know, Randyll." Aldmer did not raise his voice, but Randyll bristled as though threatened with a knife.

The council fell silent. Nazir felt he was missing something. "What's happened? Tell me." Aldmer's men shot him insolent looks, but Aldmer himself was more sympathetic.

"This is the reason I gathered you all here today. Valare was not the only city to fall. The Barta League has been destroyed. The Dominion landed a second army in their lands, and they have taken their lands and cities. They are marching west as we speak."

The news was worse than Nazir could have dreamed. Not only must they contend with the army from Valare, but another horde was coming from the east. There was shock in most faces, except for those from House Mance. *They already know.*

"The loss of the League has severed our supply lines across the sea, and from the east." Carr Mance was solemn as his father, his small rat like eyes sunken in his face. "The Leagues' army has been destroyed as a fighting force, with only a few hundred survivors from Valare. We've heard nothing from the other states. Likely they have already been lost. The leader of this second army from Klassos is a king, Vultor III. A man as cruel as he is mad."

"And speaking of Valare." Nazir looked to the speaker; one of Hinari's agents. Sil Naso. "Nazir Cessil. I bring news from Valare regarding your eldest son."

Tyrone. His name had an impact, but only a small one. "He chose to forgo his rights when he left the duties of his family and fled to that city," Nazir said calmly. Randyll and Gilbert regarded him warily. Everyone was looking at him. "What of him? What happened?"

"You can breathe, he survived the attack." Sil's face was impassive. Nazir felt something dull. Was it relief? It had been so long. "The Dominion assaulted the city, and destroyed it with sinful Kyrm fire. The Order sent a force to help the survivors, and they're now in a refugee camp, forty miles west of Manesow. But regarding your son, he has been imprisoned."

"Why?" Nazir asked, mainly out of habit. He had not seen his eldest son in nearly a decade. *I can barely remember what he looks like.*

"There are important and reliable sources who speak of treason within the walls," Aldmer interrupted. "Someone betrayed the city to them, and deliberately failed to raise the alarm when the Dominion moved ships into the harbor under cover of fog. Your son is amongst those in custody, and we intend on finding out who helped the enemy."

"Whatever the boy is, I refuse to believe he betrayed that city," Nazir said coldly. "He betrayed my family to go to that place to fulfill his foolish dreams." He struggled to keep the bitterness from his voice. The loss of his heir stung even now.

"From what I hear, he left Nazir's home, in order to go to Valare." Arban Mance wheezed slowly. "I too, find it odd." He nodded politely at Nazir, who felt his jaw tighten. Aldmer seemed to agree.

"Whatever the case, he attacked a member of the Order while we were taking the Paladin into custody," Sil continued, a triumphant smile across his face as he spoke. "I just thought you should know. Do you want to see him? It may be your last chance, after all." At his words, Randyll's arm twitched.

Nazir considered for a moment. "No."

There was movement from outside and one of the Bessian Guard entered. "My lord, he's here."

"I refuse to treat with that treacherous cunt," Randyll snarled as a man strode in. There was no mistaking his face. Mercer Duston looked around, unsmiling. He hasn't changed. He was tall and powerful, with shoulder length brown hair. There were scars and welts across his cheeks, but he looked the same as he did when his army was broken outside the walls of Valare.

"It's good to see you all, in these troubling times," he said mildly. There was a hint of amusement in his hazel green eyes. Randyll spat, and got to his feet, drawing his sword.

"You should be rotting deep under the earth."

"And yet here I stand." Mercer's face was stone. "But I am not here to rub salt into open wounds, Randyll Thendil. The hour is too late. I was sorry to hear of Adreina's death." He added, almost as an afterthought. "We received a bird bearing the words. I would have contacted, but some wounds are too deep I fear."

The remorse in his voice was genuine. Nazir almost believed it.

"She was a kind woman. I remember her well, before she ascended to the regency."

"You dare to speak of her, you fucking traitor!" Randyll stood, his sword sweeping out with a hiss.

"Sit down. Both of you." Aldmer's voice was knife sharp. Randyll's blade remained pointed directly at Mercer's heart, and although nobody spoke, Nazir could see that most in the room were willing him to use it.

"Do as Aldmer says, brother," Gilbert commanded, but he too was glaring at the turncloak. With a final murderous glance at Mercer, Randyll placed his sword on the table, slumped back into his seat. Still smiling,

82

Mercer took a seat next to a couple of Mance's captains, who recoiled visibly.

Nazir couldn't bear to look at him. *He should be buried alive, not sharing our table.*

"It has been a long time." Mercer said softly, looking around them all. "Twenty years, in fact."

"You should be on your knees, begging for forgiveness." Gilbert declared.

"You were a squealing pink bastard at your wet nurse's tit last time I saw you. Don't think to lecture me." Mercer's cold green eyes bore into Gilbert's, but he kept his voice light, friendly. "But yes, it was a serious error of mine, and my household paid for it dearly."

Nazir felt a twinge of reluctant respect for the man. He was as calm and reserved as he was back then.

Mercer gave a heavy sigh, the scars from the past catching up with him. "I paid a great price for my actions, as you all know. Four sons and eight thousand men died in front of those hell gates."

"And two thousand of my own men died stopping you," Valerie Bael spoke for the first time, lifting her sharp little eyes from her flagon wine to meet Mercer's own. Her jaw was rigid, brown teeth bared.

"Whatever treason he committed is of little consequence now," Aldmer told the council in a tone that brooked no argument. "What matters is the future."

Mercer bowed his head. "You are wise. Let me tell you what I know." He reached inside his tunic, laying out a thick wad of greying parchment upon the table. He cleared his throat gruffly.

"The Barta Leagues' forces did not patrol their coastline as vigorously as they should have," Mercer said grimly. "They assumed their neutrality would protect them from the Dominion. I appealed to them, but they ignored my warnings. The Dominion laid waste to our lands with foul weapons."

Kyrm fire. Nazir felt sick. It was yet another weapon they didn't possess, despite the efforts of their alchemists. It wasn't just the Kyrm fire of course, but all the other twisted weapons. The Dominion commanded fierce war elephants, tigers, weyverns, and who knew what else. That didn't bother Nazir as much as their horsemen did. Masters of the plain, they were at least the equal of Harloph's finest cavalry, and far greater in number

Finally, Nazir could bare it no longer, and caught Mercer's attention. "That doesn't explain how you came to be here." Nazir said slowly. "Did you just abandon the League to their fate?"

"I tried to save them, Cessil." Mercer pulled back the sleeves on his shirt; Nazir could see deep scars, half healed. "I deserve your judgment, of course, given our history. As soon as we heard news of the attack, I did what I could to help them. My son, Godwin, called the banners, and I marched as fast as I could to defend the cities, but I was too late. I offered a pact between the cities and my own, a defensive front at the Nowk Mountain pass. They refused. If they accepted, we could have stopped them."

"What news on their movements?" Arban Mance asked Mercer bluntly.

Mercer hesitated. "Little enough from my own scouts. Most of my men are still in the Nowk passes, and I've heard no news from my commanders. I fear the worst for the League. I saw what happened at Garro. The pillars of fire, the sky black as night over the old city, a relic from the old Men. All gone. I can only imagine what it was like for the others, and for Valare."

"How many men have you brought for us?" Gilbert interrupted.

"Oh, I thought you wanted no part of my help?" Mercer shrugged. "I brought just a bodyguard of two hundred men. My son has command of the greater part of my army, which I brought forward to Manesow. I figured you would require some assurances from me, before you accepted my assistance." Mercer's smile curdled. "But, to answer your question, Gilbert, ten thousand infantry and two thousand horse. Over half are still at the passes, but I brought as many as I could. I hope they will suffice."

"You are going to have to do better than that, if that you want to convince me to welcome you back with open arms," Randyll snarled.

Mercer frowned. "You misjudge me, Randyll. If it were not for my actions, the council would not be aware of the Dominion's advance, and the destruction of the Barta League. Furthermore, my army has bloodied their divisions greatly, especially in the Crane Pass. I slayed two of their chieftains in single combat myself. The Dominion have taken heavy losses, but we all have family we want to protect."

"Your death is all I would desire," Randyll muttered dryly.

"We need Mercer's men," Carris grunted, glowering at the belligerent Randyll. "Within three days, we'll have thirty thousand swords at Manesow, but we'll need another host to march east against this new threat. I for one want to see what Mercer can accomplish."

"Mercer," Arban croaked, and Mercer blinked as he turned to face the ancient man. "Do you know how many of the Dominion attacked the League?"

"At a count, thirty . . . forty thousand?" Mercer shrugged. "Could be more. Could be a lot more.

Vultor, however, does not frighten me. He is a violent, brutal man, but he lacks patience. I bled him greatly, and hopefully, he will continue to blunder. The eastern houses will make him bleed even more, but we need to join forces and crush him, before he joins the army from Valare."

"We'll throw them back," a black-skinned Thendil guard raised his fist into the air. "We're each worth a dozen of the scum from Klassos." He grinned. Nobody else shared his smile.

"This is no game," Mercer said coldly. "On the way here, my outriders did some scouting of the Valare front. I know now who leads that army. Kujudo, the Red Sand."

Nazir's blood ran cold.

One of the Pharos Order laughed. "Why should we fear him? He is just a savage."

Aldmer rounded on him. "The demon of Selpvia, the destroyer of our armies at Yang Point? Drowdrite? Because of him! Use your head, fool."

"I must say, sire, I am unconvinced of needing to ally with this traitor. Why should we?" Randyll protested.

"We cannot afford to lose any more. We need Mercer," Aldmer said in awful finality.

He's right. Nazir hated to admit it. The news about Kujudo leading the enemy's vanguard was more chilling than anything else. Everybody knew the legendary skill in battle that man possessed. If he even was a man, after all. If he was in command . . . *Mercer, you bastard. You leave us with no choice, and you know it.* Mercer appeared calm, with a neutral smile that could mean anything.

"What if the Red Sand bypasses our forces at Manesow?" Gilbert was saying. "He'll not be foolish enough to attack such a well-fortified defense, surely?"

It was Mercer who answered. "You would be hard pressed to know what lies within that demon's mind. But walls won't stop them. They burned the League's walls down with Kyrm fire, much like they did to Valare. It's nothing but rugged mountains and hills south of here, and Manesow is the only entry into the richer lands. There is nothing worthy for them in the east. The capital is the ultimate prize. If it falls, it'll be a huge boon to them, and a crippling blow to Bale's legacy. No, they will push west, into the Imperial lands, and Bawsor. It's what I would do, if I were them."

He looked around at the council. "We mustn't let that happen. With Vultor advancing, they'll wait to combine their forces before striking. We must hit the Valarian front first, and drive them back into the sea."

"The Order's men are still occupying the Kahal regions," Hinari said. His voice brittle, barely above a whisper, yet the ancient man's words quieted the room in an instant. "If the enemy dares cross into their territory, they will bleed for every inch. The Kahal will not tolerate another invading force."

"Aye, we have enough trouble quelling them," one of his aides remarked sardonically. Nazir knew what he was referring to. He had fought skirmishes against the Kahal tribes in his younger days and their ferocity would give any grown man nightmares.

"Ten thousand of our kin died fighting the tribesmen, and while they were sinful, brutal thugs, they are fierce beyond peril." Sil said. "The invasion has unsettled them to the extent that they agreed to join us in a defensive pact. Trust me, the Dominion will have little to gain from attacking south."

Mercer cleared his throat, handing a tightly bound scroll to one of the scribes attending the meeting. There was a mocking smile on his face now. "These are our terms."

Arban Mance stiffened at those words. "Terms?" Spittle flew from his mouth. "Are you so foolish to demand terms from us?"

"My price is very small, Arban." Mercer smiled pleasantly at him. "All I ask in return is my House's restoration to the Empire."

The outrage was immediate. "You have no right!" Valerie screeched.

"You dare ask us for terms, when it is you who betrayed the Empire!" Gilbert roared.

"ORDER, ALL!" Aldmer bellowed.

"I know enough to know there is no choice in the matter," Mercer called softly, above the din. "I have not been idle in my exile, and I know that you need help more than ever. Twelve thousand of my knives are sharpened and ready to defend my old home." He smirked. "Or not. As I say, the choice is yours."

Aldmer's eagle gaze regarded him.

You fucking bastard, for making us agree to this. Nazir could gag, but he swallowed back the bile. In truth, his price was not high. The terms had been laid out in detail earlier. That brought some mutters of irritation from the other members of the council. Mercer's demands were indeed few.

"True, you need me, but I need you just as much, if not more," Mercer said. "The Dominion struck my lands too. Put them to the torch. Many are dead."

"Very well, Mercer," Aldmer rose to his feet, the council falling silent. "We accept."

Mercer bowed. "As you wish. Together we can repel the foe."

"Any objections?" Aldmer asked. Nobody spoke, but Nazir could feel the tension in the room. Randyll's face had curdled, and the fury in Valerie's face was all too clear. Aldmer cleared his throat.

"Very well. We have defenses to prepare, and not much time."

A Fleshman's Penance

I was born in a world of pain and poverty, and I built a new world from that pain. I had many faces, but there is one I will follow to the death.

~ Tyir of Irene.

Tyrone's eyes itched. Dust, he supposed. There was hardly any light in the cell, and the single candle he had been given was dying, its tiny flame gnawing at the waxy stump. He strained his eyes to read. The history book was a welcome distraction. Even if each turn of the fragile pages sent up another itchy cloud, making him cough.

The Gaol armies, great and terrifying, marched on foot, clothed in the skin of beasts and man to keep themselves warm. Their steeds, mighty Palveran boars, were their lifeblood. To quote Archscribe Hemaok; "The Gaol live and die by the Boar."

The Valian explorers from the Forbidden Ocean would not find the hordes an easy conquest. The screams of the Second Valian Dynasty were many as their capital city, the great emerald kingdom of Urban, was sacked by the ferocious hordes of the Gaol during their decades long war of Suppression, which eventually spread over the entire continent of Harloph. Many atrocities were committed by both sides.

The next few pages were ragged, torn, the writing faded. *Trust the Order to ruin more of their legacy,* Tyrone thought as he thumbed through the text, angrier than ever.

It was when the great Mer kings of the North stood against the ferocious enemy that they were finally forced back, but only after great and terrible bloodshed.

Enough. Placing the History of our Ancestors, Vol VII aside, he stretched out on the ground, trying to get a little less uncomfortable. The cell was smaller than his cupboard in Valare. It was dingy and stank of shit, but at least he was alone. That was small comfort, but a comfort nonetheless. Not everyone was so lucky. Many had been forced to occupy a single tiny cell, where they were forced to stand. The Order bastards had called them rooms, but in truth they were prisons.

Maybe if I punch another one of the Order, they'd reward me with a shower. Tyrone laughed at the thought, but it soon petered out, ending in a hacking cough. He was alone with his misery and his anger. His unkempt nails dug into his palms as he clenched his fists, his body ached from the beatdowns. But the pain was nothing, nothing . . .

Grief for Valare welled up deep inside him. He couldn't shake the stench of fire and death and he thought he would choke. It had been his home for seven years, ever since he fled his home, his family. House Cessil. He did not miss it. He had no interest in politics, but his father had insisted:

"You must do your duty, in order to carry on the House name," Nazir lectured. He was relentless. "You must be the one, as my heir. When I am gone, you will run this House, and all the power and responsibility of it will be yours."

Why did it have to be his? He had two younger brothers, both far more skilled in the administrator's trade then him. Tomea and Keir were more studious, obedient and adapted for the task then he ever was. He never had interest in becoming the next master of House Cessil, even if it were his right. While his brothers studied and learned the secrets and joys of their duties, Tyrone wanted to study history. Valare provided just that; freedom and a means to pursue his ambitions. He wanted real knowledge. And he wanted to learn how to fight.

But now the city was in ruins, along with everything he knew. And everyone. Oman and Jeramine were gone, dead. His good hand clenched into a fist. He would give them justice.

His bare foot scraped against the floor, his skin blackened with dirt. *Damn them all.* His fingers flexed, desperate for any weapon. Order guards had wrestled his sword from his hand when he was finally overpowered. The days since had been a blur.

His foot collided with his pail of water, knocking it over. Tyrone roared, slamming a fist into the wall. The pain of his knuckles hitting the stone did nothing to quell his rage, or his despair.

Betrayal. That was what the Order had told them, when the last of the survivors had struggled into the hastily erected asylum camps to the south. He recalled the cold, furious eyes of Commander Sil, an ugly man brings only ugly news.

"Valare is no more. Our own blood was shed in its destruction," he told them. "We have reason to believe that someone in your ranks betrayed you, and Harloph itself. We will have to interrogate to find the truth. All men will report for voluntary confinement." That was followed by two days of long, brutal marching before they reached the great fortress of

Zachmir, which the Order had been fortifying for weeks.

The Dominion laid waste to Valare and barely a thousand made it out alive. Tyrone had spent days in a desperate run, searching for any sanctuary. Dozens dropped from fatigue and hunger daily, others from wounds. Finally, they were picked up by the Order. Not long after, whispers of betrayal began. Memories of the battle were hazy, and Tyrone's body was in so much pain that he spent most of his days and nights swaddled in linen cloths, essence of dittany stinging his body to protect from the burning Kyrm fumes. As time passed, he felt doubts. He saw with his own eyes the huge fleet approaching his home. How did nobody see it coming?

Some reacted with disdain and outright revulsion to the Order's commands. Lazarus had protested furiously against the treatment.

"How could any of my people have a part in this?" he argued, as Imperial agents and the Order's inquisitors took injured and healthy men alike into holding cells for questioning. But they wanted answers, at all costs.

Some refused to be taken into custody, and the first few days were marked with brawls. That led to Tyrone's imprisonment. He intervened when he saw an Order soldier beating an old man, his only crime refusing interrogation. Even through his own agony, Tyrone could not stand for it. It was a memory of Oman that made him charge at the Order attacker, knocking him to the ground and reaching for his throat. He would have done more if he hadn't been pulled off. It had taken four men to overpower him. Only later, when he was thrust into the small, cramped cell not fit enough to drown a mouse, did he begin to regret his actions.

The days passed in a haze of misery. He was visited in his cell by two gaolers, who checked in on him twice a day, either to leave food or treat his wounds. The bread was hard, but edible. He was tended by an elderly woman, the physician masked and clothed in woven black silk, whose gentle touches and words soothed his anger and pain. She was kind, but Tyrone was too lost in grief and anger to care. His back spasms were easing, but the burns on his left hand still had problems healing. Again, he wished for his friends to be here to comfort him. *Why did they have to die?*

When he was alone, the barred jail door locked with a metallic click and the gaoler's footsteps moving away, Tyrone could not prevent tears falling, drops of grief mingled with anger. He had been happy in Valare. *Oman was always kind to me.*

Oman had been his first friend, after he arrived in Valare. That was seven years ago when he was just fourteen. It had been a long trip; four days on the waters of the Tangent sea before the trade ship docked in the harbor. He had come across Oman while browsing one of the stalls near the dockside. *He was always a tiny thing.* Tyrone smiled. Oman's owl face peered inquisitively up at him, as Tyrone used some of his savings to buy bread. Although Tyrone found great kindness by many in the city afterwards, Oman was the one who first befriended him.

He was skilled in the art of healing though. Tyrone looked down at his bandaged hand. Moving his fingers was painful, they were slow and stiff. He remembered Oman's glare of determination, felt his power, how it aided him. *Oman's wood-arts. It saved me.*

That was something he knew little of, in truth. Magic, for lack of a better word, was spoken of in secret. It was not something brought up in public, for fear of reprisal by the Order. Oman had come from the far south in the barrowlands of Irene; a poor land, but free from the Order's persecution.

The gaolers kept attending him, and Tyrone had been too angry and upset to talk to them at first. It would be too tempting to punch them, or worse. However, once his body and mind began to recover, he started asking questions whenever a jailor came.

"Why am I in here?"

"I did no treason. None of us did. Let me out."

"Are my kin well?"

He may as well have been interrogating his chamber pot for all the answers he received.

He did catch some snippets of conversation, usually when the gaolers switched turns to stand guard outside his cell. Most was talk about daily life. The two clearly had some affiliation with each other, as both discussed their families at length. A couple of times Tyrone managed to get some useful nuggets. The Order had fully mobilized for the first time in forty years, and was in the process of fortifying the eastern passes with the Empire, to prepare for the advance of the Red Sand. He heard Manesow was where the Empire was making its stand, along with thousands of the Order. He heard the Dominion had a magic army of wolves, and were pillaging the capital as they spoke.

If it comes down to the Order fighting, we're all fucked. Other news had enraged Tyrone. The Empire was persecuting those who showed any hesitation in defending their borders, and there were many instances of families taken in the dead of night. Many had been imprisoned and executed in droves. It made his blood boil. *If that is what the Empire is now, I'm glad I left.*

After what seemed like an age, somebody spoke to him. It was a middle-aged, sharp-tongued officer who unlocked the door. Tyrone was sleeping on his cold blanket, desperately trying to keep warm as the man entered. His black eyes narrowed as he examined the cell.

"These quarters are not comely," the man commented with a sniff, breathing in the reek of stale sweat, piss and shit.

You're the ones who put me in here. Tyrone thought furiously. He kept silent. He had attacked a common soldier. This man was of much higher rank, and likely would have no qualms about cutting his throat.

"I apologize for your incarceration. It is a terrible thing for you all to suffer, but we deemed it necessary." He lifted up the hem of his flowing red cloak, stepping into the cramped space. He sniffed again. "I have to ask you. Do you know anything regarding the betrayal?"

"All I know is that the enemy attacked my home," Tyrone felt exhausted. All he wanted was to sleep, or weep, or both. "First thing I knew of the attack was guards running into my dormitory calling for us to arm and join the defense. We were . . .", he broke off, remembering. He had finished playing a prank on one of his fellow scholars in the house, a smelly, miserable cur called Key. The laughter that rang through the beds that morning as Key spluttered on the ground, soaking wet, was music to his ears then. Now it was a painful memory. They were all likely dead. He hadn't seen them since.

The officer's expression was impassive, emotionless. For a long time he did not speak.

Just get on with it and leave me in peace, Tyrone thought angrily.

The Order officer stirred. "Many of my kin lived in Valare," he said finally. He turned away. "Including my brother. I know what you are thinking, prisoner. But all I want is justice for the bastard who betrayed your homeland. We are getting closer to the truth every day."

Tyrone looked at the officer then. He could see the battle raging in his face. The man continued. "This isn't easy for us too. It's just procedure. The more we know the better. If you had cooperated, then you would be in more comfortable quarters, but the assault of a soldier of our faith is a serious crime." His lips pursed together. The single candlelight in the cell guttered and went out.

Tyrone sat in silence. "I'm sorry for your loss," he said finally. *Would I feel the same, if my brothers had died?* Oman's face swam before his eyes. His gut clenched. He did. Oman and Jeramine were his brothers.

The officer smiled then, a mere twitch. "You are kind, for those words," he said gruffly. "He was a good soldier, had a good heart and was an even better brother. We've all suffered losses." He regarded Tyrone for a moment. "You cared for your home, did you not? You must have done, to come from far away."

That took Tyrone aback. "Yes, I did. How do you know where I came from?"

"It's not difficult, prisoner. You have the look of a Balian." Tyrone didn't answer. "I know this is hard, but we need answers. Do you know anybody who may have wanted to betray the city? I do not know Lazarus." He paused, his brow furrowing. "I know of his history with my Order. He betrayed us, may Pharos judge him. But he was loved by Valare. He saved them, after all, from Mercer's rebellion. Who would betray him?"

Tyrone only knew Lazarus in passing, but the man had indeed been loved by most. He had lavishly supported the school, and defended them against critics. Not a single person he knew in Valare had a bad word against their beloved leader. "I have no idea. I was only a scholar . . . Everybody I knew spoke of him highly, and of Valare."

The officer nodded. "I thought so. I had an idea you wouldn't know anything."

Silence fell. Finally, with a sigh, the man strode to the cell door. "Very well then. As you were."

"Wait. How long do I have to be in here?" Tyrone shouted. Instantly he regretted his words. The man turned back, all pretense of warmth gone. Every line of his face had hardened.

"As long as it takes for justice to be served." With a furious final glare, he slammed the doors shut and locked it. Then, the sound of his footsteps receded, leaving Tyrone in almost pitch blackness.

Tyrone had no idea how much time had passed since the Order officer had questioned him. It was to his great surprise when the door heaved open.

"You're to come with me," a man grunted. He filled the door, blocking out most of the light from the corridor.

He had no idea of their names, as they usually didn't talk to him. There were two men who usually came, two similarly sized, bad tempered hulks. He gave this one the rather cruel name Sir Limp, as he always seemed to struggle walking.

"Why?" Tyrone asked.

"Don't ask questions."

Tyrone was long growing tired of this dingy, cramped shithole. Even walking with the sweaty gaoler was preferable. He got to his feet unsteadily, his foot buckling. The man caught him roughly with one arm to keep him from stumbling. "Come with me."

They went up the stairs, leading to the courtyard. Tyrone's eyes slowly adjusted to the sunlight, as they went outside. The cold fresh air hit him with force, his senses overwhelmed. The brightness of the sun was dazzling, but Tyrone relished in the fresh air upon his face, cleansing him. The gaoler continued to pull him by arm, cajoling him to climb the steep steps to the ramparts. Tyrone walked up almost joyfully. To be out of the cell was a wonder! The gaoler puffed his way up the steps behind Tyrone. Tyrone ran to the wall. He was standing on top of the world, looking down below.

"Follow me." Sir Limp ordered. Tyrone took one last look at the sprawling army camp, stretching as far as the eye could see. Tents and pavilions of every size and color dotted the ground below, housing what must be thousands of people. He could see archers readying great longbows, blocks of men holding ten-foot high spears drilling tirelessly. The sounds were deafening, men and women shouting and jostling for attention, training for battle. *They are massing for war.*

Tyrone followed the fat gaoler, wondering where they were going.

"You see?" Sir Limp said with a wave of one fatty hand at the scene below the ramparts. "That's our power, boy. Never forget it." A slack grin crossed his fat lips.

"What are they doing?"

"The enemy are marching on our position, and the Order has mobilized to fight the invaders. Fourteen thousand sons of Pharos you can see out there. The largest army since the great Hinari united us against the scum of Temujn and his black horde. Nothing but a bunch of goat-fuckers, the vile Voyavan tribes. Come on. You're to attend that bastard, the Paladin. Nobody else wants to go near him."

They entered one of the towers, and he stooped to go through the low door. Tyrone wrenched his neck around for a final look at the light, and caught edge of a furious conversation.

"We cannot march!" moaned a high-pitched man's voice.

"We have to. The Red Sand is bringing up serpents to attack Manesow. This is where we fight," growled another, a woman.

Serpents? Tyrone wanted to know more, but Sir Limp seized hold of his arm again, and before long he was swallowed again by darkness. It took Tyrone a few moments to remember Sir Limp's words.

"The Paladin?"

"The Necromancer, the curse of the world. Call him what you like." Sir Limp held an ugly snarl on his face. "I'm surprised you don't know of him. His reputation is legendary. He was condemned to die, and now we fucking have him again. Whoever destroyed Valare gave him to us. We should thank them for that, for now we'll have justice." A satisfied smile crossed his face as he came to a halt in the corridor.

Tyrone's blood boiled at his words. "You call it justice?" He said coldly. "Thousands died, including hundreds of your own."

There was a moment's pause, before Sir Limp slowly reached up and smacked him across the face. The sheer laziness of the assault was more stunning than the blow itself. Seething, Tyrone steeled for a fight, but the gaoler raised a huge fist.

"Don't try me, or you'll get another. You know nothing of such matters. A servant of the Pharos is tenfold of anybody from Valare. They hid the Paladin from us, along with that grey piece of filth traitor Lazarus. Therefore, their deaths are deserved."

He seized Tyrone's arm in an iron grip and pulled him down another corridor, then up some steep steps.

"While you're here you'll attend to his wants," he went on. "None of us will touch him. You may care for him as you please. He's an old man after all."

Tyrone was shaking. He tried to pull away, but the gaoler's grip was too strong. There was a sense of inevitably. *I come from one cell to another, and I have to clean someone else's shit?* He stopped dead in the corridor.

"No."

"You'll do as you're told while you're in our custody." The squat man snarled, grabbing his throat. "You're still on charge for assaulting a servant of the one true God. Unless you would prefer to return to your prison?" He chuckled then. "Or, you grow tired of your occupation? My boys could surely show you a different path." He leered at Tyrone, his eyes lingering on his crotch.

Tyrone recoiled, glaring at him. *Just you try.* Whatever the case, he would not return to that cell. Even so, the injustice of it all galled him. "Fine. I'll attend to this . . . Paladin, or whatever you call him."

Limp smirked. "Good boy. Come on."

They stopped outside a handsome oak door that looked remarkably out of place. Tyrone was surprised, expecting something less clean. He had heard snippets when he was in Valare, of a madman who dwelled within the walls, a sorcerer who experimented on the dead. Rumors he had dismissed. But then visions of the dead rising came to mind.

Sir Limp opened the door. The cell was large and lavish and Tyrone's eyes opened wide as he stared at all the splendor. The walls were draped in long silk banners in all colors of the rainbow, and bright satin cloths. Then he saw the window and his mouth hung open. He closed it quickly, trying to assume an air of nonchalance. There were two people in the room, talking quietly. An elderly man and a slim woman wrapped in a silver cloak too big for her.

"Well, you condemned cunt, here's your servant," Sir Limp announced with a mocking tone that barely masked the hatred in his voice. The elderly man in the armchair lifted his head and Tyrone stepped back in alarm. The man's cheeks were hollow, his face stretched so tightly it was as though someone had painted a skull.

Finally, the Paladin acknowledged them, looking into Limp's eyes with a mocking smile.

"You'll get what you deserve" Sir Limp said. "Hinari is going to be there when we burn you alive for your crimes."

The prisoner stayed silent, regarding Limp with indifference, even boredom.

The gaoler laughed, pushed Tyrone into the room and slammed the door shut behind him. There was a strained silence.

"Meira, leave us please, if you will." The Paladin said, gently. His eyes were now fixed on Tyrone who felt a chill under the old man's gaze.

Tyrone stepped forward into the room, taking a closer look at the Paladin. *He doesn't look that dangerous.* He was tall but thin, draped in a thick white cloak falling to his knees. He was bald, only a few white hairs remaining. He wore a gentle, fatherly expression, but there was a fire in his eyes. Tyrone couldn't look away.

"I trust you were brought here to attend me?" the old man said.

The woman got to her feet, bowing her head. She left silently, ignoring Tyrone as she passed.

"I asked you a question," the senior repeated. This time, Tyrone answered.

"They said it was this or my cell. I've had enough of that shithole."

"I am not surprised. I saw what you did. You were trying to protect someone from one of those pious bastards."

"That's right," Tyrone said.

"Not many would do as you did," the Paladin whispered.

"Is that a problem?" Tyrone demanded. He was starting to regret his impulse that day, but he wouldn't stand by and do nothing.

"No problem. I'm just surprised." There was a moment's respite before he smiled. It made him seem even more hideous. "I am well attended by my own, Tyrone."

Tyrone blinked. "You know me?"

"Not well," The man admitted softly. "I knew most that lived in Valare. Part of my occupation, and Lazarus encouraged me to know them to lessen my hatred of man." He chuckled dryly. "And I know of where you came from. Your family name is known to me. I do not know why a man of Vern came to be in Valare, however. Let alone an heir."

"I had to leave." Tyrone said uncertainly.

"I understand. Lazarus felt the same. That's why we both came to Valare." He paused. "Since I know your name, it's only fair that you know mine."

"You have many, I've heard."

"Indeed. The Paladin, Necromancer, the Demon of Man. I've had many names in my life. But my true name is Tyir of Irene."

Tyrone felt something stir inside, something unpleasant. He'd heard about him for certain.

"So, you probably heard how evil I am, thanks to our gaolers." His smile was twisted.

"He was . . . very kind."

"So, nothing new then."

Tyrone couldn't help but laugh. *He shows them no fear, despite being in their power.* "They say you're to be executed."

"Aye. They enjoy executing people it seems."

Tyir's face was emotionless as he beckoned Tyrone closer. "But that is something for another time. Can you read and write?"

"Fairly well, yes," Tyrone replied, a distinct pride in his voice.

"Good." Tyir gestured to a table in the corner, where there were quills and parchment littered across the table. "There is some work I need your help with. I will recite, you copy. No need to worry about its contents. I have my secrets, you have yours,"

He grinned at Tyrone, his eyes twinkling. "My own look after me well. This is all that I will require you for. You may as well get comfortable. There're blankets on the floor. I hope they will be suitable."

Tyrone hesitated a moment, before walking over to the table. The alternative was not an attractive thought at all. "You like the sound of your own voice, I take it?"

Tyir chuckled softly. "You could say so, I guess. I haven't thought of it like that."

Tyrone nodded, and reached for the quill.

Despite his reputation, Tyrone found Tyir to be knowledgeable and kind. He asked little of Tyrone, only writing his recitations. Tyrone let the topics wash over him; most of it was stuff he didn't understand anyway. Even so, the next few days were the calmest he had felt in a long while.

"Tell me Tyrone. What took you to Valare?"

Tyrone glanced up from his bed to look at Tyir. The stone floor was hard, but the blankets were warm and clean. He'd slept better in the last four days then he had in weeks. The Paladin was standing by the lone window, gazing outside.

"That's a long story."

Tyir sighed. "I'm due to be executed soon, apparently. I don't have unlimited leisure time. If it's a long story, you'd best get to it."

"You make a good point," Tyrone smiled.

Tyir's servants attended him several times a day. Tyrone had noticed the lack of visits by the Order for some days, an ominous sign. That suited him. He felt waves of anger whenever he thought of them anyway. Tyir's people were of the same mold, hooded and masked in black. None spoke to Tyrone, but he could feel them staring.

"Tyrone?"

He stirred from his thoughts. Tyir was watching him patiently. "Sorry. I guess I always wanted to study the past, to understand how our world came to be. I couldn't do it as a Cessil, so I left for Valare."

"An interesting path." Tyir had turned back to the window, his lips curling into a frown. "Lazarus and I founded the school shortly after Mercer's defeat. Strangely, it is difficult to do so when an army surrounds your walls."

Tyrone had heard much of that. Tales of Lazarus' heroism were rampant, part of local folklore. It made him proud.

"It was difficult at home. Oh, I know, it sounds so ordinary. A child doesn't agree with his family, flees to gain freedom from his bonds." His voice was bitter. "I had to escape. That future was something I didn't want."

"Many have sought the Barta League and the freedom of its laws for whatever they desire. You weren't the first," Tyir's voice was distant, but sympathetic. "It must have taken you some planning, to come to the city. How did you get away?"

Tyrone shrugged. "Three months of saving every coin I got my hands on until I could afford a space on the caravan to Arkane, then I took a ship to Valare. I wanted a new start, completely."

Tyrone turned to the book he was copying for Tyir, the spine cracked and dusty. If he hurried, he would be able to finish this chapter before lunch. He found the notes and prepared to get to work.

The cell door opened, the hinges squeaking. A masked and cloaked figure entered. One of Tyir's men. He had only seen a couple of his people, the woman called Meira, and a tall hooked nose man who smelled of apples and sweat. This one looked different, slender and quick.

Tyrone turned his eyes back to the book, finding the words upon the wrinkled yellow paper.

The plague swept through the plains of Harloph, countless dead rebirthed to replace the life.

It was hard to focus. Tyir and the man were conversing in whispers. Tyrone felt a chill on his neck; wheeling round he caught the newcomer staring at him. *What was that?* His mouth covered by a black mask, the man's eyes were piercing, murderous.

Tyrone turned his gaze back to his work, but his heart hammered in his chest.

Finally, he heard the door open and shut. Tyrone let out a breath, and looked to Tyir.

"They're on the move, it seems," Tyir finally murmured.

"What's going on?" Tyrone asked.

In response, Tyir wordlessly gestured for him to look outside the window. Curious, Tyrone scrambled out of bed. The window was small but gave a commanding view across the camp.

"The Order have left," Tyir said. All that remained were the ghosts of their tents. "The Dominion is marching on Manesow. Battle will soon be joined."

"One of the guards said something about their having serpents." Tyrone replied.

"No surprise, coming from the Dominion." Tyir's own voice was grave. "They're marching to their deaths."

"What are they?" Tyrone asked, a chill running through him.

"Nobody knows for sure. What I know of them though suggests they are great siege engines, for lack of a better word. They come from the far north of Klassos, forged in the recesses of the Kyrgos Mountains. Some say they are created by the heart of a weyvern concealed into the body, but those people are fools; it is a man-made weapon. A trebuchet, but they make the siege of Harloph look like children's toys."

Tyir shrugged. "From what I know, they have four of them in this army alone. Behemoths, they are, each requiring five hundred men dedicated to wielding it. Clever of them. Our brave defenders have no choice but to attack, or feel the wrath of its power bringing Manesow to rubble."

"But Manesow is the greatest fortress in the Empire!" Tyrone gasped. "Surely it can't fall so easily?"

Tyir sighed, turning away from the window to face Tyrone. "My young friend, this isn't so simple. The Empire is fighting a war it cannot win. Maybe that is why I am being brought to them? Fools! They have no hope of defeating the Red Sand in open battle."

Tyrone felt the walls close in around him; Tyir's mouth was still moving, but his words washed over him. The cold stench of the weyverns, screeching as they thrashed against the walls of Valare, his home. *Gone, like so many.* His hands clenched. He had always grown up listening to tales of the Dominion, the elder powers across the Tangent Sea, but now . . . Tyir's words finally reached him. *He's leaving.* Numbness enclosed him. What the hell am I supposed to do now?

"What about me?" His voice came out as a wavering squeak.

"I don't know," Tyir said softly. "War is fast hitting our shores, and will soon engulf us. This is only the start. Most will be lucky. Death is a blessing compared to some fates."

Tyrone couldn't take anymore. War, death, misery. Everything around him was tightening. He slumped to his knees, desperation engulfing him. It wasn't fair. He had lost his home, everybody he knew, and now he was alone, nothing protecting him from the onslaught sure to come. Then a hand pulled his head back roughly, and something hot was poured into his mouth. Darkness swiftly followed.

Tyrone opened his eyes slowly. His dreams had been cruel, full of screams. People he knew and strangers in the shadows roaring in battle and blood, as faceless horrors closed in from all sides.

What happened? He was cold. A breeze caressed his cheek. That was odd. Was the window open? He could feel weak beams of sunlight in his eyes. His head was swimming, his vision slowly clearing. He looked around groggily, searching for Tyir.

Tyir was gone. Tyrone slowly got to his knees, heart pounding. He was still in the cell, but the old man was nowhere to be seen. All of Tyir's possessions were gone too. Then he remembered.

Tyrone rushed to the window, staring, open mouthed at the sight below. The tents were still there, but now empty, flapping pathetically in the wind. Many had collapsed, others were smoldering. A couple of red-cloaked bodies lay on the ground, motionless.

Whatever was happening, he had to get out. Somebody had left fresh clothes on the table. He dressed quickly, pulling on a grey sheepskin tunic and a pair of woolen trousers; scratchy and hot, but preferable to stinking rags. He was just pulling on a pair of black boots when he heard movement behind him, footsteps.

"He's awake," said a man gruffly. "Good; I was getting tired of guarding him."

"Stop complaining," a quieter voice reproached. "It was as the master ordered." The door crashed open revealing three men.

"Tyrone Cessil," the first man said, giving a mocking bow. Tyrone stared at them. They were masked and robed in black. In spite of this, he recognized the hooked-nose one. One of Tyir's servants.

The biggest of them gestured. "You'll come with us, now." He stepped into the room, ducking to get through the door. His voice was thick, a Pyran accent.

"Why should I come with you?" Tyrone demanded. He pressed his back against the table, trying to keep the fear out of his voice.

"It's not a request." A shorter slender man said, a dagger appearing in his hand. Tyrone groped blindly behind him. His fingers closed around the hilt of a dinner knife. It would do.

"Reach for that little apple-peeler, and it'll go worse for you."

The man that Tyrone knew spoke this time, much quieter and calmer than his associate. "Come along quietly and we won't have to get . . . rough." His eyes sparkled with amusement.

"No!" Tyrone shouted. He made a bolt for the door, but his path was barred.

"Take him. Try not to injure him. The master wants him unharmed," the Pyran said. "Besides, I like the look of the lad."

The three closed in.

Instinct took over. Avoiding his blind side, Tyrone jammed his elbow as far into the left hand man's gut as he could reach. He heard angry noises, followed by the sound of drawn steel. Another hand grabbed at the back of his head. He wrenched free and hurled himself towards the door.

"After him," said the Pyran's voice. "And try not to harm him, Sleeper."

Tyrone sprinted along the corridor, heart hammering. He had to get out!

The courtyard was deserted, deathly silent. Wood smoke filled the air. There were footsteps behind him.

He had to be quick. The fort was large, but it would not hide him forever. Hurrying down stone steps, he began searching for anybody. His fellow Valarians, the survivors, they had to be around. His legs collided with something hard, sending Tyrone sprawling to the ground. Blood, dirty and metallic flooded his mouth as his teeth clamped on his tongue.

"Going somewhere?" There was a soft, cruel chuckle.

Tyrone held out the knife. "Don't come near me!" He hissed, but he couldn't keep the wavering out of his voice.

"Come now, you're trembling like a child." The Pyran chuckled softly. "You're in safe hands, lad. We aren't here to hurt you."

"Leave him to me, Horse," The smallest man whispered. His voice was light with amusement, but the sound drove a spike of fear into Tyrone's heart.

"Try and stop me!" he snarled and ran headlong at them. Tyrone no longer cared at this point. He had to get out, fight to the death if that's what it took.

The one called Horse gasped as Tyrone sprinted at them. Then something sharp dug into his neck and Tyrone stumbled. His chest constricted, his mouth turning numb as his legs collapsed. The pain was indescribable; he couldn't even scream. He choked, writhing on the ground, his mind going hazy. He clutched his chest with both hands, heard the dull thud as the knife fell from his hand. His vision was growing black.

"Sleeper, you fucking idiot," said the Pyran. "What did you do that for?"

Grim Defeat

War can only work when both sides believe they are doing the right thing.

~ Bentley Thatcher

The cell was like most; dank, stinking and full of the hopeless desperation of the condemned.

"He's ready to talk now, sire," Carris said, throwing the boy to the flagstone floor. His face was badly bruised, long hair matted with dirt and sweat. He breathed heavily as he spat out part of a broken tooth. Aldmer stood alongside Carris, hawk like eyes red-rimmed as they locked on their prey. Nazir and Lazarus looked on, neither speaking.

It is a darker world we live in, thought Nazir from the doorway, powerless to stop the torture. *It is for the greater good.* He had to repeat those thoughts several times a day, as he bore witness to more beatings, more executions. As the war spiraled out of control, so did Aldmer's regime, trying desperately to keep hold of their falling Empire. Lazarus of Valare, grey and ancient, stood by Aldmer's side, powerless.

"I'm going to ask you again. And be quicker about answering, or I'm going to start taking fingers," Carris snarled as he threw a punch into the captive's gut.

This is our military leader, our de facto Emperor. Nazir felt nausea rising in his throat. This was not justice. It was torture. *Murder.*

Aldmer moved swiftly, grabbing the boy by his throat.

"You heard my man. Your precious Piez has already paid for his treason, so tell us what you know. Don't even try and lie to me, you fucking piece of filth." This was too much and Lazarus advanced, fists clenched.

"Leave him! Piez has already confessed and paid for his sins. You killed him, remember? There is nothing to be gained from this."

"Stay out of this," barked Carris.

Aldmer regarded Lazarus, an incredulous look across his face. "Your home was destroyed because of treachery. We must sometimes do vile things, for the good of our people. This must happen, Lazarus."

Nazir thought otherwise. *Lazarus speaks true. This solves nothing.* The memory of Piez's screams was nauseating; Aldmer's soldiers had lowered the boy feet first into a cauldron of boiling water. Nobody deserved that death. The smell had a terrible resemblance to cooked ham, and it clung to Nazir like perfume. He couldn't forgive the regime, not for the manner they extracted these so called confessions.

Nazir had heard tales of what went on in the dungeons. He could hardly believe they were true. Piez and others had confessed to allowing Dominion ships into the Valarian bay under cover of thick fog. The Balian people were horrified by the news.

"Who would sell out their own people?" Nazir heard many ask at the public execution. Some called it justice, for the suffering to the free people of Valare. But this torture? *This was not justice.* Nazir felt sick with anger.

The captive struggled in his bonds. Finally, he looked up at Aldmer. He said nothing. That earned him another punch from Carris. He reeled as his head turned from the force of the strike, fresh blood pouring from his nose.

Nazir recoiled at the sight. He felt overwhelmed by shame and remorse.

"You're driving me to this. You don't want to make me angry. What . . ." Carris' words were punctuated by another blow, "do you know?" He gazed angrily down at the boy who could not be a day over sixteen.

There was a few moments of silence before the boy finally spoke. His voice was hoarse, thick with the blood.

"I'm sorry," he burbled thickly, through blood running into his lips. "Piez was my friend. But I don't know anything about his movements. I don't know why he did this."

He was bawling now, his face a smear of blood and snot. Lazarus twitched.

"I don't know anything about treason. Please, no more!" He screamed again as Carris advanced on him, carrying an ugly bar of sharp iron.

"That's not good enough."

"Stop, please!" The captive's voice went up an octave, the terror palpable in his voice. He licked his cracked lips, shuddering from the impact as Carris whipped him across the face with the metal bar. His nose snapped in a gout of blood.

Aldmer glared down coldly at the boy. "What is your name?" The boy did not reply, lying on his back, gasping in pain.

"Lazarus," Aldmer turned to face the reluctant spectator. "I heard you know your people like family." There was a mocking tone to his voice. "What's his name?"

There was a pause before Lazarus finally answered, his voice bitter. "Jared."

The boy began screaming again as though his name was his death sentence. "I don't know what you're talking about!" Jared writhed pathetically in his bounds. "I knew nothing about Piez. I had nothing to do with it!"

"His crimes are yours too!" Carris roared, whipping him again. "It's because of scum like you that we're in this mess with the Dominion marching on our homes! For that, you *will* be judged!"

"Aldmer, he is one of my own," Lazarus reminded him sharply. "Let me speak to him. You owe me that, at least."

"I owe you nothing, remember that" Aldmer replied coldly. He took a step back nonetheless. "But as you wish." His tone was grudging, yet showed the first sign of restraint.

Lazarus limped over to the boy.

"I looked after you all as if you were my own, Jared," Lazarus whispered. "Many gave their lives to defend our walls."

Jared sniffed. "I don't know anything about his betrayal, my Jaal. I swear it on my family's life . . . if they aren't already dead." Tears began to flow anew. Carris let out a cruel laugh.

"I believe him." Lazarus said firmly, looking at Aldmer. "He doesn't know about any betrayal."

Aldmer remained silent, his fierce gaze boring into Jared's bloody face. Nazir thought he saw a little of the rage in those shrewd, merciless eyes fade.

"I see," he said, reluctantly. "Carris, keep him here until I decide his fate, and see that his wounds are treated." A small dose of mercy.

Lazarus glanced back at Jared, his eyes wavering. Nazir followed against his will, leaving the prisoner alone with Carris. The boy was sure to die. Bile rose in Nazir's throat.

"Don't kill him. He's innocent." Lazarus limped in place alongside Aldmer and Nazir. "Piez may have betrayed us, though I must protest at your barbaric methods. But not him. Please not him."

"I like this no more than you," Aldmer exclaimed. "But we must send a message to any other traitors." A muscle twitched in his jaw, as he tugged at the golden chain around his neck. "We're fighting a war, you do understand that, Lazarus?"

"I watched the Dominion burn my city, thanks to your war," Lazarus replied sharply.

They took a turn, climbing up a tight bank of stairs

"I am still ruler of my people, and their fate should rest with me. We'll help you fight the Dominion. They're our foe as much as yours, don't *you* realize that, Aldmer?"

Aldmer laughed, but the mirth did not reach his eyes. "My war? You're part of Harloph. The enemy threatens us all." He stopped and turned to look at Lazarus. "I won't stand for traitors. And it's Sire, or Your Imperial Majesty."

"Sire, since when?" Lazarus demanded in surprise.

"Since the Empress died."

Nazir held his tongue. It would not do to question Aldmer's authority. In spite of the fact that their leader had not been named Emperor, he had assumed its mantle. *But would the people accept him*, he thought. *Would they have a choice?*

"My people belong to a free city," Lazarus snarled, his eyes bright. "The Empire has no power over them!"

"You aren't in Valare anymore. It's lost. You're under my protection now, and subject to my law."

Aldmer stared into Lazarus' eyes, unblinking. For a moment Nazir wondered if he was going to strike the old man.

"There are changes coming, and the war is growing, Lazarus," Aldmer declared angrily. "And I'm not going let you tell me how to deal with turncloaks."

They reached the top of the stairs, emerging onto a platform with a low wall. Nazir felt the warmth of the sun hit his tanned face, a stark contrast to the dank chill inside. Just below them were the battlements of Carin Fort, where a constant steel on stone noise emanated as masons shaped and laid stone. Further below, vast trenches were being dug, while mangonels and scorpions were rolled into position.

This is folly, he thought with a growing dread. Manesow was their gamble, nearly forty thousand marched. So much went into the defense, with no quarter given. Barely a third returned alive. The rest were either dead, or rumored shipped back to Klassos in chains to work in the camps of the Dominion. It was a disaster of epic proportions.

Even so, despite everything, Nazir could see the gritty determination etched into the faces of everyone he set eyes on. It brought some happiness back, a flicker of hope even in their times of chaos.

We will keep fighting, Nazir thought with a surge of pride. The people were broken, bloody, but they loved their land. They would fight to the death to protect their country. But now that Manesow has fallen, what hope did lesser forts have? It was said only the Sepulcher of the Order and Bawsor itself had stronger defenses than the great fortress of Manesow.

"Lord Aldmer!"

A courier hurried up the steps to them. "Hinari commands you to visit him. He's spitting blood about the necromancer. The Order is furious."

Aldmer stared at the courier coldly. "Fine. I'll tend to him shortly. Fucking Order."

117

He turned to address Nazir and Lazarus as the boy hurried away down the steps. "He doesn't realize the truth. That man could prove the difference in this war."

"It's still your intention to use Tyir?" Lazarus asked wearily. "It won't work. He has no loyalty to you, nor does he care for the Empire. And I doubt he can help you even if he wanted to. He's not as powerful as you believe."

The Paladin had been confined to the black cells upon his arrival at Carin Fort, where the remainder of the war council had moved, following the rout at Manesow. Tyir's arrival four days before had been jeered on by vast crowds of fanatical Order sympathizers.

Nazir had heard much about the Paladin; a feared fugitive from the south. There were dark rumors whispered of necromancy. He was also a dangerous criminal, who had killed hundreds of the Order in the past. Men like him had no place in the world, but Lazarus had spoken highly of him.

Aldmer dismissed Lazarus' objections with a casual shrug. "If he wants to live, then he'll do as he is bid."

The fort was next in the line of defense. Another Valian citadel, although much smaller then Manesow, it was one of the old race's many surviving strongholds in the Adnis. With the overflowing banks of the River Nurse to the east and the mountains to the west, it held a commanding post over the only path the Dominion could cross.

Nazir observed the combined Order and Empire levies working hard together to bolster the forts defenses. *With luck, we can halt them here. We have to,* he thought.

If it fell, the Dominion would be able to push into the ill-fortified flatlands until they reached the capital, with only small villages to serve as blockades against them.

"Tyir will support us, if we grant him immunity from the Order. Hinari will understand." Aldmer glanced slyly at Lazarus. "It's said you helped him escape, all those years ago."

"Aye, I did." Lazarus replied, his mouth set in a hard line. "And I'd appreciate it if you didn't bring that up, sire. They despise him more than the Dominion itself. Many tried to kill him before he was sentenced to die. I had to kill my own kin to free him."

He broke off, staring into the distance before a moment before continuing. "You'll never convince the Order to spare his life, not now. They have him again. I have dealt with assassins, bribes, economic sanctions, even the threat of war from the Sepulcher for Tyir. He has been a thorn in their side for too long. They'll never relinquish that opportunity again."

Lazarus had protested every day since Tyir had been brought to them in chains. Nazir had heard rumors of a debt Lazarus owed to Tyir. However unlikely, thinking about it made his skin crawl. *Just what was this necromancer capable of?*

"He'll come to heel. Now get out of my sight." Aldmer turned and left, leaving Lazarus to splutter. Nazir gave him a quick bow before hurrying after Aldmer.

He finally caught up with him as they entered Aldmer's quarters. They were far less lavish then Nazir had expected.

"Wait, Aldmer." Nazir reached out a hand to stop him.

"What?" Aldmer snapped, coming to a halt.

Nazir hesitated. He was in dangerous territory here. He could not repeat the mistake that Randyll had made. A fleeting regret filled him. Randyll had been

119

dragged screaming into the dungeons at Aldmer's order after he disobeyed a simple command. He brushed the disturbing thought from his mind. "You intend on using Tyir's so-called necromancy, don't you?"

Aldmer crossed to the window and stared out at the ranks of bowmen training in the yard below. "Yes, I do."

"I must advise you to reconsider. It will turn the Order against us."

"Are you questioning my judgement, Nazir Cessil?" Aldmer turned to face him, eyes narrowed.

"No," Nazir said quickly. "But we must be cautious. I don't agree with the Order's methods, not at all. But they purged our country of sorcery for a reason. Do you not know the history?"

"Of course I do," Aldmer's fist clenched tightly around his gold chain. "What of it? I did not take you for a superstitious man, Nazir."

"It could tear our empire apart . . . you must reconsider, Aldmer."

"You may address me as Sire, since we are alone. It is thanks to the Order's meddling that we are in this mess," Aldmer retorted. "They outlawed the sorcery that this Tyir possesses. The Dominion and those across the Tangent are free to use whatever knowledge they wish, but because of the Order's purges we're fighting with one hand tied behind our backs. Valare was burned to the ground thanks to Kyrm fire. The fucking Order is responsible. Tell me, Nazir, what do we have to counter with?"

Nazir had no answer.

"I am not an evil man, Nazir. I know you resent the decisions we have had to make, but it is necessary. We need to win this war, at any cost. What is one dark art against the entire empire's survival?"

"Everything." Nazir's word was soft. "We cannot win this war without our people. Listen to yourself, Sire. You are making foes and seeing invisible shadows in the dark. I know little of Tyir, but his reputation is dark, and not without reason. The Empire was born from the old kingdoms, which allied with the power of Valia before them. Our blood stems from them. And they fear the past and what truth lies within! We cannot turn to such demons!"

Aldmer smiled thinly. "There's more to it than Tyir's knowledge of necromancy. So much more." He broke off and seemed lost for a moment. "I've seen many new things, Lord Cessil. I will protect this land, and the people from the enemy, Nazir. Tyir of Irene has a great many talents and I mean to put him to use." At that, Aldmer turned and strode to his desk, throwing himself into his chair. He looked up at Nazir. "I mean to wipe his slate clean, so he can start over. He will be a hero, Lord Nazir. I'll hear no more of it. We meet tomorrow for the war council. Now please, leave me."

It was not angry like his dismissal of Lazarus, but a dismissal nonetheless. Nazir bowed stiffly and walked away as Aldmer picked up a quill and began writing.

"Excuse me, Lord Cessil."

Nazir stirred under his bedclothes in the royal quarters of the fortress. It had been another sleepless night, disturbed by thoughts.

"Should I let him in, my lord?" The old physician Saul was bustling by his bedside. Nazir sighed, and threw back the covers. It was high time he got dressed. On his bedside stood the still-full cup of sleeping draught. He had needed it more and more ever since Manesow.

"Yes. I'll see him now." The doors opened into his solar, as Adane entered. He was wearing his finest armor, a handsome silver and black cuirass protecting his chest.

"You ready to leave, Adane?" Nazir asked.

"Yes." The reply came, not without reproach. "My place is with you, Nazir. I'm no good at running a household, particularly yours."

Nazir let slip a rare smile. "Are you mocking my family, sir?" Laughter burst from Adane. It helped lighten the somber mood. "Don't let Vivian know I said that."

"I still stand by what I say. I'm a warrior, not an administrator."

"Your place is where I tell you. I need you there to look after my family."

"Why not one of the generals?" Adane poured a cup of wine from Nazir's bedside table, draining it in one noisy gulp. "Kalven, Tatin. Hells, even Kevan the Lard would be better suited to the task. He's too fat to sit on his fucking horse, but keeping a household is something he can do better than any. The blade is where my life belongs. I'm your bodyguard, after all."

"Kalven and Tatin are needed here, and I don't trust Kevan at Vern as I trust you. You are right, he is good at his role, but you know the position we're in." Nazir gestured to the flagon, and Adane passed it to him, nodding in reluctant agreement.

"As you wish. But at least give me leave to hunt down and kill that bastard, Mercer."

Mercer. The anger inside Nazir tripled at the name. "We were fools to trust his word. Once a turncloak, always a turncloak." He took a swallow and grimaced. The wine was bitter. Dregs. *If the Adnis falls, we'll lose good wine too.*

"We have riders scouting the region, from the borders of the river Tessus to the Colossus of Iris. If they find him, he'll pay. Arban Mance believes he knows where he may have gone."

"Aye, over to the waiting arms of the fucking Red Sand." Nazir clutched his silver laced goblet from his dresser and hurled it, half full at the wall where it smashed, sending purple gold everywhere. The defeat at Manesow did not hurt nearly as much as the mocking letter sent by Mercer's son, along with the skulls of six Imperial commanders captured at the ruined citadel. *Fooling the Empire once was a privilege*, scrawled the cruel, mocking words. *But fooling you bastards twice is a pleasure.*

The realm was in uproar, and it took Aldmer's own men to physically restrain some before things turned to bloodshed. The double betrayal was even worse.

Twelve thousand men we will never see again.

Against their misgivings, they had placed trust in Mercer, let him in on their plans. They had even given the order together to send the birds to the defenders at Manesow to launch their attack upon the Red Sand. Mercer had fled, never to return. No doubt he would begin his own campaign of terror against his former kinsmen, as a twisted revenge for his failed treason.

We gambled, and lost. We paid the price in blood and pride.

But it would not do to send more men after him, not at all. *His time will come,* Nazir reminded himself.

The Dominion was the greater threat. And with the Red Sand and Vultor's hosts united, they were now a torrent of destruction.

Adane still looked unconvinced. "I need you in charge of Vern. If the Dominion strikes across the Tangent at another point, particularly the capital itself, I require your expertise at those lines. And we'll need Vern to answer the call."

Nazir scowled. Aldmer had declared conscription the day after the news of the fall of Manesow, with dire consequences for any who refused service. Nazir disagreed with that too. People responded better to conscription without threats.

"We had reports of ships concentrated off the Bay of Bezle, and we need to watch our flanks while we fight both invading armies. I need an able man to watch my fleet, and scuttle it if it comes to that. I don't trust anyone else."

"Your fleet is in good hands, Lib Deem is a skilled captain. My place is at your side," Adane said stubbornly.

Damn you, my friend. Nazir tugged on his leather boots. "I know. But you know I speak only the truth. You've seen how it is here. Aldmer's taken control. Even I'm not immune. Should something happen to me . . . "

He broke off, as Adane blanched. He tried to argue, but Nazir held up a hand for silence.

"No, my friend, listen. I haven't had a day since I've seen someone flogged, or hanged. You've seen what happened to Randyll. It could happen to anyone, even me. Vern needs strong hands to lead it. Vivian is strong, but she needs help, and she trusts you."

Adane dropped onto a stool next to him. All resistance vanished. "Yesterday I came across Imperial guards hanging a family outside the walls, just because the father refused to give up his supplies. Some of them were from Arban Mance's own patrol. I could hear them laughing as they threw pennies at the father, watching his face turn blue as he choked. Two of them were just young boys. And all for nothing."

He drew his sword, laying it across his lap. "What has the Empire become, my Lord?" His confidence and bravado were gone.

It has become what I have always known to be, ruthless. "War makes horrors of everyone, Adane. That's never changed. When old Emperor Gordnor called the banners against the Uslor barons, I rode with him. You were still a child, and an annoying little shit at that."

Adane cracked a weak smile. "You were barely a man grown yourself, if I recall."

"True. We did dreadful things to try and take back control of Uslor. Villages burnt to the ground, poisoning their wells, setting fire to acres of forest to prevent the warlord's guerrilla attacks on our legions. It did no good. I lost a quarter of my men alone in one week. When you consider what conquest does to ordinary people, I wonder how the Octane judges us when we die."

Nazir took a deep swallow of his wine. They were painful memories. After seven years, Uslor was still independent. Gordnor paid with his life.

"I still remember who Aldmer was, before the war. He was just a simple soldier, a minor officer of rank. I knew him as well as any. I even respected him. I cannot say that I do anymore."

Nazir got to his feet. "You better get going, my friend," he said. "That is your lord's command. When you return to Vern, send a message to the Fennick family with my seal. They are to raise five hundred bowmen and march to Vern to reinforce it. All my bannermen are also to send reinforcements to Arkane and the Gates. They will keep a lookout for attack. It's my job as Steward of the West."

The vital sea-front fortress was their main defense in the west.

"Take as many of our own men with you as we can spare. I'd rather have them safe in our city, then wandering the plains against outlaws and raiders."

"What about looters?"

"Hang them. Also send word to the Derwoods. You know why."

"I know." Adane nodded, then leaned forward and embraced Nazir, gripping him with surprising strength. Nazir could do little but pat him awkwardly on the back, before they broke apart.

It's for the best.

Adane was loyal and well-liked by his men, perfect for ruling Vern in his stead. That, and his wife held him in high regard. It was better that way. Everybody in Vern knew that Vivian's opinion mattered as much as Nazir's, possibly more.

I have no choice. He could not risk losing him to one of High Command's purges.

"Go. And give my regards to your father."

Tears pricking his face and falling into his black stubble of a beard, Adane turned to leave, but stopped at the doorway. "We should sue for peace, my Lord. What are the chances of bringing the Dominion to the table?"

Nazir turned to reply, but Adane had already left.

There was a deathly silence in the yard. *The Octane are angry.* Nazir shouldered his way to the front of the crowd. Even in his thick cloak, the chill wind was like a knife on his cheek, and he was glad of the press of people. Above him, the clouds were thick and overcast, the dull purple of the early dawn sky penetrating them with feeble rays of sunlight.

There was a somber aspect to the morning wind. *The gods do not approve.* He had tried one final time to persuade Aldmer, but his plea fell on deaf ears. Aldmer was kinder this time to Nazir, but only said it was "part of the plan." Nazir did not dare to ask what the plan was.

It had been a ruthless and draining negotiation with the Order, regarding Tyir. Hinari and his subjects had been horrified by Aldmer's plan. Aldmer was always one step ahead, and went as far as threatening to withdraw all support if they refused his demands.

They'd heard disturbing reports from the far south, of the Order's expulsion from the pilgrim city of Tarantown, outlaws causing trouble in the Kahal and clashes with Uslor. There were even whispers that the Keidan themselves were threatening conflict.

Nazir was no fool. He knew just how much they wanted vengeance, to execute the man they had condemned. Ever since they had declared their intentions, there had been open fury from the Order's agents. There were even reports of clashes between Order and Balian troops.

But here they were; the Empire was about to make a pact with a demonic madman. He'd heard talk throughout the encampment. If even half of what they said was true, they were shaking hands with evil.

Despite his misgivings, despite every fiber in his body, Nazir could sense a desperate justification to the plan. For all his faults, and bastard though he was, Aldmer somehow had the right of it.

The Red Sand, the great Dominion commander had linked up with the barbarians of the butcher King Vultor, despite all their efforts to stop that from happening. United, they were pillaging and burning their way west, marching towards Carin Fort.

So far, the Empire could not stop them, but not for lack of trying. The army did all it could, but were hopelessly outmatched. To make matters worse, Mercer's men were running riot in Vence, their protectorate in the south. They were too poorly equipped to fight bandits, let alone a battle-hardened army.

If Vence felt that the Empire was not protecting them and surrendered to the Dominion, or even worse joined them, their entire position in the region would be compromised. And all this with only a fraction of the Dominion's strength.

Across the sea lay the hulking shadow of their eternal enemy, where hundreds of their legions waited, ready to invade. A hidden dagger is always more dangerous than a brandished sword. If they moved south, the Empire may as well surrender on the spot.

Aldmer and his two justiciars, Carris and a cruel brute called Valron, stood on the raised platform of stone, his silver-robed guards on either side like frozen sentinels. Between them knelt an obviously old man, hooded, gagged and bound.

Nazir felt a cold tingle as he looked at the prisoner. The watching crowd was thousands strong, a motley crew of fresh Empire conscripts, peasants, resentful Order priests and veteran legionaries. The Paladin finally came into view, flanked by prison guards.

He doesn't look that dangerous, Nazi thought. Tyir was tall, with sparse gray hair falling lank to his shoulders.

The crowd watched him pass, some whispering but the Order were particularly vocal, hurling abuse and death threats. Shouts of "Hang the Irene pig!" and "Kill the demon!" were some of the kinder insults.

Slowly, the elderly man reached the platform, standing before Aldmer. The crowd fell silent.

"It is an honor to meet you, Tyir, or Paladin, if you prefer." Aldmer's voice rang strong, easily heard now that the crow had fallen silent. He had dressed handsomely for the occasion, in a thick black tunic edged in gold. Around his neck dangled a pendant bearing his sigil, two crossed spears.

Tyir didn't look at him, instead his gaze swept through the assembled masses.

Nazir watched from his place in the crowd, just to the side of the platform. When the necromancer's cold eyes met Nazir's, something told him that the old man was not scared, just amused.

"I trust you know why you have been brought here," Aldmer went on. "You stand condemned by our great allies the Pharos Order, sentenced to death for your crimes."

Allies? You damn near threatened them with war, Nazir thought coldly. Some of the Order in the crowd shouted then, and one near Nazir even shook his fist at the stage. The ring of spears surrounding the platform slammed into the ground and silence reigned once again.

Tyir turned to Aldmer and in a voice crisp and cold replied. "And yet . . . instead of dealing with their happy faces, I've been dragged hundreds of miles, to answer to the likes of you. What am I to make of that?"

Some in the crowd bristled, but Aldmer's men were fixated on the Paladin.

"We have the power to absolve your crimes," Carris declared to Tyir. "The Sepulcher's word is powerful, and carries much influence across our lands. However, under our own council, we can arrange for your entire criminal past to be erased. Make you a free man."

Tyir laughed at that. "I am no saint, nor do I want to be. I have killed hundreds of the Order. Many whose relatives watch me now. Thousands more have died during my days as a sword sell. Not to mention my experiments. They won't forget my crimes easily, nor do I want them to."

He speaks of murder like he's playing with a baby. Nazir felt his gut twist. Making a pact with demons indeed. The kneeling captive stirred, struggling. His words were muffled by the gag, but it sounded like pleading to Nazir.

Aldmer was the next to speak. "Hinari, in his greatness, has agreed to remove your stain upon his children, if you meet our requests."

"I hate to think what threats you made in order to get him to do that."

"You'd be unwise to turn this down, Paladin," Valron barked. He wore the seal of the royal guard on his beautiful red cloak. "Take this as a warning."

That only made the Paladin laugh. "This dallying is wasting time." Tyir affected a bored indifference. "Why am I here? Surely not to feel the cold, at any rate."

Aldmer took a few steps forward.

"Very well, to business. As my comrades have said, you are offered redemption. We will promote you to hero of the Empire. You are aware of the dangers that face Harloph, and every day the situation grows darker. The Red Sand has killed many of our faithful subjects, and more innocents are dying by the day. We are at war. This is possibly the most important war in the history of the Empire."

Tyir's smile was just as light. "Some would call that blasphemy. Many in our realm would argue that it was the blessed Pharos during the Cold days that fought the most important war in our history, when he prevented the Daem Vein from using the darkest arts to destroy our world. There were other wars too, I trust . . ."

"You aren't here to debate with me," Aldmer cut in. "Nor are we here to bleat about ancient history. The

Chaos is not relevant here. What we need is help. I admit it; we are in a brutal struggle for survival."

He let that hang in the air. Whatever muttering in the crowds had died.

Tyir's eyes narrowed. "I don't know what you are suggesting."

"We're no fools, Tyir of Irene." Aldmer's voice hardened in those words. "We know the shadows of the sorcery you brought into the world."

"My art, you mean."

"We also know you were responsible for the Valare incident. We have eyewitness accounts from many of the survivors who swear upon their families lives that hundreds of dead walked again, and their reanimation threw back the Dominion forces. It seems they have a weakness after all."

There were shudders in the crowd, whether from disgust or awe Nazir did not know. Some shouted abuse at Tyir. Nazir felt dirty, something unclean clinging to his skin even through his thick layers of clothing. *Dead rising?* He too had heard stirs of such things in the free city, but he had dismissed them as rumors, myths stirred from the fear and trauma of battle.

"You would be right about that," Tyir said. "Even the cruelest men will break if met with the unknown."

Tyir's pockmarked face showed only contempt for Aldmer. "You should offer me more gratitude," he continued. "Were it not for me, the Kyrm fire the scum unleashed on my home would be used against your precious cities, I'm sure. But instead, Valare paid the ultimate price, as did the cities of the Barta League. They burned so you might live. They destroyed them out of fear of me." There was a hint of menace to his voice now, but also full of bitterness.

Carris was unmoved. "Your life is ours. The Order would have killed you, if not for our mercy."

"Your mercy is to use my power for your own whims," Tyir replied, his retort like a whip. "My life is not yours. It is Lazarus to whom I owe my life. Why should I assist you against the power of the Red Sand? I'm afraid that necromancy won't help."

"That hasn't stopped you though, has it?" Aldmer replied, his voice darkening. "We've heard a great deal of your exploits, Paladin. You have other names too, and none of them kind. Necromancer and Alchemist. From the Kahal to Irene, it is said your name comes as easily as those from folklore."

"My past has been dark and bloody at times," Tyir snorted. "What of it? What makes you think I should help you?"

Aldmer's next smile was twisted. "Because we hold your life debt. Show him the prisoner." Aldmer nodded to Carris, who wordlessly obeyed his command. He grasped the prisoner's hood, and ripped it off, revealing his face.

The crowd jostled and shouted, the noise deafening. There knelt Lazarus, his stunning mane of white hair slick with blood, his face bruised and swollen.

"No!" Someone shouted from the crowd. Nazir saw someone punch their fist into the air. "Lazarus!" the man bellowed.

Lazarus slowly lifted his head, his eyes almost lost amidst the mass of ugly bruising. His lips were cracked and bleeding. He looked out at the crowd, seeing the raised fist. A horrified gasp formed. "Cassel," Nazir saw him mouth. "Run!"

Aldmer pointed to the man in the crowd. "Bring that man here and kill him." Aldmer commanded softly. "In front of the old man."

There was scuffling as guards forced their way into the mass of people, grunts of pain and the sound of steel hitting flesh. Nazir was paralyzed, stunned by what he was witnessing. *I should have gone home with Adane.* It took six men to batter Cassel into submission. Bloodied and beaten, his face smashed open by mailed fists, he was dragged onto the stage.

"Aldmer!" Nazir could take it no longer. He stepped forward. "Stop this. It's getting us nowhere!" He shouted above the growing din of the crowd, as an increasing number of people screamed obscenities.

Cassel struggled to his feet, reaching out a consoling hand to his master before another mailed fist smashed into his mouth, sending blood and the ruins of broken teeth flying. He collapsed, lying supine, unmoving. Lazarus let out a groan, a sound only terror and grief could produce.

"I'm guessing you recognize this man?" Aldmer shouted above the noise, glaring with ill-repressed triumph into Tyir's eyes. "Here is your choice. You will serve me, or you can watch your friends die."

"Don't do this," Tyir whispered. "This serves nothing."

He's terrified, Nazir realized with a jolt.

"He is innocent. Leave him alone," Tyir pleaded.

"Tyir," Lazarus struggled to his knees, but was punched to the ground by one of Aldmer's guards. "Don't help them!"

"You're fools!" Tyir shouted above the din. "The art won't help you win!"

"This is your final warning!" Aldmer shouted. A smirk fell across his lips as he walked slowly across the platform to stand beside Lazarus who was quietly sobbing next to the unconscious Cassel. "Help us, or watch him die."

Tyir was torn, his feet rooted to his spot. Around him, guards formed a ring to prevent him from running to his friend. "Lazarus," he whispered. "Don't . . . help them." Lazarus said, looking up. "Your chance is gone. Carris, kill him." Aldmer stamped hard, on Lazarus' back, forcing him to the ground; there was a crunch as his spine broke. Lazarus barely had time to let out an agonized scream before Carris stepped forward. Showing only silent indifference, he reached out a hand and wrapped it around Lazarus' throat.

Nazir couldn't hold on any longer.

"Stop this madness!" He roared. There were groans and cries from the crowd, growing fury alike even in their soldiers. As Lazarus was lifted into the air, Carris Montague hesitated, but only for a second. He slashed Lazarus' throat.

"That is what happens, when you disobey," Aldmer screamed.

Lazarus' lifeless body slumped upon the ground. A pool of blood spread over the stone, the stench reaching Nazir's nostrils. The air was choking. Tyir was silent. Aldmer gave Tyir a glare of deepest disgust. Spitting on Lazarus' corpse, he turned his back. "We're done here. If he won't obey, hand him back to the Order. Let them kill him."

The crowd cried out in anguish. Nazir heard a great rush of wind, then the ground vanished under him.

The blast was so loud it lifted dozens off their feet. Nazir's eardrums throbbed as he was thrown, landing atop another man. An elbow shot out of nowhere painfully into his face, and Nazir smelled blood. The air was searing hot, and growing hotter. There were screams, and someone bellowed orders.

"What's going on?" He could hear Aldmer's furious voice, the twang of arrows, but the air around them was thick with dust; Nazir could barely see. Lights danced before him and he could not focus. He started to black out, the promise of oblivion almost welcome.

No! He wrenched his eyes open, keeping them wide even as the sky grew hotter. There was a powerful, overwhelming stench of smoke, and something else, something more sinister.

Clamping a hand over his nose to stem the free flow of blood, Nazir wrenched himself free of the tangle of bodies scattered on the ground. The billowing smoke masked everything around him. There were many feebly stirring while others stumbled to their feet. All around him screams and the sound of steel on steel, fragmented by the crackle of flames. He reached for his sword.

Something grabbed him by the ankle. He turned his head, and felt his chest constrict, the breath in his throat dying. He looked into the boy's eyes, no older than seven. His flesh was purple, his cheek a congealing ruin and he stank. But his eyes were clear, unblinking.

The dead rose at Valare. His stomach clenched, and Nazir wrenched his leg away from the reanimated child as he stumbled. He had to run, but where?

Arrows whistled through the air, there were screams and grunts as people fell around him. Then two naked shapes lunged at him from both sides.

Nazir was thrown off balance as two corpses, a man and an elderly woman, latched themselves onto him.

Both were completely bare, the young man's spine visible through his skeletal form, maggots clinging to pus encrusted lips.

Nazir felt vomit rise to the back of his mouth, as he lifted his sword. His head was pounding, the blood flowing from his smashed nose, but it did not matter.

The dead were walking. It was the Paladin, the Necromancer . . . the Alchemist.

He reacted quickly, the dead's movements were clumsy and Nazir was able to parry their stumbling attacks, catching both in the stomach with his blade.

They slowed, but did not stop. The wounds were grisly as Nazir pulled out his sword, but they were still moving.

The dead can't die.

He ran. The smoke around him became thicker, the smell foul, clogging up his senses. It smelt like blood, but that could not be. Then he saw flames. Great billowing pillars, igniting across the horizon. Crimson and orange, their heat threatened the air itself.

Soldiers shouted in panic, each with looks of sheer terror upon their faces.

"The Octane have mercy." Nazir said as felt his bowels loosen. The panicked crowd ran from the growing inferno. Several turned on each other, such was their desperation.

The stables. I have to reach the stables! Nazir stumbled, half-blind. People bumped into him, whether foe or friend he did not know, nor did he care. He felt something heavy smack into his side, the blow cascading through his body, the force knocking him to the ground. He could not breathe, his mouth opened as he desperately tried to suck in air. His vision blurred and he lurched over to vomit. Then he heard voices. He knew them; Aldmer's men.

"Kill the traitors! Kill Tyir!" Someone was snarling in the distance; Aldmer.

Spitting blood, Nazir got to his feet.

"Find the necromancer! Bring him to me!"

Someone else was shouting, screaming, an Order official no doubt. There were people running everywhere. Nazir headed for the deserted stables.

Incredibly he found a horse already saddled, pulling against the reins that held it tied to a hitching post.

He pulled the leather strap free, and with great difficulty hoisted himself onto the horse's back. The stallion bucked, nearly throwing him off, but he managed to gain the saddle.

Aldmer would see this as treason, But he no longer cared. He had to get away.

The horse snorted, nostrils flaring, eyes wide in terror as he tried to calm it with a pat to its neck.

"Easy! Easy!" Nazir soothed.

More voices, someone screamed his name, but he paid no heed. He kicked his heels into the horses flanks and the animal took off, as desperate to escape as its rider.

A soldier reached up to grab the reins, but Nazir kicked him away. Across the courtyard, the tall palisade gates were closing. Nazir spurred the horse forward.

End of the Long Game

Once, long ago, a wraith clad in grief proclaimed
"The Shadow that will plague the world."
There was still time yet.

~ Tyir of Irene.

"The master is in Vengar. We'll march at first light." A man's rough voice, faintly heard. Tyrone's head was swimming, eyeballs burning in their sockets. He felt as if he were floating in a dark ocean of pain.

"How is he?" Another voice, soft, feminine.

Something pressed hard on Tyrone's throat. He coughed and was rewarded with spasms of pain.

"Still out of it. We'll see what happens. I must say, I'm surprised. He's responding better than expected." The man chuckled. "I may have been wrong about him after all."

"This was your fault. You were ordered not to harm him, Sleeper." The female's voice again, now full of reproach. "Tyir will spit blood over this."

"I know . . . I know. I expect to pay for it later," the man's voice rose in angry retort. "Though if Horse keeps mocking me, I'm going to shove a knife in his guts."

Tyrone felt himself falling, felt jagged rocks cutting into his flesh. Warm and wet liquid trickled down his arms and legs. The voices faded...

Raindrops, soft and padding against canvas. He knew that sound. Tyrone slowly opened his eyes. He stirred feebly. He was lying on a bed of furs and skins. The smell of damp animal was pungent, but at least the mattress was warm and comfortable. Raising a stiff hand, he let out a gasp. His felt hot, his skin on fire. Bile rose to his throat and before he could stop himself, he was sick.

"Easy." Soft words and softer hands were on him. "You've been out for a long time." The girl's voice was familiar.

Tyrone stretched a leg only to groan in sudden agony as he felt it cramp. He shut his eyes tightly against the pain.

"Here, drink." His head was tipped back, a cold fluid dripped into his open mouth. His throat clenched as he swallowed; the substance was chalky. He retched some of it back up immediately.

"Damn it, Sleeper." The woman's grip was like a vice. In his current state he couldn't struggle. Slowly, Tyrone's vision began to focus.

His speech was slurred, throat cracked and dry. He licked his lips. "Water. I need water." Every word was a trial.

"Of course. Hold on." Cool water dripped into Tyrone's mouth. He lapped at the stream eagerly. Slowly, his surroundings came into view. A young woman hunched over him, a hood obscuring most of her face, but he could see her eyes, pale blue and unblinking.

"There. You're finally awake."

I'm in a tent. But where? He slowly reached up an aching hand to his face.

"Who are you?" Even in his state, Tyrone could sense something unnatural about her.

"Later." She lifted her grip on Tyrone's head as he pushed himself up slightly on his elbows, squinting outside the gap in the tent. The pitter-patter of the rain continued, accompanied by a gentle breeze.

"Where am I?" Tyrone asked.

"Doesn't matter," the girl replied. "Still in one piece. You'll need to recover."

Tyrone felt his head sway alarmingly, his vision going. His stomach contracted painfully as he vomited again. It burned his lips and mouth as it splattered everywhere, the pain in his chest so great that Tyrone was swallowed by darkness. Someone shouted for help, then he passed out.

He was not out for long this time. When he awoke, he heard something new.

"Is it true what they say? That Lazarus . . ."

Voices again, calm. Tyrone felt helpless. His memories were stirring. The men who attacked him in the Order's prison. He felt strangely cold, indifferent. *If they're going to kill me, they best bloody well get on with it.* He lay still, too weak to move.

"Aye, it's true, Ombrone." An elderly man, different to the first, thick with anger.

"He was murdered because our master refused to aid them in their futile war."

"Lazarus?" The first voice again. "It can't be! Who killed him?"

Shockwaves flooded through Tyrone. Lazarus? No. A cold feeling spread through his chest.

"That bastard Aldmer. May the false faiths grant him peace." There was a pause. "He's hurting, I see it. I don't know how to help him."

"We can claim vengeance." A different woman's voice, hard and brutal.

"Aye, we can. The Rapier is coming . . ." The voices tailed off, and footsteps fell away into the distance.

Lazarus is dead. Tyrone's chest was heavy, a void beneath him, swallowing everything around him.

Even his agony dimmed. His eyes pricked with tears. *The Empire killed him?* He felt himself swallowed by darkness again, into even deeper misery, slipping further and further down. He felt ashamed to be Balian. *The Empire did this.* The ocean of darkness came like a tidal wave. Tyrone gulped, lost again in its depths of misery.

"I brought you some food."

Tyrone fought the darkness. He opened his eyes. Amazingly, most of the pain was gone, but he remembered.

"I was captured. That's why I'm here." His voice was strong again. He sat bolt upright, wincing.

"Easy!" The woman's tone was scolding as she pushed Tyrone back. Tyrone struggled, but every movement was weak, and the woman handled him as though he were an infant.

"You're healing well, but please be careful. You've been out for nearly three weeks. You need time to recover. It would not do for you to die now."

Three weeks? He could see clearly now. It was the woman he had who had first attended him. Her hood was lowered, revealing a pale, heart-shaped face and white hair which fell past her shoulders. Tyrone felt a surge of anger.

"Answer my question, please. I deserve to be told what's going on. Am I a prisoner? If you're going to kill me, then just do it."

She almost smiled. "My master sends his apologies. He deemed it prudent that you recover first. The Sleeper's actions were not kind to you, I confess that. Stupid bastard." Her voice lowered into a snarl. "He is a fool. But you have my word, no more harm will come to you."

"Why should I trust your word?" Tyrone retorted.

The woman's eyes narrowed. "If we wanted you dead, we wouldn't be talking now. But our master doesn't wish that. And your home has been destroyed, lost in fire." Tyrone glared at her. "Home is such a loose term in this world, where it can be gained or lost in an instant."

Her strong hands grabbed Tyrone and pulled him into a sitting position. He looked down and saw he was naked. Blushing, he jumped to cover himself.

She nearly smiled again, but stopped short. A crude wooden platter was shoved into his hands, bearing a simple feast of hard bread and cheese. "Eat and dress. Then I'll take you to our master. He's waiting." She made no move to leave.

"You're . . . going to watch me?"

A smile crossed her pale lips. "You must be hungry." She turned away softly. "Eat. I won't watch if that's what concerns you." There was a hint of amusement in her voice. "But who do you think undressed you in the first place?"

Tyrone sat up, wrapping the bedding around him. There was a cold breeze, early morning sunlight peeking through the tent. His stomach rumbled and he realized how intensely hungry he was. The bread was hard, the cheese thick and waxy. It was the sweetest meal Tyrone had ever had. The girl kept her word and didn't watch.

When he had finished eating, he pulled on a scratchy leather jerkin and woolen trousers. He stood up shakily, and the sound of his movement brought the woman out of her reverie and she turned, a smile adorning her face at the sight of him.

"Come."

He followed her out of the tent, gently placing weight on his legs. They obeyed his will, but slowly. The area around him smelt of smoke and meat cooking. There were broken and derelict houses all around. *I know this place.*

"This is Vengar." His lips were cracked and sore. He ran his tongue around them, wincing. "I came here once when I was a child."

The buildings were simple, wattle and daub affairs, mostly, with some slightly grander constructions having shingled roofs, while most were thatched. Those that still had a roof, anyway.

"We'll leave soon." She looked at Tyrone. "Can you walk unassisted?"

Tyrone gritted his teeth at the word child. "I'll manage."

Manage he did, but every step hurt. He had never felt so drained. He wanted to lie down and collapse. There were people everywhere. Most ignored him, but a few stopped to stare. He could not see their faces, many covered by black masks and hoods, only cold eyes showing. The woman led him through the remains of the village he once knew.

He looked around the ruins as they walked. He had been eleven when he was last there. He had journeyed with his father, though he didn't know why. Vengar wasn't a Cessil province, it was on the fringes of the Empire. He couldn't remember much about it, nor its inhabitants, as he was more interested in fighting with his two little brothers.

Has it really been ten years? He felt a sudden sadness at how old he had become.

The buildings were in disrepair, many covered in a forest of ivy, a small tree growing from the thatch of one roof. Evidently, somebody had pillaged the place; debris were littered everywhere.

Tyrone remembered his family with a pang and felt guilty for the first time in years. Alarmed, he quickened his pace. There were more people in the distance, some gambling, some training with swords while others hacked down wood with axes.

Great, black longbows lay propped up against walls, some used by men taking aim at the distant trees, while others sharpened well-crafted blades on whetstones.

They were mostly quiet, talking amongst themselves in mixed languages, some Tyrone understood; either the Common voice, or North Mer from Klassos.

Many seemed to be from the south, a dialect Tyrone knew well. He caught a couple of snatches of Pyran, though in a rough accent he could not understand.

On they went, a small dirt path snaking through the village like a meandering river. Finally, they came to a halt near the center where a large fire burned. Around its perimeter, four cloaked figures squatted, kneeling before a hunched man in a cloak. His back was turned to them. But Tyrone heard his voice clearly as they approached.

"Jaques. Take twenty men and scout out the path north of here. Kelzar, go with him." He sounded familiar. "Search the path for bodies. Bring them into the village so I can raise them. They can serve as scouts when we march."

"Rapier's men should arrive soon," one of them replied. "Old Jackal spotted their vanguard."

"Good," Tyrone heard the elder reply. "It's about time too. Was beginning to think he hadn't received my message. Would have some explaining, I know him too well."

"Aye, he's coming. On his fucking elk, no doubt," the other chuckled bracingly, a Pyran. He was by far the largest of the group. "Still no word from the Dog." That last sentence was with some heat.

"Makes no matter," said the leader smoothly. "He'll join us soon enough. What matters right now is speed."

"Can we really trust him, Horse?" A third. "The man's a demon in human skin."

"I wouldn't let him hear that, Kelzar," Their leader laughed. "Go, now. Take Jaques with you."

"That's One-Hundred-Jaques to you," The man grumbled, rising to his feet. The Pyran let out a booming bark of laughter.

"Deeds matter, not names." The leader turned around as two of the men nodded and got to their feet. His hood masked most of his face. "So," his tone was soft. "It is good to see you on your feet, Tyrone."

Tyrone's stomach clenched. He tried to open his mouth, but his throat had gone parchment dry.

"You caused quite a stir. Sleeper," he called, and there was a steely menace to his voice then. He turned to the fourth shadow. "Remove your hood and stand up so that Tyrone can see you."

"Do I have to?" The smallest of the four complained, lowering his hood. Tyrone recognized the man at once. *This is who did this to me.* Tyrone recoiled.

Sleeper had a youthful complexion, his skin smooth and unmarked from age, with thin, blonde hair.

He's no older than I.

Regardless, every movement betrayed discipline, and a cruelty beyond human.

"Nothing to fear, Tyrone." The man soothed, as Sleeper turned to face him. "Although I must admit, I did fear for your life. Even Sleeper was surprised you're still here, and he's the only man in my company whose talent for poison rivals my own. I guess I'm thankful he knows as much about healing as he does of maiming."

With a swift movement, he lowered his hood, his twisted features thrown under the flickering of the warming fire. Tyir? Nobody could forget that face.

"Now, Sleeper. At what point did I tell you to poison Tyrone?" Tyir looked even older than Tyrone last saw him. His face sagged, though every line was etched deeper. "I'm very particular with my orders. I said to take him in heel. Not once did I tell you to nearly kill the lad."

Sleeper shuffled his feet. "He came running at us, Paladin." He looked away.

The one called Horse sniggered, clutching his mouth with a great sweaty hand.

"Silence!" Sleeper snarled at him. His partner only laughed harder. "Oh, fuck off, Horse."

"Tell me, Sleeper. How many men did you kill, before you joined the Scars?" Tyir regarded him through a cold gaze, but his eyes sparkled with amusement.

Tyrone was burning for answers, but only one mattered. What the hell was going on?.

"Come on," Tyir encouraged Sleeper with a grin. "I'm giving you the chance to brag here. We don't hear that often."

"You might not, sir, but I fucking have to." Horse put on an expression of mock horror, throwing up his hands. "Please, don't give him this! I'll never hear the last of it."

"Four hundred . . . four hundred and twenty . . . four hundred and eighty seven," Sleeper replied, shooting Horse a malevolent glare. "Wait, do you mean just the past two years, or my whole life?"

"It doesn't matter," Tyir replied through clipped tones. "Answer the question."

"What about the other bitch?" Horse chortled. "A few months ago? That makes it four-hundred-and-eighty-eight. Though I'm sure you're lying, you little prick," Horse sniggered, clapping him hard on the back.

Sleeper bit back a retort; Tyir was watching him, tapping his foot. "Fine, I'll round it off and say five hundred, it makes it easier."

"Exactly." Tyir glared at him, and Sleeper's face flushed red. "I gave you orders to take him with you. Not to put him to the point of death. But if I knew a boy would frighten you, I would have put you on another task. Like peeling vegetables. Or would you like to tend to Rapier's elk?"

Sleeper turned pale. Horse was roaring with laughter now, thumping the mud with his fist. Tyrone recognized them now. The men who had come to his cell. Sleeper's response was violent and quick, a dagger held tightly against the bigger man's throat.

"Shut your mouth, Horse, unless you want to be choked with your own fucking intestines!" Coughing with mirth, Horse wrenched himself free and grinned at Tyrone.

"Sorry lad. Our friend here is a little . . . unhinged." He lumbered forward and seized Tyrone's hand, swallowing it in the depths of his own enormous paw.

"It's good to see you awake. Anybody who can survive this prick's shenanigans is a friend of mine." He grinned. "Name's Horse, my friend. Tyir mentioned you're a Cessil."

"Aye." Tyrone replied nervously, as he shook the dark haired giant's hand staring up into his wide, beaming face.

"Good to meet you, lad, or Tyrone, should I say. Where are my manners? Can't say I'm fond of the Cessils, but then I'm not fond of any from the Empire. Fucking vandals, the lot of them. No offense to you though." He grinned insanely the whole while, not letting go of Tyrone's hand.

"I'm sorry, Tyir." Sleeper fell to his knees, his hood knocked askew. His skin was pale, hair short and blonde. "I failed in my task."

"Take heart. He's still alive, at any rate." The look Tyir gave him was grim. "And I think it's Tyrone that you should apologize to. As must I."

Sleeper looked at Tyrone. "I'm sorry." It was brusque, and very formal. "We misled you, but it was necessary. My master deemed it vital."

"That will do." Tyir spoke again, not unkindly. "Now go."

"To look for Rapier?"

"Yes. When he arrives, bring him to me." Tyir turned then to the Pyran as Sleeper gathered his things. "Now, Horse, take a dozen men and go back the way we came, right along the Barrow road to the north-west. Watch the road. Anyone comes, kill them. If they are too many, return and sound the alarm."

"As you wish, Tyir." Horse clapped Sleeper on the back. "Let's go," he said. He turned to Tyrone. "See you soon. I hope." They left quickly, leaving Tyrone with Tyir and the woman who had brought him.

"Tyrone." Finally, Tyir rested his eyes upon him. "I hope you can forgive me. I deceived you, but it was necessary. I'm also sorry for leaving you when I did, but I had no choice in the matter. I had to take you out of the equation, as well as rescue you from the noose. You were due to be executed in the Empire's custody, by order of Bane Aldmer himself. No idea why, so don't ask. I figured keeping you there was a better option, which is why I got Sleeper to bring you to me once I had a better idea of what was happening. If only I knew . . ." His voice shook and died.

Execution? "What did he want with me? Surely it was the Order that wanted me? I attacked their men, not Aldmer's." He sat down where Sleeper had knelt, upon a ragged bundle of skins.

"That's what I thought," Tyir admitted. "From what I heard before Aldmer's men took me out of my cell, the Order intended on setting you free, but Aldmer had plans for you. What they were, I don't know." He shrugged, gazing into the fire. "I couldn't let you die for them. But, that is then and this is now. We have greater concerns to deal with."

I'm an outlaw. Tyrone blinked in surprise at the very idea. He didn't know how to react. "Why did you save me?" He blurted out.

Tyir snorted. "You helped me in the prison. You were not the only one to lose your home. I lost much too. The Empire should be throwing itself at my feet in gratitude. If it were not for me, the Dominion would be using Kyrm fire on their capital by now." His jaw clenched. "Apparently, the Dominion laid waste to the rest of the Barta League in the same manner. Kyrm fire is costly, and dangerous to master." He gave a helpless shrug. "At least I was able to save one life."

Tyrone kept silent, trying to suppress the great weight crushing his chest.

"I saw how you fought," Tyir went on. "I just didn't want another soul to fall to fools. And Sleeper also told me how well you fought against him. You've impressed many." There was a pause. "Meira, leave us please." The girl rose to her feet. "I would like to speak to him alone. Check what we picked up so far."

"As you wish, Master." Meira bowed her head shyly and departed

"A good lady . . . Now, Tyrone." The flames glowed brighter, warming their skin. "I invite you to ask me some questions, though I may not answer all. Even the masters have no truth of everything."

Tyrone was beginning to feel better, but he did not let his guard down. "How long have I been out of things?"

"Three weeks. We needed you sedated and unconscious to give you the best chance of survival. The venom Sleeper poisoned you with is usually quite lethal. You must have shocked him, forcing him to resort to that. He was one of the finest assassins in the south before I recruited him. You heard Horse. He can't stop teasing him, poor bastard. I tasked them on getting you out of that hell, after I knew Aldmer's intentions. I underestimated you. I'm sorry for that." His jaw twitched.

"I know your next question. The war. The Order marched to join the Empire, but they were defeated at Manesow, and the Dominion has been sweeping west ever since."

"What?" Tyrone felt his heart pound. "They lost? But Manesow has never been taken!"

"Until now." Tyir's gaze flickered to the flames. "Kajudo of the Red Sand is a true master of war. I told you about the serpents. How cunning of him." His face twisted, his features becoming even more menacing. "Vultor leads the army from the League, and I fear they've joined forces at last. The Red Sand knew that by unleashing the serpents, he'd force the Empire to go on the offensive. To their credit, the Empire didn't lose for lack of trying. Anyone else and they would have prevailed. But the Red Sand is formidable. They were massacred. Oh, they made the enemy bleed, but it wasn't enough."

There was a pause as Tyir's mouth twisted into a ruthful smile.

"I was not so lucky to escape. The Order knew they could not lose such a valued captive, so they marched me two hundred miles to Carin Fort. They couldn't bear losing their precious captive. I guess they wanted an audience when they took my head." Tyir spat into the fire, his gnarled hands clenched.

Tyrone remembered something. "I heard your men say something regarding Lazarus." His throat tight, he glanced at Tyir. The tears in his eyes confirmed his fears. "It's true?"

"Aye." All trace of kindness in Tyir's voice died. "The Empire will pay with blood, I promise you that."

The Empire? Tyrone felt nothing but emptiness, anger. *Valare was my home, more than my family ever was.* He had never spent much time with Lazarus. He was a kind man, and everyone in Valare adored him.

"The Empire killed him?" He could scarcely believe it. "Why?"

"Aldmer." Tyir spat out the lone word. "They wanted my power to help them combat the Red Sand's advance."

"Your power?"

"Tyrone, use your head." Tyir's rebuke was not harsh. "Hinari excommunicated Lazarus for his crime of freeing me from my execution chamber in the Sepulcher. The Order threatened their own blood for my sake. Aldmer wanted that my power, to aid them in their futile war. I refused."

It made sense then. "They killed Lazarus to make you co-operate."

"Yes. They made me watch as he was tortured and slaughtered like a pig. I would have burned them all, but my faithful friends kept me from my impulse. I guess I should thank them, but I was prepared for some small vengeance. I raised some readied vessels, turned the place ablaze and escaped. My only regret is that I was unable to take Lazarus' body with me. I may have been able to . . ." He swallowed. "I have more bad news, Tyrone. Tai Cassel is dead too. They murdered him when he tried to stop them killing Lazarus."

It was another blow. Tyrone was always strong and fast, and no stranger to weapons, but it had been Cassel who had trained him. *Another man I shall avenge.*

"He never liked me, you know. I met him in Valare shortly after Mercer's back was broken at the walls. He was devoted to Valare. In truth I liked him. He challenged my beliefs, and his loyalty to Valare was pure."

"Why would they kill him?" Tyrone closed his hand into a fist, wincing at the stiffness of his movements. "He was no threat, just a man who did his duty."

"Because they could. Just like Lazarus."

Tyrone felt cold, despite the warmth of the fire. "You really cared for him."

"Have you have been to the Sepulcher?" When Tyrone shook his head, Tyir nodded in understanding. "Their prisons put the Empire's to shame. Indeed, I have been in sewers more luxurious than that shithole. I was there for execution."

"Why?"

Tyir shrugged. "For my experiments. But if you want the truth, it was because I aided one of their enemies, during the Kahal's rebellion. You've heard of that I trust?"

"Yes, I've heard," Tyrone said quickly, eager to hear more.

"These men you see," Tyir said, gesturing expansively at the camp. "They started there. Our strength now is a mere shadow of what it was. The Kahal clans were fighting to throw out the Order.

They recruited many men. I joined them. Why not? Easy gold, easy blood, and it provided subjects for my research. When the rebellion was finally quelled, I was captured by the Order. They sentenced me to death without trial, not that it would have helped in my case."

He smiled briefly as he looked down at Tyrone. "I was languishing in my cell when Lazarus entered. I felt a connection with him, one I hadn't felt for decades. I helped him, and he helped me. Finally, it came to the day of my execution. But Lazarus saved me. He broke me free, even killed his own kin to help me escape. We slept rough for weeks, before we fled to Valare. He protected me, sacrificed everything."

He turned away, almost shyly. "I owe a great deal to that man, and he died for me. A life debt is the most powerful of all, Tyrone."

Silence fell before them for a while, both lost in thought. Tyrone felt pity engulf him. His concern seemed to show on his face, for Tyir spoke up then.

"You fought valiantly in Valare."

Tyrone felt unease at how much he knew. He did not see Tyir at all during the battle, although now it was like wading through smoke, groping blindly for memories. "I was just doing my duty, like everyone else."

The thought reminded him of something Tyir had mentioned earlier.

"You said the Empire should be thanking you." He broke off, remembering. It was as though he could smell the burning flesh and wood around him again, the smoke in his skin, in his mouth, in his hair. But even more, he remembered the cold, shuffling flesh advance in waves, the reanimated corpses forcing the elite Dominion soldiers back. He finally understood the truth. "That was you, when the dead rose?"

Tyir regarded him closely for a moment, as if considering whether to reply. "I did say I would answer your questions. Yes, it was me."

Tyrone's mouth had become papery. He licked his lips, gathering his courage. "I saw dead men walk again!" He had heard whispers in Valare of the Paladin's exploits, of his dark and deserved reputation. But to see it. "No one can do that!"

"Do you doubt my power?" Tyir's replied amusement, one eyebrow arching. Tyrone shook his head, accepting what he knew to be true.

"It was a horror."

Tyir averted his gaze, looking into the flames. "Lazarus forbade me from participating in the battle. He realized the Dominion would target me, but I could not sit back idly and watch our men fight and die. I had to help." He laid a hand gently on Tyrone's shoulder.

Tyrone jerked away from his touch. "But I saw the dead on the ground rise. I had killed one of them just moments before. He fell by my hand." Tyrone covered his face with his hands as if that would deny the truth. He could see it, smell it, the memory as real as it was that day. "He had my spear through his body, and he rose before me!" He looked at Tyir, expecting . . . what? Contrition?

"We all do our duty, whatever it may be. We were struggling to hold them back. You saw their invasion fleet." Tyir turned away, revulsion in his eyes. "It was my fault. They used the Kyrm fire because of me. I'm the reason that Valare burned."

No, Tyrone thought. *We would have been defeated in the end.* He could see that easily. For all their courage, they were too few, the invaders too many. That was the brutal truth. He shuddered. "That was no natural power." He stood, swaying slightly.

Tyir rose too. His eyes were blazing, but he had regained his composure. "What do you know of such things, eh?" He turned and called out for the girl, Meira. "It seems I must prove my power to the lad."

"Master? Is this wise?"

Tyrone jumped as she appeared behind him.

"It has to be done."

The girl did not reply. Tyrone turned to her, but she was already gone.

"Follow me, Tyrone. This is a rare occasion."

Tyrone followed until they came to the border of the village. *I played here.* Tyrone recognized the giant oak tree at once, the largest he had ever seen. It reached higher than the rest of the trees around.

A body lay there on the ground. A young man, no older than Tyrone. Blood, crusted and browning had congealed on his head, and there were gaping holes where his eyeballs had once been. They were not alone. Meira was there, along with a large group of perhaps of fifty men.

"I am ready, Tyir," she whispered, bowing her head. Tyrone could see her fully for the first time. Comely, was his first thought. Long blonde hair ran down her back, far past her shoulders, but in the growing darkness it seemed to glow like molten silver. Her cheeks were hollow, her eyes more so.

"Good. Time is short, but we need to move. There is much to be done." Tyir turned to Tyrone then. "Join Meira, and bear witness. Many think they know what power is. Some say wealth, some say strength. I, say it is knowledge. Knowledge that few dare to follow."

Meira reached forward and pulled Tyrone to her side. He meekly followed, heart pounding. He could feel the other men's eyes on him, but he could not turn his attention away from the corpse. There was a faint stench of death, but not as foul as he had expected. The body seemed to be fresh.

"Tyrone, tell me. What do you know of sorcery?"

Tyir knelt on the ground. The assembled men moved swiftly, jostling each other for position as they formed a circle around their master. Meira laid pulled Tyrone back from the center of the circle into the expectant crowd.

"Sorcery? Very little," he admitted. "The Order enforced their laws well. When I had the courage to ask once, I was shouted down."

"So much ignorance, and for too long." Tyir clasped his hands together, as though in prayer. The watching men had fallen silent. Even the wind had died away.

"I've spent my life searching for knowledge to tap into the underworld's infinite power. Now, Tyrone Cessil, you shall see that the Torn World is possible. Keep silent, my Thousand Scars and bear witness. I am still the man I was when I forged your blades, I promise you." He began to murmur; strange words in an odd cadence.

Tyrone did not understand. "What *is* that?" He whispered.

"The language of the old ones," Meira replied.

Tyrone could scarcely believe his eyes, but he could not tear his gaze away. A blue aura began to envelope the corpse, a gentle hissing emerging from the body while Tyir continued to chant softly. A sudden screech filled the air, so sharp it made him cringe. Meira had fallen to the ground.

Tyrone stood rooted to the spot, transfixed, as she began to convulse violently. He made to aid her, but strong hands grabbed him from behind, holding him fast.

"What?" He struggled, turning to one of Tyir's men who was restraining him. "Look at her!"

Blood began to drip from Meira's open mouth. Her eyes were vacant as she continued to convulse. Nobody paid her any attention, focusing on Tyir and his ritual.

What's going on? Finally, Meira stopped shaking, let out a gasp and lay still.

Tyrone looked at the corpse, but the aura had vanished. Tyir's chanting was slowly easing, the foreign voice vanishing. Then the body stirred.

Slowly at first, the creature began to stand, its limbs shaking slightly. Tyrone felt something warm and wet release inside his trousers, as he stared into the corpse's bloody eyeless sockets. The 'man' groped its way to its feet.

It's moving . . . it's moving! He gazed down upon Meira's lifeless form. *But at what cost?* There was a cold sense of fear inside him. *Tyir killed her to prove a point to me.*

The restraining arms loosened their grip on him and Tyrone knelt at the girl's side.

"You don't understand. Come, it's alright." One of the other men took him firmly by the arm and pulled him gently away from her body. Tyrone heard sniggers, but let it wash over him. "Leave him be, Scars. He doesn't know our ways," the man said.

The sound of hooves thudding amongst the trees came to them and Tyir rose to his feet, the corpse still standing, swaying slightly.

"That you, Rapier?" Tyir called out. There was a triumphant smile marking his lips.

"Aye. Starting without me?"

There was a rustling in the trees, as a huge, hulking shadow came into view. Tyrone almost did a double take, staring at the apparition emerging from the forest, riding a . . . giant elk. Tyrone blanched as the men cheered. The animal was enormous, standing six foot at the shoulder. The man riding him was easily seven feet tall, Tyrone judged. He was clad in black robes, his face under a blood-red hood. Behind him came a throng of men, and a couple of women. All were armed with great hornwood bows, scythes and spears, axes and swords. Some of the weapons appeared to be wet with blood.

"It's been a long time, my old friend," Rapier rasped. "When I heard your call, I marched north as fast as I could with my men. I only apologize I could not bring more. I haven't been able to rally everyone. Iron Dog is still gathering forces." His voice was gravel and ice. "So, the Scars have been revived then?" His hooded head glanced around, face hidden by shadow. Only his eyes were visible, glowing red. "War is glorious."

Tyir looked to Tyrone. "That must have been some shock to you, child." He smiled gently. "I'm sorry about that."

"What does this mean, Master?"

Meira! Wheeling sharply, Tyrone took a stumbling step backwards, his legs crumpling from under him. He sprawled upon the muddy ground, looking up in shock.

"You didn't tell him much, did you Tyir?" Horse shouted from the new band of arrivals, cheerfully. The air rang with the men's laughter, and Tyrone felt his face burn.

"Leave him be." Meira's reproach shut them up; the laughter died. She reached down, pulling him to his feet.

This doesn't make sense! Not unless . . . Then it dawned on him. He pulled away from her grip. Her cold hands, her rising from the dead. There was only one explanation.

"What exactly are you?" *She's dead. She's some dead thing.* Part of him wanted to turn and flee. Rapier turned his gaze upon him, and Tyrone recoiled from the intensity of the man's gaze.

"Who the fuck is this?" Rapier's voice was soft, but no less frightening. Tyrone shivered. Nobody laughed this time.

"It makes no difference. All that matters is he's here." Tyir declared. He was panting with exhaustion, his hands shaking.

"Is this it, then? We're going to war again?" Someone asked.

"Yes. The Thousand Scars will bleed the world." Tyir whispered.

There was a sudden outbreak of cheers as he spoke, his words evidently carrying to the greater number of people present.

"It has been too long. In my heyday as the Paladin, I founded this company. Necromancy has its price, and for many years I waged war to gather the means to further my knowledge. Now our sword shall be sharpened to a new purpose."

Rapier dismounted the great elk. "Those were good times," he said. "Nothing speaks louder than the drums of war." Rapier emitted a chuckle. "While you were safe north, we kept loyal to you, Tyir. We destroyed three of the Order's patrols on the way to this shit holdfast. Now I know what you want, I only regret I didn't bring you more bodies to play with."

Tyir nodded solemnly. "Strife shall engulf this world, but it is only the beginning." He looked at his men, his eyes resting briefly on them all. "Now my war begins! Lazarus went to the Empire as ally. They murdered him. I will not sheathe my blade until he is avenged. What say you all?"

Every man and women presented answered his call, some drawing their weapons. As one they exclaimed loudly, "The Thousand Scars shall bleed the world!"

"None shall leave your side, Tyir of Irene, until your will is done." It was Sleeper. He took a knee, bowing deep. "If you had a kingdom, I would serve you as though you were my king."

Someone sniggered. "Why don't you suck his cock and be done with it, Sleeper?" A voice called from the crowd.

"Fuck you, Rancil," Sleeper snarled, hand reaching for a dagger.

"Pathetic though his sentiments are, I share them. And if I don't come with you, Sleeper would only miss me." Rancil was a short, hunchbacked man with a square jaw. "He needs my manliness as an example in his life. Give him something to aspire to." He grinned wider, showing a mouthful of brown, cracked teeth as he thumbed the edge of a bearded axe.

Rapier strode forward. He walked with a slight limp, his bare feet black and veined.

"Lazarus is dead, Tyir?"

"Aldmer killed him. I tried to save him, but I failed," Tyir replied.

Rapier's breath rasped. "I'm sorry for your loss, Paladin. I know what he meant to you."

"Thank you," Tyir's reply was soft.

"What would the Empire have done with you, Tyir?" Sleeper asked. "We all know the limits of your necromancy." There was a stirring and muttering from the crowd at this. "It's true. What they require from our master would not be possible. I mean, there is only so little they can achieve."

"Unless. . ." Tyir began, and Sleeper fell silent.

Tyrone looked into the old man's eyes. There was a momentary flicker of fear, and Tyrone felt his stomach drop. *There's something he's not saying.* Then, it was gone just as quickly.

Tyir turned to face Tyrone. "Now, regarding you." There was another pause. "What you want is up to you. By now there is no confusion about who we are, or what we are going to do. We shall take up arms against our foes, until Valare and all our enemies are avenged. I brought peace to the Empire. They repaid me by taking the life of the greatest man I had ever known." Tyir fixed Tyrone with his gaze. "If you want to leave, I will arrange for an escort. Or, you can swear into my service. In truth, I would welcome somebody of your skill. And a fresh face too, at that."

Rapier laughed scornfully. "Him?"

"Silence, Rapier," Horse glared at him. "He fights well. He'll be good for us."

"I don't take orders from oafs, Pyran." Rapier turned his hooded head towards Tyrone. "Fresh meat bleeds more easily. I will see for myself."

He took a step forward, drawing the largest greatsword Tyrone ever seen. Tyir put a cool hand on Tyrone's shoulder.

"That will do Rapier. If he joins us, it'll be a long time before you can test his mettle." Tyir grabbed Tyrone's chin, lifting it up so their eyes met. Tyrone didn't struggle. "The choice is yours. I saved your life, but only you can decide your path. Tell me quickly. We march tomorrow and I need your answer."

Before Tyrone could say anything his legs buckled, and he collapsed, white-hot pain searing through every muscle in his body.

"You've pushed your body too far," Tyir whispered. "Go and rest, but I want an answer in the morning. For at dawn, we bleed the world."

A Thousand Scars

*Many have died. And yet, I fear if I do what has to
be done, it will plunge this world into ruin.*

~ Pharos Animar

Tyrone lay in bed, unable to sleep, thoughts racing.
Where could I go? A sinking depression consumed
him. Tyir had admitted that he was a necromancer.
His people were murderers and thieves, the lot of
them. He had no desire to be part of that. And yet,
Tyir had saved his life.

His body throbbed with a dull, burning pain as he
sat up, wincing. *I have nowhere else to go.* A lump
came to his throat, so painful he couldn't swallow.
Valare is gone. His bladder ached.

Desperate to relieve himself, he stumbled out of the
bed and quietly dressed, adding a thick leather cuirass
over his clothes. He was still unsteady on his feet, the
pain in his limbs making every step an ordeal. Nearby
were voices, loud and obnoxious, cut with snatches of
drunken singing.

Above was a brilliant full moon, so it was possible to
see his surroundings. Tyrone found the source of the
voices quickly. He began to walk in their direction,
looking for a quiet spot to piss.

"Been awhile since I last saw you, Jaques," a woman
said throatily. They were sitting in a circle, four in
total, her and three men. "We didn't really get chance
to talk before now. Come, tell us, who was the last
bitch you had? I see at least a dozen new scars. How

handsome you have become," she purred. "How long has it been; four, maybe five years?"

"Six. It's been too long, my dear Sybill."

Tyrone now had a clear view of them. The one called Jaques held a lute lightly in his hand, letting it dangle from a leather strap.

"I was plying my trade down in the Kahal," Jaques said, "before I heard Tyir's call and rushed to join. I volunteered to bring him out of Carin, but it never happened." He spoke softly and formally. "I never forget a debt, so here I am. You come with Rapier?"

"Aye. You know how much I like killing Order boys," Sybill replied. "How is it down there? The war affecting them?"

Jaques gave her a handsome smile. "Not much from what I saw. The Order has them well controlled. Still a lot of hate for the pious cunts, no doubt, but the Dominion's invasion has forced them to join forces with the Order families occupying Kahal. They've been fortifying the river passes and the river Iris for months, just in case the foreign scum move south. I doubt that'll happen though. Their beef is with the Empire, not the Kahal. But they still burn with a desire for justice against the Order invaders. It won't take too much for that fire to spread."

"I've seen you've gotten busy, at least." Sybill said. "But you're changing the subject. Your scars. Tell me!"

Tyrone halted, curious, not willing to pass the group until he heard Jaques' tale.

"Ah yes, that. Pretty ugly cut just a couple days ago. Me and couple of the lads were in an inn not far from here. The barkeep was disrespecting us, you see; tried to cheat me out of some coppers."

"I hope you robbed and killed the bastards, Jaques, if they tried to cheat you," a one-armed man growled. A squat, muscular man, he had a patch covering one of his eyes, and his left arm was nothing more than a stump. "I know how you deal with those who disrespect you!"

"Oh, I sure as hell did, Reynold. But not him. I don't fuck men. His daughter on the other hand . . ." The men laughed and Sybill let out a shrill cackle of hysterical mirth, clapping her hands together with childish glee.

"I knew it! I knew there was a girl involved. Do tell, do tell!"

"Did you write a song about it, Jaques?" The question came from a stocky man with long dirty hair tied back behind his head. "I wondered why you were so late out of there."

Even in the dark, Tyrone could see the man's pug-like face twist with malice.

"You could've told me," he continued. "I would've joined the fun."

"Shut the fuck up!" Sybill snarled at him.

Jaques raised a hand for silence. "Jackal, it's cos I wanted the meat for myself, you know what I like."

Tyrone began to circle around them, as quietly as he could. Jaques was talking again.

"Anyway, I wanted another ale and the bastard refused me. The old innkeep was rushing me, and I wanted a another drink. Treated us like shit the whole time we were there. Well, it was the last straw for me. His daughter came into the room. Pretty girl, sixteen, maybe seventeen? Well, you know me. I wanted a new scar. I shoved the innkeeper out of the way and grabbed her. The old man tried to stop me, came at me with a knife believe it or not, but I grabbed it and rammed it in his throat. Poor girl was a bit out of it when I was done with her. I felt a little bad, so I threw down the coppers her pa tried cheating me out of and left. Poor girl. No daddy and no maidenhead

164

anymore!" He broke off laughing, the others laughing with him.

Tyrone stopped in his tracks as he found himself looking right into the man's eyes.

"Look what we have here," Sybill said softly. "Boy!"

Fuck, fuck. They were all staring at him. Sybill was a strong, strapping woman in her late forties, with a mane of long copper hair. Tyrone averted his eyes. Her face wasn't unpleasant to look at, far from it, but her broad eyes sparkled with a dangerous cruelty. Her lips stretched into a predatory smile.

"Ah, the new meat. Tyir must think right by you. Does he?" She asked softly. She rose to her feet, advancing on Tyrone. He could smell alcohol on her breath. Tyrone took a step back.

"Where you going, lad?" Reynold pointed at him with his one good arm. "Tyir said for you to rest. You got a decision to make. Go."

"I needed to piss," Tyrone said shortly. *I must not show fear.*

"He thinks he's better than us." Sybill smiled wider, her hand darting under her bodice and pulling it open, baring large breasts. "You think we're monsters, don't you? Come, spend ten minutes with me and I'll show you I can do good work too. Call it an initiation."

Tyrone said nothing, but he looked away, thankful for the dark that hid his blushes.

"Leave the lad alone, Sybill," Jackal grunted. "He's not used to the likes of us."

"What's wrong? I was a whore in Bawsor. I fuck better than girls half my age." Sybill's eyes flashed. "Stop that look! He thinks he's better than us. Some fucking lorded-up, soppy little shit!"

"You mean to run off and fuck us over, don't you lad?" The one armed Reynold lurched to his feet, greasy curtains of maroon hair jumping about his face. "We can't have that. You're probably too craven to fight with the likes of us, that's fine. But you think of betraying us, and . . ."

"I wasn't!" Tyrone snarled back, but he felt his legs give way. *Don't show weakness. They won't give you any mercy.* "I need to take a piss! Can't I do that without being judged by idiots?" The insult tumbled out of his mouth before he could stop himself. Everyone fell silent. *Shit.*

Sybill advanced on him. "So the little pup has a mouth. Good."

There was a flash of steel as Jackal rose to his feet. Suddenly the ghostly wail of a warhorn blared. As one, they all turned to face the sound.

"The sentries," Sybill whispered. "Someone's coming."

The warhorn sang again. Someone close called out, "Outlaws! To arms!"

Outlaws. The confusion fogging his brain evaporated. Tyrone sensed movement all around. One-Hundred-Jaques grabbed a long knife from the ground. Tyrone looked for a weapon, the need to piss forgotten.

"You heard!" Jaques snarled at anybody and everybody. "To battle, all of you!" He seized a crude, heavy longaxe, and threw it to Reynold who caught it easily with his only hand, and hurried past him.

"Time to taste blood!" The one called Jackal cackled. He ran up and seized Tyrone by the shoulder. "Get back inside your tent. We'll take care of this."

And be called coward? Tyrone thought. "Not going to happen," he replied. "I'll fight." The air was pungent with the smell of wood smoke. In the distance, Tyrone could hear arrows whistling, and the sound of steel, but he could see nothing of the enemy.

"Like fuck," Jackal snarled. His grip on Tyrone's arm tightened. "You're wounded, boy!" He drew his sword. "Go! We'll take care of this!"

Tyrone felt the heat in his face rise. "Look!" He began, but his eye caught something moving towards them; ill-clothed and ragged men had broken through the lines of fighting that raged around, and were nearly upon them. Instinct took over.

"They're coming!" Throwing Jackal's hand off, he snatched up a sword lying next to a blanket on the ground. He assumed a fighting stance just as the first of the brigands reached him. The man held a small shield and a spear, and he thrust at Tyrone, the spear point jabbing at his face. Tyrone stepped forward, and the outlaw stumbled back in alarm.

Holding his blade tightly, Tyrone lunged with all his strength. The point caught his attacker in the armpit, causing him to roar in pain and slump down as his knees gave way. Tyrone kicked him to the ground and ripped the small shield from the dying man's grasp, gripping the handle of the buckler so tightly he thought his fingers would burst.

Something was on fire. There was smoke everywhere, stinging his eyes, but Tyrone could just make out the frenzied action through the chaos. He saw Jackal, caught in ferocious combat with two outlaws, their steel clashing so quickly their movements were a blur. Tyrone was stunned by the speed of the swordplay. As he rushed to help, something caught him in the small of the back, throwing him off balance. The impact knocked the wind out of him as he fell hard, his sword flying out of his hand. Gasping for air, he got to his knees. One-Hundred-Jaques was battling three attackers in the distance, next to the big tent; flame and smoke from the canvas high in the air. Ragged breathing warned

Tyrone, and he groped in the mud for his weapon. His fingers closed around the hilt of the sword, and he swung it just in time to meet the knife held by a heavily padded man. It was a clumsy block, but Tyrone's desperate swing threw his attacker off balance, the man's eyes widening in surprise as he raised his knife to attack again.

Adrenaline pumped through him, spurring him forwards and Tyrone seized his chance, plunging the point of his sword deep into the outlaw's chest. As the man dropped his dagger, Tyrone tugged the sword free and left him sprawled in the mud. He saw Jackal and another of Tyir's men surrounded by more outlaws.

I have to help them. There was nothing for it. Taking a deep breath, Tyrone charged in.

The outlaws were too busy fighting Jackal to notice Tyrone, and he drove the point of his blade into the back of one of them. Tyrone caught the swing from another assailant, blocking with his sword. With the buckler in his right hand, he deflected a blow from an axe, wrong footing his attacker, giving him the opening he needed to drive his sword deep into the man's back, causing him to spasm frantically on the ground as his spinal cord was severed.

That did the trick. Three more brigands were fleeing; Tyrone caught a glimpse of Rapier stalking after them, chanting something in a foreign tongue. Tyrone's head was aching fit to bust, and his legs burned with the exertion.

"Fall back!" Someone bellowed. Then he saw the enemy break, men fleeing, cut down by arrows or hacked down by pursuers. Horse let out a roar of fury as he grabbed hold of a screaming outlaw by the throat, dragging him towards him.

It's over, we won. Tyrone fell face down, the smell of the dirt and blood rank in his nose. Darkness overtook him. He knew nothing more, until someone grabbed him by the scruff of the neck and pulled him onto his feet.

"You look like shit, if you don't mind me saying."

It was Jackal. The right side of his face was caked in congealing blood, but otherwise he looked unharmed. The sun had risen while Tyrone had been out of things and the early morning light shone down on the camp.

"I feel it," Tyrone replied groggily. Every inch of his body was burning with fatigue. He looked around. Tyir's men were looting corpses.

"This looks nice," one of them chortled, holding up a white necklace with a shining black stone. Its previous owner lay on the ground, his decapitated head lying beside the body.

"You don't want that! Give me it!" Reynold laughed harshly, his boot slamming against the severed head as he spoke. It rolled grotesquely towards them, coming to a halt resting against Tyrone's ankle. Pushing away the sick feeling in his stomach, he moved away from it.

"Bandits. That was foolish of them," Tyir chuckled as he came into view, holding a slim longsword. "More meat for my experiments. We leave within the hour, once we get everything prepared." He turned to Tyrone. "You alright?"

"He saved my life," Jackal spoke before Tyrone could, clapping him hard on the back. "Drove his blade right through one of them." Then Rapier was there, looming over him.

"As you say, Jackal."

"I knew you had it in you," Tyir bowled over Rapier's contempt. "I think it's time that you made

169

your choice, Tyrone. Do you want to leave, or will you fight with us?"

Tyrone hesitated. He looked at the assembled men and women, some of whom were bleeding. If he left, he would almost certainly die. If he stayed, they would likely kill him anyway. Not much of a choice.

"Aye, I will join with you, Tyir, if you will have me."

"Welcome to the Thousand Scars, lad," Jackal said cheerfully. The others watched him coldly.

"I must warn you," Tyir said, his voice rising. "This won't be easy." Tyir took a step towards him, the slightest of warnings, but one which made Tyrone's blood shiver. "Many have committed the darkest crimes with me. We're all killers. Remember that we're fighting a war, and demons stir in men. We will kill and torture to gain what we need. I don't ask you to follow my example, but I do ask for unwavering loyalty. Nor can I guarantee your safety. If we are caught, we will die in the most painful way possible. And if you betray me, well . . ."

"Regardless, I will go with you, Tyir." Tyrone paused. "Just don't expect me to call you master."

A couple of onlookers cursed, while others tittered. Tyir laughed softly. "Very well." He turned to Rapier. "You command my vanguard. Pick forty men. You're my eyes and ears."

"As you wish, Paladin." His voice was filled with a savage triumph.

"Meira, you will help me reanimate the vessels we have. Thanks to these fools, we have even more now. Lessens the chance of failure. Begin."

"Of course, my master." She bowed her head. "This body is your gift, and your weapon."

They left the camp later that morning. Horse had delivered a gift to his tent; clothing scavenged from the dead. Boiled leather and comfortable animal skin trousers with a stained jerkin, it was better than Tyrone had previously had, even though they stank.

"He's not going to need it, whoever it belonged to," Horse said, looking him up and down. He hoisted a bag on his shoulder, barely noticing its weight as their party reached the outskirts of the village, its border marked by the remains of an ancient wall. Trees were scarce, many having been felled. "You might be a warrior yet, lad."

Rapier had personally requested Tyrone's presence. "I want to know what belly the boy has for our needs," he had rasped to Tyir at the choosing. His master merely nodded consent, and Tyrone went into the vanguard.

"There's some villages to the south-east, three or four days ride from us," Jaques declared. They were sixty in number, though a third of them were the staring, vacant bodies raised by Tyir, shambling obediently. The mere sight of the reanimates made Tyrone's skin crawl. "Tyir told us to raze the village of Caribou, and wait for him there."

"We came past it when we were on our way here," Sybill clucked impatiently, washing in a nearby pond that buzzed with flies. "Few defenders, lightly guarded. I wanted to put the place to the torch, but Rapier wanted to meet the master. Finally I'll get a chance."

She caught Tyrone looking, and gave him a wide, feral smile with a wink. Tyrone turned away. The events of the night before were still on his mind.

"Trust the large men to do the heavy lifting." Horse swore under his breath as he tied the heavy bag of supplies on his back. "I'd be better up front, but never mind." His grin faltered as he looked down on Tyrone, who couldn't help feeling intimidated. "You hurting, lad?"

"Some," Tyrone said uncertainly. Rapier was lumbering towards them, that ugly great sword on his back. There was something inhuman about him. Horse caught Tyrone's eye and winked.

"We have a holy task at hand, men, for the Paladin. We will not fail." Rapier said in a thundering voice. "The Thousand Scars will bleed the world!"

"The Thousand Scars will bleed the world!" The men around Tyrone bellowed, raising their left fists into the air as one. Tyrone didn't join in. Horse put a hand on his shoulder as Rapier approached.

"Look at me, new blood," Rapier said.

The demand was clear. Tyrone dared not refuse. He looked up defiantly into the demon's face, still lost under the hood.

"Your chance to prove yourself. I only give one chance." Rapier gave a single curt nod as he waved them ahead.

"Don't mind Rapier. He's like that to everyone," Horse muttered as soon as Rapier was out of earshot. "Don't tell him I said that." Tyrone managed a weak smile. "Here, I have something for you." Horse grinned, handing him the bow he had been carrying. Tyrone was surprised. There was no mistaking its artisanship. Tyrone hesitated.

"Go ahead! It's yours, lad!"

Tyrone whistled as he handled the bow. It felt natural in his hand, the skill in its build apparent. Four feet long, but light; he could balance it in one hand. Its curve was deep, the tips of the bow pointing away from him. He felt his stomach drop.

"It's from Pyra." Tyrone exclaimed. There was no mistaking the smooth ripples of the stelwood, a ghostly grey tinged with emerald green, laminated with horn and sinew.

"That's my boy. It's my legacy and that of my people." Horse's eyes were dark behind his heavily scarred, wrinkled face. His cheeks were lined with deep scars, some fresh and others only half healed. "Why do you think the sigil of the Pyran lands is a bow crossed with a sail? It is the heart of my people, and the weapon of the song of my home." He grinned wider, showing a mouthful of browning teeth. "Go on," he nodded, as Tyrone still hesitated. "I have one of my own. This one is yours."

"Are you sure?" Tyrone had to ask, astounded.

"Of course! I always keep a spare. You really think I'd give you my only bow?" His chortle was loud over the crunch of the undergrowth as they trudged through it. "I like you, lad, but not *that* much!"

Tyrone gently slung the bow across his back, its weight surprising him. "The Young Bow was my childhood hero, back when I was younger," he admitted. That was one of the few studies he hadn't minded learning.

"You have good taste in heroes then. Tyrus the Great was a formidable man. A legend from my homeland," Horse agreed, his footfalls landing heavily. "Pyra is an old and biting land, filled with peril and hardship, but Tyrus took the two things the Pyrans possessed and nearly destroyed Bale's legacy. The bow and the sail."

Tyrone nodded. "It was said he pushed the Empire to the brink of destruction, thanks to these bows." *I am holding the greatest bow ever crafted.* Made of Stelwood, only in Pyra, their price overseas was incomprehensible. "My father once ordered a dozen of these for his personal guard," he suddenly remembered. "He was in a rage for days when he heard how much they cost. He still bought them."

Horse laughed. "I don't doubt that for an instant. Pyran bows are rare on the continent, especially since the trade routes were closed by the war." He scowled. "Tyrus the Great took twenty thousand bows with him along with his fleet." Horse let out a happy sigh. "Then when the Dominion marched upon Hzarn's walls, the same bows held them at bay for twelve years." He nodded stiffly at Tyrone. "Use that bow, Tyrone, and you will truly contribute to the Paladin's fight."

Tyrone's side flared, the pain forcing him to a stop. Sharp like a stitch, it almost made him double over. Concerned, Horse pulled him back onto his feet.

"That poison still troubling you?" Horse asked in a low voice.

Tyrone gritted his teeth, the ache in his pelvis ebbing. Tyir and Sleeper had warned it would take a while before he was free of its influence.

"Yes." Weakness irritated him, his own more than anything. Horse made a clucking sound with his teeth.

"Damn you, Sleeper," he berated the assassin, who had caught up alongside him. "You see the pain he's in."

"Fuck you, Horse," Sleeper shot back, but had the decency to throw Tyrone a guilty glance. "It will heal in a few days, I promise. Unfortunately, you must be patient. Although," he grinned at him then, "be thankful you can still walk. One man I gave a taste of that venom to had his legs melt off him within hours." He shrugged, a swagger returning to his steps. "Come on, we need to move. We have a lot of ground to cover."

It had been two days since they left the ruins of Vengar, and while trudging through endless grass plains and forest was exhausting, dull work, Tyrone was thankful for Horse's company.

"So tell me. Why do they call you Horse?"

"That's easy." Horse had a ready smile, which he flashed at Tyrone as he pushed through the thick and ferns. "I got it cuz of the sound my foes make before I kill them."

"What, they neigh at you?" Tyrone smiled. "He's lying to you, Tyrone." Sleeper cast Horse a challenging glare as he labored behind, grunting. "It's a nickname from his old life, when he spent all his days in his father's stable."

"Hey, horses are beautiful creatures!" Grumbling, Horse shook his head and increased his pace, the others hurrying to match his stride.

Even Sleeper proved to be amiable when he wasn't scowling. A similar age to Tyrone, he was intelligent and resourceful, even offering to carry Tyrone's gear as payment for his misjudgment. He soon regretted that impulse, much to the party's amusement.

Tyrone lengthened his strides to keep up with Horse, the sounds of the forest dead in his ears. His fellow brothers grunted alongside as they walked in a column. The air was cold against his badly shaven cheeks, but thanks to a mottled green travelling cloak, he was warm enough. There were no roads, only a narrow dirt path carved through the trees. They were on the outskirts of the Empire now, yet they still found old ruins, little lost hamlets and watchtowers of its old rivals. Tyrone knew little of the history. The Empire had an annoying habit of destroying the lore of the older kingdoms, so names like the Undines, Mesyphra, the Cadik, Tyke and others cropped up less and less.

Tyrone was growing fond of Horse. Booming and manic oaf he was, he had been the kindest to Tyrone by far, besides Tyir. Sleeper still unnerved him. The assassin fell into place alongside Tyrone, matching pace. As for the others in the party, they disturbed and scared Tyrone more then he dared to admit.

One Hundred Jaques, the horribly scarred musician so-named for cutting a gash into his body for each victim he had tortured. There was a gangly, rat-faced bastard called Ombrone the Scarred, who collected teeth and hung them around his neck. Then there was Sybill of Bawsor, the whore who had been imprisoned by the Empire for robbing and castrating twelve clients, and had fled east into Kahal where she joined Tyir during the civil war.

Then there was the Uslorian exiled prince, only nicknamed Tongue-Kin for his obsession with mutilating his victims. A few names Tyrone didn't know, but he was sure they were just as cold. They had to be, fighting for so long. Horse had filled him in about their history during the long march.

Rapier was the worst. His fellow Scars treated him like a god, almost with as much awe as Tyir. Tyrone had heard he was once a soldier of the mysterious Keidan, before defecting to Tyir's company during the Kahal civil war. He had known about that brutal rebellion during his youth, and the stories chilled him even now. Just the word Keidan made Tyrone shiver.

On the second morning where they had camped around the ruins of an old Balian watchtower, his great elk would not waken, and Rapier delayed their march by nearly three hours to pray over his fallen steed. When one of the Scars tried to slice a chunk of meat off the elk for breakfast, Rapier took his head off his shoulders in a single stroke. Nobody stopped him. Horse claimed the man's boots and sword for himself.

One of the undead came stumbling, a gaunt, middle-aged man with a brutally twisted neck. Its eyes were vacant, staring into the unknown. Tyrone watched it curiously, aware of the cold sweat under his clothes. The sight of the dead always unsettled him. They made no noise, but they stank. They were on the flanks, stumbling sentinels.

"Don't fear nor pity the dead, Tyrone," Sleeper told him. "Only pity the living."

Tyir had raised nearly one hundred of them in Vengar, including the bandits from the night raid. He had split them between the four parties, claiming "reconnaissance purposes," but Tyrone remained confused by their role. When he asked Sleeper what their purpose was, he and Horse both chuckled.

"When the flesh is few in number, Tyir utilizes the dead. In a war, there is no shortage. Their destruction gives our enemies no advantage. Of course, necromancy does not revive their old skill in battle, but the fear alone is an effective weapon."

From what he seen of Tyir's necromancy, the results were hit and miss, and the undead were shambling, ineffective wrecks, capable of simple tasks but poor fighters. They were slow, and certainly had no intelligence. Their humanity had died with their bodies, and had not been resurrected.

As the sun rose higher, Tyrone let his mind wander. There had to be another use for necromancy, he was sure of it. Bold as Tyir's notions of vengeance were, their host was tiny, less than two hundred men. Even with the dead bolstering their ranks, it was still not enough to attack villages on the borders, let alone invade the Empire. There had to be another plan. His fellow Scars made idle talk about more men to the south-east, who were being gathered by a man called Iron Dog. His name became the butt of many sarcastic jokes over the days, most often being "Lame Dog" for his dawdling to reach them.

The forests around them were thinning, and he could see more clearly through the gaps in the trees. On and on they continued along the trail, until the night stars rose above them.

"We'll stop soon," Rapier rasped.

Sure enough, they came to a halt in a clearing near the edge of the forest, surrounded by a ring of trees stretching high above their heads. They made camp. A deep pool lay at the bottom of the steep hill, and Rapier immediately set off to make his nightly ritual of praying, not to return until morning. Some set up tents, while others patrolled. Tyrone took his time to stretch his legs and take more of the antidote that Sleeper had given him. It was a bitter, vile tasting liquid and he had difficulty keeping it down, but it was necessary.

"Take it four times a day, otherwise the poison will consume you," Sleeper had told him as he handed Tyrone the tiny bottle, grinning all the while.

Tyrone retired to a dry bit of ground to rest, regretting that he couldn't assist in the construction of the camp. Nobody complained, but Tyrone felt a twinge of shame. He knew little about the company, and liked many of them even less, but he felt duty bound to help where he could.

That night, as their party slept; some in their tents and some on deerskins under the stars, Tyrone lay awake, watching the heavens. He could hear quiet footsteps as guards patrolled the camp, hearing snatches of conversation. The corpses that had accompanied them had long since been spent, many of them collapsing in the forest and not moving again. Needing to piss, he got up and passed Horse near the edge of their camp. The big man stood, looking out, his bow at the ready.

He smirked, pointing into the gnarled trees. "Make your water there lad, but don't go far. And don't worry, I won't watch."

"Glad to hear it," Tyrone retorted. Horse sniggered.

After relieving himself, Tyrone made his way back to the circle of sleeping men, looking for his spot. As he reached it and settled down, he heard voices.

"I hope that boy's ready for what's coming." It belonged to Ombrone. Tyrone heard the clattering of his grisly necklace as he moved. He had a feeling he knew who they were discussing. He laid still, his ears pricked.

"That boy has ears, you know. Surely he'll be listening. It's a dark path he's following," said another.

"Tyir had his reasons for saving him, I'm sure. He'll prove himself soon enough. Our master has never led us astray." There was a pause, followed by Ombrone's sigh.

"Strange of him. But if the runt betrays us, he's gonna answer for it." Then came the sound of steel being sheathed. Tyrone's heart hammered, his anger rising to the surface. But it was no good to complain. Remember who you're with. He strained to hear more, but they didn't speak again. Slowly, Tyrone fell into a restless sleep.

He was roughly woken after what seemed only minutes by a boot pressing on his chest, and he glared blearily at the perpetrator. It was Ombrone, hair matted and hand curled around a curved sword. The hilt shone in the moonlight.

"What the fuck are you doing?" Tyrone demanded.

"Language." Ombrone's green eyes glittered darkly. "Rapier wishes to speak with you, lad." His were deep shadows. "Come, he's waiting by the pool." A shudder ran through Tyrone. "Don't give him cause to hurt you. *He's not a patient man.* With that sinister warning, Ombrone left him.

He walked away as Tyrone took off down the hill past the watching guards. Some were smirking openly at him. He found Rapier kneeling by the pool, sharpening his blade. A red mist billowed across the water. The sword was monstrous in size, nearly six foot in length. Rapier looked up, but Tyrone couldn't see his face. A black void seemed to mask his features under the hood.

"Do you fear me boy?" Rapier rasped.

"I might. Though I have no reason to." The words came tumbling out of Tyrone's mouth before he could stop them. Rapier watched him, not speaking. On impulse, Tyrone groped blindly for the dagger Horse had given him. Rapier chuckled, a softness more chilling then his rages.

"That will be the only insult I will allow you, Cessil. Your bravery will get you killed, boy. Don't bother reaching for your apple-eater. Raise a weapon against me, and it'll be the last thing you do." He paused. "So you wish to become a Scar?"

I have nowhere else to go, Tyrone thought. But the necromancer had saved his life. "I am Tyir's man," he said slowly. What choice did he have?

"Good answer. While Tyir is gone, you answer to me. As First Sword of the Scars, you'll obey all commands from me without question. Any disobedience and I'll have your head. We are blades for Tyir, and we must keep ourselves sharp at all times. Do you understand?"

"I do."

"Good," came Rapier's satisfied reply. "One more thing. You ask why you should fear me. I'll give you that reason now." He raised his hands to his hood and pulled it down. It was all Tyrone could do not to scream and run. What should have been a face was gone, replaced by a gaping hole of crusted blood and pus. No eyes, only bloody holes. They glowed like embers. Tyrone felt a rise of bile in his throat. Rapier wasn't human.

"This is the reason. You'll do well not to question." Rapier's words rang through the trees as he pulled his hood back into place. "So now you know, Tyrone Cessil. Go. Leave me to my prayers."

Tyrone went.

Bleeding the World

I have made many mistakes. I only hope that my next one does not condemn us all.

~ Pharos Animar.

Tyrone stirred, awoken by his night demons. He shuddered as he remembered Rapier's face, the horror under the hood. The man looked nothing human. He opened his eyes, feeling hot rays of sunlight beating down on him. It had been another difficult night. Sleep would not come easily.

Music reached his ears, the twang of a lute's string. One-Hundred-Jaques was playing with his lute on a flat rock, singing with his eyes closed. Other Scars were awake too, some skinning rabbits or cleaning their gear. Stretching, Tyrone downed his morning antidote, grimacing as he listened to the killer sing, his voice clear and strong.

> "Sorn *of the Light, hear us*
> *Quiet in the wind.*
> *Our children are sweet souls*
> *Praying to your light.*
>
> *Let the halls fill with love,*
> *And Duty*
> *And Peace.*
> *And may the Sorn rally march us to war,*
> *To begin our path to justice."*

Jaques finished the last note. Opening his eyes, he noticed Tyrone's presence.

"Good morning, Lord Cessil," he said with a wink and easy smile. His pale blue eyes glittered mischievously as he stood before bowing low. "I was just getting some practice in. It's shocking, but a long road of murder and plunder gives me few chances to practice."

"Don't call me Lord Cessil," Tyrone replied.

"Touchy." He shrugged, his hands cradling the golden lute. "Well, I don't wanna know your life story, so don't even try."

Tyrone bit his tongue. It was hard to believe that someone with such a honeyed voice could do the things he had. Tyrone did not want to think about it.

"You sing well," he said uneasily.

Jaques bowed his head. "I thank you, for that. Like a sword needs a whetstone, a voice needs training. Music is a song for the creative, much like how war is a song for the blood-hungry. Do you recognize the song? It's rather well known down Kahal way."

"Not to me. I'm a northerner, and I never really enjoyed old music," Tyrone replied, shrugging. Jacques eyes narrowed at that.

"Heh, just when I thought we could become friends. It isn't that old. It was written after Augustin Carrow's early successes against the Order. Ah, the Kahal rebellion. After they sacked Iris Keep, the song was born. *The Sorn's Revenge,* the minstrels called it. A brutal war it was. Both sides committed horrendous crimes," Jaques mused. "The Sorn's Revenge is a symbol of the Kahals' suffering, and their attempt to regain freedom."

"Tyir said you all fought during that war."

Jaques smiled a nasty smile. "Not all you see here. Sleeper, Tongue-Kin, Meira didn't fight then. They're new recruits, or new compared to some of us." He reached inside his robes and pulled out a leather flask, which he drank from deeply. He wiped his mouth on the back of his hand. "Many of my friends died during the war." His handsome smile faltered. "The Thousand Scars disbanded after Tyir was captured, but when we heard he had fled to Valare, we remained active. Rapier and Iron Dog, they kept most of us together, though where half of them are now is anybody's guess. He's never idle, the Paladin. Iron Dog needs to hurry," he added with a low growl. "I love a new war. Gives me a chance to deal with some new girls too, if you get my meaning. Nothing I enjoy more than pretty cunts." Jaques finished, tipping Tyrone a massive wink. "Want a go on my lute?" He offered. Tyrone shook his head.

"No thanks," he said in what he hoped was a neutral voice. Jaques shrugged amiably and took a swig from his flask as Tyrone walked away.

This is who I must associate with, Tyrone thought. It didn't bode well for his future. But he must live with what company he had. At least there were some positives, he reflected, as he saw Horse and Sleeper approaching, both looking rather bedraggled.

Before Tyrone knew it, they were on their way again. Rapier had decreed that they needed to reach the holdfast of Caribou quickly, to beat the other parties.

"Tyir likes to keep us entertained. All who help me sack Caribou before the others, gets double plunder," he decreed, and the men were quick to obey. It made for fast and painful trekking through even more forests, with only dirt trails, and Tyrone often struggled to keep up. Horse had offered to help but he refused; he didn't want to give the outlaws any more reason to call him weak. He had already heard many mutterings amongst them and several pointed glances in his direction. Tyrone ignored them with Horse's encouragement. He had a point to prove.

The dead were no longer with them; most of the twitching corpses had been abandoned, slumping to the ground, decomposing rapidly. When Tyrone asked Sleeper why, he could only shrug.

"I know little of Master's workings, to be honest," Sleeper admitted, as they made their way up a steep hill. Some were grumbling at the work, though out of Rapier's earshot. "But the dead are with us for only a short amount of time."

"I don't see the use of them, that's all," Tyrone replied, pushing himself on. It made hard work especially with the toxins in his body, but he was a natural climber. His efforts won him a few approving grunts from the others, and Ombrone threw him his water skin. "Forgive my lack of knowledge; such sorcery is unknown where I come from." He took a drink from the musty animal skin, a thin watery ale.

Horse laughed bitterly. He was having more difficulty then most ascending the slippery slope. "Understandable lad. It's unknown many places now." He frowned then. "They usually last a lot longer than this. They barely made it through a day."

"I know what you mean," a man grunted behind them, using his spear as leverage against the slick slope. "There's something wrong, I can feel it."

Rapier kept them walking the rest of the day with no breaks, despite complaints from his party. As red streaks of sunlight covered the sky, Rapier finally called a halt and the group paused for breath.

"The village of Caribou lies ahead." He pointed ahead. *Finally*. Smoke was rising from a hill in the distance, a tall wooden palisade surrounding the village. "And it seems unmolested. The more for us."

Tounge-Kin cackled at that. Tyrone had seen the smoke long before. He knew little of the village, only that it was an important trade hub on the borders of the Empire, where Order and Kahal territory met. He was thankful; the long day of trekking through the forest had exhausted him, and his legs were screaming for release. The worst part was yet to come. Tyrone didn't want to kill innocents. *If they see your weakness, Rapier will kill you.* He had no choice but to fight.

They made their plans quickly. They were well covered by the ring of trees surrounding the village, Rapier picked four scouts to deal with any lookouts. They didn't have to wait long for the archers to return; a freckled ranger named Posin at the head.

"All done," he grinned a black smile at them. "Fuckers didn't hear a thing. The fools only placed a few lookouts at the edge of the village. Their defenses really need work."

Rapier emitted a cruel chuckle under his hood. "As much as I like a challenge, sometimes an easy conquest is a better song for my Lady. Proceed with the attack." He drew his greatsword and led the charge.

"Kill anyone who resists" Horse roared. "Anyone who yields will be spared for Tyir's necromancy. The Thousand Scars shall bleed the world!"

"The Thousand Scars shall bleed the world!" They chanted their war cry. The archers went in first. Tyrone drew his sword too, a heavy blade scavenged from one of the bandits killed in Vengar. It felt unfamiliar in his grasp. *I have to kill innocent peasants.* Swallowing the bile, he followed the Scars into battle.

They lost one man. The wooden palisade surrounding Caribou was undermanned, the townsfolk taken by surprise. As the first volley of arrows flew over the wall, Posin and Sleeper set alight the wooden stocks sending flames and thick smoke billowing into the air. Once they charged through the gate, all that remained was the slaughter.

Tyrone followed, doing what he could. One grandfather charged, holding a sturdy two-handed battle-axe, but he was unarmored and Tyrone simply stuck him with the blade, felling him. Horse was in his bloodlust, beheading a fleeing man with one stroke after his archery had done the damage. Tyrone had never seen such skill with the bow as Horse. Two peasants had arrows through their eyes.

Rapier was the cruelest of them all in battle, his cloak whirling around him in a murderous smoke, taking on all challengers. Amidst the sound of battle, roars of "Kill the Keidan demon!" were loudest as petrified townsfolk rushed at Rapier with crude pitchforks and rusty blades. They all perished. By the end, Rapier's blade was red from point to hilt. The slaughter was over in minutes, but for the peasants, their suffering had only just begun.

Next came the pillaging, and rewards. Horse led men into the homes to ransack what they could find, while Tongue-Kin and Ombrone found two peasant girls in a burnt-down farmhouse, half-naked and bloody, weeping over their dead mother. Tyrone felt sick and turned away as Tongue-Kin tore off his shirt bearing his scarred chest. Hooting, half a dozen Scars followed, Jaques leading the pack of wolves.

"You need to share!" he grinned.

"There's plenty around, stick your cock in one of them!" Tounge-Kin shot back, thrusting hard into the sobbing girl. Shrugging, Jackal walked away to help drag bodies over to a pile, as two Scars held down the other crying girl's arms and legs as they loosened their clothes. To avoid the grisly sight, Tyrone joined Jackal, lugging the heavy corpses across the ground.

An arrow would put the girls out of their misery. But he knew that if he tried, the men would deem him weak, or worse, a traitor. He couldn't take that risk, despite his conscience. Unable to take the screams any longer, he walked over to Rapier and Horse.

You're no better than those monsters, he thought with revulsion. It was all he could do not to throw up.

"The mayor's sealed himself and about fifty others in his house," Horse was saying to Rapier, as he stood brooding over the pile of dead. Horse flashed Tyrone a grin he didn't return as he wiped blood and gore off his boots on the face of an old man's corpse. "At least this fella had some use in death," He chortled. "What should we do? Smoke them out?"

"They're no trouble to us locked in there. They know if they leave, we'll kill them," Rapier thundered, shoving the point of his blade into a still living peasant's chest. He twitched and moved no more, eyes staring into the underworld. "It's not as though we're going anywhere. Leave them for Tyir."

He looked around at them all. "Get a fire going and prepare to stay, feel free to take what you want, but keep some food supplies intact. For your sake, not mine. Round up any survivors, do what you want to them but keep them alive for now. Use them for your pleasure if you wish."

Rapier shook his sleeve loose, revealing his hands for the first time, black and swollen. Tyrone couldn't turn away from the sight. *They're dead, just like his face.*

Clapping Horse on the shoulder, Rapier left the safety of the walls for his evening prayers, leaving his men to play. For something to do, Tyrone took a quick walk around the ruins of the village to see what he could find, doing his best to ignore the screams and shrieks from the survivors as the Scars played. It proved almost impossible; everywhere, the Scars feasted.

Many of the houses had been burned to the ground as the fires rampaged out of control. Scattered across the gardens and pathways were the burned corpses of the townsfolk, many caught in the flames as they tried to escape. The southern wall remained intact, but even here the bloodshed had spread; a dozen bodies littered the gateway. One was still alive. Tyrone approached him. No older then Tyrone, the wounded soul was sobbing pitifully for his mother, his left leg a bleeding ruin. The sight and smell made Tyrone want to retch. *This is the true horror of war.* He knew for a long time the consequences of it, but Valare and his experiences since had shown the truth to his eyes. He was no longer the boy training for battle, believing it to be heroic. Was this his future?

Tyrone knelt beside the boy; his eyes fever-bright as he continued to cry. His brown smock was stained reddish-brown. Tyrone drew his dagger and exposed the dying peasant's throat. *He'll be no use to Tyir, nor will he gain anything from living like this. This is mercy.* Tyrone closed his eyes as he ran the razor-sharp edge across his throat. The boy let out a desperate last rattle as his mouth bubbled with blood and lay still. *You're at peace now.*

He sat beside the body for a long time, watching the sun fade in a haze, the sky bleeding. The view of the hills before him seemed to stretch forever, with the horizon mapped by great mountains, their gnarled faces glaring upon the world. He knew those mountains well, the lands of Sirquol. *Old Valia.* A chill ran through him.

"Mercy is a tough act, boy. You needn't waste it on these."

Tyrone snatched up the dagger and jumped to his feet as Sybill sauntered over, her clothes ripped and bloody. To complete the vision, she cradled in one arm the severed head of a man.

"Decided to go for a stroll?" Her eyes looked down distastefully at the bodies, and the peasant boy who Tyrone had killed. Shrugging, she lifted up the head of the man, talking to it.

"Look at these here. Was this your boy, papa?" She mocked. The head didn't reply. "Of course you don't speak. You're dead." She threw the head on the ground. Sighing, she turned back to Tyrone. "You ended his pain. Why?" Her tone was more curious then hostile.

"As you said, mercy," Tyrone muttered, his back to her. He didn't want to look at her.

"Aye. With only one leg, probably wouldn't have been any help to Tyir anyway," Sybill mused. "You aren't used to this, are you boy?"

Tyrone turned to look at her. Her pretty face bore no malice this time. "Why would I be?" He retorted. "I never asked for this." Sybill's eyes bored into his, dark and unblinking. Finally she sighed.

"We're far different from the lorded lifestyle you're probably used to. There are those in the Scars who give no shits for that kind of stuff. Just remember who you're with. We aren't innocent little farmers who bow to the whims of lords. Our enemies are our meat. I miss my other girls. Kleeze, Alera. They're with Iron Dog still."

She sniffed. "You may not want to indulge your desires, but we do. Don't judge, and you may yet do well with us." She turned away. "Come. Rapier's sent out scouts south to look for any enemies, and the men have meat and beer ready. You should join us. No offense but you look like shit. Even I wouldn't fuck you in this state." With a cackle she sauntered away.

Bemused, Tyrone followed her back to the center of the village, where the Scars sat in a ring around a makeshift cooking spit, drinking and talking wildly. The remains of a ten-foot tall wooden totem still smoldered, the top sculpted in the shape of an eight-headed man, the Octane effigy. *The Scars are clearly no respecters of faith.* One was prying out the sixteen jeweled eyes with a knife, encouraged loudly by Jackal and Rancil. Rapier was still absent.

"Tyrone my lad!" Horse bellowed, waving a drinking horn. He was already tucking into a hunk of charred meat, dripping with grease. Tyrone sat down next to him; the long-haired lout to his left gave him a grudging nod in greeting before turning back to his food. The ring was loud with eager talk as the men shared words. As Tyrone helped himself to the half burned, half raw meat, the conversation turned to their plans, and Tyir's call to war.

"We should march east into Kahal to join with Iron Dog, it's where our strength lies," Ombrone brooded. He sat opposite Tyrone, drinking deeply from a wineskin. "We'll have nearly two thousand men then."

"Iron Dog? The cunt is a slow fucker and didn't come when Rapier marched west. He didn't join the Paladin's call!" Jaques grunted, his sharp eyes unfocused. His chest was bare, revealing his newest scar across his left breast, still bloody. "We can't rely on such."

"I dare you to say that to his face," said his drinking buddy. "He'd split your head open like a log, and you know it." Jaques' snarl of reproach was drowned out by a gale of laughter, as the man sitting by Tyrone's left leaned forward to speak. Tyrone could smell the stale drink on him, his long hair filthy and stinking.

"What do you think?"

Horse shrugged. "He should've marched to meet us, but our men are scattered. It will take time to bring them all together. Many went to ground when Tyir was taken, though we did keep up the fight. It was dull at times though. Do you remember when Tyir got taken, Korin?"

"Those were the days. We were truly fucked then. The men were ambushed, near Laros," Korin added to Tyrone, chortling gaily.

"We got surrounded by nearly a hundred Order cunts, and the leader called for Tyir to surrender, or watch his men die. He did nothing of the sort. Broke the arm of the one closest, stole his sword and we charged. Lost half of our men in the process, while the Order lost over fifty. We ran them the merry way for a while, more of us joining the master. Finally, Tyir saw it was hopeless, and bought us time to flee. A week later we made it to the river Iris. Then Tyir handed himself over."

He shook his head. "Iron Dog and Rapier kept the men together. And now we're back to our roots. Our *glorious* roots." He took a swig from a bottle of wine, made a face and hiccoughed. "I wonder why the Empire wanted Tyir. Master wants revenge badly."

"The bastards killed Lazarus." Horse grunted. "We'll serve Tyir to the end." Both of them lapsed into a brooding silence, letting Tyrone finish his meal in peace. The rest of them were talking jovially. *They may be monsters, but at least they get on well together.* Sybill had taken Posin away by the hand, her topless form rewarded with cheers, while Jaques played on his lute. Tyrone was cramming a hunk of black bread into his mouth when a horn blew by the gateway.

"Tyir comes!"

Tyir's party strolled through the gates to the cheers and roars of the men; it seemed the remaining parties had united before reaching Caribou. All looked tired and worn, except Tyir who looked as fresh as when he began. A few nursed some wounds. Those around the fire bowed their heads, as though he were a great lord.

"Good to see that you lot know the importance of eating," Tyir said mildly as he approached the circle, which shuffled around to accommodate the new arrivals. His travelling cloak was stained with dried blood. Meira was with him, her head bowed. Many in the circle departed for their nightly duties as Tyir called for food.

"I see the dead you've gathered for me," Tyir said to Horse as he bit into a chunk of meat. His voice was surprisingly bitter.

"Village was easy to sack; some others are holed up in the main house over there," Horse jerked his thumb to the manor house in the distance. "What do you want done with them?"

"Let them stew for a few days," Tyir replied. "I've had a bellyful of people for now." He acknowledged Tyrone with a curt nod as he sat down, drinking deep. Meira looked at Tyrone. The memory of her death came back as powerful as before, and he dropped his gaze.

The unease must have settled in his eyes, for Horse nudged him gently. "Is anything amiss, Lord Cessil?" Unlike the others, Tyrone didn't mind it from him. Regardless, he still flinched at the title.

"Lord Cessil is no more a part of my name now then Pyra is of yours." He kept his gaze fixed on Meira. Horse reached for a wineskin.

"Here." He offered the skin to Tyrone gruffly. Tyrone nodded in thanks, and took a long swig. Instantly he recoiled, the contents inside so powerful it made his eyes water.

"Fucking hell," he spat. Horse brayed with laughter as Korin clapped Tyrone hard.

"You have nothing to worry about, Tyrone," Horse added. "She's fine." Tyrone said nothing. Horse leaned in closer. "You're full of questions, I'm sure," he whispered.

Tyrone swallowed painfully. "What exactly is she?" he blurted out. Horse didn't smile.

"I wouldn't ask her that directly. She's been a great asset to Tyir, but she can still kill you in a heartbeat."

A suspicion overtook Tyrone. *If she's not dead, then something must be wrong with her.*

"Every day it's as though Tyir's past becomes darker," he muttered. Horse laid a heavy hand on his shoulder.

"Don't let Tyir's modesty fool you; his knowledge of the hidden arts is great," he said gravely. "She is not dead, though, but his vessel. His greatest prize."

"What do you mean?" Tyrone was surprised to hear himself whisper. *Do I really want to know?* He took a deep swallow of the mead to calm his unease, this time embracing the potent fire in his throat.

"Well . . ." Horse hesitated then, his eyes flickered over to where his master sat silent. "You aren't blind. You've seen what Tyir can do. He has spent his whole life studying arts now forbidden." He broke off, looking uncertain. "It's not up to me to tell you, Tyrone. If you want to know, go and ask him."

Tyrone held back, but Horse had made his choice for him. "Tyir!" He said loudly, making his master look up. "Ty-boy has a question for you."

"What the fuck are you doing?" Tyrone hissed, but Horse only clapped him on the back and rose to his feet. "Need to answer the call of nature. Come Korin! Let's leave Lord Cessil to it." He grinned. Chortling, Korin got up and followed Horse, the two of them throwing cruel, mocking smirks at Tyrone.

Thanks, he thought acidly. Tyir and Meira both look at him expectantly.

"You have a question, Horse says." Tyir said calmly. Tyrone spluttered for a reply, but Tyir waved him down. "No need. I already know. Your question is regarding Meira, and what you saw. Must have been quite a shock."

Tyrone didn't reply. He looked at Meira, who returned his gaze with the same dead eyes. *She's dead. She has to be.*

"She is what I call my greatest asset. Do you know why I spent my whole life studying the art?"

When Tyrone shook his head, Tyir smiled. "I was born in what is now the ruins of Irene, to the south of Harloph. Not even the Empire's reach ever extended there. So much blood was shed in the country; the scars of the Chaos itself still remain. Even as a young boy I was amazed by the secrets of the world. I visited a village close to the Gaol Mountains, and saw the rituals which the common folk there partook in. It opened my eyes."

Tyrone was taken aback. "I thought the Order outlawed all study of the arts?"

"Only in their lands. The south is free of Pharos influence. South of the Armumian Mountains, where it is said the last of the Gaols live, the surviving tribes lingered, and still try to practice, although few do. Only the Valians have been able to get a grip of the sword that is sorcery."

"Do we have time for your whole life story?"

Meira glared at him, but Tyir only laughed. "He has a point. I was fascinated with death and what happened after. Of course, nobody can truly say what happens, but the dread realm's existence cannot be denied. Many open the bodies of the dead to learn secrets of the living, but I wanted to go further. I opened the living, to explore the dead, that path of knowledge which is now forbidden. All arts have a cost though. I spent my whole life trying to find a means around that, and finally I learned. In order to revive those sent into the Dread realm, one must offer up a sacrifice of equal proportion, life. A living sacrifice is the price to reanimate the dead. A cruel cost, I've killed hundreds for that goal."

Tyrone understood. "But how?" It was the girl who spoke then.

"When I first met my master, I was on the brink of death. The Peaceful arrow, as some called it. He saved my life, and in return I am his. It is a beauty to serve."

She broke off as Tyrone stood suddenly, his heart pounding. *The Peaceful Arrow?* He was no fool. *The carrion plague . . . and she touched me?* He felt himself shake. When he was six, he remembered some poor wretch in Vern was rumored to be infected with it; he was executed on the spot by his father's men, in fear of it spreading.

Tyir laughed then. "I know what you must be thinking. True enough, Meira still carries the Peaceful Arrow, or the carrion plague, as some men have call it. You have nothing to fear however. Did you think I sent Sleeper to take you by mere accident? Timyir venom is deadly but it carries immunity to the plague. A strange flower blossoms from its killing qualities. To be honest, you were most likely safe from pestilence anyway. It is a very small risk for contamination and corruption in an infected body, but I dislike taking chances. Why not make use of such a gift? So you can breathe, you're safe, from that at least."

Tyrone struggled to come to terms with it all. His animosity towards Sleeper lessened with Tyir's revelation.

"Back to the question at hand. I studied the practice of the living for many years, and finally I found an answer. The carrion plague is nearly incurable, and it has no mercy for any creed. Therefore the only way I could have saved Meira's life was experimenting on her body. At the point of death, she accepted."

Tyrone looked to Meira, but was met again by an icy, indifferent wall.

"I then realized she was the perfect vessel, and she became the source of my power." Tyir took her hand in his, his eyes fond and warm. However, there was something cloudy in his expression Tyrone couldn't decipher. "I would be groping in the dark for knowledge without her. So you have the truth of it Tyrone."

Tyrone was at a loss what to say. The fires closest to him had burned down into cinders, their embers glowing in the night. He could hear a faint pounding in the distance, sobbing and screams. *Those trapped in the manor.* Tyrone felt sorry for them.

"We'll need to take care of them, but not tonight," Tyir said. He winced as he rose to his feet. "The survivors could have vital intelligence. Maybe we'll stay here for a few days. The walls give us enough protection from bandits, and should any enemies come across us, we'll give them a lesson in pain."

The manor held out for two more days. Tyrone had just broken his fast on charred horseflesh and watered-down ale when the disheveled mayor was thrown out by his own people, his extravagant golden robes shredded. Cries of "Coward!" and "Murderer!" followed him as the door was slammed shut and bolted. Tyrone caught a glimpse of dozens of scared and bedraggled faces staring from the windows.

Ombrone and Jaques threw the whimpering man on his back. Tyir ordered him to be fed and the man was given a slab of what looked like roast pork which he ate ravenously.

"Mercy, mercy please. What do you want?" The mayor was crying as he ate, grease all over his face.

Tyir's demand was as cold as his reputation. "Surrender the people. You have no means of resisting.

"I have a family. Please, my wife. Your men said you have her." His flock watched from the broken windows, shouting and cursing at him.

"We found her," Sleeper interjected kindly. "Surrender the manor, and you can see her. She's been well looked after." Some of the Scars tittered, and Tyrone had a sinking feeling in his stomach.

"Very well. They are yours. Just spare her, and me, please. Have all our wealth, just spare our lives." His words were drowned out by an outbreak of fury from inside his house.

"Fucking scum!" roared a one-armed man, waving his badly bandaged stump.

"Got me daughters in here!" screeched a hard-faced mother. Jaques held a bloodied dagger to the mayor's throat.

"What should we do with him, Tyir?" He asked.

"Kill the craven. Bring out the survivors." Tyir replied, already walking away.

"But you promised!" The mayor whimpered. "At least let me see my wife! Where is she?"

"Look inside you, fool. You met her already, fat man!" Jaques laughed loudly, prodding the plump mayor in the stomach. Tyrone could only look on it horror as the poor man doubled over, violently vomiting the remains of his wife all over himself, chunks of barely digested meat and fat.

Tyir, your dogs are rabid, Tyrone thought queasily. He walked away, the mayor's death rattle in his ears. Tyir's coldness had stunned him. *He's a necromancer, murderer and commander of these demons. What did you expect, Tyrone, a hero?*

Fortunately, torturing the survivors hadn't fallen to Tyrone. He doubted he had the stomach for it, something Tyir seemed to understand. He was set to work on the southern gate as a lookout. After his prayers, Rapier had left Caribou the night Tyir arrived with twenty hand-picked men to scout ahead; Tyir commanded them to learn more about the city of Tarantown, five days ride from the village. They had captured a few horses in Caribou, and the stable was unmolested.

The morning's guard duty was dull, although Tyrone's boredom was mollified when Horse tripped over a tree root while patrolling, falling flat on his face. Posin laughed so hard wine came spurting out of his nose, while Horse raged. Giving Posin a look of imminent retribution, Horse shuffled shame-faced into the village.

Another three days passed with little incident. The townsfolk were all dead; either tortured to death, or used as sacrifices for Tyir's necromancy, and now mindless husks were stumbling in their place. Tyir however seemed to be struggling with them, and his failure darkened his mood. Tyrone often heard him cursing and retreating into the woods. Many of the dead stank of rot, and struggled to move. None survived for more than a few hours. Why had he raised them? Tyrone had to wonder.

"The master's art isn't going well, it seems," Sleeper mused one night, as he and Horse shared a keg of ale. Tyir had returned from the forest, white-lipped and angry, and refused to speak to anyone, not even Meira. He sat on his own away from their circle, staring into the fire silently. His fellow Scars gave their master a wide berth. Tyrone wanted to ask him what was wrong, but couldn't pluck up the courage.

Horse only gave a helpless shrug. "It has its risks and failures. Even Tyir's skill isn't perfect. He's modest about his limits." He tilted his head back and emptied the keg, the ale spilling over his mouth. A green-eyed, ebony beauty who Tyrone didn't know glared at him grumpily and stormed off to find her own drink. Horse shrugged, wiping his lips.

"Kara is going to make you regret that," said a nearby Scar.

"There's plenty of spoils," Horse snarled back. He turned to Tyrone. "What was I saying, before we were rudely interrupted? Oh yes, Tyir. Even so, it's the beauty of necromancy. Nobody loses but the enemy."

Tyrone was still confused. "But for these failures, it must mean something?" Horse shrugged, throwing the wooden keg onto the ground with a lazy yawn.

A horn blew in the distance, a powerful ringing filling the evening air. Posin's voice came from afar.

"Rapier approaches!"

Sure enough, the giant demon came strolling through not long after, blood splattered on his robes, followed by his weary party. None of them rode the horses they took from the village. Tyir rose to his feet at once, no longer sullen.

"What news, First Soldier?"

"We came to blows with an Order patrol two days past, near the northern road into Tarantown. We slaughtered them on the spot."

"Any casualties?"

"Three dead on our end," Rapier replied. "Master, one survivor was very willing to talk. Tarantown is no longer in the custody of the Order; they got expelled months ago. Hinari keeps sending men to the town. The Pharos scum are mobilizing for war, they said, no doubt to try and retake the city. Seems that trouble is brewing."

"Who's in command of Tarantown now?" Tyir sat up; this was new information.

"No idea. From what we found out, the Order doesn't know, nor do the Empire. They seem like a rogue faction, possibly mercenaries." Rapier replied. "I know your reasons for Tarantown, and I agree with them. I recommend we move on."

Tyir smiled, the first time in days. It was an evil thing. "Very well. It seems I must go ahead with the plan. Strong as Meira is, she cannot sustain the sacrifices forever. That and we can see who these new rulers of Tarantown are." His leer faded. "We shall have to tread cautiously. If only we had Iron Dog with us. We need some way of sending him word. He should have joined us by now."

"When he stops wiping his arse, he'll come," Rapier's reply was thick with anger. "With your command, I could return to the east and bring the storm onto the Order filth."

Tyir chewed it over before nodding. "Rapier, prepare the men."

"I can bear the burden perfectly well!" Meira hissed, taking Tyrone aback. He hadn't even heard her approach. "I bore the weight of those we raised when we tried to save Lazarus, and I could have done more if you didn't stop me."

"I didn't want to burden you further," Tyir replied, his voice as calm as Meira's was angry. "I couldn't wait longer; as soon as I heard of Lazarus, I had to try and save him, and anyone else from Valare. I swore an oath to *them* as well. But I had failed in that too."

There was a cold silence, as Meira's eyes softened. "You saved him once. His death wasn't your fault."

"I only saved him once," came the sharp reply. "And that's a mystery I still don't understand. Maybe Tarantown will provide answers."

"I hope it does, Master," the undead girl whispered.

"It's decided then. Rapier, we march at first light. Let the men know," Tyir commanded. Rapier bowed low and lumbered into the darkness. The necromancer turned to Tyrone.

"Your true test begins. So far, it's been easy. If all goes well, Tyrone, our vengeance will take its first steps in Tarantown." He turned heel and left.

Tyrone flexed his sword hand, stiffly. He could feel the fight coming closer. Hopefully, when they reached the pilgrim city, Tyir's true plans would be revealed.

Returning to the Roots

The first victims of the Betrayed called it
Tarantown: The city of Graves.

~ Lazarus Oltor

The mournful cries of a murder of crows filled the dawn as they settled to feed. It was a stark contrast with the silence of the high forest. Littering the road were the bodies of the Order trade caravan, picked apart by Tyrone and Sleeper's ambush. Pale and bleeding profusely from one eyebrow, the lone surviving merchant scrambled like a butchered pig away from Sleeper's advances.

"Let me go, please, I swear to Pharos that-"

"You're in no position to swear anything," Sleeper said softly, holding his dagger against the man's throat. The merchant spluttered and writhed on the ground. Sleeper chuckled, enjoying the man's terror.

Tyrone leaned his back against the trunk of a tree. *This man is a soldier?* It had been so easy. Granted, they were only peddlers, but it was two against a dozen, most of them armed. Tyrone had expected a desperate fight. It was more of a rout. The crossroad was littered with the fallen; the only injuries Tyrone and Sleeper had suffered were a slashed open doublet and a broken shoe.

"I serve the great Pharos Order!" The man coughed up bloody spittle, eyes staring wildly. He didn't look like a merchant, in truth. He was big and strong, and had swung his bastard sword with considerable

203

strength. It lay five feet from him. When he made a grab for it, Sleeper kicked it out of his reach. The man gasped. "You're in our territory, and the Sepulcher will know of this!"

"Don't threaten those who hold your life in their hands." Sleeper chuckled, looming over him. "Don't worry though. Just answer my question and I'll let you go. How far away is Tarantown?"

"Tarantown?" A trickle of blood dripped from the man's mouth.

Losing patience, Tyrone strode over and grabbed him by the collar. "He asked you a question. How far?"

"I- why do you want to know?"

Sleeper sighed, brushing gore out of his greasy blonde hair. "I'll make it simple, little man. Either you tell us what you know, or I burn you alive." He reached inside his robes, pulling out a draw-string pouch. The merchant stared at it, wide eyed. He began to sob.

"Fire is such a pure death, don't you agree?" Sleeper went on. "And you shall never join Pharos. The soul cannot live if I char your body into ashes, can it?"

"No! Anything but that; please!" The man screamed, tears running down his cheeks. "It's a day's ride, just follow the road. The forest roads are dangerous at night. We were on our way back; they refused us entry."

"Who's they? Answer me!" Sleeper snarled.

"I don't know, I don't know," The merchant coughed again, his lip trembling. "There. I told you everything I know. Please, let me go. I have a family!"

"So did the Kahal, before your kin butchered them." Sleeper caressed the merchant's cheek, a facade of mercy. "Unfortunate." His dagger ran across his throat. The merchant gurgled.

"And that is how you end someone painlessly."
Blood spurted from the man's throat.

"Painless? Doesn't sound like you." Tyrone replied, but the joke was thin. He looked into the eyes of the dead man, feeling a weak pang of sympathy. *He was an enemy, but I didn't see evil.* "We're lucky we came across a patrol after camping out on the road for two days."

"The Sepulcher will naturally keep their men on the roads, trying to find a weakness in Tarantown. We know the new occupiers closed the gates to them." Sleeper shrugged.

Tyrone tugged at the corpse's handsome weapon belt. Fancy leather. "I may as well take this," he pondered. "He's not going to need it, after all."

Sleeper smirked. "You're learning. The dead have no need for trophies. Take his shoes too. Fancy man, this one. Good quality leather, to boot."

"That was a terrible joke."

The two turned and walked back through the trees to their camp. It made for uncomfortable travel squelching through dead leaves and mud, but safer than the road. "I don't see why they insist on wearing cloaks like that," Tyrone wondered aloud. He shook his head. "It makes little sense to me."

"Well, don't forget this is their territory, so to speak. They want to show their authority," Sleeper replied.

Tyrone's thoughts were swirling through his head. Finally he decided to gamble. "Sleeper, a question."

"What is it?" Sleeper's reply was short as they wound their way through the gaps in the trees. A bird trilled.

"What are we looking for in Tarantown? Surely there will be too many of the enemy to deal with."

"The famous crypts, I thought that was obvious." Sleeper's lip curled into a sneer as their tents came into view. "Thousands of preserved corpses, Tyrone. Think of it. Thousands to be added to our force. Dead flesh is expendable, living is not. A necromancer knows that when he learns his art."

"But I'm not one, am I?" Tyrone replied, keeping in step. Sleeper smiled.

"Tyir is planning a war, and he'll do it on his own terms."

Surely any old corpse would do, Tyrone thought, but then remembered what Tyir had told him. The undead had a short lifespan. *Then why must we travel for miles for days on end, into a guarded town? He decided to leave it be.* But what was so different about the dead in Tarantown?

The fire was burning low as they reached the camp; Tyrone was pleased to see it. Sleeper made his excuses and went off on his own. Tyir called Tyrone over. He and some others surrounded a smoke pit, breaking their fast on what looked like chicken. *Or at least I hope its chicken.* He hadn't forgotten the business at Caribou.

"How far away is Tarantown from here?" Tyir asked him in a tired voice. He wasn't eating.

"It's not far. It shouldn't be more than a day away." Tyrone unbuckled his leather belt and sat down heavily, rubbing his thighs. The smell of charred meat was making his mouth water.

"Any problem with patrols?" Horse laughed. He tore a chicken leg apart with his fingers, sucking at the tender flesh. "You were gone long enough."

"We only saw one merchant convoy. Sleeper and I dealt with them easily enough," Tyrone shrugged and reached for his share of chicken.

"Look at the great warrior!" Horse grinned at Tyrone as he stuffed the remains of the chicken into his mouth, chewing loudly. "Good to see, my friend, good to see. Right!" He announced, struggling onto his feet. "I'm gonna take a big piss."

"Lovely," Tyir mused, as Horse left them, swaggering into the trees. "We'll break camp. I want to get to Tarantown as soon as possible."

Tyrone looked around, the unease in him growing. There were so few of them left. When Rapier left their camp four days earlier with most of their force, there were nearly two hundred. Less than fifty remained.

"Still no word from the others?" He took a big swallow from Horse's wineskin, only to regret it moments later as he coughed the potent mixture back up. *Fucking hell, I should have expected it.* Grinning, Posin thumped him on the back.

"Rapier should have contacted me by now," Tyir paced up and down in front of the fire. "I want to take no chances when we break into the catacombs."

It was a few moments before his words reached Tyrone, tears still streaming from his eyes. "Break into the catacombs?" Sleeper was right.

"Yes. There is pure blood in those tombs, thanks to the devastation wreaked in the Valian wars. They are preserved, and they will become a vital asset to my army. We lack the numbers for total war yet. I gave Rapier the command to split our force and go back east to gather our forces." There was a silence as Tyir glared into the fire. "Besides, Rapier is the true warrior in my army, and he is better suited for what lies ahead. He can also contact Iron Dog in the Kahal. With our enemies growing daily, I have no choice but to act."

"I still don't follow," Tyrone looked to his master. "Why not any old body? They decay, but surely with your power it would be no trouble?" He noticed Tyir's face darken at his words, saw his lips tighten.

"It's necessary. It is all to do with blood. You'll

understand more in time. There's much even I don't know yet." Tyir scowled up at the sky, purple streaks painting the heavens. "But do I have a choice?" With that, he rose to his feet, looking around his company. "Break camp," he ordered. The Scars obeyed at once. "We know that the town ahead is under guard. Whether they are hostile to all outsiders is unknown. But we know they haven't cut off all trade. We'll enter in groups, masquerading as pilgrims. It may be our only chance. Let's move."

As the remnants of the company packed their belongings and weapons, they were split into small groups. Tyrone found himself with four others; Sleeper, Horse, Meira, and a rat-faced man called Palion, of whom Tyrone knew little.

"Travel light, and pick up what you need in town when you arrive," Tyir said to them, before they set off. "Such a place is like to attract trouble. With luck, Rapier will join us with more men soon. Once we enter the catacombs, we'll know what to do next. Good luck, you know the signal."

With that, they split into their respective groups and departed. The camp stank of the dead, but none rose to go with them. Tyir no longer tried to raise them. Something was amiss. Maybe Tarantown held the answers.

"I could get used to this," Horse said cheerfully, as the small group trekked unsteadily through the same narrow path Tyrone and Sleeper had found. There were sharp rays of sunlight penetrating the trees. The air was crisp, refreshing, as he ran his fingers across his coarse beard. His hair was long and unkempt, a tangled mess.

"Rapier should have sent word to us by now." Palion did not smile. He wasn't a handsome man, but he was tall and powerfully built, with thick bushy eyebrows and a crop of filthy black hair. He was cold, but soft-spoken. More than once Horse had challenged the gentle giant a fight, but he got little response. He had a habit of fingering his pair of throwing axes at his belt, caressing it almost lovingly. "We should have gone to the Voyavan steppes to gather men. Or even Uslor. They hate the Order as much as we do."

Meira shook her head. "I doubt that, Palion. Uslor's been a mess for decades, and Voyava is a world away."

Horse lumbered in front of the pack, but even his considerable frame was dwarfed by Palion's. Sleeper groped in his cloak pocket for a small drawstring bag, a scrap of leather smelling of charcoal.

"With luck I can find some more ironstone for my stash," he mused. "We nearly exhausted our supply, and we used too much against the Empire." He shook his head. "It's expensive stuff. What was Tyir thinking?" Tyrone jumped at his sudden ferocity. "He must have known he couldn't save him."

"He wanted to rescue Lazarus," Meira said softly. She was walking quicker than the others, and Tyrone had to increase his stride to keep up. "We lost a great deal in that attempt."

"We did," Sleeper agreed. "But we try, and strive again for greatness. It's what we do." He pulled his coarse woolen hood over his head more tightly. "This cloak stinks. And it itches."

"It had a dead man in it, Sleeper. What you expect?" Horse laughed.

Tyrone ignored their squabbling; he was thinking of Tyir. The man was clearly struggling, that much was plain. He pushed the concern out of his mind. *Surely that's our main goal? To raise the dead?*

The journey to Tarantown took most of the day, and it made for dull progress following the path through endless forest. Several times they passed signs of war; grisly remains of burnt wagon trains, the smell of death pungent, and rotting bodies encrusted with maggots. Finally, they made it to the entrance to the town, the sky tinged with pink. The great wooden double gates were old and worn, guarded by a couple of soldiers mailed in thick plate, carrying eight-foot spears. The banner upon the gate carried the sigil of ancient Valia; two crossed swords intertwined with a phoenix.

Tyrone had heard much about the city in his childhood. It was where man and Valia first made their fated alliance, all those millennia ago. A handful of guards awaited them. Meira took the lead.

"State your business," A guard barked lazily, when their group arrived before them. He knelt heavily on the butt of his spear, his eyelids drooping.

"Wish to see the great catacombs, sir." Meira's reply was humble and soft, her eyes downcast under her hood. The others stayed silent.

The guard squinted uneasily at them with a bleary eye. For a moment, Tyrone thought they wouldn't be granted access, but then he nodded. With a great creak from within, the doors opened.

There were a few townsfolk on the streets, and the market town, while large and filled with aspiring traders, had few customers. The traders began shouting and jostling for their attention as soon as they came into view.

"Customers! Come to me, fresh ham for sale!" and "Bearskins, fresh from the Gaol mountains!"

Once or twice, Tyrone even heard a few shouts about rare boar flesh, something that struck his interest. Horse looked longingly at it, but a glare from Meira and he backed down.

"You'd be wise not to sheathe that blade of yours

while we're here." Palion warned, as they made their way into the marketplace, their hoods up. "I thought there would be more people." He mused. "Tarantown has its history. It is where the Pact of Yarin was forged between Valia and Man, and even greater deeds were done here besides. I expected pilgrims to be in their stinking droves here, but all I smell is the typical shit." He sniffed at the air.

It smelt nothing out of the ordinary to Tyrone. Just the same as a normal town. For such a legendary place, Tarantown seemed very ordinary.

Sleeper walked over to a trader. "Excellent, they have ironstone." It was a makeshift apothecary, the title of the store, Jacksone Wares and Fuels embroidered on the wooden roof. A horrible burning stink emanated from it, so pungent Tyrone felt his eyes sting. Scowling, Horse thumped him on the back as they followed Sleeper to the stall. The owner saw him approach and waved frantically at them.

"Praise the Octane, finally customers!" He was an old man, hunched with long grey hair. He bowed his head at them, smiling broadly. "What can I do for you?"

Sleeper looked around before replying. "I see you have ironstone. A rare item. I'd like to purchase it. I want it all."

There was a surprised look on the trader's face, but he kept smiling. "I do take pride in my wares," he admitted, glancing at the traders alongside him. They were going about their business, but stopped every few moments to throw him jealous looks. "Got lucky with this batch." Tyrone could scarcely blame them; they were the only ones in the marketplace. "A rare ask even in busy times, I must say. An alchemist, I take it? I know its properties."

Sleeper didn't reply.

"Well, woe betide me if I were not to lecture a customer. In these times, I will take what I can." His hands fumbled with a silver lion brooch on his cloak. "But it is a rare substance, and a powerful one," he said, all business like again. "Not cheap."

With an easy smile, Sleeper reached a hand into his pocket and pulled out a heavy bag of gold. "I'm sure this will cover your expenses." He threw it cheerfully to the man, who opened it with a groan of longing.

"This seems to be in order, sir." He handed Sleeper the bag of ironstone, and Tyrone got a whiff. He gagged. It was a sour and unwashed stink of sweat and sulfur, much like what he experienced in his time in the mines of Azult.

"First sale I have made in weeks." The trader was talking again feverishly. "It has been rough business here. First the war in the north, then my town gets taken over by strangers. I would rather have them though then the Order."

"What news from up north?" Sleeper asked. "I have brothers settled in Bawsor, and I haven't been able to contact them in weeks." He shook his head solemnly. The trader's heavy-lidded eyes glistened.

"It's bad up north, I can tell you." He coughed hard into a filthy brown handkerchief. "We don't get much activity here no more, most of the townsfolk keep themselves to themselves. We still have goods trickling in from the north, but price of foodstuffs have tripled since the Dominion landed. Brayson and the new boys do their best though. But as to your question, I'm sorry, but I know little of the war."

He glanced around nervously before beckoning them closer. "I'm glad for these new people though. Right before they kicked the Order out, they came here with a bunch of Empire blokes and took a bunch of our people off, dragged them away with swords at their throats."

His nose crinkled at the smell of ironstone. "Had similar problems with Awakened scum too."

Sleeper rose his eyebrows. "Awakened?"

"Religious scum, that's all I can say." His jaw twitched. "They used to patrol in droves, screaming nonsense. Mayor Brayson issued decrees and drove them off, but people are still scared. Thankfully none since the new boys took over, but still . . ." The seller broke off, looking awkward, his pasty face even paler, his voice lowered into a harsh whisper. "The new men in charge of the city have stepped up patrols. Tarantown is safer now at least, for me and the wife."

"Yet I don't see any patrols," Palion gestured around them.

Tyrone stepped forward. "Who are these new men? Men of the Octane, or of the Order?"

The merchant squinted at him, eyes furrowed. "And who are you, may I ask?" Sleeper gave a jerk of his head.

"He's with us." He reached forward and grasped the merchant's hand in his own, and the old man gasped. "Many thanks for assisting in these difficult times." He glanced at Tyrone and the others. "Let's go."

"Wait," Meira urged, and addressed the merchant. "This new faction, who've taken over the city. Who are they?"

"They've been here for months. We call them heroes, Brayson called them the Ironhearts once." The merchant shrugged. "They come from the far north, apparently. Means naught to me. They step up their patrols in the city at night; I watch them come and go from the taverns where my wife works, armed to the teeth, but they don't bother us common folk, and we don't bother them. I can't complain. I need to pack up, get down the inn with the lads for dice." Mumbling to himself, he bowed them away from the stall.

Horse waited until they were out of the marketplace before speaking. "What the fuck is an Awakened? First I've heard of them." There was silence. "Ironhearts? Don't know who they are either. Whoever these men belong to, they're an enemy to the Order, and maybe the Empire." Horse stopped, looking thoughtful. "Maybe we can recruit them? We should tell Tyir."

"We aren't here to find out. Our task is to enter the catacombs," Palion snapped.

"Tyir will be pleased." Sleeper whistled, pocketing the bag of ironstone. "It's expensive stuff. In truth I was surprised to get any, let alone so much. We should look at the rest of-"

"Not now," Meira said coldly. Sleeper's face darkened. "The rest will get here soon. Master is concerned enough without us failing here too."

"What do you mean, Carrier?" Horse grunted. The group fell to a stop. Meira glanced around to make sure nobody was listening, then whispered.

"Master fears he's been losing his power. You've noticed why we haven't brought bodies back to our camp every night, and our vessels are dwindling?" She turned away. "We find somewhere quiet and lay low. Then we wait for Tyir."

This is not our place. The air was musty, stale and old. Tyrone shook his head trying to adjust to the darkness. "What is this place?" His voice echoed. *The cavern's enormous. I can't even see the ceiling.* He shivered. Indeed, he could barely see anything.

"It is the site of the Dread Night." Tyir reached out a hand and touched the jagged rock face. When he pulled his fingers away, they came back caked in black dust. "The Boarmen's war against the second Dynasty died on this very spot. Thousands of Valians died

214

here. The Battle of the Black Slopes, if it could be called a battle. It was a massacre, as the Valians could do nothing to stop the tide. The Second Dynasty was besieged, close to destruction. But then the Boarmen made a fatal mistake. Drunk on their victory, they attacked a convoy of merchants of the Mer Kings, a mistake that cost them their lives. But that is another story entirely. You saw the statue outside, I trust? It's where the Mer kings signed the alliance with the Dynasty and created the bond of eternal majesty. In less than thirty years, the Gaols were forever broken, their armies crushed by the bond between man and Valia. The name for this place is Chaghalas, or in Valian, Graveyard. That is what I need."

Tyrone wrapped his thin cloak around himself more tightly, feeling the chill, his skin gooseflesh. The night had brought with it a horrible cold and deep underground, it was even worse.

Tyrone turned to Tyir. "Meira mentioned something. You've been unable to reanimate, unlike before I mean."

They took a step, the band in single file now. The ground was uneven, sloping downwards, slowly at first, and then increasing in steepness.

"Yes." There was a bitterness in Tyir's voice, but amusement too. "That girl should keep her mouth closed. The art of necromancy is not guaranteed, after all. Many times even I have failed to bring a soul back from the Well. This is not new. I'm used to failure."

"It's still a cause for concern, Master." came Meira's soothing voice from in front. "I am sorry, Master if I displeased you, but the boy had a right to know if he is to join us completely. As do your men. We serve you for life, and our lives are yours."

"No harm done," Tyir replied. "I mentioned that blood is a vital part when it comes to sorcery, Tyrone.

Valia could wield it, but at a cost. Man tried, but were never as skilled with magelore. Did you know it was part of the Mer Kings price, for the Valian alliance? They realized too late that the blood of man is too weak to bear the cost of sorcery. I read in some old lore that the men to the far west could use magic, far better than we can. All too often, that has been proved. In the Torn World, everything is different. Oh, how I would love to visit it someday."

At last, Tyrone understood. *He plans on using the Valian dead.* His hand reached for the hilt of his sword, taking comfort in it. Well, he thought with an empty smile, *At least now I know.*

Down and down they walked at a painfully slow pace. Horse wanted to hurry, but stopped moaning when Sleeper asked him cheerfully if he could keep Horse's boots once he fell screaming to his death. Finally, after what seemed like hours, Tyrone's feet landed upon solid ground, but almost as soon as they did he stumbled on the unsteady gravel, almost falling.

"Good. We're in the deepest part of the catacombs. Everyone spread out and search the graves. And keep an eye out." Tyir's breath steamed the air. Their combined torches cast a powerful light on the surroundings, and Tyrone could see quite well enough. There were row upon row of crudely packed graves, the filthy sediment baked hard in the chill. *Hundreds of dead. Hundreds of allies for Tyir.* Now that they were much deeper underground, the cold was even more biting, and even with the welcome warmth of the torches Tyrone could not stop shivering. *It's so cold they will likely be well preserved. It seems Tyir could well indeed have the army he seeks.*

Some of the graves had headstones, pale as skulls.

Sleeper knelt to examine the closest. It had been marked with a simple gouge in the sediment, bearing a symbol of three teardrops.

"Here." He pulled off his cloak and handed it to Tyrone. "I should have noticed beforehand. This chill can kill you."

Tyrone took it, looking at him curiously. "What about you?" He wrapped the robes around himself, reeling at the smell. Still, it was better than freezing.

"Cold doesn't affect me. I served with the Jebatu for years. We spent weeks at a time holed up in an ice cell as part of our training." Shrugging, Sleeper turned his torch on the first grave. His eyes narrowed. "The grave is disturbed. See the gouges in the ground?"

It had been torn open, with nothing as much as a scrap remaining. *Someone has beaten us to it. Or something.* He could hear low voices from elsewhere around him, then Sybill.

"This grave is empty, Master."

For the next hour they heard nothing else than the discovery of more empty graves. They continued to search the crypt, looking at every grave they came across until Tyrone was panting with exhaustion, sticky sweat freezing on his cheeks.

"Something is amiss, Paladin," Ombrone said finally. "Every grave we have seen is empty."

"This cannot be," Tyir replied through clenched teeth. "I shall not leave here empty handed. Split up. We search everywhere."

Every grave Tyrone inspected had been disturbed, in some cases torn open. Finally, they gave up.

"What's the meaning of this?" A wolfish red-haired Scar snarled, throwing his weapon to the ground with an echoing clank. "Surely, there is no one else capable of resurrecting the dead apart from our glorious Master?"

"Quiet!" Tyir snarled. He made his way down another road, open graves all around them. His pale face was contorted, eyes narrowed into slits. "This cannot be. Every grave is empty. I was certain, of this."

Somebody spoke, but not a Scar.

"Clearly, Tyir of Irene, you were wrong. About many things, it seems."

Tyrone whipped his head around, the torches illuminating the new arrivals. Men everywhere, all in white cloaks and armor. Dozens of weapons pointed at their hearts.

"Who in god's fuck are you?" Horse reached for his bow.

"Make one move fool, and you will be cut down where you stand," one of them laughed. "We have ten times your numbers here and more coming."

"Only a coward hides behind his men," Tyir said coolly. "I know that voice though, I'm sure of it. Who commands you?"

There was a brief silence, followed by a gentle, sarcastic clapping. The darkness rang with laughter, though marked by mutterings.

"You know me well, though much has changed."

Many torches bloomed into life, illuminating the violated tombs. There stood dozens of men holding powerful Pyran bows, or swords and spears.

Tyrone's heart raced. *We're trapped, and vastly outnumbered.* Tyrone counted over seventy, and more coming.

A young man came through the parting soldiers still clapping. *He looks no older than I am.* There was a certain impish wickedness to his face. Drawing his bow, he notched an arrow, pointing it directly at Sleeper's heart.

"An arrow is a cowardly weapon to kill someone,"

Sleeper warned the boy, who only laughed.

"That's as may be, but it will go through you all the same. There are no prizes for killing your opponents honorably. A foolish argument from somebody who fights with poison."

Sleeper's mouth opened with a snarl as he reached for the ironstone, but Tyir shouted at him to stop.

"I remember your face," Tyir said softly to the enemy leader. "Even now, after these years, although you were little more than a squalling, snot-nosed little boy when I last saw you. Tell me, Krause., Where is your commander? The great Gollet Longspear? I yearn to see his face again."

"He's dead. No thanks to you, Paladin." His lip curled, his cheeks pinched and worn at the corners. "The men want you dead for that, Tyir. We loved Longspear, and your teachings killed him." The last few words came as a pain filled snap. Tyrone heard the tightening of many bowstrings. He shut his eyes as Tyir spoke again.

"I am sorry to hear it. I cared for him too. It was he who came to me, you know, desiring to learn the art for his own ambitions."

"I will hear no more," Krause said softly. "You will pay for my fallen leader." Tyrone opened his eyes again, saw him raise his hand.

"Be careful," Sleeper said gently, stepping in front of their group, though their numbers were dwarfed in comparison to that of Krause's men. More were appearing from inside the tomb, filling in everywhere from behind pillars. "Tyir is my master, and I will protect him to the unwaking void, as will all of us." He reached inside his robes, pulling out his blowdart.

"That's not going to work . . . Sleeper, you're called?" Krause smiled pleasantly. "Your poison has no power here. We've been tracking you for a long

219

time, Tyir. And we know you, and your weapons. I know a Jebatu when I see one. Besides, do you really think you can slay us all?" He turned his eyes upon Meira, who was pushing up her sleeves, bearing her snow-white skin. "Ah yes, your ultimate prize, Tyir. Just in case you get any ideas, it won't work either. We know."

Bastard. He checks our moves before we even make them. Tyrone gulped. Just who were they? He tightened his grip on his weapon. They knew everything.

"Are you here to kill me, Krause?" Tyir called out softly.

"Why are you here, necromancer?" Krause demanded, ignoring Tyir's question. "Tarantown is a strange place for you, Tyir. It is a pilgrim's refuge. Most unlike you." Krause walked confidently towards them, his free hand indicating the open graves. "You wanted to rob these tombs for your art, didn't you?"

"You are as smart as I remember, Krause," Tyir replied. "Did you have something to do with this?"

"Of course not." Krause gave a jerk of his head in irritation. "They were gone before we came to Tarantown. Now, answer my question."

"If you answer mine," Tyir bit back.

"You were leaving a great deal to chance surely?" Sybill asked then, and Tyrone knew she was impressed.

"Longspear left this company in good hands. If you are good at anticipating the human mind, nothing is ever left to chance." Krause glared at them through bleak eyes. "He taught us great things, and especially that to know your enemy you must think like them. It is easy enough. He meant the world to me and to Lance Ironheart too. You remember him, don't you?"

"All too well," Tyir said. "Lance loved Gollet like a

father. What is a Bawsorian diplomat doing here?"

"Most of us would like nothing more than to see your head on a spike."

"Why don't you then?"

What the hell is he doing? Tyrone thought with alarm. But the enemy did not strike. Even at this distance, he could see Krause's stance waver lower.

"Two reasons." He scowled. "One is blood. If I give the order, you'll be killed, certainly, and all those who stand by you. The men I have with me here are only a fraction of the force we have to track you down. But you have already bled us greatly, and I care for the lives of my men. It would prove to be a great cost for which I am sure Lance Ironheart will never forgive me." There was a gentle, almost childlike edge to those words. "We're his men now, to the very end."

Tyir did not take that amiss. "Bled you greatly? But we haven't fought you . . . " He paused, the truth now dawning. His face turned grim, a mask of death. "I see. You already tracked down Rapier. Explains why he never returned."

"I'm sorry, were you expecting him?" Krause spat. "Aye, we tracked down your monster and your men. Don't worry; most of them are in safe hands. You picked your companions well, I have to say. Clever of you, to split your forces."

"I command the Thousand Scars." Tyir said mildly. "It's wise not to underestimate me. How many of mine are dead? You owe me that much."

"Maybe forty, including Rapier." The retort came out as an outburst of fury, and to Tyrone, shame. "Four to one we had in numbers, and yet you still killed more."

"Forgive me, if I couldn't care less for your dead?" Tyir replied, his words sparking roars of outrage from the Ironhearts. Krause shouted for order, and it came, though the men still muttered.

"Seventy dead just for that thing. We were too cautious, I admit it. Your Rapier was the worst. He took out a dozen of my men before falling, and good men all. Veterans of many campaigns."

"Your bastards nearly took my eye out," An archer grunted, pulling back an eye-patch.

Tyir was unmoved. "Rapier was always a formidable fighter. He served me well." He stepped forward. "That's one reason, what is the other? You mentioned Lance Ironheart."

"I did," Krause said simply. "We have orders to bring you to him. He hasn't been idle either, these past months. Something foul is happening, and for some reason he wants to talk to you. If it were me," he added imperiously. "I would kill you and be done with it, but I'll respect Lance's wishes."

"Not an option I relish." Tyir looked around. The Scars nodded. "Let's play a game then. What happens if I refuse?" Tyrone closed his hand around the hilt of his blade, ready for the signal. *I'm prepared to die for these men I still scarcely know.*

"Simple. My men will kill every one of yours, and take you to Lance in chains. I have my own duties to fulfil."

Tyir thought it over. "There is definitely something amiss," he said. "Graves robbed, people being taken off the streets at night, and if Lance suspects something?" He looked around at his men, expression furious, but determined. "Very well, Krause. You give me little choice." The bitterness in his voice was palpable. "I will go with you." He looked at everyone, some with weapons drawn. There was mutiny in most of their faces. "Yield." Horse had his weapon out, raised to full height. "That includes you, Horse!" Tyir hissed. "Lower your weapon. Now."

For a moment, Tyrone thought Horse would disobey. Finally, he let out a snarl, hurling it to the ground with an echoing clang. "Fine!" He bellowed, his roar echoing throughout the tomb. "For you though. Not for them."

"There, we yielded," Tyir glared at the surrounding Ironhearts. "But any harm comes to my men, and there will be blood, I swear it by every god known to this earth."

Krause applauded softly, the sarcasm thickening. "You did well, Tyir. We shall leave immediately." He leered. "Worry not. Your men will be safe. You made the right choice." His cockiness congealed into hatred.

"Come then, Paladin," he said, beckoning him forward with one finger. "Lance is waiting. Take the others to a holding cell."

Counterbalance

Our hope lies in nightmare. It will destroy our
enemies . . . and us as well.

~ Pharos Animar.

Forlorn, Lance Ironheart paced back and forth in his chambers, impatience biting with each step. Days of preparation had led to this moment. Any moment now, surely. It had been hours. Thirty-two years old, his usually clean and tamed jet-black hair hung in greasy layers down his back, uncut in months. Finally, footsteps on hard stone alerted him and he stopped, facing the closed door. It flung open and a panting Isran Reus entered, a robust man clad in gleaming ringmail and a fox-fur cloak. The top-ranked man of the Ironheart army bowed deeply on arrival.

"What news?" Lance demanded.

Isran grimaced, but his heavily lined face was alight with success. "Krause has the Paladin."

Lance wiped his brow, unaware how much he had been sweating until now.

"He did exactly as you predicted, Lance." Isran frowned heavily. "He's been hunting for corpses." His voice was thick with distaste. "We found him in the old crypts, sniffing around. Not that he found any."

Lance nodded. *I know him well after all.* The painful memory of the skirmish a few days ago stuck in his mind? "Who was he with?"

Isran waved a hand. "No need to worry on that

224

score, sir. They all surrendered to Krause without a fight, forty to fifty of them. Cowards." His voice was grim, but smug with triumph.

Lance gave a snort of hollow laughter. "Tyir is many things, but he is not a coward. Neither are the Thousand Scars." He looked back down at the parchment on the table he had been studying, covered with ancient runes in a language he struggled to understand. Tyir's capture couldn't have gone better. All his men were taken into account too. At last, he felt a faint relief. "We were lucky. The Scars are dangerous."

Slanos' battle with the Rapier had cost Lance nearly a hundred dead and wounded, all told. But that was a necessary loss. Rapier was Tyir's most dangerous servant. Lance had heard tales from survivors, and broke into a cold sweat each time. His men were battle hardened, having spent years in service first under Gollet, then him, yet Rapier had torn through them so easily. Lance shivered. He would lose no sleep now that Tyir's strongest weapon was dead.

Isran made a sound between a sneer and a snort. "Slanos underestimated them, that was all. He should've given me the command to go after Rapier. I wouldn't have cost us the lives of so many men, and good friends at that. What you going to do when Tyir arrives?"

Lance glared at him. He knew exactly Isran meant. "I don't know," he sighed. "But I need to hear him out first."

"I know what I want. His head on a fucking spike," Isran spat. "He killed Gollet. Or let him die, which is the same thing."

"No. They are not the same. Not quite. But I understand your concerns, but . . ."

Isran's hawk-like face regarded Lance bleakly, his

225

narrow face full of old grief. "Much as I love you, Lance, you just don't understand. He was our commander. Our friend. Gollet was . . ."

"You go too far. He was my friend too." His eyes met Isran's with such ferocity, even the battle-hardened killer recoiled. Instantly Lance felt remorse and he clutched the silver pendant around his neck, bearing the portrait of his sister. Hatred and anger burned through him, then grief, even stronger. His legs buckled. At a stroke, Isran was by his side, one arm around his shoulders.

"Lance! I'm sorry, I didn't mean to . . ."

"I'm fine," He pushed Isran's hand away, his anger fading. The feeling of helplessness burned through him.

"The Empire will pay for what they did to you, and for your sister," Isran said through clenched teeth. Lance looked outside the window overlooking the marketplace. All was silent: a clear, cold night. The inhabitants of the pilgrim city had so far treated their arrival well.

"Isran." Lance's voice came out as a soft whisper, afraid. "Can we trust our men?"

Isran cleared his throat, aghast. "There are three thousand, Lance. All loyal to your cause." He paused. "I know your worries. Believe me, I do. But do we really need Tyir for this?"

You know full well we do, Isran. That was Isran though, stubborn to the last. "He's our best chance. He knows more about those foul arts more than anybody I know. I'll hear no more about it."

Lance turned from his lieutenant's gaze. He shivered, but not from cold. It all came down to Tyir and his knowledge. Lance remembered the research, the months of careful weeding through stacks of ancient lore taken from the Tarantown library. It made his skin crawl. Tyir had studied necromancy and all the strange history of Valia. It was this knowledge that had killed Longspear. They needed Tyir alive, and furthermore, needed him complicit. "I want no harm to come to his men, Isran. We need him on our side."

The hate in Isran's expression had mollified somewhat, but there was still a marked reluctance in his voice. "As you wish, Lance. Though they're evil fuckers."

"They are that." Lance knew the horror stories that had spread amongst his men about some of Tyir's company. One-Hundred Jaques was a name that kept cropping up, and of course Rapier was legendary. But they were mercenaries, and did what they must in order to survive. *Just like our men*, Lance thought. He had no delusions about those who followed him. "But we need them alive all the same." There was a knock on the door. "Let him in."

"And kill him, I say."

Lance slammed his fist against the wall. Isran, usually calm, stepped back in shock. "You swore to obey, did you not? My command is that Tyir lives. Now, open the door, damn you." His hand throbbed in pain. *Not the smartest thing I've done today.* Lance shook his hand, swearing under his breath.

Still shaken, Isran opened the door revealing Tyir of Irene, flanked by Krause and two of his men.

"I bring you the Paladin," Krause announced, voice tinged with pride.

"Thank you, Krause," Lance said politely. "I wish to speak with Tyir alone."

"That isn't wise," Isran said at once, his eye fixed on the necromancer. "We can't leave you with this scum."

"You're disobeying, Isran," Lance reminded him with a raised eyebrow. "Leave."

"Come on." Krause pulled Isran away. "We'll remain outside though. Not even your order can stop that." They left, muttering amongst themselves.

"Lance Ironheart," Tyir said softly. His eyes darted, taking in the surroundings. "It's good to see you again after all these years. But I don't appreciate the circumstances."

"It was necessary, Tyir," Lance replied. "I only wish there was less bloodshed. I needed to see you."

"Why am I here?" The necromancer folded his hands calmly before him, looking more like a mendicant than the mass murderer Lance knew him to be. "Do you mean to kill me, in penance for Gollet's death?"

There it was again, their blood-stained history rising like a wall between them. "Your perception hasn't changed, Tyir."

"No. But a lot else has." Tyir's voice wavered slightly. "I was sorry to hear about Gollet. He was a fine man, although I cannot exactly call him a good man. I wish I could've saved him. When did he die?"

"Two years ago." Lance turned away. It hurt to speak of him, even now.

"Yet his men now follow you."

Lance looked into his enemy's eyes. They didn't mock.

"I wanted to save him," Tyir repeated softly. "How was he, in his final days?"

Gollet had screamed night after night for months after Lance had brought back him to his family manor, his body and mind fractured, his face ghastly and emaciated. It had been four agonizing years before his shattered body shut down and he finally passed. Once a mighty man, he was tiny in death.

"Lance?" Tyir's voice reached him, bringing him back to reality. The memories hardened his resolve.

"He was broken. He saw terrible things. I had to restrain him myself. You have no idea of the pain he was in." Lance spat. "You should never have taught him. He would still have been alive were it not for you."

Tyir sighed. "He was a sellsword, Lance. Your intellect has left you blind in one eye. He approached me, if you must know." Tyir gestured wordlessly towards the chair in the corner of the room. Lance nodded, and the old man sat.

"That's better," Tyir's satisfied smile slipped away. "He wanted to learn necromancy, to use the dead as I have. But he wanted more, to become a legend. I tried to convince him of the perils of using the dark arts as well as the futility, but he wouldn't listen. I'm no teacher, I warned him that. He refused any help. You know how stubborn he was. I should have done more, I know that now. Maybe, I should have refused him outright."

Lance nodded, but didn't speak.

"Are you going to kill me?" Tyir asked again.

"No," Lance replied, much too quickly. Tyir raised an eyebrow. "But you've seen my men, Paladin. You know how much they want you dead. Regardless, it's done. There's another reason why I have you here. I need your help."

"I've long been accustomed to the fact that many want me dead. But you say you need me." Tyir's voice lowered into a snarl. "Why? You've killed my men, captured me. Now what do you want?"

"We have the same enemy. I've sacrificed much in the last few years. But we share a common goal, survival."

Tyir's eyes narrowed suspiciously. "Now it gets interesting. Okay, I'll listen. Not that I have a choice. Tell me, how long have you been here? Reports have been unreliable from the south in recent months."

"We've only been here a few months. I needed a place to plan. It's been a dark time for me." Lance swallowed. "I left the Imperial Council some eight months ago, shortly after the Empire lost their hold in Klassos."

"Aye, Lazarus mentioned that." Tyir stretched, suppressing a yawn. "Drowdrite was a disaster, the Kingdom of Beiridge collapsed not long after. A catastrophe we all know. The Empire were fools to march to war alongside such an ally. When King Aulozon died at Drowdrite, his kingdom died with him, making the Empire's holdings ripe for the taking. But enough of that. I did wonder about you. Some say you deserted, but I know you better than that. I've always known you to be a man of morals."

"I never deserted," Lance growled, clenching a fist. He had heard the talk before, and its injustice bit deep. "I resigned because it was a failure. You weren't there, you wouldn't understand. The Empire has become corrupt under Aldmer's control."

"The Bale Empire has likely been corrupt for generations. They always are."

Lance ignored that. "I had enough and left. Then things got worse, and I had to flee. I discovered things, you see. When they found out, they tried to destroy me." It took all his willpower not to punch the wall again.

"What exactly did you discover?"

Lance watched him closely, took a deep breath. "What do you know about the Counterbalance?" The effect was immediate. Tyir didn't say anything, but his face spoke volumes. His breath quickened and his eyes grew wide. His brittle grip upon the chair's armrest tightened. Finally he spoke.

"How would you know of it, Lance?" Lance said

nothing. Tyir closed his eyes. "Aye, I know a little. It's an old legend. Most of our history got purged by the Order following the Chaos. If not for our scholars, I hate to think what would have happened to our knowledge of the past."

He gave Lance a hard stare. "I'm surprised that you know about it however. Why would you even ask . . ."

Comprehension slowly dawned on him. The chair crashed on the floor as Tyir surged to his feet.

"No. That's not possible. Aldmer tried to recruit me but . . . how would the Empire even know about this? Don't tell me they're trying to do it? Even they wouldn't be so stupid."

Lance nodded grimly. "You see now? Shortly after my resignation, I learned of some disappearances, dozens of them. Council members too. Aldmer replaced them with his close allies. One of the missing was my friend, Hardenne. It surprised me, because Aldmer and he were close. Why would Aldmer get rid of him?"

Lance shook his head. "I made some enquiries into his disappearance, but found nothing. Except that Aldmer held secret meetings inside the old catacombs in Bawsor for months. I remained in the capital for a couple more weeks after my resignation to investigate further, employing my agents to spy on the new regime. Many members, mostly those in favor of Aldmer, gathered there often. That's when we first heard of the Counterbalance. And necromancy. We heard it many times. And something about a ritual."

Tyir's face if possible, paled further. "How do they even know about of it? This is madness. Who were they with? Somebody has to be behind this."

"Someone by the name of Raphael. Head of . . . ."

"The Pharos Order in Bawsor," Tyir finished for him. "He oversees their operations in the North, answers only to Hinari himself. I see it now." He was breathing hard, bright-eyed. "They would have some knowledge of it, maybe old lore left over from Valia's times. I know some of it survived the purges. But why would the Order do this, when they despise their own history? It makes no sense. They can't be pursuing the Counterbalance surely? This is bad, very bad." He lapsed into silence. Flushed, he righted the chair and sat back down.

"What is this Counterbalance? I've researched as much as I could, but I've had no luck. If the Empire is interested in it, I want to know how serious it is."

Tyir gave him a pitying look. "If what you say is true, then imagine your worst nightmares. Necromancy is a difficult art. Costly. You fools think my power is great but I'm just a novice." His laugh was just how Lance remembered it, bitter and full of cruel memories.

"What's that to do with the Counterbalance?"

"If you'd let me finish?" Tyir continued, impatience biting. "I can't help if you keep interrupting me." Lance bit his tongue.

"When Valia came to Harloph long ago, they brought the knowledge with them. And when they died, it mostly vanished. The Order's purges after the Chaos saw to that. Humanity's grasp of magic has always been poor, even necromancy, arguably the easiest path. Of course, that could just be how life is here. Neither Valia nor the new race of men who invaded Harloph had any trouble with sorcery." His smile was a thin-lipped leer, ghastly. "We're limited to reviving the dead in puppet form, little more than reanimated husks for simple tasks. I turned to necromancy initially to study anatomy, then I saw the damage they could do in war. Men are easy to break. Raised corpses cannot fear. Controlling them is difficult; the cost to revive the dead is great. It needs living flesh to sacrifice, and reanimated bodies do not last long; their link is too weak. Even I lack the skill to create true legions of the undead. I'm a failure."

Lance regarded the older man shrewdly, but wisely held his tongue. *I heard what you did with Lazarus.*

"The Counterbalance is on a whole different level, with the power to resurrect a limitless force of living death. Restored to full power, it's said it can even revive dead animals into warriors for their bidding. I read ancient scripts speaking of terrible beasts slaughtered in battle rising against their killers, exacting their revenge."

Tyir's eyes were bright, glistening. "An army, unstoppable and the match of any living soldiers. After all, the dead vastly outnumber the living. You know of the Octane birth, I trust?"

A sickening nausea took hold of Lance. "How could I not?" It was the legend that had brought him and Gollet together in the first place.

"The Counterbalance began then, inside the Mora plane where dark creatures and devils ruled. Well, it's said they ruled. I guess we don't know for sure what they really were. In the Begotten War, the Octane gods used the Counterbalance to create life from death, an army of the dead to defeat the Messeahs and escape their dark world. And so our world was born. Several times across history, the living tried to harness the power of the forbidden magic, and the last attempt destroyed the great Valian Alliance, plunging us into a dark age which has lasted centuries."

"The Chaos?" Lance croaked. "Pharos' Bane?"

"That's the one. The Order scholars never went into detail regarding what truly happened of course," Tyir wore a bitter smile. "The alliance struggled internally, as two vastly different races would. Man wanted to learn Valia's secrets; the Valians were torn between helping their saviors, and isolation. Those who followed the old ways split to form the Magnus, and civil war broke out between the two sides. The Man-Valian alliance tried to raise an everlasting army of the dead to use against the old Valians, but it backfired, and the Magnus took control. What became the Chaos engulfed Harloph. Pharos sacrificed his life and defeated the rebels, but at the cost of Valia, leaving only his followers and a smattering of human tribes. Desperation leads often to catastrophe." He shrugged. "That's all we know. History is written by the victors, of course. Who's to say it is correct? But that's why we are men of learning, above the rabble of fools. We strive for the truth."

"And that's what the Empire wants," Lance said in horror. "It makes sense. They're fighting a war against a far greater enemy, one they cannot hope to defeat. The Counterbalance is their only hope. What they believe is their only hope." *What lies have they been told? What has Aldmer done?* There was always hope in war.

"If it can be believed, Aldmer is playing with a weapon of exceptional power. I cannot even begin to think of what could happen. The Counterbalance ripped a hole in our world. It would take untold amounts of work and sacrifice to even make the attempt. Resources beyond our comprehension, both in material terms and the amount of living flesh needed to carry out such a ritual. It takes at least the same amount of living flesh sacrificed to breathe an imitation of life back into a vessel. To permanently resurrect a living army, the cost will be cataclysmic. But this is the Empire we're talking about; they're at least the equal of what Valian power had in this land, if I could guess. They have . . ."

"The resources to do this," Lance finished for Tyir. It was still the superpower of Harloph, commanding enormous power. Easily enough to challenge the might of Selpvia, despite what everyone said. Dread filled him. "There must be something we can do. How do we stop this?"

"I don't know," Tyir said slowly. "I don't exactly appreciate the 'we.' But there might be something. It's an ancient book of spells and lore, written during Valia's golden age. The Aegis Mora. It's a legendary artefact, covering all the secrets and histories of the Old world itself, right to the teachings of the Valian masters; including the darker forms of magic used by them, dating back to the Old Ones. Included is the Counterbalance itself, as it is told. Pharos used it to help end the war apparently, translated much of it himself."

"Have you ever seen it?"

Tyir's lip curled. "No. Only scrawls and tiny excerpts, when I was a prisoner of the Keepers of Sirquol. I may have stolen some searches. The Keepers really lacked for security." His smile widened. "I don't know why they were so angry when I escaped. Anyway, it made a few references to the Counterbalance. After the Chaos, copies of the entire manuscript were kept and sealed in certain places, but most were destroyed during the Purges. From what I remember, I'm afraid only one copy exists within our reach; in the bowels of the Sepulcher."

Lance scowled. Their only hope lay in their enemy's hands. "The Order are no friend of ours. They're massing on both sides of Tarantown. They took my expulsion of their forces very poorly and are allied with Aldmer. We'll be at war with them soon enough."

Tyir laughed shortly. "I guessed as much."

"And of course we know your history with the

Order," Lance said dryly.

"Naturally." Tyir snorted. "As much as I am loathe to admit it, we have no chance against the Order currently. Weak though they are in spirit, they will still overpower us, even if we join forces. They command at least five times our numbers, not even counting the Empire should they come our way. There would be many who would take up arms against the Order, but that would take time we do not have. Besides, I've been a prisoner of the Sepulcher once before. The only time I'll ever return will be to torch the putrid filth to the ground, and condemn their children to the death they deserve." The final words came as a venomous snarl.

Lance shifted uncomfortably in his seat. "So we can't get that copy. Then what? We can't stay here and do nothing."

"Simple." There was a hungry look in Tyir's eyes. "Hope is never lost. We go for the real one."

"The original? Where?" Lance demanded.

"The only place it could be."

For a moment, Ironheart considered the Sepulcher. Death would be almost certain. But even death was preferable to some alternatives. He remembered Gollet. *There are things worse than death.*

"The Keidan" he said

"Aye, the Keidan, that lies in Tarantown's shadow. The sacred grounds of Lyth. A fortification which no army has ever breached, and no outsider has gotten out of alive. There's our salvation." Tyir finished. "Doesn't sound hard, does it?"

The door crashed open; Isran entered, closely followed by Krause. Their faces were bloodless.

"So, you heard," Lance said, dumbstruck.

"The Keidan, sir?" Isran muttered. "What is this madness?"

"This is our only chance," Tyir said. "You know as I do the bodies in the crypts are gone, which can only mean one thing. If you want to stop the Empire, the Keidan is our only way to find the truth. Both the Empire and the Order could destroy us in an outright war, so time is not on our side."

"Each of our men is worth ten of . . . " Krause began angrily, but Tyir cut him off.

"Maybe, but how many men do you command? Two, three thousand? The Order has you five to one, and that's not including the armies they have north helping the Empire. It will be suicide without more men. At least with the Keidan, there's a chance. They haven't declared war on us, unless there's something you want to tell me. In which case I'll be on my merry way."

"We aren't Bawsor Dune, Tyir," Lance said sharply. *We aren't stupid enough to march into Keidan lands, get drunk and desecrate their sacred shrines.* He needed sleep, and time to think things over. More importantly, he needed Tarantown. He addressed his two generals. "I want a meeting with Brayson first thing. We need Tarantown's aid. You two will join me, along with the fat one."

A ghost of a smile cracked Krause's lips. "Slanos?"

"That's him." A common joke with the men. Lance turned to Tyir. "Thank you, for helping." He braved a smile, but it felt like lockjaw. "It's not easy, I know, in your position."

"Not at all," Tyir replied, not nearly as civil. "I still don't appreciate threats, Ironheart, but in light of what you've told me, it can be forgiven, at least for now. Where have my men been taken, if I dare ask?" Krause and Isran backed away from his stony contempt. "I swear, if any of them have been hurt, then I'll . . . ."

Isran let out a snarl, but Krause stepped in. "They're in our custody, and are fine. We put them in suitable quarters over in the Vla District. They're comfortable, and it's more than they deserve."

"And they'd better be kept that way, if you want any help from me."

"It'll be so," Lance said quickly, before Krause and Isran could reply. "We share a common goal." His two generals met his assurances with a wall of silence. Convincing them to put aside their hatred of Tyir wouldn't be easy.

"Tyir. I want you present at the meeting also, along with those you deem most able."

Tyir bowed his head. Krause cleared his throat. "Agass," he called out through the open door. A harried looking man entered. "Take Tyir to his quarters."

Agass was an old and brittle man, with one side of his face black and dead from an age-old wound. "Yes sir." He offered Tyir his arm with more grace than Lance expected. "Come." His voice shook with age.

Tyir went quietly, leaving Lance alone with Isran, who let out a long, deep whistle. "That was awkward. I'm sorry if I made that worse. I know we need to be diplomatic."

"It's fine," Lance replied.

"Can we trust him?" The blunt question hung between them. "I didn't mean it like that," he added quickly. "It's just that . . . you know what I mean." Lance glared at his lieutenant. "This isn't easy for any of us," Isran went on. "It's just like the fable of that Witch, when the family made the pact to save their child. I don't like it."

"It's the fable of the Lily Crow, Isran," Lance corrected him with a small smile. "I like it no more than you do. But we have no choice." His vision wavered and he staggered slightly, on hand reaching out to the wall for support.

"Lance!"

"I'm fine, Isran," Lance spat, his free hand clenching into a fist. "As for Tyir, we're in this together. We're both outcasts, both hounded by Aldmer's regime. Where the Counterbalance is concerned, I fear we have no choice but to trust his judgement, for now at least. And if we have to come into contact with the likes of the Keidan, then he will prove useful there too."

"Making common cause with our enemy to fight something greater," Isran's hands curled into fists. "I don't like it."

"If we don't, we all perish."

"We're behind you, sir," Isran said, clapping him on the shoulder. He nodded his head at the door. "I'll send Gabriel to you first thing in the morning."

"Tell Brayson I want the meeting hall tomorrow. He'll want to be there too, it concerns him and the city. If we're going to negotiate with the Keidan, we'll need his cooperation. Furthermore, we need to convince him to use the wealth of Tarantown to aid us. It grieves me to further impede on him, but we need him more than ever. Any problems with the townsfolk?"

Isran shook his head. "None. Thanks to us, the garrison's food supplies are triple what they were while it was under Order occupation, so we have the general support of the populace. I fear Brayson will be harder to convince though. He's still expecting us to pillage the town and rape his people." He gave a helpless shrug.

"The Order treated the city horribly during the occupation, Commander," Lance reminded him, more sharply than intended. "Of course he's wary of outsiders." It had indeed taken many weeks for the populace to start trusting them, even after they liberated the town. *This world is cruelest to the innocent.*

"I know," Isran stated. He turned to leave, but Lance called him back.

"Another thing, Isran. Regarding Tyir's men. I want none of them to come to harm. As much as you hate Tyir for what he did, they had nothing to do with it. We need their help as much as we need the Paladin's. Keep your men in line."

"They aren't normal," Isran muttered. "I've heard some stories regarding a couple of them already, and even if they are half-truths, it makes me want to spill open their fucking guts and make them see their black hearts. We've lost a couple of men to them already."

"They're mercenaries; they fight for gold and plunder. Need I remind you of your time under Gollet's banner?" Lance said. "Tell me that none of you ever did anything wrong during your campaign, and I'll call you a liar."

Isran's face flushed. Lance smiled. "Didn't think so."

That wasn't the only concern. Some had been captured, but the bulk of Tyir's company were still in the east, and news of their master would surely reach them. *We'll deal with that when the time comes.*

"You've made your point. You have my word; no harm will come to them." Isran bowed low, stopped at the doorway. "That girl of Tyir's, Meira. She can tend to Tyir's needs. I've done as you've asked in keeping her in isolation. Is it really true that she . . ."

"Yes, it's true," Lance interrupted. "And she could be our downfall. If we're going to win Tyir's cooperation, we need her safe. You know what she is, and what she carries. I don't know if it's true or not, but I'm taking no chances against them. You've already taken precautions I hear, but we don't know enough about her or Tyir's ways. If Tyir chooses to unleash whatever sorcery her body possesses, it will end us all. Keep her alive and unspoiled at all costs."

"Alive? But isn't she-"

"Yes. She's called Carrier for a reason. You get that Isran?" Lance said heatedly. He was growing tired of his insolence. He took a deep breath and held if for a moment. They had a darker path to follow now. "Keep them all safe and happy for now. Tyir's cooperation is paramount."

"I heard you the first time." Isran replied in a dull tone. "We're walking into darkness, aren't we?"

Lance felt very small. Aldmer had seen to that. "We are. Keep an eye on them, that's all. Goodnight."

"Goodnight sir."

The door closed, leaving Lance alone. Sighing deeply, he walked to the window. He understood exactly how Isran felt, despite his assurances. He had to convince his men, that Tyir alive was more important than revenge.

He sat on the straw filled mattress and looked down at the parchment in his hands. It was the final extract of Gollet's last words. His eyes started to blur, tears threatening. "Damn it," Lance whispered, wiping his eyes. Crying always disturbed and confused him, even as a boy. His sister often wept whenever she was sad or in pain. He had only cried when they all died. But that seemed like a lifetime ago, and they were gone where they couldn't return. This time, when his sister lay broken and destroyed in his arms, Lance could do nothing to save her.

He knew that the Empire was planning something dark, but nothing could have prepared him for this. When he learned that the Paladin was approaching Tarantown, it was an opportunity to get information.

Now, he almost wished that he hadn't. What could they do against such power?

Wiping more tears from his eyes, Lance read the last line as he had done a hundred times before. The words were scrawled roughly, broken, disturbing.

My body is failing, my mind broken. Shadows in the midst, I see my forebears. Don't let the gate fall!

Some instinct told him it was all connected.

"No!" The overweight Brayson slammed the table with his huge fist. "I will not hear of it! Are you all mad? You mean to take this artefact, a prized possession, from the Keidan? You know what they are!"

"Of course we know what they are, Lord Brayson." Gabriel Artini rolled his eyes. When the fat mayor turned away, Lance's scribe made a throttling motion behind his back.

Brayson looked close to tears. "Is this the only way?" He turned desperately to Lance.

"Positive." The only light came from the filtering rays of sun seeping through the windows, casting an eerie shadow upon the room. Lance looked into the mayor's eyes. *He's like a scared child.*

"This is the only way, in order for us to find out the truth. You've heard Tyir's words for yourself. We're dealing with a threat beyond our comprehension, and we must find a way to stop it."

The two sides had come together for the first time. Isran, Krause and the giant Slanos representing the Ironhearts, and Tyir along with two men he'd introduced as Horse and One-Hundred-Jaques. Both were big, powerful men who easily rivalled his strongest, their very presence menacing.

Better human than demon. Rapier's death was vital to keep the power balance in his favor. Lance's scribe and Gabriel were seated to Lance's left, facing the head chair taken by the reluctant Brayson Toney. It took some time for the vastly different sides to sit in the same room as each other, but Lance and Tyir's persuasion finally paid off. Even so, the constant glowering and snarls from them all was beginning to fray Lance's temper.

"This is folly," Brayson bleated, his face sagging. "The Keidan has never been breached. It is madness. The Order could attack any day now!"

He was a large, ungainly man, with a bulging belly and thick, pudgy hands that worried at each other.

"You took this town from them and I'm forever thankful for that, but they hate the Keidan! If they hear that you're even speaking of them, they'll send their full might against these walls, and we won't be able to stop them!"

"You underestimate our command here, Brayson," Isran said curtly. He was seated to Lance's right, deep shadows under his eyes. He and Fortescue had spent hours talking into the night. "The Order is nothing compared to our prowess on the battlefield. We are well prepared for any threat. Should the Order be foolish enough to attack here, we'll beat them back. But, as Lance said, we are dealing with more pressing concerns than the Order's whims. We need your support on this. If our fledgling bonds break now, we're all doomed."

"Big words, coming from a man who threatens us with blades," One-Hundred Jaques snarled back across the table.

The mass rapist. Lance felt queasy looking at his brutish face.

"If I may, Lance," called Tyir quietly across his seat on the table, as Isran opened his mouth to argue. "You will allow me to speak."

Lance nodded his assent, his men giving Tyir glares

of deepest loathing. Brayson's face was white as curdled milk as Tyir rose to his feet.

"Mayor Brayson," Tyir began. "We have good reason to believe the Empire is attempting a dark magic beyond all power, and they must be stopped. The bodies in your crypts are missing, and people have been disappearing in the streets for months, long before Lance's company liberated you, yes?"

"Aye," Brayson whispered. "It is so."

"Whether the Order or the Empire is behind this is anyone's guess. But we need to act. Whatever your fears are of the Keidan, I ask that you trust us, as you have trusted Lance. We need you."

Some of the color returned to Brayson's cheeks. He took a deep breath and finally, nodded. "As you wish." He leant back in his chair, his hands together, fat, bruised sausage fingers interlocked. "Forgive me. I sound so weak and foolish," he muttered. "I should have done more to save my people."

"You're a good man," Gabriel said slowly and deliberately.

"I've been weak, but that is done." Brayson sighed. "So much peril lies ahead. I've trusted you and you helped me. You saved this town from the yoke of the Order. It is only fair that we help. There are just so many dangers from outside Tarantown, and I will not allow my people to suffer. Only a few days ago I got a report from one of your scouts, Elric? They came across a village in the Kahal, the town of Niehrin. Was a beautiful place, I went hawking there once with my father. It's been completely torn apart. Homes flattened to the ground, nothing but ash and rubble, and a few . . . body parts. I have heard other reports in the Kahal too of similar tales."

"He's one of mine," Slanos boomed, beet red in the face. "He never said anything like that to me." There was an awkward silence. *What could have caused such a terror?* The Order were often brutal in their repression of the Kahal, everybody knew that. Lance cleared his throat.

"We need to focus on the task that lies ahead."

"Right you are, Lance," Brayson replied, relieved to change the subject. "This book, you say," Brayson shot across the table to Tyir. "It's inside the Keidan, correct?"

"Correct."

"How do you intend on getting it? They won't just hand it over." Brayson wiped his brow, sweating profusely in his brightly colored robes of silk. "I know them well enough. You're putting a great deal to chance. And if this book is the only source of knowledge, what if it's already been stolen? This must have been in planning for a long time. What if this ritual has already begun? We could be risking open war for nothing."

He has a point. A cold dread stole over Lance. *Could he be right?* Tyir came to his rescue.

"I've already considered that possibility," he said quietly. "I've been thinking about this all night. I believe we would know already if they've achieved the ritual. There are certain ways, certain signs." He coughed, shaking his hands out of his long sleeves. "We still have time. The Keidan is our only way forward."

"But we don't know that for sure!" Brayson countered. They glared at each other. Slanos cleared his throat.

"Regarding the Keidan. As the scum said. I have another idea."

"My name is Tyir, thank you," Tyir say coldly, but Slanos ignored him, snorting. Isran and Krause looked their comrade warily; a big, angry man, with a mood to match his strength. A bubble of snot burst from his hairy nostrils.

"I'm guessing we cannot use force here," Slanos said.

Gabriel coughed and looked up from his furious scrawling, and Brayson gasped. Lance looked to Slanos, wondering if he had lost his mind.

"I know that look, Lance, but hear me out. We have good men here. If it comes to it, we can go and force the issue and take this Aegis Mora thing. Why not make the Keidan to give us what we want?"

"I hope not all of your senior commanders are as foolish as this one, Ironheart," Horse shot at Lance. "Begging your pardon, Mayor Brayson, but we'd be as fucked as the whores in your brothels." He tipped the blushing mayor a massive wink.

"Tyir, keep your men in line!" Gabriel snapped over them. "We need to be diplomatic about this."

"It's alright, Gabriel," Slanos soothed, though his face had purpled dangerously. They were forbidden to carry weapons in the mayor's presence, but Lance knew the commander's lack of patience. "Go on then, Horse. Tell me why I'm wrong, little one."

Horse's grin curdled as he regarded Slanos with disdain. "Little one? You're smaller than me, and far less attractive. But fine, I'll humor you."

He lent forward. "Why are you wrong? Because the Keidan's strength is an unknown entity." Horse paused to take a long slurp from a flagon of ale provided for them. Brayson gave a deep sniff of disapproval, but otherwise said nothing.

"We know a little about the Keidan, thanks to our work with the Reaver. Our other enemies, at least we know their power, even if we're outmatched. The Keidan have existed for thousands of years. It survived this long for a fucking reason. The Order went to war with them shortly after the Chaos, and failed to bring it down. It was built during the time of Old Valia. Outright war with them is suicide."

"Fine! It was just an idea," Slanos barked, his cheeks beet-red. "Do you have a better one?"

"Force is not an option, we need the Keidan on our side," Tyir said, before Horse could retaliate. "The last thing we want is a war with them. We need access to their land in order to find the Aegis Mora. Of course, I don't expect them to hand that over freely . . ."

"If at all," Lance finished for him. *This looks bleaker and bleaker.* "What do we do?"

"Unfortunately, I know little of the Keidan's ways," Tyir said gently. "I'm certain none of us do. Rapier would have, but you killed him. Well done for that."

Horse stood up, giving the Ironhearts a mocking clap. Jaques glowered with a look that could cut glass.

"He slayed dozens of my men!" Slanos said, flaring up at once.

"And whose fault was that?" Krause added, cuttingly. Before the argument could escalate, Brayson banged his knuckles hard on the table, bringing it to an end. To everyone's amazement, the mayor was aflame with passion.

"Fortunately for you all, I know." Everyone turned to look at him. He was smiling now. "I haven't been idle either. As soon as Lance told me about the crypts being pillaged, I made my own investigations."

He yawned widely. "Don't look so shocked, there's some intelligence behind this bulk," he slapped his wide belly. His expression turned serious as he continued.

"Tarantown has held a trading pact with them for decades. The Keidan send merchants here to do business. They require livestock and other things, and in exchange we get gold. We will just have to appeal to their other tastes."

"And what are those, exactly?" Krause asked. Although shooting contemptuous looks at Tyir and his entourage, he hadn't joined Slanos' attack on them.

"Well, how do two differing sides find common cause? A common enemy," Brayson replied, linking his fat fingers together. "It's no lie that the Order and the Keidan have clashed for centuries. During Carrow's war, Hinari sent armies to fight the Keidan and try and achieve what his forebears couldn't, but the Keidan beat them back, even sending a force to join Carrow's rebels. They made peace shortly after, and it humiliated the Order, let me tell you."

"I never knew that," Lance said.

"It's true." Tyir spoke up, favoring Brayson with a rare smile. "Yes, Brayson's right. That is our road. There will be a heavy price to pay, of course."

"You mean blood and flesh?" Brayson replied, and Lance was surprised to see a twisted smile across his fat lips. "We have hundreds of Order prisoners. They should suffice." He shrugged, a vengeful leer twisting his lips.

Sacrifices for their rituals. Lance shuddered. He had no love for the prisoners they had taken during the takeover of the town, but they deserved better, surely? But if the Keidan wanted sacrifices, they would get them.

"There's an agent of the Keidan who operates in these lands." Brayson went on. "He goes by the name of Little Bird. He also recruits for the Keidan and holds considerable influence in their circle. I know him well enough, and have given him no cause to mistrust me. I think he'll be our best chance to make this deal. Although I have grave doubts that they'll ever hand over such delicate information."

"In that case," Jaques grunted, "we'll have to try to

keep that quiet."

"When's the next time he's likely to come through here?" Krause asked.

"Five days. Gives us time to prepare. I'll send word to him, to broker this meeting," Brayson replied. "It's the least I can do."

"Our thanks, Brayson," Lance said. "Once we've made the plans, I'll address our forces." But he was battling with his doubts. So much they didn't know, and so much to lose. Everything hinged on the meeting to come.

My New Brothers

The Thirteen Scrolls must be secured. Where else but the only place in the war that has not been breached?

~ Pharos Animar

Tyrone lay awake on the thin mattress, listening to the snores and occasional whimpers from his fellow Scars. The cell was too cramped for ten, let alone thirty people. It stank of stale sweat, piss and shit from the nearly overflowing slop bucket. He no longer gagged from the smell, but it remained deeply unpleasant.

Tyrone had grown used to not being cooped up in prison conditions. Groping in the dark, his fingers closed around his hidden dagger. Tyrone burned with a silent fury. Any moment now, the Ironheart bastards would barge in with yet more threats and abuse. Perhaps this would be the time he taught them some manners with Jaques' gift.

"I don't trust these Ironhearts," Jaques had said, passing the blade surreptitiously to Tyrone as they lined up for their evening gruel. "Keep this with you at all times!"

Tyrone took it without argument. He was not afraid of the sellswords anymore, but the Ironhearts were an unknown entity. *It's a fine day when I prefer the company of a murderous rapist over them.* That was a bitter pill to swallow. What had happened to his comfortable life? They were in hostile ground, in a town under control of an army that hated Tyir. Their capture made Tyrone angrier than ever. He surrendered so meekly.

That stung them all. Tyir was a legendary fighter, feared across the land. Yet he gave himself up to these men without so much as blooding his blade. That was five days ago. Tyrone sighed, and moved his hand away from the small hilt.

Attacking them would be suicide.

That was the worst thing. They were powerless to stop the abuse. The Ironhearts vastly outnumbered them: hundreds of determined, well-armed men and women followed Lance Ironheart. Footsteps scuffing on stone alerted Tyrone, and he sat up. Then someone hammered on the cell door.

"Get up, all of you," a man grunted. Tyrone knew him by his voice, and his stink. Sure enough, the door opened and Slanos lumbered in. His white-coat guards followed him, as did the miasma of his stench. All were wearing the same self-satisfied smirk of triumph, as though they had beaten them in gladiatorial combat single-handed. Tyrone hated them on sight.

"It's your lucky day, scum. There's work to do, and you'll do your share. Get up, the lot of you. Lance says you're all to be treated well, so you'll get a shower and that's more than you deserve."

Another man arrived, slightly out of breath. He grabbed the enormous man's arm. "Lance wants to see you, Slanos."

The fat man shook him off, making an obscene hand gesture at the still groggy Scars. "All of you get the fuck out of here before we kill you! Don't think we won't, we already had to deal with a couple of you cunts."

Tyrone clenched his fist, closing his eyes. He wanted

251

nothing better than to ram his dagger deep into the obese bastard's eye and watch him twitch. Sleeper leapt from his bunk, naked but no less dangerous.

"It is cowardly to threaten unarmed men." With eyes a mask of death, Sleeper stepped closer to Slanos. "That scared of us, are you? Maybe you'd like to settle this here and now?"

"Don't make this harder than it already is," an Ironheart warned, his voice rumbling through his bronze helm.

"You don't want to mess with me, scum." Slanos' smile was even uglier than his face, covered with scars and welts. He raised his huge arms wide as a challenge, the unwashed stink coming off him in waves.

"Give me one minute and you'd die, you piece of shit," Horse rumbled, rising naked from the floor. Slanos' slack, greasy lips widened, but he didn't speak.

"Come on, all of you, get up. You got chores," the Ironheart guards demanded. Fury now pounding through his skull, Tyrone leapt out from his bunk and glared at them all. The other Scars obeyed, but not quietly; their tirade of curses met with a slur of threats and abuse from Slanos.

"Let's go you fucking traitor's spawn. You think I can't be harsher than this? You should be thanking us with bended knee for sparing your miserable lives! Come on, you shits, hurry!"

"Back off, or I'll slit your throat and rape your corpse." Jaques snarled. Tyrone was ushered down a corridor, Ironhearts pressing them from all sides.

Tyrone trudged down to the shower rooms. He was surprised at the turn of events. A shower would be welcome. But how did they even have showers at all? He asked Sleeper, who told him about the deep thermal wells that had been sunk long ago, supplying the area with ample superheated water. It was a marvel. Shame he could not appreciate it, under the circumstances. He looked at the Ironhearts as they passed, making sure to remember each face as the Scars had taught him. It was little use.

There was anger on some faces, but fear too. Tyrone smiled a little. On the first night, the madman Tongue-Kin snatched a sword and killed two Ironhearts before they could react. It quickly turned into an all-out brawl, stopping only when the Ironheart lieutenant Krause intervened. By that time, Tounge-Kin and four Scars lay dead, along with ten Ironhearts. After that, they were manhandled, beaten and forced into a workhouse. None were fed until late the next day. He kept his mouth firmly turned down. Any sign of amusement would be met with a beating.

He was at the door to the shower room when someone tapped Tyrone gently on the back.

"What?" he said, startled.

Tyrone whirled round, coming face to face with an Ironheart around his age. His face was pale, but bore a friendly smile. He handed a towel to Tyrone.

"Uh . . ." Tyrone couldn't think of a reply to this. He took the towel from the boy. "Thanks," he muttered.

"Go," the young man said, nodding to the showers. Tyrone obeyed. The water was piping hot, helping to cleanse his body and his fury.

Once they were showered and changed, Tyrone was ushered with the rest of the company outside, the promise of a good evening meal if they worked well providing some motivations. Having been confined to the cramped cells for two days, the Scars obeyed. The only incident occurred when Sybill nearly punched an Ironheart officer for making lewd remarks about her. But the look she gave him probably neutered him. Fewer insults were hurled at them that morning, a surprise to them all. Something odd was going on.

Separated from the others, Tyrone was led into the great walled garden of the ancient city by a giant, cheerful lieutenant the other Ironhearts named Illie, where he was handed a trowel and ordered to weed the potato plants and rows of beans. Once again, no insults, which the Scars took with decent enough grace. There were already dozens attending to the large garden, many of them commoners, but he spotted a few white cloaks, and a couple of Scars. He was left at one patch, joined soon after by Horse, looking most peculiar in a woolen jerkin four sizes too small. He looked so ridiculous Tyrone fought down the impulse to laugh.

"Fucking Ironhearts," he grumbled, wielding his trowel like a sword. The earth was damp to the touch. Inhaling deeply, Horse began to turn over the soft earth around some of the plants. The scent filled Tyrone's nostrils. He smiled.

"Just look at me. I'm a commander of the Thousand Scars, yet I'm being told to weed these damn gardens like a fucking commoner, and I can't refuse because they keep threatening to have Tyir killed." Horse worked furiously, taking out his anger in the soil.

"Tyrone, how much would you bet me I couldn't ram this into an Ironheart's skull?" He mused quietly.

"Careful," Tyrone breathed, looking around. He began to turn over the soil, the tool clumsy in his fingers. It slipped out of his grasp and he cursed. Horse chuckled.

"Let me help. And I was joking. Although if that piece of shit Slanos doesn't stop goading us, it'll be the worse for him." Horse broke off as a guard strode towards them. Tyrone kept his head down, worried they were overheard. However, his fears evaporated as the soldier took off his helmet, sat down beside an elderly woman and helped her pick tomatoes, filling his helmet when her basket was full.

"They're a strange bunch, these Ironhearts, aren't they?" Tyrone muttered so only Horse could hear him. His trowel dug deeper into the soil, rooting out the weeds. He reached down with his hands to tug them out; sweating with the exertion. *This is going to be another long day.* Still, it was better this than being stuck in that stinking cell, or worse.

"Depends what you mean by strange. Even amongst the cruelest of orders, you'll find some kindness," Horse replied. "Their hatred of Tyir is well known."

"They won't kill him, will they?"

There was a pause as they both feigned working the soil, for the Ironheart was still in earshot. Finally, he and the old woman moved away, carrying their precious cargo, allowing Horse to talk. "Honestly, I don't know," he admitted. "I only know a little of these Ironhearts, but they don't hate Tyir without reason. Years ago in Valare, their previous commander, Gollet Longspear, came to Tyir asking for training on raising the dead. He died trying to emulate our master."

"Really?" Tyrone said loudly. Horse shoved him and he fell silent, feeling foolish.

Of course it could be taught, otherwise how would it be passed down? He shook his head.

"Then what are they planning? If they want Tyir dead, what they doing to do with us?" A thought of exactly what they wanted crept up on him, leaving him in a cold sweat.

"Your guess is as good as mine, Tyrone." Horse coughed, his face already red and shining with sweat. "Best we keep it at that, lad. We have work."

They were kept working for the rest of the day. By the time they were finished, Tyrone was dripping with sweat, aching all over and covered in dirt, but he felt an odd sense of achievement. As the sun sank, the townsfolk departed, but Tyrone was ushered back into the showers to wash off the sweat and dirt. For that, he was grateful; he smelt awful. He entered the shower room, coming face to face with Sleeper, muttering to himself darkly as he stripped, revealing his back and shoulders. Tyrone was amazed. Every inch of Sleeper's back was covered with ugly scars.

"You know, talking to yourself is a sign of madness," Tyrone said with a grin, shutting the door behind him. Sleeper whipped round so fast he nearly slipped. Tyrone chuckled until he caught the look on Sleeper's face, and wisely held his tongue.

"Don't you fucking test me, Tyrone. Not in the mood," he snarled.

Shrugging, Tyrone stripped and stood beneath his own shower, pulling the chain and reveling in the hot water cascading over him. There was even a lick of soap, which he quickly snatched up. Sleeper showered quickly, finishing and dressing, leaving with a swathe of muttered threats. Tyrone decided to take his time, wanting to avoid Sleeper for as long as possible. His thoughts again turned to Tyir, and what this Lance wanted with him.

As he finished showering, the door opened and several Ironheart soldiers entered, laughing and joking. One of them mimed the breaking of a nose. Slanos was amongst them. Tyrone could recognize the stench anywhere. He tried to ignore their banter.

"Look, one of the traitor's spawn," Slanos drawled, pointing a fat finger at Tyrone. The Ironhearts had cruel, mocking grins on their faces. "What you doing here all by yourself?"

"Washing," Tyrone replied coldly. He reached for his soiled clothes, feeling a chill that owed itself to more than his nakedness. They were all looking at him with predatory expressions.

"Showing me cheek? Oh no you don't." With a snarl, Slanos clicked his fat fingers. Four of his cronies pounced on Tyrone. He struggled, punching and kicking, but it was no use. They were armed, and he was not. He had the little blade concealed in his clothes but if he attempted to use it, they would cut him down in a heartbeat. All his anger simmering under the surface broke through in a torrent.

"Fuck you!" He drove his fist into a face that recoiled with a roar. The savage sensation of triumph flared only for an instant. Two held his arms behind his back in a tight grip. One of them had a knife pressed tightly against his throat, his great hairy arm pressing against his face.

"Fucking piece of shit," one of them whispered harshly in his ear. "You're mad, fighting us."

"Idos, you alright?" Slanos lumbered over, his boar hide boots squeaking on the wet floor. Idos clutched his nose, blood leaking through his fingers.

"Aye, commander. Bastard scum can hit hard for a scrawny kid," he muttered thickly. Slanos gave him the once over, his ugly features brought closer to Tyrone. His piggy, thick lips parted. Two of the Ironhearts had hung back, watching the scenario unfold. Neither had participated in the assault. Tyrone flung them a desperate glance, a plea.

"What could a weak shit like you be doing in the Paladin's company, I wonder?" Slanos demanded, peering into Tyrone's face. His rotten, brown teeth and the stink of his breath brought a wave of nausea to Tyrone's stomach. "Little boy got a hard on for necromancers?"

Tyrone spat in his face. Slanos let it run down his cheek, breathing hard. "Commander, this isn't necessary," someone protested by the door. Tyrone recognized him as the young man who had offered him the towel that morning.

"He assaulted one of our own, Iris," Slanos snapped. "And you'd do good not to backchat me in future, boy."

"Look, I'm just doing what I've been told," Tyrone said, trying his hardest to keep his voice steady and calm. The grip on his arms tightened, and he felt them starting to go numb. "I've done nothing to you."

"Tyir fucking has!" Idos shouted thickly, his voice muffled by his hands clamping his nose. Blood dripped between his fingers "He killed Gollet. And he put Lance through hell!"

"Tyir did that, not me!" Tyrone insisted. None of them paid him any attention.

"We should send Tyir a message, fuck up one of his own," growled the one holding the knife to Tyrone's throat. He felt the blade press harder against him. "I'll cut this bastard's throat."

"Lance also gave orders to leave his men alone, remember Slanos?" Iris implored from the doorway. Slanos paused, fist raised, ready to drive it into Tyrone's stomach.

"He's right. Lance needs Tyir for our plans. That won't happen if we harm his men." said the knife man reluctantly. He made no move to take the blade from Tyrone's throat.

Plan? Tyrone couldn't make head or tail of that remark. He winced as the steel bit lightly into his skin, just grazing his throat. He forced away tears of impotent rage. *I won't give them the satisfaction.*

"Good point," Slanos muttered finally, a moment of defeat. He let out a deep, long sigh, before his smile turned into a leer. "Still doesn't mean we can't teach this one a lesson, though, right lads? And he's even naked. I do love that. I'll go first. Idos, you want a turn after I'm done? I know you like em' broken in."

"Fine by me." Idos beamed, his eyes boring straight into Tyrone's.

Reckless, foolish abandon came to Tyrone then. "What's the matter? Too weak you can't take me on yourself so you need to get your little boys behind you? You're a bunch of fucking cowards."

A horrible pain crunched in his stomach, and Tyrone slumped to his knees. That wasn't wise. Why couldn't he keep his mouth shut? An explosion of pain ripped through his legs, his knees hitting the ground hard. He felt the Ironhearts moving in on him, jostling to get into position. The one called Idos pressed down hard on his shoulders, pinning him to the ground. The men were laughing and hooting, shouting obscene things, the one holding the knife to his throat sniggering the whole time.

"Nothing wrong with a bit of rape, where no-body will see it," Idos chuckled, wiping his bloody nose onto his fingers before smearing it on Tyrone's face. "The boy's gonna pay for hitting me."

"Get his arse ready and wet. I'm going to show him the meaning of the word respect." Slanos whispered, chuckling as he began to undo his breeches. One of the men spat a glob of phlegm and snot onto his hand, before Slanos shouted, "Actually, fuck that. I'll go in dry."

Tyrone's fighting instincts kicked in. As the men pressed further on him, he began to thrash furiously.

"Look at him! The bitch wants it bad!" Slanos sneered. "Don't worry, little doggy. Uncle Slanos is here to give it to you."

For a moment, the pressure on his shoulders eased up and Tyrone wrenched himself to one side. He was free! He rolled, quickly coming to his feet. He leapt at his clothing, found the discarded knife in his soiled robes and snatched it up, slashing wildly just as one of the Ironhearts reached for him. The steel bit through cloth and flesh and the man swore, grasping his cut arm as blood splattered on the wet tiles.

"Fuck this!" Idos said, and the Ironhearts drew swords. Idos and Slanos were up front, pressing Tyrone further until his naked back hit the wall. There was no way out, but he felt no fear, his only thought to take as many of them with him before he died. Before he had the chance, the men rushed him, holding against the wall, pinning his knife hand.

Idos grabbed for Tyron's throat. "Bleed the cunt."

Tyrone flinched as he felt two fingers probed at his arsehole.

"Slanos! What's going on here?"

The pressure on his throat slackened. Tyrone craned to see around the Ironhearts. Iris had returned with a man dressed in distinctive black armor. He was taller than Slanos, with a hawk like visage and a stern, no-nonsense demeanor. Slanos' men backed down at once, one falling to his knees.

"Slanos," the newcomer said coldly. "I asked you a question. What is going on here?" He took a step closer into the room, his eyes sweeping the showers. The Ironhearts backed away from him, lowering their weapons, even Idos. Slanos lurched around to face the man in the doorway.

"This Scar assaulted one of my men, Isran. I was going to teach-"

"It's obvious what you wanted to teach him, Slanos," Isran snapped. "Your breeches are down. YOU LOT!" He roared, so loud that they all jumped as he stabbed a finger at each of the Ironhearts surrounding Tyrone. "You're all on probation. Hard labour for a week, no pay. Lance will hear of this. Now get out. You've been taught better than this! What would Gollet think?"

"We answer to Slanos, not you," Idos muttered under his breath. Isran took two swift steps and seized him by the collar, lifting him bodily into the air. Tyrone let out an exalted breath.

"You say something, Idos? I will not stand for scum in our ranks, do you get me?" Isran said, his face inches from Idos, who whimpered. Tyrone felt a stab of satisfaction as he saw the man's complexion blanch.

"That boy attacked me, nearly broke my nose," Idos jerked his head at Tyrone.

"He also stabbed me, look!" The one who Tyrone had slashed held his arm out as evidence.

"Any more words from any of you and I'll stab you myself," Isran warned. "This is not what we stand for." When they made to argue, Isran took a step towards them. "Do you really want to test me?"

They obeyed without further complaint, filing past Isran. Some looked apologetic, others angry. Idos had tears in his eyes.

"You two, get those injuries checked out. But this isn't the last we hear of this." Isran warned, before turning on Slanos. "I expect better from you, Slanos. I'm going to have to talk to Lance, you realize that, don't you?"

"They're our enemy," Slanos replied, though the arrogance in his voice was gone. He did up his breeches, shooting Tyrone a contemptuous look. "They serve the Paladin, and he killed Gollet."

"I know all too well. And scum though some of them surely are, we can't condone this behaviour. Look at yourselves. Most of those in our custody are deadly fighters, and we've lost enough men! We have too many enemies." Isran thumped him hard in the chest. "Lance is right. Things need to change. Look at this," he waved a hand across the room, in particular to the pools of blood on the ground. "One lad against seven of you, and you still suffered injuries."

Tyrone winced, holding a hand to his stomach. Slanos said nothing.

"These aren't weaklings we can push around. Lance needs Tyir, and thus we need them safe." Isran sighed. "Come on, let's go. I expect better from you in future though, commander."

Finally, Slanos gave him a curt nod. "You not coming Isran?" He grunted, squeezing through the doorway. Tyrone felt his eyes on him, and turned away. The pain in his gut was fading now.

"Soon. Go, I'll catch up." Isran let the door close and turned to Iris and another Ironheart.

"Iris, Saul. Clean him up and take him back to his quarters. You did well today." Their faces flushed with pride as Isran looked down at Tyrone. "I'm sorry about that. Are you hurt?" His voice was stern but not unkind.

Tyrone pulled on his clothes quickly, not looking at them. *I'm going to feel that tomorrow.* They were still there, looking patiently at him. "Some. They just cornered me after I was showering. I swear, I was only acting in . . . ."

Isran held up a hand to silence him.

"You don't need to explain, lad. I'm thankful at least some of my men are decent." He paused, his jaw twitching. "Rest assured I'll take care of this. I'll leave you to it." Nodding to the two boys, Isran left. Iris and Saul hurried forward at once. Tyrone drew his knife closer to him as a warning, but Iris shook his head.

"We're not your enemy, don't worry."

"He's not likely to believe that, Iris," Saul pointed out. They looked at each other and pulled out their swords, dropping them to the ground.

"There," Iris said. "You're armed and we're not."

262

Trust us, please. We're here to help."

Tyrone nodded and lowered his dagger, letting them close. The two Ironhearts were young and strong, easily supporting his weight and he sagged against them, his strength fleeing with his rage.

"There's a clean robe for you, and I got alcohol to treat your wounds. You badly hurt?" Saul asked, shaking his greasy black hair out of his eyes with worry as the one called Iris handed Tyrone a grey woolen cloak from his bag. Tyrone grabbed it and shakily pulled it on.

"I'm alright. I didn't get hurt much. Slanos punched me in the stomach but I'm okay," Tyrone replied shakily. He took a deep breath. That was close. The wool was warm against his skin.

Iris touched his shoulder gently and inched his head back. "There's a cut, but not much blood. It's not deep. Slanos is a prick at times. I'm sorry. That was unacceptable," he said darkly.

"He'll probably sit on the privy tonight for another of his three hour squats, shitting and cursing. I never liked him," Saul grimaced. "Isran is a good man, he'll deal with it."

"Not that I'm not grateful, but why? Aren't I meant to be your enemy?" Tyrone asked, taking a gingerly step.

The boys looked at each other. Saul shrugged. "You seem decent. No matter who you are, it was wrong what my comrades wanted to do," he replied. "Besides, it seems we may not be enemies much longer."

"Well, thanks," Tyrone replied. They lapsed into an awkward, almost shy silence.

Iris watched him closely. "Well, you have our names. What's yours? You look young to be mixed in with that lot," Iris said.

Tyrone let slip a smile at that. "I could say the same for you both."

Saul laughed. "He has us there, my friend."

"We are, but that's not answering the question. What's your name?"

"Tyrone." He paused. "Tyrone Cessil."

"Ah, an Empiran," Iris replied.

"No longer," Tyrone retorted. He stumbled, exhausted. "Forgive me," he said. "But can we do this another time? I need to sleep. I get the feeling it's going to be another long day tomorrow."

Iris and Saul exchanged a glance, before they nodded. "Of course, Tyrone," Iris said, bowing. "We'll take you back to your cell."

The air was thick with wood smoke, the smell of cooking meat, rowdy bellows and drunken shouts. "You, you're Tyrone, right?"

Tyrone looked up from his tankard of spiced wine and stared at the men sitting at the table around him. He blinked.

It was the feast of the Faun and it had been a long time since Tyrone had eaten so well. Great slabs of sizzling, charred meat of all kinds lay on wooden platters. Wheels of cheese, hot bread and cold beer flowing like gold, the bounty of Tarantown for them all. It was time for the great festival, celebrating the Octane's glory. The twentieth of Tyrone's life. He couldn't remember all of them, of course. It might have been his twenty-first, he did not know. Since Valare, he had lost all track of time.

It marked the peace between the Scars and Tarantown. Lance had called the whole population, every man and woman in the town for a meeting. His fellow Scars were allowed to join the feast too, although they were scattered amongst the enormous rows of tables, lost in a sea of strangers. Tyir was also going to be present.

Things had improved considerably for Tyrone since Isran's intervention, though his fellow Scars were none the wiser. Tyrone didn't bother explaining it to them.

"I asked you a question. You're Tyrone, yes?" A strong, fair faced soldier opposite him demanded, leaning across the table. He was softly spoken, with straw-like hair cut short.

"Combrey doesn't like when people ignore him," Iris chuckled next to Tyrone, draining a wineskin. "Another!" He cheered, reaching out to grab a flagon.

His mouth full of meat, Tyrone looked around, searching for his fellow Scars. The great wooden tables each sat a hundred. Around him were mostly Ironhearts, with a couple of younger locals who eyed the Ironhearts with awe, begging them for stories. Most were only too happy to oblige.

From what Tyrone had grasped from snatches of conversation, most of the Ironhearts were mercenaries in Klassos, initially under the now fallen Beiridge Kingdom, before emigrating to Harloph with their beloved Gollet. Like the Scars, they knew each other well.

"He's right. I dislike being ignored." Combrey hiccoughed, wiping his mouth with the back of a hairy hand. He waved and a serving girl sidled up to him.

"Bring me that smoked wood cheese from the far table over there, girl," he ordered. She bowed her head and hurried off. He looked back at Tyrone. "Well boy?" He barked suddenly, making Tyrone jump. "I'm not going to ask again."

He's a prickly one. Tyrone decided it was just easier to give him what he wanted. He really didn't want a conflict. "Aye, I am," he replied uncertainly. Iris and

Saul were seated nearby, and although he found them easier to get along with then the others, the memory of what happened in the showers still lingered. The Ironhearts on his table however seemed decent, and treated him well enough.

"Young, to be serving in a company like the Thousand Scars," Combrey said. In the background, Tyrone heard a snatch of singing and a lute playing. He had no idea what the song was.

"I daresay you're right." Tyrone grabbed a chicken leg from the platter, dripping in black onion gravy and bit into it. The rich flavor danced in his mouth, and he sucked his fingers clean.

"Well, you don't seem like a monster, like some of them," Combrey went on. Tyrone raised an eyebrow. "Don't give me that look. How did you come across the Paladin?" The question came out in a slight rush, his tone sharpening as he said Tyir's name, but not hostile. "Just a question," the man shrugged.

Tyrone chewed his mouthful slowly, pondering a reply. Saul and Iris were listening. Is he judging me? Tyrone thought, regarding the Ironheart veteran.

"Tell me how you came to meet your leader, and I'll tell you how I met Tyir," Tyrone said, smiling warily. His eyes were itching with fatigue.

Iris chuckled appreciatively. "He has you there, Combrey."

Good-natured laughter rang out somewhere. Combrey scowled at Tyrone, but his eyebrows twitched. "Very well, very well. It's a boring story, in truth."

"Good thing we have time then," Tyrone replied, bringing more laughter from those in the vicinity. Look at me. I'm funny to them.

A twitch appeared at the corners of Combrey's mouth. "I first came into Gollet's service when I was campaigning in Klassos, against the Jiakini tribes. Vicious vassals of the Dominion they are, but they like fighting as much as they like drinking, and both are natural to me. Well, Longspear recruited me into his army, and it just went from there. When he passed away," Combrey swallowed, swaggering in his seat. "Lance required our help, so I gave my allegiance to him. Longspear valued his friend greater than anything, and Lance saved him, so it's the least I could do."

Tyrone turned to Iris and Saul on either side. "What about you two?"

"Late recruits. We're both from the Empire. Bawsor, strictly speaking." Saul muttered, clutching a mug of ale. He was taking quick, shallow breaths in between sips. "I served as Lance's squire. I saw it all. What happened." His voice shook and his shoulders slumped.

"Tyrone was about to reply, but it was too late. Without a word, Saul pushed up from the bench seat and stalked away, losing himself in the dancing crowds. "What . . ." he began, but Iris put a hand on his shoulder.

"I'm sorry about that," His smile had died, his eyes forlorn. "Saul lost a lot that day. He doesn't like talking about it. You didn't know."

Tyrone looked between them. Most of the Ironhearts around him had stopped laughing and joking amongst themselves and were now brooding quietly. Whatever it was, it had hit them all hard.

"I'm not the enemy," Tyrone continued.

Combrey held up a hand. "I know you aren't," He growled, exhaling a deep, sad breath. "And, I guess your fellow Scars aren't either. There's just a lot of bad blood between us and the necromancer. Seeing him again brought it all back." The joyful mood on their

267

part of the table had died.

"Yes, I know. He was responsible for Longspear's death," Tyrone said. *I need to be careful here.* Beneath the table, he gripped the dagger under his robe. To his relief, the Ironhearts showed no sign of anger towards him, only a broody silence. Combrey spoke again.

"Tyir killed him." He paused again, and Tyrone could see intense anger burn in his eyes. "That monster destroyed our leader. But we will avenge him. You look young, to be honest, to be part of the Paladin's entourage. You are aware of his past, right?"

Tyrone regarded him coolly, pushing the messy platter of bones away from him. He no longer felt hungry. His insides tingled. He saw it again; dead corpses lumbering towards the attacking Dominion in Valare. He knew all too well what Tyir was.

"If I didn't I'd be a fool. I was in Valare with him for years. Of course I do." He leaned forward, looking Combrey in the eye. "You all hate him. I'm not stupid. But I also know that if you truly wanted to kill him, you'd have done so by now."

The older Ironheart next to Combrey placed a hand upon his shoulder, a bald man with deep lines in his shrunken face. "Many in our company wanted Tyir dead, when the Longspear died." he said softly. "And when Krause finally captured him down in the crypts, we thought we'd finally have that chance. Then Lance spared his life. That was the biggest shock of all. Gollet never held any grudge or dislike towards the Paladin, you know. He was his student, and he only felt respect and trust. Even as he fell." He sighed then, his shoulders sagging.

Combrey looked a little calmer now. "True, Jain." His words were begrudging, but as he looked at Tyrone, he thought he saw a little guilt in the fearsome brown eyes. "Scars will always remain." He turned back to Tyrone. "Now, Tyrone, don't think you're getting away with this so easily." He smiled. "How did you come to be in Tyir's service? We know their reputation, and forgive me for saying this, but you don't look like the killing type."

Some of the Ironhearts around him chuckled.

I can show you, if that's what you truly want. Tyrone gripped his dagger more tightly. Fire burned inside him again. "Spar with me and you might find out," he said quietly.

Combrey barked with laughter. "Brave. I didn't mean to insult you. Besides, I heard from Idos that you shouldn't be underestimated. Bastard," he muttered under his breath. "I don't condone his behaviour. There were a few of us who cheered when we heard. He deserves more than a punch in the face, next time. If you do, we sure as hell won't turn you in." The elderly Jain winked at Tyrone. "But enough of that. What is a boy from the Empire, elder son of one of the great Houses, doing here?"

Tyrone hesitated again. He wasn't going to divulge that story yet. "My true home was Valare." His voice prickled, and he felt the rawness of it well up inside him.

"Your home?" One of the Ironhearts cut in. "Lance had a great love for that city. So did Longspear. But, you have your father's . . ." He broke off at the look on Tyrone's face.

Tyrone raised an eyebrow. "May I finish?" Beside him, Iris was smirking, a couple of the women near Combrey chuckling audibly. Even Combrey looked amused. The serving girl returned, placing a wooden board of crumbly white cheese and grapes on the table. Combrey rewarded her with a gentle kiss on the hand and a sweet word, causing her to blush red and hurry away. Down the far length of the table, a red-faced Ironheart was regaling to young boys about his war victories. When one of the boys asked gleefully if he could hold his sword, the chuckling soldier took him to his smiling parents on another bench for a chat. All of them were beaming.

He knows his courtesies, Tyrone thought. Horse was right. They were indeed not ordinary sellswords.

"Do tell," Combrey offered.

And so he told them, all the way back from when he participated in the defense of Valare. He remembered the smell, the sound of battle. His friends, everybody he had known and loved, dying in the inferno. He talked about joining Tyir's group, though left out the darker details. As he talked, he turned his thoughts to everything that had happened the past few months.

Four months ago, he was in Valare, training and ready. He was so sure of himself. But now the future seemed uncertain, full of danger.

"I see," Combrey nodded sagely, when Tyrone finished his tale. "That explains what we heard from the capital. Lance has his agents everywhere." He looked uneasy. "So . . . Tyir reanimated the dead to avenge Lazarus? That explains . . ." He broke off, deeply disturbed. Jain gave him a withering look.

"Yes." Tyrone struggled to keep his temper. "They killed him before his eyes. He tried to avenge him. I have never seen such pain in anybody's face when Tyir broke that to me. You could tell how much he loved him." He was a good man. Cassel had always admired Lazarus, and died trying to save him. That made Tyrone think. He had joined Tyir for a chance of vengeance. But against whom?

A horn blared.

"Up there," Combrey pointed.

"Finally," muttered a busty, tanned woman with short, violet hair, draining her tankard.

Craning his neck, Tyrone saw a stone podium. Lance Ironheart, Tyir and a huge, balding man stood on the platform, waiting for them. The noise began to die down, although Ironhearts pumped their fists into the air, cheering.

"Lance! The Ironhearts! For Tarantown!"

There were no cries of "bleed the world" from Tyir's men, Tyrone noticed. Probably for the best. Lance Ironheart raised a hand for quiet, and slowly the roar died.

"Our worlds have collided as of late, and not for the better," he called out, his voice strong and steady. "Many of you have suffered at the hands of our enemies. I too have suffered. We all have inner demons. But we need to join forces, and bad blood between our sides is not going to help with that." Tyir stood by his side, silent and impassive. "Tyir of Irene and I have put aside our differences for the greater good. He has confirmed my worst fears. *Our* worst fears."

The Ironhearts erupted into noise. It took a full minute for the bickering and jostling to fade.

"The Order and the Bale Empire are conspiring to unleash a danger beyond anything in this world. They must not succeed. If their plans come to fruition, everyone will perish." Lance went on. The silence of hundreds of people awaited his every word, clinging onto them like a lifeline.

"Separately, or causes are doomed. We will join our strength, a single mailed fist, and fight the common enemy together." Lance raised his clenched fist to more cheers. He turned away as Tyir approached the platform, watched by hundreds of distrusting eyes. The Ironhearts on Tyrone's table were all glaring at him; Combrey's hand clutched his steak knife so tight that his hairy knuckles turned white.

"We are not friends," Tyir said loudly. "I know that. I am no friend to any of you. However, Lance speaks the truth. Outside these walls stir an enemy who plots to end everything we all hold dear. Beneath this town, the bodies of the ancients were stolen. We can only guess their purpose, but whatever they are planning, we will stop them."

"What are they planning? Tell us!" someone demanded drunkenly, five rows down from Tyrone. His fellows roared their approval at the question. Tyir exchanged a look with Lance and the fat man, before continuing.

"I will tell you what we know. The enemy intend to bring a necromancy ritual of terrible power into this world," Tyir called, his voice rolling over them all. "It is known as the Counterbalance, and if they succeed, the Chaos will happen again. We cannot allow that!"

Counterbalance? Tyrone was lost for words, as were the men around him, judging by their faces. Silence reigned and only the occasional cough broke the sudden stillness. The mayor of Tarantown stood.

"In three days, we make our stand. To aid in our survival, we have declared a joint pact with the Keidan," he said in a wavering voice. "This is our way forward, and the friendship between Ironheart, Scar, Tarantown and the Keidan will endure. The Keidan come to our walls, and we must make it happen. I thank you for our words."

"They will be here soon. We must prepare," Lance bowed his head in prayer. "That is all." The two descended the platform.

The uproar was deafening. Tyrone let it wash over him. He knew of the Keidan. A memory flashed before him; the Keidan was shadow, its very existence seldom spoken of. Even the natives spoke of fear and mistrust of the underground citadel, the black towers that were said to have been scorched by sorcery.

Everybody knew of the fanatical cult dwelling within the dread forests, its history drenched in murder and espionage. Even thinking about it sent shivers down the back of his neck.

"Some say they strip the humanity from the acolytes, in order to pursue their faith." Combrey glowered.

"Aye. Monsters. But if Lance says it's necessary, then we will do our duty," Jain mused.

"What is this Counterbalance?" hissed another.

Tyrone sat back in his chair. An insurmountable threat loomed over them, and all that stood against it was a rabble of cut-throat mercenaries led by a necromancer, and an army that would happily kill them. He grabbed the nearest tankard and swallowed a deep draught. *I shall need a lot more than this.*

Poisoned Whispers

Purity is now Corruption.

~ The Red Sand

No wonder the Empire failed to quell Faxia. Even half-starved and desperate, the clansmen were a fearsome force. Nazir Cessil looked on grimly as the enemy shield wall clashed with his own. It was their sixteenth attack in nine days, and it had worn his small expedition force ragged. Every night he was nervous, afraid of another sally from the hill fort they were besieging. An ancient nomadic race, the Faxaens had never tolerated the arrival of the New Men. The Bale Empire was no exception. No matter how many incursions the western lords made into the mountains, they couldn't drive the Faxaens out, nor bring them to heel.

This is folly. The tribes will never fight for the Empire. Our war isn't theirs. The plan was brave, Nazir gave it that. In light of losing more ground against the Dominion in Harloph, Aldmer had ordered the western houses to recruit the fierce tribes across the Gale river, bringing them into the Empire as mercenaries. Nazir had no choice but to obey. He was on thin ice over his desertion at Carin Fort. The date of Aldmer's verdict was later that day. *Go after my family, Aldmer, and I'll hunt you through the endless void of the Mora for eternity.* That was a certainty.

Behind a wall of spears and sturdy shields, the small

force of elite archers under Carr Mance notched their arrows for another volley, shouting encouragement to each other. Nazir commanded a force less than three hundred strong, made up of volunteers from his own bodyguard, House Mance, House Deem and House Fennick. Most of the western forces were back across the river, training levies and preparing to march back east against the Selpvian army. If the Octane listened to their prayers, the clansmen of the west would bolster their numbers considerably. The Faxaens were formidable warriors, after all. Even the women fought, and viciously at that.

Well, we've had some small success. A couple of tribes had been convinced in the last few weeks, though this lot were proving particularly troublesome. When they got close to the great hill fort of Nicracte, the gates opened, unleashing a pack of howling warriors who formed a shield wall in the narrow valley blocking the only route forward. When ordered to stand down, they retaliated with a hail of javelins and stones and charged. Nazir had no choice but to fight.

This defiance had been repeated elsewhere according to his scouts, so they knuckled down and prepared for a siege. It was futile. This was one of the most feared of the hill clans, led by a ferocious chieftain named Vultrog.

Tales of his barbarism had reached even Bawsor, his vile acts told to children if they misbehaved. *They cannot hold out much longer,* he told himself, as the fighting wore on. All he had to do was wait. They had enough food to starve them out if need be, and the Faxaens were a poor people. Their crops had failed this year. Once or twice at camp, lookouts reported accounts of them eating their own dead.

With their latest attack defeated, the tribesmen were spent. After another hour of waiting, horns blared from warriors upon the ramparts, and Nazir ordered his men to disperse the shield wall. They did so, warily. *They don't like being here.* The rugged hills and mountains of Faxia were never friendly to them.

At last, the fort gates opened with a wet creak, and the host trudged out sullenly, hundreds of them. The brutal ones have joined their wild gods, and the flock approaches. With luck, it was the agreement Nazir needed.

Rallying his warhorse, Nazir moved to greet them. His honor guard followed on horseback, less than twenty. Nazir was cautious. The ground was slippery in the muddy quagmire, unsuitable for their horses, but it was important to show strength before the superstitious clansmen, who had rarely seen a horse in their lives.

"Careful now, sir," A Deem noble growled from atop his nervous filly. "These savages will strike without notice. I say we attack, and slay them all. Punish them for going against the Pharos." He spat a glob of phlegm. His squire held aloft the banner of the Pharos Order, its golden phoenix aflame on a bed of red.

Nazir silenced the Deem noble with a look. *He should never had brought that banner.* He had a mind to banish him back to the camp. The Valian conquerors had failed to take Faxia in their heyday, and the Order were reviled by the clans.

"They're broken Hermes, just look at them," Carr Mance adjusted his helm, a black horror shaped into a dragon's mouth. "They have to submit."

Hermes snorted, glowering at the barbarians.

Submission. Nazir had his doubts on that. Faxae did not bend easily. *Nor does it look like they're broken.* The crowd was mostly malnourished women clutching babies and vacant-staring children, but many of them were men, strong and armed, who made a dense front line before their kin. They were holding mostly halberds and wore their famous hard-leather armor, flaked with the volcanic glass that gave the clansmen such a reputation.

The three chieftains stepped in front of their people. The largest of them Nazir recognized at once: Vultrog. Seven foot tall, he held a two-handed battle-axe in one hand as a child would hold a rattle. Even from this distance, Nazir saw his necklace of shriveled, grisly penises. Trophies. It was chilling to think each trinket dangling from the silver chain was a body part belonging to a man from the Empire.

Vultrog began talking in a language Nazir didn't understand, but he didn't need to. His kinsmen let out a yell of approval, the throng of warriors hurling abuse, shouting and brandishing crude blades and halberds.

"Vultrog demands you eastern scum leave our lands." An elderly, balding man with a magnificent black beard translated for their benefit. "We know what you seek, and have spilt the blood of our own. You . . ." he frowned, a smile on his torn lips, "Fucking goat whores have no place with the Faxae."

Nazir was expecting that. He had to go softly. Hermes opened his mouth to speak but a glare by Carr Mance stopped him. Nazir cleared his throat.

"The Empire pledges all men of Harloph to join them in the fight against the greater enemy of Klassos, the power of the Selpvian Dominion. All of Harloph will perish to their swords if we don't band together. Divided we'll fall, but united, we have a chance."

The hostile clansmen watched with hateful eyes. *They love us not.* Hermes snorted with contempt as he looked down upon them from his warhorse, but to Nazir's relief he didn't speak. He wasn't alone in his enmity. Many of the nobles were disgruntled with treating with old enemies.

"We aren't friends. You folk claim ours," a particularly savage looking spearman grunted.

"Empire men are our enemies. They kill our men, rape us," mumbled a mad-eyed woman in silver-spangled rags. Around her neck dangled a necklace made from severed fingers.

"There is no help between us," the third chieftain declared. He was the most elaborately dressed in brightly colored furs and skins, his small head wrapped tightly in a bearskin turban. Even Vultrog stopped spitting, falling docile at his words. "The northern sheep do not concern us. They have not harmed us. Bale has. You have no place here with your arrogant ways. Looking down at us from your demon dogs."

Nazir could see the spiteful rage and discontent in their eyes. There was nothing for it. With a nod of approval from Mance, the nobles dismounted from their destriers. Taking the lead, Nazir stepped forward, feeling a cold sweat upon his neck. It wouldn't do to show fear. *Keep calm.* The throng of warriors were still hostile, but Nazir thought he saw some of their anger lift at their action.

Vultrog pointed the tip of his spear in their direction and spoke again. "Vultrog in his greatness, demands to know why the clans should help you?" Behind him, the clansmen closed ranks around their vulnerable in a hedgehog of spears and halberds, silent.

"We aren't friends, that is true," Carr Mance spoke for the first time. "We haven't been friends, we'll never be friends. Blood has been spilt on both sides and the Empire has committed atrocities, much like your people. This," he raised his voice, for the clansmen began hissing in fury at his words. "This is no longer important. While blood exists between our people, the Dominion will extend its hand across the world. As we speak, the Empire fights and dies to hold them back. The Dominion will enslave us all if we do not stop them."

"Faxaen's don't care for Klassos cunts," someone shouted. There was an outbreak of screeches and war cries from them in their tongue.

Vultrog raised his axe into the air and bellowed. "Vultrog in his wisdom decrees the Faxae don't fear these Dominion. The Volcrenion will take their hearts for his will."

"You will all die!" Hermes blurted. Some of the other nobles shouted their assent.

"Hermes!" Nazir shouted, but he took no notice. The tribesmen bristled as Hermes drew his sword. *This will turn into a bloodbath if we aren't careful.* Vultrog had stopped shouting, instead glaring at Hermes coldly. Then he made another screeching grunt.

"He asks what you mean, easterner. And no lies, or he shall cut out your heart and feed it to our Volcrenion."

"It means as I say, I speak the truth." Hermes held his temper in check. "The Dominion will kill us all. Not just us men of Bale. Your clansmen of Faxae. The Pharos Order. Voyava, Irene, Kahal, the League, the Corpselands. The men of Undine, the men of Uslor. All will fall and break under their iron grip, if together we don't stop them. I'll freely speak truth; I'm not fond of you, any of you. Your kind have butchered dozens of my folk, and carried off more. The lands you raid belonged to my uncle, Ovilion of House Deem. You ruin him with your attacks. He killed himself, when you took all he had."

"You Easterners are no better! We live in poverty

and squalor in the hills, segregated by your Empire," One of the largest Faxaens complained. "We pay your taxes, and your men pillage our lands. I lost half my family to your raiders." More shouts of indignation followed their warrior's proclamation.

He has a point, Nazir had to admit. *Both sides are raiders, when seen from the other.*

"The past I don't care for. The future matters." Mance tried, but his words were drowned out by Vultrog lurching forward, axe in hand. His eyes were red and bloody as he roared again. Behind him, the remaining fighting men joined in unison, raising their weapons.

"Speaking this as you kill our men!" The clansmen were in a frenzy, some of the more daring advancing across the no-man's land, already littered with their own dead. The tribesmen carried vicious-looking spears and cudgels, their edges razor-sharp with volcanic glass.

Nazir looked around, seeing the pot near boiling point. The archers quickly reformed behind the wall of spears and large shields, notching arrows into their longbows. Nazir reached for his warhorn and blew it.

The shrill blast stopped both sides in their tracks. Their horses whinnied in fear at the noise but didn't bolt. Nazir stepped forward. *I will not fail.*

"I'm not asking any of you to forget your dead! We won't forget ours. We'll never be friends, that's true. Nor will I ask you to fight for us. I'm asking you to fight for yourselves!" Nazir paced back and forth. The clansmen had stopped shouting; they were listening.

"Both have bled, but if we are divided, we'll fall against the true enemy. Your clans are fierce and formidable, but it won't matter against the Dominion. Our enmity began centuries ago. It won't end, I'm certain. But against Klassos' evil, we will all fall. I ask you to think of your children, and their future."

Silence finished after his speech. Nazir felt the bite of the wind as it picked up. *These lands are bitter and have no mercy for us easterners.*

The elders, including Vultrog were conversing fast in their native tongue, the brutal and foreign sounds rough in Nazir's ears. At Mance's command, the Empire's archers relaxed, the spearwall dispersing.

That was too close for comfort, Nazir thought.

Bloodshed was only seconds away. Eventually, Vultrog let out a howl of badly-disguised outrage and hurled down his axe glaring in Nazir's direction. His shoulders hunched with defeat. The oldest of the chieftains nodded and slowly, Vultrog stepped forward, grunting in a quieter voice.

"He accepts. Vultrog does not trust you, but has seen the omens by Volcrenion. This clan will fight."

Was that all it took? Nazir looked on, aghast.

"Will we be fed? We have suffered greatly," said a whispery mother, clutching a bundle of rags in her thin arms. A weedy arm no thicker than a straw poked out of them, clutching the dirty cloth.

"We'll provide you with whatever you need in return for your allegiance. It's time we make cause against the greater enemy," Carr Mance said kindly. The promise of food encouraged more to come forward, particularly the women and elderly men, who Nazir saw looked weak and hungry. Many of the fighters joined too.

"Volcrenion demands blood. Maybe Klassos hearts will appease him," grunted one particularly big and hairy warrior, running his thumb across the edge of his giant two-handed battle-axe. He looked down upon the corpses of his fellow dead. "That one fucked my wife," he grunted at one of them with an arrow sticking out of his sheepskin cloak, drenched in blood.

Opening his trousers, he pissed on the dead man.

It took the best part of an hour, but finally their new allies were ready, their possessions and meagre food stocks packed onto carts. In total, seven hundred joined. They were emaciated, weak and many sick, and less than half were armed. No wonder they chose us as the lesser of evils. Even so, Nazir felt some satisfaction.

At least I got the easier task. Deep into the hills and mountains of Faxea lay the largest and most belligerent clans. The elderly Arban Mance was given command. Unable to leave his position in the east, he ordered his men across the Gale into the Faxae territory. That was two weeks ago; none had returned so far. Probably none ever would.

Packing up their camp, the Balians, along with their uneasy wildmen allies, began to move back into Balian territory. Nazir rode along with Carr Mance, who was less keen with his father's rule. For hours, Nazir listened to the young man's anger as a light drizzle turned heavy.

"This is foolish," he raged at Nazir as the Augustin bridge loomed into view: the only way across the River Gale for days. The march was slow, the horsemen in the front followed by rows of spearmen and archers flanking the tribesmen in the center. In the rear were the rest of their cavalry. Scouts ranged ahead, on the lookout for any ambush. Although it was unlikely, Nazir took no chances. The glens and hills surrounding their march like overbearing storm clouds, hanging over their host. *We're like a lone rabbit, on open ground.* They were a perfect target for an ambush.

"What is Aldmer thinking?" Carr Mance went on. "Making peace with the Faxae I can understand, but they'll never fight for us, not in force. We've been fortunate enough with the few we have."

"We've employed the Faxae clans as mercenaries in the past," Nazir replied slowly. "Several hundred fought for us during Mercer's betrayal." Even more had fought for the young Pyran king Tyrus the Great, a century or so before.

"Those were different; savages who only think of plunder and gold," Mance snorted, his youthful face hardening in an instant. Nazir kept silent. "My father just wants to keep his loyalties and his gold. Three thousand men I know and trust are following the Empire's goose chase, when they'll be better suited against the Dominion."

He looked around carefully to ensure they weren't being overheard, then spat. The howling wind sent the phlegm back into his cheek, but Carr didn't care. "Fuck the council, and fuck Aldmer."

"There are unfriendly ears, Mance. Careful," Nazir warned, but nobody paid them attention; they were too busy struggling with the rain. Turning his head, he could see the natives were faring considerably better. Carr Mance's outburst was a surprise. *At least one of them shares my feelings.* But it was too dangerous to speak of dissent.

Randyll had proved the truth of that, dragged into a prison cell after speaking against Aldmer's regime. Nobody knew what happened to him. Countless others had been imprisoned, lesser known men nobody would mourn. Some ugly rumors were filtering through the Bael ranks that their matriarch Valerie was in trouble, for some argument with Bawsor.

"My father's sent too many men." Carr fretted, his hair hanging limp and dripping from his freckled face. "Does he really think we're any safer from the Dominion because we're in the west? The sea is not the land." Carr shook his head, soothing his horse who had balked at his cursing. "Shhh, it's okay Finn. Calm, it's alright. Is there any word from your captain?"

"None. Last I heard from Lib Deem was after the Battle of Nouga, and that was a month ago. I've heard nothing else since regarding my fleet."

Nazir had thrown himself into helping the western lands of the Empire for war. As yet untouched, it was their best chance at rallying fresh troops. But it was the unknown danger across the sea that Nazir feared most.

Sure enough, the Dominion had tried to storm the formidable Gate island protecting the Gale with a naval landing. In his last report, Lib Deem had scored a victory over them, but at the cost of dozens of ships. If the Dominion succeeded in taking the island fortress protecting the mouth of the Gale, the Empire's entire position in the West would be compromised. Even worse, the beautiful city of Arkane was in danger, the second most important city in the Empire. None of the riders Nazir had sent to find word of his admiral had yet returned.

"Your trial is today, is it not?" Carr Mance was saying. Nazir's mood if possible, darkened further.

"Aye."

Red-faced, Mance made his excuses and rode on ahead. *He's scared it'll happen to him.* Nazir wasn't afraid, no matter what the verdict. The Empire still needed him and his men. He'd defend his family to the death if need be. He remembered what Aldmer had done to Lance Ironheart just to force that necromancer's hand. That was why he deserted the east.

Their force slowly made their way down the hill and over the bridge, guarded by Palane bowmen. They were called wasps, thanks to their distinctive tunics of yellow and black. But these wasps packed a much deadlier sting than their tiny namesake. They gave Nazir a bow and let the company pass, throwing churlish glares at the foreigners. Nazir ignored that. He thought back to Carin Fort, and the events there. Aldmer wanted that Tyir man for his necromancy, but why? He was clearly desperate, which was why he had Lazarus killed when Tyir refused to co-operate. Why would the council turn to necromancy? It was no trivial force; scars from the Chaos still remained. The Order had done much to purge magic in Harloph, after the Chaos, so how was it possible? What happened at Carin Fort was real. Clearly, necromancy was very much still being used, in spite of the Order.

Unless it was something else? Tyir claimed his powers were limited. He knew that the dead at the fort were Tyir's making, but they were painfully slow, little use to the war machine. So what did the council want with him?

The thought stayed with Nazir all the way into Adas Keep. Dismounting, he let his horse be led away. Carr Mance took the new allies away to be fed. In the courtyard he saw some of Aldmer's men, and the brutal form of Carris Montague amongst them. His heart hardened at the sight. *So, it's time.* He felt a deep tingle coarse through his lean body.

"Nazir Cessil," Carris boomed, seeing him. He was wearing his blood red justiciar robes. He strode over and took Nazir's hands roughly into his own. He squeezed them, smiling warmly. This welcome surprised Nazir who stared around in mute confusion.

"I bear word from Lord Aldmer himself. Is there somewhere that we can talk in private?"

Nazir regained his composure. "Yes," he replied. "The barracks would suffice." *You won't set foot in my chambers.* "Let's hurry. Can't say this rain agrees with me all that much."

Carris barked orders for his bodyguards to leave him, and the two walked quickly across the muddy yard into the barracks, the downpour now torrential. There were several young conscripts inside wrestling, egging each other on, but they fell silent and bowed when they saw Carris.

"Out, all of you," Carris ordered. Nazir noted the resentment the men showed but they obeyed. When they were alone, Carris let out a deep sigh.

"Forgotten how hard the journey is to these parts. The Palanes really need to get their roads fixed. I lost four horses on the way here."

"They lack the resources to make such repairs." Nazir replied coolly. Aldmer decreed their gold taken away to fund the new army was what he really wanted to say, but that wouldn't do. A long table with benches stood opposite the bunks and they sat down on opposite sides.

Carris forced a smile. "It's good to see you, Nazir. We feared for your life after the necromancer attacked us. Bastards." Just like that, it was gone. "He had no right. Aldmer will have his head, he has sworn it."

You killed his friend in front of him, Nazir thought. *Of course he'd attack.* The anger must have shown on his face.

"You feel pity for him? Is that why you left your post? Aldmer was interested to know why you spoke against our decrees so often."

"No pity. But there are cleaner ways to go about it, that's all. As for me leaving my post, thousands fled the fort that day. Did you have them investigated too?" Nazir shot back.

"Cleaner ways don't win wars, Cessil. You know that better than most." Carris stared at his fingers. When he spoke again, his voice was softer. "The Red Sand marches closer to Bawsor daily, joined by that barbarian, Vultor. I was at Yang Point, Nazir." The authority and confidence in his voice was gone now. "When our legions were routed, Vultor had all prisoners boiled alive. Alive. The suffering of our folk at their hands has been appalling, Nazir. Our men are stretched trying to hold them back, and more lay in Klassos waiting to strike. Either we unite, or we die, Nazir. Aldmer knows this, and recognizes your heroics in the great war. He is a good man, Nazir. We only ask for loyalty."

Nazir stared at him. *Good men don't execute people for standing up to them. And good men don't order the rape and murder of a diplomat's sister just because he resigned from his council.*

"You think harshly of Aldmer, I see that. You may mislike him, but he's our only hope for ending this war." Rising, Carris made for the door. "I'm pleased with this day. I hope that this marks the end of any further concerns about you, Nazir Cessil. You are a fine man, and one worthy of the Empire. By your leave, sir." Carris Montague bowed low.

Something in Nazir broke at his words. "Please, a moment. I have a question?" He had to choose his words carefully, but he could no longer contain his curiosity. The thoughts of the more moderate on the council had stayed with him for months, namely Hardenne and Petere Cordon in particular. They were good men, and Nazir found it unsettling to have just lost word of them, but the war had driven them out of his mind until now.

"Of course, Cessil. What is it?"

"You are chief Justiciar on the High Council. I only wish to express my concern about some whom I haven't seen for a while. Hardenne Nomar and Petere Cordon. They vanished from the Council months ago.

I'm just curious to where they went, that's all. Were they unwell?"

"Hardenne and Petere resigned due to ill health, and wanted to return home to see their families." Carris didn't meet his eyes. "You know Hardenne, he had family in Klassos. When we received word of the fall of Yang Point, he despaired for his family and fell into a depression." He shook his head. "I had my misgivings about Hardenne, but Aldmer holds him in the highest of regard. We granted him compassionate leave on those grounds. He was desperate to hear news of his family. We eventually found out they died when the Dominion took Manesow. Yet another reason for us to destroy them." Carris placed his hand on the door. "I will ask for them, if it will put your concerns to rest, Lord Cessil. Farewell."

Nazir kept his expression neutral until the door closed. *He's lying.* He didn't miss how quickly he replied, nor his reluctance to stay in the conversation. Did something happen to them? Nazir felt a wave of exhaustion overtake him. Maybe, a few hours sleep would calm his demons. He looked at a nearby bunk. The conscripts wouldn't mind would they? Yes, of course they would. With a sigh, he stood and made his way back to his own quarters.

Nazir awoke with a start. The fire had died down to mere embers, but his chamber was still warm. In spite of this, his body shivered. He stumbled out of bed, naked feet hitting the ground, eyes taking in the darkness. A shadow moved. Nazir wheeled round, his heart thumping. There was somebody in the room with him.

"Who are you?"

The figure moved and light burst into life as the stranger advanced, holding a ball of brilliant blue flame in one hand. The sorcery illuminated his features, masked by a pale snow robe. His face was shadowed by a hood.

Nazir was paralyzed, unable to move. *This isn't fear.* The intruder, by some art, had frozen him in place.

"You're in no danger, Nazir Cessil." The stranger's voice was light, friendly. Holding a finger to his face, he uttered a word and the flames vanished, casting them back into darkness. "If I release you, will you stay your hand? Your word on it? I'll allow you to nod. Just once will do."

Nazir nodded. What choice did he have? The restraints holding his body lightened, and Nazir crashed painfully to the floor, taken aback by the sudden return of feeling to his limbs. Nazir looked at his weapon on the ground. The stranger chuckled.

"That won't do. You gave me your word. Don't make me resort to other measures. Killing is not our profession, but I assure you that I am perfectly capable of it."

His arm twitched and Nazir started, but nothing happened. The coldness in the man's voice made Nazir shiver, but he didn't back down. *Who is he?*

Curiosity and common sense prevailed over instinct. Against his will, he turned away from the blade and climbed to his feet. He stared into the man's hood, trying to find his eyes. They were pale, gleaming emeralds.

"There. That wasn't so hard was it?" The man said pleasantly. "I have no intention to harm you. Now we can talk business."

Nazir glared at him. "I'm Nazir, lord of House Cessil and commander of the Western Army of the Empire," He stared down the hooded man. "You'll tell me who you are, and why you are intruding in my quarters. I have guards nearby."

"A feeble threat. There are ways for a man to find paths around guards, and neutralize them if necessary. However in this case, they weren't a danger, so I left them in peace. They're unharmed; you have my word on that."

"Why should I trust a word you say?" Nazir retorted.

"Because you're still alive."

Nazir didn't reply. He had no choice but to back down. His eyes now used to the darkness, he found a symbol etched into the cloth of the man's cloak, a black orb. He knew sigil. *The Whisperers.* Never before had Nazir felt so vulnerable. What were they doing up here?

"Why are you here?" He asked. "The Whisperers are of Lomchar, not from the north." That was only what he heard. Nobody truly knew where they came from, only that they existed.

"The Whisperers are only contracted when we have information to give," The stranger replied. "Why else would I be here? Come, the hour is late, and I have little time for pleasantries. That and I'm sure you need your rest. You're fighting a war, after all." He muttered something under his breath. Nazir willed himself to calm down.

"Do you at least have a name? You know my own."

"Certainly, if that is your wish. My name is Raven."

Raven, Nazir thought. He had to be lying. Even so, it was a name, and that was a start.

"Very well then, Raven. What do you want? We don't employ the Whisperers. I have my own spy network, and I know the price your organization demands."

Who would employ them here? They were a relatively new group, with Nazir only hearing about them a decade ago. Their existence came as a surprise.

Many in the Empire viewed them as untrustworthy. The arrogance of their kind, believing only they had power and knowledge, unlike the lesser-known south. This one though . . . *he wields dark powers.* It had to be some trick.

"I'm not an enemy, only the friend of a friend. You guessed correctly why I'm here. As a Whisperer, it's our duty to share information we're contracted to give." He stared haughtily at Nazir. "Our chapter was paid for this information, from your friend."

Nazir's eyes narrowed. "And who is this friend?"

"He asked not to give his name," Raven replied softly. "And we are honor bound to obey. We also ensure any information we receive through our network is genuine. The Whisperers hold lying to be the greatest sin. We don't assess a fine when people lie to us. We send an army."

He uttered a word, and a gold bound scroll shimmered into existence, hovering before Nazir.

"Here it is. There are the terms to this contract."

Terms? Nazir liked that not one bit. "What do you mean?"

"We take our client's wishes to heart, and his only term is that you keep this secret. Words are more powerful than war."

Nazir took the scroll. It shimmered in his grip like molten silk.

"We'll know if you have broken this contract. We'll always know. Watch the world turn, Nazir Cessil. Farewell."

Nazir bristled. *You dare threaten me?* Before he could say anything the room turned pitch black.

"Wait!"

When the darkness finally lifted, he was alone. The scroll was warm in his hand. Keeping one eye on his door, he unraveled the scroll, curiosity getting the better of him. *Who would employ the Whisperers to get this to me?* A cold chill ran through him. Evidently, magic was returning to the world, despite the Order's fanatical attempts to purge it. Or maybe it was always there, lying dormant ready to rise. *Magic is an archer with no training.* They couldn't risk using it, surely?

The room seemed very small now as Nazir read the missive. He stared at the words, incredulous. *It could not be.*

He read the message again, its words short and blunt, damning.

No. This cannot be true. He closed his eyes, trying to block out the truth. Try as he might, he couldn't unsee the words. Everything they were fighting for was a lie.

The Dominion had nothing to do with Adriena's murder. It was Aldmer.

The Aegis Mora

I will march to Sirquol, to join forces with what remains of King Garren's army. I know what I must do. Why then, am I crying?

~ Pharos Animar

"You look nervous, Lord Ironheart," said Tyir. "Don't be. This is the first step to discovering the truth."

Lance stared at Tyir across the courtyard. The necromancer had not moved for the past hour, his head bowed low. The weather that morning was stifling, the muggy air clinging thick as swamp mud.

"Nervous? We're about to try and broker a contract with a murderous cult, while surrounded by enemies, and all in order to stop a ritual we know little of, nor do we know if we can stop it." His hands clenched into fists. "Of course I'm nervous."

Tyir shrugged and closed his eyes, murmuring the song "The Tears of Aul" in a soft, mournful tune.

Lance let out a sigh and stared down at the flagstones. Tensions were high in the town. Already that morning, four Ironhearts had broken into a fight over the imminent meeting with the Keidan. Two had died, a third on the brink in the hospital wing, the latest of an outbreak of scuffles. *They fear our brokers, but what other option do we have?*

The locals were worse; many refusing to work, the talk of retribution from their Order captors rife in the taverns. Lance would have liked to have kept the Counterbalance information just to the commanders of the hastily drawn alliance, but Brayson would have none of it. He wanted his people to know the truth of what they were facing.

The last thing Lance wanted was uproar in the streets. After talks with the Tarantown government, street patrols were tripled, extra sentries posted at each gate, and militia training increased. The yard square was packed full of soldiers for the meeting, disciplined Ironhearts bristling in their exquisite enamel plate and chain-mail.

They were drawn up in a tightly packed wall of spear-points with a line of archers behind with the deadly stelwood bows from Pyra, trained in the old ways of the phalanx.

Up on the walls and atop the gate overlooking the road stood more archers. He wasn't expecting a battle, but better to be safe than sorry.

We have no backup plan. That was the most frustrating thing of all.

Inspired by Gollet, Lance was a strategist first and foremost. If he made a plan, he made sure to have ideas in reserve, ready for anything, but this had defeated him. Never before had Lance felt so helpless. If it went wrong, if the Keidan decided to attack, they would stand no chance. Not even old Valia could defeat the Keidan during the height of their power. What hope did they have? Sure, his men were disciplined and veteran soldiers, but this was the Keidan they were dealing with.

Get a grip on yourself. He had to put his trust into Brayson, and his influence with this 'Little Bird.' The mayor stood with him, clad in thick bear furs that enlarged his already great bulk. There was no joking and laughing from him today. He was putting on a brave face, but Lance didn't fail to notice the silences, and twitchy movements. The mayor was clearly stressed.

Isran had voiced everyone's concerns. "These Keidan won't be easy to placate," he said bluntly that morning. "I hear that the Keidan are an ancient and demonic sect, their history is soaked in blood."

He was there now, tapping Lance hard on the shoulder, graver than Lance had ever seen him. "Is this the only way?" He hissed. "We can't give them what they want. It's inhuman, even for the Order."

He may be right about that. Lance surveyed the Keidan offerings; fifty prisoners from the Pharos Order, captured when Lance freed Tarantown from their control. Roughly equal between men and women, all were malnourished and sobbing in their prison rags, some sporting badly-healed injuries. They finally had a purpose, though Lance didn't like it.

I would have preferred to execute them myself, rather than subject them to this. Even Isran had balked at the sacrifice. Neither Tyir nor his own entourage cared for their well-being. *No surprises there.* The enmity between the Order and Tyir was absolute. Even so, Brayson had argued that it was the only way to broach a contract with the Keidan.

"The Keidan aren't like normal men," he had warned as they made their plans. "They don't take gold or gifts. They demand blood and flesh for their services." For the first time since Lance knew him, he wore a cruel, vengeful smile on his waxy lips. He wanted vengeance for the suffering of his people. Lance couldn't blame him for that. Tarantown had gone through hell under the Order.

Tyir was the calmest of all. "They are still human, Isran, with a world and purpose just like ours." The necromancer gave him a wary smile, brushing a few loose strands of white hair from his eyes. "Everyone has a weakness."

Lance wondered what was going through his head. In spite of their uneasy alliance, he still felt anger whenever he looked at the necromancer. *This plan is on your head, Tyir. Do not fail me.*

"I just wish we had another way," Krause said. One shaking hand coiled around the hilt of his sword. "If what you told us is true, Tyir, we need to stop Aldmer before he completes what he's planning."

"To be honest, Aldmer doesn't concern me right now." Tyir said. Everyone in the vicinity turned to stare at him.

"Say what you mean, Necromancer," grunted an Ironheart crossbowman.

"It's Tyir to you," Tyir bit back. "Those conspiring with them are the true danger. Whatever the case, Aldmer doesn't have the knowledge to do this alone. Somebody is using him. We need to find out whom and destroy them. Although I think we have a good idea who it is."

Isran grimaced, yawning. "You think it's the Order." Lance said.

"Who else could it be?"

A horn blared from the wall.

"The Keidan approach. We have company!" bellowed the brutal voice of One-Hundred Jaques. The line of Ironhearts locked their large round shields together.

"No!" Brayson hissed at them. "I told you! No weapons. We're dealing with the Keidan, remember?" The wall of spears and halberds dispersed quickly. Lance thought he caught a flash of irritation in Tyir's eyes as he joined his side.

Jaques shouted down to them again. "Tyir, Ironheart. You should come up here and see this. There's an awful lot of them."

Lance shared a look with the necromancer. Doubt

clouded his eyes. Together, they climbed the steps to join the vigil overlooking the gate; a motley crew of his own Ironhearts, levies from Tarantown, and some of Tyir's men.

None of them looked comfortable, although the few Scars had ugly grins on their faces. The Keidan had declared they would arrive from the southern gate, so it was that one which harbored the welcome party. From their vantage point, they had a clear view of the surrounding area: the rolling hills and woodland, the main brick road leading south towards what Lance knew to be the wild barons of Uslor. On the horizon far in the distance, Lance could also make out the ghosts of the mountains, snow-capped and foreboding. The mountains of Sirquol. His gut tingled uneasily. Sirquol, the mountain under city of Valia, the place where Pharos had stopped the Chaos.

"There they are." A Tarantown local pointed. There was a column of men marching to the gate, flanked by the Ironheart escort Lance had sent to escort them. Too many. Two hundred men in black, at their head two men in white cloaks, riding sturdy ponies. This was a message, and not one he liked.

"No banner." Tyir mused. "Rapier always said, but it's been years since I've last seen them in the flesh."

The mayor came up behind, wheezing a little from climbing the stairs. "They never carry them. The Keidan is a way of life, a lifetime of service to the High Lady. It's no faction but a nameless world. Banners are, in Little Bird's words, a 'human concept, pointless to their creed'. They take their Valian origins seriously." Brayson's foul breath brushed Lance's cheek. He wiped his sopping brow with a spare hand. "Damn it," Brayson swore. "He never spoke of this. Little Bird always takes a small escort with him when he travels for protection, but never have I seen so many at once. That's Little Bird, right there," He added, pointing at the head of the delegation, drawing nearer by the second. Lance saw a small man, his face masked by a thick grey hood.

"You know him from here?" Jaques rumbled.

Brayson gave a nervous chuckle. "I've known him for years, Jaques. He's come through this road countless times for his trade. Believe me, I know him when I see him." His moment of bravado collapsed. "I don't recognize the one beside him though." The one riding alongside Little Bird was taller, more confident. Lance felt uneasy just looking at him.

"His robes are white as snow. . ." Brayson sucked in his breath, his face turning pasty with fear. "The mark of the Eldar Circle. The Keidan are making a show of force. Open the gates!" He bellowed to the gatekeepers down below "Come, let's go and greet our friends, shall we?" Without so much as a backwards glance, he made for the steps.

"Our Tarantown friend has a nervous belly," Tyir muttered, before following.

Lance waited a moment before he began taking the stone steps two at a time. The Eldar Circle sounded very elite, another grim sign. The scraping of metal as the portcullis was raised sounded loud in the quiet.

The Ironheart escort came through first, splitting off to either side. Then came the silent ranks, five abreast, of Little Bird and his entourage.

They didn't speak or even seemingly to breathe, Lance noticed. *They all look the same, all in the same uniform. No armor. Can't see any weapons either.*

Little Bird dismounted and stroked his mount's mane with one hand, lowering his hood with the other. Taking its bridle, he beckoned over a stable-boy.

"Take good care of him. Anything happens to him,

you die," Little Bird said, turning away. He was a short, thin man in his mid-thirties, with a pointed rat-like face and cropped neat brown hair. He headed straight for Brayson.

He doesn't look that dangerous, Lance thought. That was foolish. Neither did Tyir.

"Little Bird. I wasn't expecting . . . well this," Brayson said coldly, looking at the poor stable boy as he extended a hand. "I requested you and you alone," he added, staring hard at the little man.

Suspicious, Little Bird took his hand and shook briefly, his small black eyes darting to the boy who led his pony away.

"My loyalties to the Lady exceed my dealings with even you, Mayor Brayson." The Keidan man's voice was high and haughty. "But I thank you for your welcome nonetheless. This request however was most peculiar, so I responded in kind." He chuckled. "Strange times. You have friends. I don't recognize them." he nodded towards Lance and his men. Brayson turned even whiter and nodded curtly. "Where are your fellow leaders of this town?"

"Away. These are allies. I don't recognize your friend," said Brayson pointedly, nodding towards Little Bird's associate who had just dismounted. The Keidan men fell to their knees in a bow, heralding his arrival.

"He insisted on coming," Little Bird replied with rather a cruel smile. He went to his knees as well, head bowed. "May I present Armadis, High Protector of the Keidan, and chief silencer of our great Lady." Armadis lowered his hood, his face covered by a white mask.

Lance stiffened at the sight of him. *They come in force.* It was a mere title, spoken without malice, but the words seemed to chill the air. He didn't fail to see the change in Tyir's face, a tiny, involuntary movement but one which spoke volumes. *This was a mistake,* he thought, not for the first time.

"Do you have our gift?" Armadis asked as greeting, his gaze assessing each of them in turn.

Isran clenched his jaw but held his tongue. Armadis' gaze turned coolly from him onto Lance, who glared back defiantly. The High Keeper's lips were not visible through the mask, but something told Lance that he was smirking. The man's eyes were potent jet, piercing. Brayson cleared his throat.

"We do." He clapped nervously, and gestured for the captives to be brought forward.

Lance almost turned away from the grisly sight. Some of them were not going quietly. Many were sobbing openly to the heavens and their god for mercy, others shouted abuse. Lance's lip curled. Why did he feel sorry for them? *They must have killed and persecuted many during their occupation of the town.*

"Fuck you, unholy scum!" one roared as he was dragged, struggling in his bonds. He opened his mouth to hurl more abuse at Lance's men only to trip and fall in front of the two Keidan leaders.

Little Bird stumbled back with alarm, but Armadis marched forward and bent down, grabbing the man, lifting him bodily off the ground. Lance heard his battle-hardened generals gasp at the sight. The prisoner was huge, and dwarfed Armadis, yet he handled him like a baby.

"Good. The gifts of blood. You've done well, child of Tarantown," Armadis said to an aghast Brayson. The captive's struggles stopped as he glared, panting into the deep black pools that showed through the white mask.

"Your fucking blood-soaked standard will fall to the

Order!" He snarled. "Even as I join Pharos, more will take my place." He spat, his spittle landing on the Keidan leader's mask. Armadis let him go, and removed the mask. He retaliated with an icy frown, and then a surge of something black smoked out of his fingertips. He touched the man, almost gently on the arm. The captive began to shake, sweating.

"What. . .no!" He burst into flame. Trained and battle hardened men alike shuddered at the sight. A few Ironhearts dropped their spears and fled, but most stood firm, too enthralled or disgusted to turn away from the spectacle.

"Hell save us." Brayson swore, blanching and retching as Krause wrenched him away. The stench of charred flesh filled the air. Within moments, only a blackened, scorched skeleton remained. Lance didn't look away, although he wanted to. The memory of his home burning before his eyes, the smell of charred flesh, the suffering. He pushed it out of his mind. He had to be strong.

"You won't join Pharos. This is a gift to you, my Lady." Armadis whispered. He flung the smoking carcass aside.

Lance stepped away from what remained of the corpse, Isran and Brayson on either side supporting him. He felt a sick, heavy hopelessness fill him. What were they dealing with? He burned him alive in an instant. For a moment, he was lost. He didn't know what to do. *We can't reason with power like this!* Tyir stepped forward.

"I'll speak first," he whispered to the stunned Brayson. Tyir stepped into the no-man's land between the two forces, addressing Armadis. "You're here to broker a pact with us. Men and Keidan stand alike to fight the common enemy." Tyir bowed low in a rare act of servitude. "If you will ally with us."

"I recognize your face, Tyir of Irene," Armadis replied. He had a handsome face and chiseled jaw, as though crafted from the Kahal Mountains itself, his long black hair silky. "You fought during the great Kahal war, alongside the Carrow rebels. Some of our own fought on their side too, after the Order continued its hostilities against us and pillaged our sacred shrine."

"Indeed I did," Tyir said mildly. "I practiced my art greatly during the war. I met my salvation towards the end."

An art you say you've lost, Lance found himself thinking irritably. Isran and Krause were glaring at Tyir. Lance pushed those unwelcome thoughts aside. He was their ally now.

Armadis' smile curdled. "You presume our friendship though, Tyir. You took one of our finest men. The First Soldier, one of our greatest sentinels." His voice was still light as ever, but stirred an unspoken threat. Lance's eyes caught Tyir's men on the battlements; some made obscene hand gestures.

"Rapier served me well. His death bought me time to survive, and find a new way." Tyir said, but with more bite. The High Keeper bowed his head as if in acknowledgement of Tyir's praise for his former vassal, and the unpleasant moment seemed to pass.

"Very well. We have no quarrel it seems." Armadis turned to Brayson. "Do you have suitable quarters for us to broker this deal?" His eyes swept the area. Lance knew he was surveying the ring of steel that enveloped them all. Armadis' face hardened. "This is not how you plea for the Keidan to help us, meeting us with a show of force." He said slowly. "Pathetic your mortal guards are, this was a mistake."

Krause's mouth opened with a snarl, and for a horrible moment, Lance thought he saw Isran's hand move to his sword. Little Bird's sharp eyes darkened as he too, reached under his cloak. But the sight of the burnt corpse still lay between them, and Isran backed down.

"So then," Armadis said, as though nothing had happened. "You have a place where we can talk?" Brayson nodded, sweating more profusely than ever. Lance let out a relieved breath he hadn't even realized he was holding in.

"We have a place prepared for your arrival. Come, I'll escort you." Brayson bowed low before him, extending a welcoming yet shaking arm. Armadis' smile was fixed, unpleasant. Ignoring Brayson's offer, the High Keeper turned to his fellow watchers and held up four fingers. Instantly, four of them moved to his side.

"You'll have your own men overseeing the meeting no doubt. That's fine. As long as I have my own," Armadis said. Brayson nodded stiffly, and Lance caught his officers giving each other nervous looks.

"What should I do, greatness?" Little Bird asked him. "I can oversee the sacrifice if need be."

"You'll be with me. Your experience will be of use to us, and the Lady," Armadis said smoothly. "The soldiers will handle the sacrifices. It's what they do."

"Not in the courtyard." Brayson drew himself to his full height, his eyes hardened with determination. Armadis turned to face him with an air of cool indifference. "Your men have your own ideals and I'll respect that, but respect the laws of my city too," he demanded. "You aren't the Order, that much is plain."

Armadis' face flushed as color filled his cheeks. It was only a fleeting moment of emotion. "You're right. We aren't." He raised a hand in the air, and the men behind him each seized a prisoner. "Take them outside the gates. Tarantown's laws hold here. Also, I need some of your stable-boys to attend my horse."

Brayson nodded stiffly giving the order. Two nervous boys hurried over to where the snow pony stood, its doe-like eyes blinking dolefully at her new handlers. She was a beautiful little thing.

"Any harm befouls her, sons of Tarantown, and nothing of you will remain." Armadis left them shaking.

The Keidan soldiers led the offerings outside the gates. More sickened than ever, Lance reluctantly followed Brayson and Tyir through an empty side street to a quiet inn run by a friendly old man called Trog. There were no signs of the locals. Brayson had ordered a day of work-free activities for them. As they walked through the narrow streets however, he caught a glimpse of scared eyes peering from behind curtains as they passed.

Lance and Brayson arrived first. Directly outside creaked a sign in the breeze, its rusty metal hinges bearing two golden horses entwined with each other. Faded almost to nothing, "The Six Fillies" was etched upon the sign.

With a hefty sigh, Brayson opened the door, leading them into the inn. Warm, friendly smells of wood smoke and roasting meat hit Lance the moment he entered; the familiarity of it calmed his nerves.

The room was spacious. A fire had been lit for their arrival, its red and orange fingers licking the air and filling it with warmth. A portly old man came hurrying towards them, flanked by his burly, sullen son, carrying an old, battered crossbow under one arm. The old man nearly tripped upon sight of the Keidan, falling into a deep bow.

"Good to see you, masters. Everything's prepared."

"Well done, Trog," Brayson said with false bravado, taking him by the hand and bringing him to his feet.

"We won't be too long, hopefully."

Trog tried to smile, but his wrinkled cheeks paled as he looked at Armadis. The Keidan lord didn't smile but wore a look of polite curiosity, and Trog blanched. Recovering, he finally noticed his son's antics.

"No, son, stop," He snapped at the lad. "Go, attend to the barrels, there's a good lad." Lance felt a pang of sympathy for them as the boy lowered his weapon, blushing furiously. He left the room through a side door, stumbling.

"Nice establishment, haven't been here before," Little Bird said as he sauntered through, passing a dumbstruck Trog, looking around his surroundings with an air of vague interest. The inn was deserted, several wooden tables and chairs neatly organized for them. On the largest table in the center of the room sat a platter of bread, cheese and thick cuts of beef.

"Let us sit then," Tyir said as he and Krause entered the inn together, shutting the door behind them. Together, they reached the center table and seated themselves: Lance beside Isran and Krause, with Brayson on his left. Tyir took the right, while Little Bird and Armadis sat down opposite them. The four Keidan men who had followed them remained standing behind their master like frozen relics, their faces still covered. Trog was stiff as he walked over.

"Do your . . . friends require refreshment?" He asked, addressing Armadis with a tone of forced politeness.

"No," Armadis replied. "The soldiers cannot take sustenance." Trog if possible, turned even paler. "I'd rather not have him present for our negotiations," Armadis nodded to Trog as he addressed Brayson. "Send him away." He flicked his wrist at the poor innkeeper. Isran shot him a nasty look, his face purple. Trog bristled.

"It's alright," Brayson said kindly. "Go downstairs. Rest assured you'll be well paid for your services today. I'll call you if you're needed."

"No, I'll go wait outside," Trog replied, turning away. "I know the dangers we're in right now. I'll get some of my local lads to stand guard with me. BOY!" He bellowed. There wasn't a reply, only the clunking of metal from below. "Damn the lad. I'll get him and we'll head out the cellar door, get out of your way," he bowed his head swiftly at the mayor and departed as quick as his old legs would allow, leaving them with the shadows. Little Bird cleared his throat.

"Your friend seems nervous. Anyway, let's begin. Mayor Brayson. We've been dealing for many years, even during the Order's occupation. We've done well, you and I, and the Keidan has no cause for discontent with you." He paused, and Lance noticed Brayson's hand clench into a fist on the bench. "I'd even go as far to say we are friends."

A good sign. Brayson's fist relaxed.

"This is a new request, and is quite unprecedented. Tarantown has never asked for such a pact with the Keidan in its history. Master Armadis demands to know the reason."

Brayson opened his mouth to speak, but Tyir put a hand on his shoulder. "Let me talk." he said softly. Brayson nodded tremulously, and leaned heavily in his chair. Tyir turned to the Keidan delegates.

"My Thousand Scars have allied with Lance's Ironhearts, along with the people of Tarantown. As a unified people we have joined forces to fight the common enemy, and we have reason to believe that the Keidan should add its strength to ours, for the enemy is planning to use a weapon that threatens everyone's existence."

"Your enemies are different than ours," Armadis

said at once. He leaned forward, his spindly fingers locked together as though in prayer. "The Great North War between Bawsor and those from the northern realm means nothing to us."

"I'm not interested in helping the Empire, if that's what you're thinking," Tyir said, his voice lowering into a snarl. "That's not why we need you. My concern is the Pharos Order, and the knowledge they could be giving Aldmer's regime. This is important. I know you're fighting them too."

"Minor skirmishes," Armadis waved a casual hand, shrugging. "The Order has been our enemy since the Keidan's creation. We have a great power and knowledge. They have never succeeded in defeating us. The Keidan was born under ancient Valia, before the Chaos. Pharos entrusted his legacy with the Keidan. Pharos' own blood have tried to besiege our great fortress many times, deeming our creation to be against Valian beliefs. They failed, and we grew our forests with their blood. The Keidan do not view them as the enemies you believe."

"It does amuse me though," Little Bird said suddenly, and Armadis fell silent. "Tyir, you've been pressed into helping the likes of these Ironhearts," he gestured crudely in Lance's direction. "How touching, for you to fight alongside those who want you dead. And Ironhearts? How arrogant for a man to name his men after his own namesake." He laughed.

Seething, Lance made to rise, but Krause seized his hand, while Tyir threw a hand to cover Isran, who got to his feet. Lance took a few deep breaths, but still felt the blood rush to his head. How dare they? The Keidan made no sound or movement.

"You know a great deal about us, in such short space of time," Tyir addressed the one called Little Bird, before turning to Brayson. "I hope you aren't behind this, mayor," he added with a drop of menace.

"Not at all!" Brayson spluttered turning red, but Little Bird chuckled.

"Relax, your secrets didn't reach me through Brayson. He's loyal, through and through. I'm a frontline spy for the Keidan. It's my job to know about those who seek our assistance. Don't underestimate my intelligence network, Tyir of Irene."

Tyir said nothing. Armadis made a soft cough, bringing the conversation back to the essentials.

"Even so, we are aware that some events change matters. You propose a military alliance then. Not uncalled for, in such times. The Keidan have made military contracts in the past, so it's not impossible. What is your strength?"

Lance had been prepared for this. "Thirty four hundred of my own," He declared. "With a thousand still in training. They are Klassos born, trained in the old ways of the Guardian of the Porte." That was only half a lie. Gollet's brother had served a brief period in the Selpvian religious elite. "Highest quality of weapons and training, with Pyran longbows."

Armadis said nothing, but Little Bird gave them a small smile. "I hear that the strength of stelwood bows far outclass anything else made in the current world. Even old Valian bows lack the power and range of Pyra. They will have taken losses though, against their enemies, and certain rebellion." Lance saw Little Bird wink at him, and felt his mood curdle.

"I am no military genius, but I currently have eight hundred militia in training, with the ability to double their numbers if need be within a month," Brayson added.

"I only have two hundred of my own mercenaries under my command," Tyir admitted. "But there are many in Kahal, at least a thousand who can join us quickly. I sent out riders." Lance noticed a scowl on the necromancer's face then, his face darkened. The two exchanged a silent look. He had not forgotten.

Armadis set in silence for a moment. "Not much power to call by then," He sat up a little straighter. "Always know the strength of your foe. The Order still commands some sixteen thousand in the Kahal alone, their armies in the east are at least twice that number. And that's not to mention their army in the north. The forces of Bale, your enemy, let's say another one hundred thousand, although they are occupied for the moment, battling the Red Sand's armies. Even so, it may be prudent to . . ."

"Hold on, your greatness." Little Bird squinted at them all. His eyes widened with sudden understanding. "Sorry, Armadis. There's something more to it. Many despise the Order, and would gladly join an effort to destroy them. But there's another reason you called for us, isn't there?"

The question hung between them. *How could he know?* Lance exchanged a panicked look with the mayor. Armadis saw through them at once. His expression darkened with mistrust.

"You speak of knowledge and trust." All pretense of warmth vanished. "If you want any chance of a deal, you need to tell us the truth. Now, or we leave."

The tension in the room increased. Lance looked round at his fellow conspirators; Brayson looked nervous, Tyir determined. It was as they feared and expected; the Keidan knew everything. *It's time.* Lance cleared his throat.

"Lance Ironheart is it?" Armadis said. "You provide the bulk of your alliance's strength, so I'll call you leader. Very well. Tell us everything. What you want, what you suspect, and why you came to us. Believe me when I tell that you if you lie, we will know."

"As you wish," Lance began, letting out a deep breath. "We suspect that the Order is feeding knowledge to the Empire about the necromancy ritual known as the Counter-Balance, and they plan on using it as a weapon to defend themselves against the invading armies of the Dominion."

"The Counterbalance?" Little Bird's eyes narrowed.

"Don't interrupt," Armadis warned. Little Bird's face flushed, falling silent, as his master looked at each of them in turn. His gaze stopped on Lance, who didn't back away. "I know a little of what you speak. I highly doubt it is possible, judging by the power of the sorcery required. It requires a vast sacrifice of life-force, beyond anything in the current world. But go on. What makes you think this?"

Lance hesitated as he struggled to marshal his thoughts. *What should I say?* Everything hinged on this. Isran put a consoling hand on his shoulder, and the touch galvanized him. Slowly, he began to talk of his suspicions, going back to his time serving in the Order's council, his anger at their failure to fight the war against the Dominion, his overhearing of secret meetings under Bane Aldmer's regime with Raphael, and the discussion of the Counterbalance.

"Ah, Raphael, I know that name of course. I see," Armadis said finally. "Yes, he would have some knowledge. It's possible he got the information somewhere, I somehow doubt our inferiors simply destroyed all the wealth Valia gave them, though I wouldn't put it past them. A powerful weapon no doubt. The Counterbalance has that potential, but I still stand by what we know. It is an impossibility. Why would the Order do such a thing, or even know of it? No, I don't believe it. Even if they did discover knowledge of the Counterbalance, how would they perfect it? It'd take unlimited power and sacrifice."

"You know the answers as well as I do," Tyir whispered. "The Aegis Mora doesn't just belong in your domain. A copy lies within the Order's possession."

It was the wrong thing to say. Armadis got to his feet. "The Aegis Mora, you say?"

The Keidan have two faces. Lance recalled Brayson's words of warning that morning. The face of their majesty and warmth, their aura. And the face they wear for their enemies. There was no mistaking Armadis. Every line within him cold and derelict, void of pity or kindness.

"It's the Aegis Mora you want isn't it?" Armadis demanded. "That's your wish, to delve into its contents? You intend to find out once and for all about this wild scheme?"

There was no need for them to say anything. The Keidan guards had moved from their vigil and were gliding silently over to their masters. Krause rose to his feet, his voice strangled. Armadis threw back his head and laughed. It was a pitiless, brutal laugh, sending shudders down Lance's spine. *Whatever this one is, he's not human.* His heart hammered in his chest. Krause remained rooted to the spot, his hand frozen reaching for his blade. Armadis finally stopped laughing. "Never. We'll not help you. This is beyond the Keidan's wishes."

"Don't you care what could happen?" Tyir asked, rising to his feet too, all pleasantries now dead. "You've been fighting the Order for centuries, and this is possible. As a necromancer, I-"

"The difference between yourself and the old powers are beyond your wildest dreams, Tyir of Irene," Armadis interrupted, expressionless and cool. "Your necromancy is primitive and frankly, weak." His nostrils flared. "Do you really think you're an equal to the old Order? Or even hope? No. The Valians we know had power far beyond anything man can ever hope to achieve through the Mora, and that's only on this side of the world. As for our war with the Order, their whims mean nothing to us. The Keidan knows no equal."

Lance got to his feet, his chair scraping back with a screech. Armadis shot him a look of contempt.

"Did you lesser men honestly believe the Aegis Mora was yours to take?" Armadis declared, his voice rising all the while. "It has existed in our vaults since its conception. Even we cannot access it."

Tyir stood his ground. "I'm telling you, Lance spoke the truth. The Order and the Empire are attempting the Counterbalance. You must see that!"

"Impossible!" Armadis snarled. His eyes glowed red. There was a scream from outside, and the High Keeper broke off from his tirade, looking at the doorway.

"What was that?" The screams from outside grew louder, and the sound of heavy footfalls. Isran blinked, confusion spreading across his face. The look Armadis gave them was full of loathing. "Is this some kind of cowardly ambush to force our hand? Very well then. War it . . ." The door into the inn crashed open, the innkeeper Trog stumbling through. His face was bloodless and grey, foamy blood at his mouth.

"Trog, I thought I-" Brayson began, but stopped short, eyes wide as Trog fell forward to the ground, the broken point of a spear embedded in his back.

Brayson let out a primal roar of mingled fury and shock. Before any of them had a chance to react, a flood of men burst through the door. All carried weapons; crude scythes, rusted swords and one bearing a giant two handed battle axe. They were a dozen in number, wearing rotted and ragged clothing

Lance had never seen before.

"Protect Lance!" Isran shouted, and he and Krause lunged forward into the battle. One hand firmly clutching the large mayor's midriff to stop him falling, Lance threw off his cloak, eyes darting for something he could use as a weapon; he found a fork on the table used for spearing chunks of beef. Holding it tightly in one hand, he brandished it in front of him, ready to kick and stab for all he was worth. One of the attackers hit a Keidan soldier over the head with a club, while three others advanced on Armadis and Little Bird, who were standing on the other side of the great table. Little Bird's face twisted in fear as he brandished a dagger. Armadis remained calm.

"Now," Armadis said softly, and pushed forward with his foot. The table was hurled through the air as though it weighed nothing, straight into the path of the attackers. Meat and bread flew everywhere, the contents of the mead flagons smashing to the floor as the attackers were trapped by the table's great weight. They didn't speak or make any sound as they struggled to lift the table pinning them.

They were outnumbered, the fighting thick and fast. Krause and Isran launched themselves against three of the enemy, their weapons clashing with a constant clang of steel, but another had broken past them, advancing on the mayor who was still crouching over Trog, trying desperately to revive him.

"Brayson!" Heart racing, Lance threw himself in front of the mayor, raising the fork. The points were sharp, easily enough to defend himself. His attacker was young, yet made no sound, his eyes boring deep into Lance's own. They didn't blink, but seemed to stare openly into his soul. *What's wrong with them? Who are they?*

The boy lunged forward and Lance thrust with the

fork, but even before the two weapons made contact, his opponent was thrown off balance, Tyir blindsiding him. Thankfully, the attacker wore no armor; the Paladin's sword pierced the man's left side to the hilt, but there was no blood. The marauder crashed on top of a chair and the two fell to the ground in a clatter of wood and flesh. Tyir recovered quickly, scrambling back onto his feet, but was now defenseless, his sword still buried in the body of the fallen boy, but their attacker recovered even faster, springing up.

The boy shambled forward again, this time aiming for Tyir. Swiftly, Tyir dodged the clumsy sword swing and grabbed hold of a meat cleaver from a nearby table, his eyes on the boy at all times. Lance lunged for the attacker. His charge forward caught the boy by surprise, and as he spun around to face Lance, his sword arm still outstretched, Tyir swung the cleaver with all his strength. Cold tempered steel bit through wool, flesh and bone, and the attacker crumpled, the sword falling from the almost severed arm.

Tyir seized the weapon with his free hand. As he aimed the cleaver at the boys head, Lance caught a glimpse of Isran, who had hacked off the arm of his combatant, yet the wounded man calmly got back onto his feet as though nothing happened.

Six of the twelve had fallen, but the others were battling hard. Lance rushed to join the fight, spearing one of them through the back with a scavenged sword. Not once did they make a sound, nor give any indication they were in pain.

The room was littered with severed limbs and heads, tables and overturned chairs, but the remaining attackers kept fighting with a ferocious determination.

Krause was being pressed further and further into a corner by two of them, his excellent skill holding them both off, but he was running out of space, and Lance knew that meant death . . . he had to help him. Isran shouted for his comrade but he too was hard-pressed, even with Tyir's help, whose speed and prowess was startling.

"Move aside!" demanded Armadis.

Lance turned his head to the High Keeper and saw the black glow in his hands. Seizing Isran and Tyir by their collars, he threw them and himself down onto the ground, where his leg connected painfully with a broken chair. Eyes watering, he felt a sudden surge of energy, then a searing heat. Lance looked up; saw the combatants burning. Still, no sound from them, not even a whimper. Their charred bodies fell to the ground motionless, smoking.

Armadis wasn't done. With a contorted snarl, he threw out his hand at the final two attackers battling Krause, who was on the brink of being trapped. It was a testament to his discipline that he didn't flinch away from the two now human torches, but he did stumble away as he blind-sided them. In a short while, smoke filled the small room, leaving a haze of chaos in its wake.

Lance reached forward and clutched his right leg, swearing. Tyir got to his feet first, offering both he and Isran a hand up. Isran refused it with a brusque dismissal, but Lance accepted gratefully and was hauled to his feet. Victorious, Armadis whispered a stream of musical words, and the smoke cleared away.

"Thanks for that," Lance said to Tyir. Tyir didn't seem to hear. He was busy surveying the scene. Upturned tables and chairs littered the floor, broken and ruined. Many of them were charred black from the High Keeper's powerful spell.

"No, Trog! TROG!" Brayson shook the man again and again, but the innkeeper was dead. There were footprints on his back where the attackers had run over him. Lance felt a huge surge of regret at the sight. Brayson draped his cloak over the body, covering him in a sea of purple velvet.

"Lance, look at them. Something is very wrong here," Tyir whispered. The dead littered the floor of the inn, many of them scorched from Armadis' fire. None of the bodies were moving now. Krause knelt over one of the broken tables panting for breath, clutching his shoulder. The leathers of his shoulder pads, were soaked in blood.

"Krause, are you alright?" Lance asked at once, picking his way through the wreckage to get to him. Krause made a pained smile.

"I'll be fine. Just a graze."

"You're getting that checked out before you do anything else."

"You saved us," grunted Isran. He was staring at the Keidan, and the High Keeper in particular.

Emotionless, Armadis snorted. "I was aiming for the enemy fools who believed they could kill a Keeper of the Keidan. Do not mistake it for anything else." Two of the four Keidan members were dead, the survivors kneeling by their sides. A chant emerged from their hoods, the music tugging at Lance's soul. It had a beautiful, mournful melody.

"What was this?" Little Bird pointed his bloody dagger at Brayson, who was still white-faced and shaken. "Was this your doing?" He took a step forwards, his jaw clenched.

Krause threw himself in front of the mayor before Little Bird could strike. "Try it and die!" He snarled. Lance and Isran both made identical movements for them.

"No!" Brayson barked, his forehead sticky with sweat. "Why would I?"

"Lies!" Little Bird spat.

"They had nothing to do with this attack, Little Bird. Leave him alone." Armadis said sharply.

Little Bird nodded and stepped away, abashed. His superior turned over one of the fallen with his foot. Cold, dead eyes stared up at them all, the face as pale in death. The same as they were in life. "Little Bird, something is amiss. Can you feel it?"

"Feel what?" Little Bird asked, shuddering as he looked down at the corpse.

"I felt it," Tyir said, voice clear and cool. "Look at their bodies, all of you. No blood, and the smell is cold. Even the ones you burned. They didn't make a sound, nor did any of them show any sign of pain."

Little Bird's gaze darted between each of them in turn before finally sheathing his weapon, a purple flush in his cheeks. "Very well, Mayor. I forgot myself." He looked around him. "Then what is this?"

"I do not know," replied Armadis softly.

Isran stared at them. "I'm sorry for your loss."

"It means little." Armadis stood over the bodies of their fallen. "They don't have names, these soldiers. None of them do. They gave their names to our Lady. They are only cattle."

He raised a hand to his face, surveying it with distaste. His slim and brittle fingers were covered with black smudges, with an acrid smell of burnt flesh.

"Too soon," he muttered. "I still need to get stronger, learn more. I never expected to use my knowledge twice in the same day."

"We need to go outside." Isran was saying. "How could they just sneak into the inn like that, without us noticing? I'll go and . . ."

"Not on your own," Lance said sharply. Isran stopped, affronted. Lance wasn't paying attention. He was focused on the Keidan commander. The

317

expression on Armadis' face hadn't changed since they entered the inn, but he caught a flash of recognition in his eyes.

What does he suspect? Either way, something bad was going on. *Tyir's right.* No blood spilled from any of them. How? Then it hit him. *No, it can't be.* It didn't make sense, but the truth was staring him in the face. He was about to voice the suspicion, but Tyir then confirmed it.

"These men were never alive."

Lance looked down at the oddly dressed corpses. Tyir was right. He remembered the boy who had attacked him before. The unblinking stare, the lack of blood. The attackers had been dead from the start. Necromancy. The thought filled him with dread. *Is this the Counterbalance?* Was it the end?

"I thought that too, Tyir." Armadis said, giving the Paladin a withering look. "This is no ordinary, weak necromancy. Or magic for that matter. This is something unprecedented. Even so, they died like normal men, beheaded, stabbed or burned. They didn't seem to feel any pain, or emotion for that matter. Well, it seems burning really does break the hold over their souls."

Isran rounded on Tyir. "Did you have something to do with this?"

"Isran!" Lance shouted. Isran turned back, his face hard and furious.

"What? Necromancy is his art, right? If we get attacked by undead spawn, what do you expect me to think?" Despite his words, his tone suggested that he too, knew the truth.

"As our guest has already kindly pointed out, Isran, my skills with the art of necromancy are limited, and primitive," Tyir reminded him, his penetrating gaze flashing. "I can only bring a limited reflection of life.

This is something far greater."

He knelt down beside one of the corpses, now thankfully motionless.

"Look at their clothing. It's weathered and rotten, not to mention out of place with our time. Not only that, their movements were human. Raised vessels are slow and lumbering, with the intelligence of a Pharos pig. They attacked us as though they were living, sentient men."

"What does that have to do with anything?" Isran asked.

"Common sense. Shut up for a moment." Tyir picked up a rusty halberd from one of the dead. "Look at this for instance." He held it out to Lance. "I have some knowledge of weapons, having worked alongside Lazarus for years, but you're the expert here. What do you think?"

Lance surveyed it carefully. It was unlike any weapon he was used to handling. His men generally used high quality Pyran steel, or weapons scavenged from the Order. It didn't have the marks or the craftsmanship of the Empire nor the Order, although it was similar in design to Pharos craftsmanship. Voyava? No, they used wood and bronze most of the time, and rarely utilized halberds in battle, instead relying on mounted archers. Nor did it match the quality of the steel from Uslor or the Kahal.

No mercenary companies I know of. They certainly didn't belong to anything from Klassos. Recognition was dawning on him. There was only one explanation for this. It was closest to the architecture of the Order. It was unmistakable. "This is Valian. But then, that means . . ." He looked up at Tyir. His grim expression confirmed it for him.

"Do you believe us now?" Tyir asked Armadis, who glared stonily down at the Valian artefact, yet said nothing. Isran and Krause stood frozen in place, neither able to speak. Brayson cleared his throat.

"Lance, what's going on?" He stammered.

I don't even know myself, but there is only one logical explanation. "The crypts below, the stolen corpses. The cold kept the bodies well preserved," Lance said shakily. It was all making sense. "The legacy of Tarantown. We all saw it, and this is proof. How it's happened, I have no idea. But those who attacked us are from your catacombs. The dead are walking. This is necromancy, but not anything a normal man would be capable of."

"It cannot be the Counterbalance," snapped Armadis. "Impossible. However, this is certainly not just necromancy. There are safeguards meant to stop this happening, old laws. Which suggests . . . ."

The door to the inn swung open with a bang, and they all braced themselves for another attack. Three men rushed through, red faced and bloodied. *They're ours*, Lance thought with relief. Isran and Krause lowered their swords.

"It's only us!" Sleeper held up his hands as a defense against the array of blades. The young assassin rushed over to Tyir, but he fobbed off his servant's aid. Slanos and Iris followed, both white-faced and pale.

"I'm alright Sleeper; what's going on out there?" Tyir asked. Sleeper burst into rapid speech.

"Should never have let you go without protection, it's a nightmare outside the city, the town's in panic, Brayson," he paused, giving the mayor a brisk nod before continuing. "The Keidan were sacrificing the Order prisoners as planned, when a force burst out of the forest and assaulted them. We had the gates open and went to help. We came to their aid but a group broke through and made it inside the gates. They must have killed silently to reach you, and that's when we feared. The whole road is littered with dead. Tyir, we saw the bodies for ourselves, and I had to check on you. They're . . . ."

"Dead. We know," Tyir finished for him. "Many casualties on our side?"

Sleeper grimaced. "Not too heavy. None of us, though Sybill took a knife through the breast and Ombrone nearly lost an eye. We lost twenty Ironhearts, thirty or so of the town's militia. The Keidan barely suffered any casualties. I'm sorry, mayor," Sleeper added at Brayson.

"That Combrey is overseeing the effort back at the gate. There were about a hundred of the creatures. We 'killed' them all. One of your Ironhearts ordered us to burn the dead. The Keidan are making their own preparations. I don't know what they're doing."

Brayson seemed unable to speak, white-faced and streaked with tears.

Tyir turned to the Keidan commander. "Well Armadis, Do you believe us now? This is a darker form of necromancy, not one I'd ever dare pursue. And the only alternative is the . . ."

"The Counterbalance. I know your theory, yet your intelligence of the forces outside your league is weak," Armadis snapped, but with less conviction than before. "I'm not convinced. Such a ritual requires time and power, something that is hard for life, this side of the Forbidden Ocean. You're deluded if you think you're the only necromancer in this world. There are powerful spells that can raise the dead other than the Counterbalance."

He broke off as one of the Keidan screamed. Before any of them could do anything, the sentinel burst into flame.

"Gods!" Brayson yelped, jumping back as far as he could as the man became a human torch. But these flames were a vivid purple. Then from within the inferno, a disembodied voice rumbled, echoing throughout the ruined interior of the inn.

"High Protector, call to arms immediately."

Little Bird had his hand over his mouth, his eyes wide. "It's the Gatekeeper. He only calls when . . ."

"I hear you, Gatekeeper. What's happening at the Tower?" Armadis walked to the burning corpse. The purple flames grew brighter, so much so that Lance had to shield his eyes.

"The Keidan is under attack. The False Order has thousands surrounding the central tower, and holds us under siege. We're calling all outside forces to the heart to crush the threat. Return to the citadel immediately. This is a total order, handed by the Eldar Council."

"The Eldars?" Little Bird whispered quietly. He muttered something under his breath, but Lance couldn't hear what.

"This is not something to take lightly, Little Bird," the disembodied voice crackled. "You both know our toils, and much of our strength is tied up elsewhere."

Little Bird gulped and fell silent. "An attack." Armadis repeated. "At once, Gatekeeper."

"Come swiftly." The voice died, and the flames vanished instantly. The body which had borne the fire collapsed, its robes burnt away leaving only blackened, charred bones and shreds of flesh.

"We need to leave at once," Little Bird said. "This is my fault, Armadis. I asked for a larger escort. If I hadn't, we would . . ."

"This is no fault of yours," Armadis assured him. "Two hundred sentinels wouldn't have made a difference; we would still have been under siege. Regardless, this is troubling. First the Valian corpses rising in Tarantown, then the Order attack us. They haven't risked such an assault in many years."

"Is the heart at threat, do you think?" Little Bird's eyebrows rose. "The Order can't do that, surely?"

"Enough of a threat for the Gatekeeper to sacrifice one of our own, insignificant though it may have been," Armadis replied coldly. "The Order's actions have been strange of late, with their activity in the east amongst everything else..."

"Something you would like to share with us?" Tyir cut in, risking the High Keeper's ire.

"It's little concern of yours," Armadis replied smoothly. "And still, there is the matter of the dead. We'll leave immediately." He cast Lance and his party a queer look. "This meeting was clearly a lost cause."

Lance grabbed his arm. "Wait!" Their only chance was about to go. Armadis stood still but his eyes locked onto the mercenary leader's then down to the hand holding him. Lance let go and held his hands, palm out, backing away a step. "Armadis. You say you need men, and we need your help. We haven't lied, and you saw the truth of it. We're mercenaries, and we can help. I fight for a price. Let us fight with you, and give us what we seek. An alliance."

"Commander!" Krause hissed, his usually calm look shattered with fear. "We can't."

"Quiet, Krause," Slanos thundered over him. "You know we have to. You have my support, Lance." He puffed out his beefy chest. Behind his back, Sleeper chuckled with an evil grin.

"We have over two thousand men ready to march immediately," Isran said, recovering at last. He stood tall, the lion-hearted general again. "Though we need to keep men behind at Tarantown to hold it." Brayson looked relieved at his words. The High Keeper stood rooted, but he was no longer moving to leave the inn, nor did he respond when Little Bird gestured for them to vacate. Lance grabbed his chance.

"You'll want proof from us, I'd imagine," He went on. "And we need you. We'll march by your side against your enemy, for they are our enemy too."

"Especially since there's a necromancer at work behind the scenes, one with strength greater than my own," Tyir chipped in.

"Master," Sleeper whispered. "Could this mean the Counterbalance is . . . ."

"I don't know," Tyir replied. "From what we know of it, the Order could take months or years, but right now, this takes precedence. The Keidan may well have a point. Anyway, we need access to the Aegis Mora to discover the truth, whatever it may be. The only way we can do that is helping the Keidan."

"It's three days march, and through difficult terrain," Armadis said bluntly, although Lance saw his reluctance start to slip away. We nearly have him. "It's a dangerous route through the mountain passes. And can you organize over two thousand men to march at a moment's notice? I doubt your men can . . ."

"I told you, we can leave immediately." Isran interrupted. "We've been preparing for war for months, for such a situation like this. We're trained for any situation, and most are veterans of many campaigns. There's no stronger mercenary army then ours, and at such a small price, just your word to help us fight the true enemy. Lance wouldn't lie to you. He's the greatest man I know, besides Longspear."

Little Bird watched them closely, his face flushed. Finally, he nodded, his sharp little eyes wild and fierce.

"I believe them, Armadis. And we could use them. The Order has been stepping up its attacks lately, and they could be useful. As shields, if nothing else."

"We can't just hand over such powerful knowledge

on a whim, you know that," Armadis said coldly. "But, something is happening that I do not understand. As you've said, there's a greater danger. For the Pharos Order to mount an attack such of this, directly on our sacred ground, what could Hinari be thinking? The balance of power in the world is shifting, and not for the better."

"We need the Aegis Mora. Those who are trying to perform this ritual have the full might of the Order and the Empire behind them, and possibly both. You may be the Keidan but their strength alone is considerable, and even more powerful if it's a combined force," Tyir said. "If you value the salvation of your sect, then help us, but first let us help you. Besides," he added, in a voice which could cut steel. "What are the odds of these dead attacking us here, and your spire coming under assault from the Order? This is linked, whether you like it or not."

There was nearly a minute of silence. "Very well then," Armadis finally conceded. "I can see your point. But don't think you've won. You're an asset. It's likely you will all die, but you could at least be of some use. We shall have a non-aggression pact, at least for the time being. If you prove yourself, then I may support your word to the Eldar Circle."

Lance bowed his head. "Thank you." It wasn't ideal, but it was the best they could hope for. He had seen enough just that afternoon. Brayson was right. *We need them on our side, even if it's not an alliance as we would prefer, but to avoid fighting them ourselves. It's why I allied with Tyir.* He suppressed a shudder as he glanced at the Paladin. Lance cleared his throat.

"We'll march immediately. Send word to the men."

Contract

"The deep of the Mora, The gall of the Solr.
Who took us all to fate.
And the great Octane who rose to power,
Broke through their grip, today.

The Chaos of new Valia,
The Counterbalance of old
Destroyed the new world's dreams.
Now they return to their true home,
And old Valia stands tall."
~ The Beginning, by Labra Sol.

Lance Ironheart stood alone outside the commander's tent. Only the ghostly glow of the torches remained in an ocean of black fog.

There is an evil to this darkness, something unnatural.

Even the moon refused to show itself. There would be more light in a coffin. An old Pharos priest back in Bawsor had taught him lore and religion when he was a child. He had called the Keidan "the land where light dies." When Lance enquired further, the tutor angrily changed the subject. Now Lance understood.

This is all wrong, he thought. He had argued to wait for daylight on arrival, but Armadis had insisted on an immediate strike. Lance's commanders agreed, and it was a mark of unity when Tyir and his Scars took their side over his.

"The Order won't expect an attack from the rear,

our scouts have seen to that," grunted Slanos with a rare smile as he addressed the hated necromancer, Tyir.

"The scourge's roads have led us behind the scum, and it's time we fuck them up the arse before they know we're here. It's not easy hiding two thousand men."

Lance was no battlefield genius like the soldiers who had sworn allegiance to him, so he let them go, but he felt no better about it. *They have a point, and Armadis wants to see what we're made of.* *So be it. Let him see what Gollet's legacy truly is.*

Indeed, the paths of the Keidan had led their forces to the rear of the Pharos army: roads known only to them. The lands were sacred ground whom only the Keidan and a few 'lucky' souls were allowed access.

The few scouts the Order had placed around their forces had been dispatched silently by Keidan sentinels under Armadis, along with the help of Tyir's Thousand Scars. Their performance was greater than even Isran had grudgingly admitted. Less than forty of Tyir's men had joined them, but they were formidable in their kind of ambush warfare. Lance glanced back at the mouth of the head tent. Isran stood there, arms folded.

Lance grimaced at his right-hand man's misery. He had wanted first command, but Lance forbade it. Krause was injured and remained in Tarantown with Combrey along with a thousand men to bolster the city should any Pharos soldiers come knocking, so overall command of the Ironheart relief army came down between the original trio who first founded the company with Gollet: Isran, Slanos and Fortescue.

Instead, Isran commanded the reserves, six hundred strong. They would be used to reinforce any point of the battle-line which showed signs of weakness; they were about to attack an army twice the size of their own after all. *Discipline and quality defeats numbers most of the time, but numbers sure as fucking hell help,* Gollet had said once. The memory brought a wan smile to Lance's face, before it once again soured. Thinking of his friend was painful.

Lance had never taken part in a battle except the brief takeover of Tarantown, and even then he was positioned in the rear-guard at the request of his men. It was an incredible sight to behold. Hundreds upon hundreds of his soldiers, who had fought years of campaigning with the late Longspear had deployed for battle: formations of formidable longbowmen, followed by deeply packed formations. Slanos led the assault. They sent in the archers first.

"Sound the battle horn," Armadis had commanded, standing next to Isran and Lance. A veteran of a hundred battles, Isran Reus reached for his warhorn, crafted from the skull of the vicious red-Hunter hounds of Klassos, and blew deep. Its thick booming rumbling through the air like the cry of a great beast roaring in bloodlust. The call was taken up by more horns, before the Ironheart archers, armed with stelwood bows, launched a devastating volley of arrows to join battle. Then marched the first lines under Slanos. *I pray you all return,* thought Lance. This wasn't what he planned at all, but he had rolled the dice.

The battle plan was simple enough. It hadn't taken long for them to notice how ill-prepared the besiegers were for a counter-attack, and quick strikes by Tyir's outriders, experts as they were in espionage, eliminated any possibility of their presence being discovered.

"The Order's strategy has not changed since their founder's days," Slanos had reasoned, as they made their final touches, minutes before the first horn blew for battle.

"Their tactics are as ancient as their dead legacy; a line of longbowmen, behind a shield wall of spears and pikes. Like us they have no cavalry, so we have no problem of being out-flanked. They lack any real mobility."

"So do we. If only we had horsemen," Fortescue had lamented. He missed the old days in Klassos commanding heavily armored mounted bowmen under Gollet, but Lance was relieved they had no cavalry.

Horses would never have made that journey, not the horses we have at our disposal.

The two pale ponies led by Little Bird and Armadis were sure-footed enough, but Lance suspected they were Keidan exclusive, bred only for their purpose. It was difficult enough traversing the so called Anciair trail by foot, let alone by horse. Two thousand strong, the alliance made up of Ironhearts, Tyir's hand-picked personal guard and the Keidan survivors under Armadis toiled through the exhausting march.

The path was barely negotiable in some points, the only clues to the ruts being the icy puddles, so narrow they had to travel three abreast at times, strung out along a long, brutal line. *If we were attacked, we would have been finished.*

It was so dark at times, not even a thousand torches could penetrate the depths of the forest. There were only small sounds of rustling bushes and the howl of the wind. Armadis had assured them that there was animal life in the Keidan lands, and it was a greatest relief when Lance heard birds dolefully hooting. Their rest stops were brief, urged on by the Keidan.

My heart goes out for my Gollet's boys, hungry and tired for battle.

Several Ironhearts slipped and perished, some collapsing of exhaustion, but nobody stopped for them. However, the veterans serving under Lance Ironheart, battle hardened by years of campaigning in Klassos, persevered through the heavy terrain of ice and snow, while the few Thousand Scars led by Tyir were men of even hardier stock. With their undying morale, the lesser experienced fighters soldiered on, bolstered by their comrade's courage.

It didn't take them long to make a plan of attack. A heavy barrage of missiles would initiate a charge thrust at one point in the Pharos camp, which was poorly fortified, ill-suited for a siege. Seven hundred bowmen supported eight hundred foot soldiers in the opening assault, with the archers exchanging bow for blade when the arrows ran out.

They had the range Lance knew: the Order likely relying on their yew longbows with the odd Valian relic, a beautiful and formidable weapon, but rare and hard to maintain. Four fifths of the Ironheart army fielded stelwood bows, with the others making do with double recurved, horn and sinew bows from Klassos.

The close-quarter work was done with a formidable front line of spears, halberds and glaives, devastating against cavalry as well as lesser armed footman, with each man carrying a sword when the line inevitably broke. A strong reserve was held back, should they need to send reinforcements to any part of the line. There was an air of supreme confidence, yet Lance was still uneasy.

"They do have twice our numbers," Isran pointed out. "I counted at least four thousand, if not more."

"We've won battles with worse odds. Remember the charge at Geruland," Slanos said, showing rotten teeth as he smiled. "And from what our scouts have discovered, a lot of their strength is strung out thanks to the Keidan's relentless attacks, and they cannot flank the fortress without suffering heavy casualties."

That Gatekeeper had recalled all Keidan forces, Lance remembered. It would have been better if they knew more, but Armadis was unwilling to discuss the Keidan's operations, and the 'men' with him didn't speak.

"All we need to do is shatter one of their defensive points and the day is ours. Besides, every one of our men is worth a dozen of their scum. We'll take care of them, I swear it." Slanos slapped his belly, his jowls wobbling. "I won't sheathe my sword until they're beaten."

Just so long as it doesn't claim your life, Slanos, Lance had thought. Slanos was brutal and at times a sadistic barbarian, but he remained one of Lance's staunchest supporters. *When he isn't slumping back into his old tricks, he is a solid commander, and the men look up to him.* He needed them all for the struggle ahead. All he could do now was wait.

Lance didn't know how much time had passed. It had been a while since a runner from the front line had arrived. The rearguard's position was very hastily erected; there was no time to build defenses in the rush for battle, but Isran had tasked some men to lop down the smaller trees to make a palisade to protect them from a possible flank attack.

It took Armadis some convincing to let them chop down their sacred trees, but he eventually agreed. The tent was on the top of a slight slope, and it was there which they struck a defensive position for their tactical reserves.

I only wish we could see more.

With the night sky still alive, he could barely see anything but the dim glow from torches carried by his men, as they battled the Pharos Order. But though he could not see, he could hear. The sound of battle, clashing steel, whistling arrows and the roar of men in pain and anger came to him clearly. In the far distance, the end of the steep valley was marked by an old rock formation, a dominant sentinel like the king from the game shatak. *The Keidan Spire.* Just the sight of it turned Lance's blood run cold. Never in his life did he expect to be here, let alone fight for them. But here he was.

Lance had heard many tales about the Keidan. Of course, he was born within the rites of the old Balian Empire, and had seldom dealt with the whims of the ancient sect, no matter what some people whispered about the Empire's beginnings. However, nothing he did could prepare him for the sight of the Keidan's dwelling.

The Keidan stronghold itself was less than Lance expected. Whispers spoke of a formidable fortress forged with the blood of its enemies, raised from the stone of a thousand gods and impregnable to all. Even so, he found himself underwhelmed by its appearance.

It was just a mere black rock face to him, though they were at a fair distance. And with the Order in their path, Lance wasn't getting nearer anytime soon. Still, not so impressive. Once they made their way out of the deep, lush forests, the sight underwhelmed them all. Armadis was quick to prove their conceptions false.

"The Keidan is a labyrinth of an infinite void. All of it is underground, much like how the Valian explorers built Sirquol. No mortal force can ever hope to take it." The battleground wasn't what Lance would have liked: a ring of deep, lush grass fields around the citadel, which looked like a large tomb carved into a rock face at the end of a wide valley of hills. To the left stood an even wider plain leading into the thick blanket of forest surrounding the Keidan lands. *We should have fought it there,* Lance had thought, but that would mean giving the Order time to deploy on their own terms. *Never let the enemy fight their own battle.* Gollet had said that often.

It was desperately dull just waiting, but the reserve forces couldn't risk lowering their guard, so they remained on high alert. Nobody had put down any ground to sleep, but Isran placed many of them on patrol around the half-built barricade, keeping an eye out for runners.

Most of the Keidan that had travelled with them had melted into the surrounding trees flanking the battlefield. Only the mysterious female identity they worshipped as their unwavering goddess knew what they were plotting, though a small guard remained in the small camp with their master, where they ignored the Ironhearts completely.

Courier points flanked by Pyran bowmen were cleverly placed around their position, so they could gather information about the battle. Lance let out a grateful sigh as some of the mist thinned yet still shivered as the chill bit through his clothes. His chainmail shirt was uncomfortable and heavy, the metal links digging into him even with the padding. Lance ground his teeth together at the feeling. He was made for council meetings and plotting from the sidelines, not for this, but his men rightfully argued their commander couldn't lead his men under-dressed.

The mist continued to evaporate and he caught a glimpse of the battlefield. In the distance, a mass of men fought each other in a mob of chaos and noise; some disciplined formations of Ironhearts remained just about visible, but there was little to distinguish friend from foe. He could make out some of the red robes of the Order however, and the size of their host was alarming. It was incredible to think the Order could muster such a force, especially since they were at war in the north. *Sure, they had large forces east in the Kahal, but why even attack here?* The more Lance thought of it, the less it made any sense. *Why would Hinari do such a thing?*

A runner rushed in from the right, panting hard. He took a moment to get his breath. "Sir Ironheart, I bring word from the eastern forest. Our right flank is under heavy pressure. However, Keidan men have swept in from the west and are closing in fast. Pittain asks for reinforcements on our own wing." He was red in the face, a slender lad whom Lance judged no older than twenty, a recruit from Tarantown. The Keidan returning to their home. They had arrived at the right time.

Isran heard and stepped forward. "Bernan, send word to Tigane. Take two hundred men from here and reinforce the right flank. Hug the trees." The runner sprinted off again. "I should be leading the men out there," Isran growled at Lance when the young man departed the vicinity. "I feel useless here."

"You've done it many times." Lance replied. "You all told me your war stories, as did Gollet many a night." The two shared a small smile.

"True." Still unhappy, Isran rubbed his hands together. The mist had closed in again, obscuring the battlefield from view. "The visibility is fucking appalling. Come on, let's get inside. That fire is bloody strange, but at least it's warm." When Lance hesitated, he said, "We'll know when we have more reports." With a frustrated glance behind his back, Lance followed Isran inside.

It was a lot warmer, largely thanks to a purple fire that hovered in the air, conjured by Armadis. Lance gave it an enthralled look as he entered. *How could he create such a thing?* Every moment with the Keidan presented a dozen new questions.

Tyir, Armadis, Little Bird and Isran were present, circled around a large smooth rock on which they had drafted their battle plan. Sleeper had joined them, as well as Slanos' squat lackey Idos and Carver Jack, the self-declared best fighter in the Ironhearts. Half a dozen men had the uneasy honor of looking into the command tent; four Ironhearts and two Scars, who seemed rather bored with the proceedings. Tyir and the Keidan elite regarded him with curt nods.

Little Bird was sitting on the ground, but rose at their arrival. "I heard voices. Runners?"

"Sending reserves to the right flank," Lance replied, distracted momentarily from the mystical flame. "More of your people have returned, and are attacking the Order's flank."

"Good. That is good. Strange." Armadis said in a silky voice, but fell silent. Little Bird shot him a furtive glance, his upper lip curled, but he too was silent. Lance glared at them both.

"What's strange?" Sleeper grunted. They ignored him. Lance seethed. He was getting rather sick of their secrecy, but there was no point trying to force the issue. *You're not helping yourselves, Keidan.* This whole place was unsettling. A whistle of wind blew up from outside, making the flap of the tent flutter like a bird stuck in a trap. *Maybe that's what we are. Trapped.* This wasn't their place.

Lance's stomach rumbled with hunger. They had brought some supplies, but they were meagre; there wasn't time to muster a large supply train like they usually did. Every soldier carried their own provisions, which was something Gollet's veterans were used to. A faster way to deploy certainly, but

Lance would have welcomed the extra supplies. *This is the way of war.* Armadis however had declared the forests were rich with fruit and small animals, and gave them permission to forage. Despite the generosity, few dared to breach the imposing wall of trees, an unknown entity.

"I wish we could see more out there. This mist is as unreliable as Slanos' cock," quipped Carver with an easy smile. Idos glowered stonily at that comment. Lance stared him down with a stern gaze. He hadn't forgotten about that messy business in the showers with the Scar boy.

"It's a natural phenomenon, the mist from the north." Armadis caressed the smooth stone with a soothing hand. "The Lady sends it to protect our faith in times of war. Not that we need it," he added with a sneer. "The False Order imitate the Valians poorly. They cannot hope to accomplish anything with this farce. They would have been slaughtered with or without your help, though I admit so far you have exceeded my expectations. They haven't broken, nor have they died poorly."

"The Ironhearts never run. You would do well to remember that," said Carver in a low hiss. Tyir voiced the very thought running in Lance's head.

"If they are so low a priority for your kin, then why were you recalled here in the first place? Answer me that."

This time, the High Keeper's ice-cold wall showed the first signs of cracking. "The Gatekeeper's word is law. He speaks, and the flock obeys. However . . ." he hesitated, and this time, Lance could see confusion stir in those unforgiving eyes. "I have been thinking on it, during our march. Why is the Order here? Why would Hinari attack, with such danger in the north? They have been more active of late."

Lance's gaze met Tyir's for a brief moment. "Is this something you can share with us, or not?" he asked, in what he hoped was more polite then he felt.

"Well . . . the Order has three main sectors of operation, and three leaders. There's Raphael, head of the north,-"

"Aye, who has been helping the Empire with the C-"

"Paladin. I am giving you a rare insight into my thoughts. Kindly keep silent," hissed Armadis. Sleeper stepped forward, but Tyir stopped him with a look which would freeze blood. Sleeper gave a barely distinguishable nod, and Armadis went on.

"Anyway. There is Raphael to the north, Hinari who commands the Order from the Sepulcher, and of course their territories in the Kahal to the east of here, under the inquisitor, Antoch Kramer. These Order fools clearly came from the east, the same way Bawsor Dune did doing his hapless attempt to sully Keidan customs."

"I know of Kramer. He was central to defeating the Kahal rebellion," Tyir replied.

"Indeed. However, all three sectors answer to the Sepulcher and Hinari. So it begs the question as to what they are planning."

Little Bird blinked and began pacing up and down around the fire, Isran watching him with a scowl. Sleeper stood by his master. Lance ignored them, thinking of Armadis' words. He had no idea of the workings of the Pharos Order, particularly in the south. Who was this Antoch Kramer? "What about the Kahal?" He asked, risking the High Keeper's scorn. "You spoke of increased activity." To his surprise, they were again rewarded.

"We've kept an eye on the region for obvious reasons. Nothing out of the ordinary," Armadis added. "Many troop movements around the province. Some localized Kahal revolt, nothing new there. The past few months whispers of skirmishes between Redure forces and Kahal rebels, or Skyini moving in from the south. The Order have stepped up their methods to quell dissent. They've been stepping up patrols, reinforcements from the west. We heard something about prison camps, but again, old news."

"They know something; which is why you need us," Tyir said as he turned to look into the flames. "If Hinari sends such a force against you, High Keeper, then he plans on wiping you out. The only reason that makes sense is to stop you from interfering with his plans for the Counterbalance. They have always enjoyed a close relationship with the Empire, and if they succeed in their goals, nothing will be safe. You know this even more then I, Armadis."

Armadis retired to a corner and fell into a seated trance, ignoring all of them while chanting. Twice more, reports filtered in from the front line, both messages carried by a different runner. Lance knew each of them by sight but only one by name, but Isran knew them all.

A true leader must know his fighters as though they are his own blood.

"The Order has been pushed back. Our bowmen inflicting heavy casualties, while their own fall short. Their ranks are in disarray," said a flamboyant, white-haired Timoxan, fresh from the battle under Slanos. The fighting was still fierce, judging from the noise in the distance. Lance wondered if they should commit some of their reserves to exploit the breakthrough, but the Timoxan assured him with a smile that it wasn't needed, and Slanos hadn't requested reserves. With a quick drink of water and a bite to eat, he left. *All is going our way, so far.*

"Fighting is hard. Fortescue had to pull back his line

338

in order to avoid being surrounded," Isran said.

He recommended they send a hundred rangers to reinforce the left flank, but Carver disagreed, arguing that sending them to the center instead and deploying them in a reverse echelon formation would be better.

"Fortescue is a sound man. He'll keep the line in good order, and the Keidan will prevent the Order from pushing through them. Even if they break, our reinforcements wouldn't get there in time and will be destroyed piecemeal. Better to keep them refusing the flank so the Order cannot threaten the rest of our line." Armadis agreed with Carver, and so the order was carried out.

Again, Fortescue hadn't made a desperate plea for reinforcement, but in a way, that made Lance uneasy. Both Fortescue and Slanos were warriors and prickly men, leading from the front. Both also had the stubborn resistance never to give up: never had they fled from battle once they joined it.

For all we know, they could both be dying, and the crows lie about their fate. He stopped himself. *Don't think like that.*

Lance chewed over the High Keeper's words. What was going on with the Order? It was a sloppy offensive at best, a disaster at worst, certainly. Lance left the tent. The cloak of night obscured everything. Combined with the intermittent fog, even the sentries were blind. Not being able to see the battle frustrated him. Going back inside, he found something which broke through his fatigue: Isran in deep conversation with Tyir.

"A question if you'd please, Tyir?"

Lance stopped dead. Isran was being polite to Tyir, even friendly. *How long was I out there?*

"What is it, Isran?" Tyir replied.

"Your necromancy," Isran began, his moustache

twitching like a fly. "I've been thinking about it for a while. You haven't used since we found you in the crypts of Tarantown. Why?"

Tyir gazed back at him. "I was under the impression that raising walking corpses would cause a panic in the town. You boys don't need another reason to want me dead, do you?" The coolness in his words had reached dangerous levels. from the corner of his eye, Lance caught Sleeper glaring at Isran as he sharpened his knife on a grindstone.

"Isran," he said warningly, but his lieutenant brushed it off, still calm and friendly.

"I'm not getting at that, Lance. It's alright," Isran soothed.

The conflict in his face was evident, but to Lance's admiration he was keeping his cool, speaking to Gollet's killer whilst resisting the urge to behead him, as he had threatened many times.

"For once Tyir, this is not an interrogation. I've just been curious. Why haven't you used it? It may have given us more manpower to fight." Isran struggled to get the words out, disgust filling his face. "No. Forget what I said. But I'm still intrigued. You haven't used that foul power of yours, despite it being your mark. I'll even say I expected it. Why?"

Tyir was silent for a moment. "If I was able, I would, Isran. You ask insolent questions, but I guess there's no harm in telling you now. Why do you think I came to Tarantown? I needed what was in the crypts, but the enemy got to them first."

Tyir paused, raising a clenched fist. Every line of his face was rigid in anger, his gaze frigid. "I wanted those preserved Valian soldiers for my own, I'll admit it. I mobilized my men, and prepared my strategy for vengeance against the Empire, the Order, and all who stood in my way. I planned on make the Empire pay

340

taking Lazarus' life. The Order too, can join the Mora plane in an eternal suffering. I wanted to drive them into the dirt where they belong. But since that day, I've lost myself."

With a tremble in his voice, Tyir then opened his clenched hand, his veined, brittle fingers flexing. "I've been unable to raise the dead. It's never exactly easy, but it seems to be getting harder, with not the results. Whatever's happened, it's broken my necromancy. I don't understand it."

Lance looked at him, perhaps properly for the first time in his life. He knew exactly how Tyir felt, the helpless loss of power. His sister and home had been destroyed when Aldmer suspected his meddling. Was it grief that had shattered his ability?

I started this. I cannot forsake my path now. That hardened his resolve. He glared at the High Keeper. *You have to believe us now,* Lance urged, praying Armadis would hear his thoughts. *Our men are fighting and dying for you. Have the decency to help us in return.*

There was noise from outside . . . horns, then a roar of voices. Cheering? Lance turned to face the entrance as a runner arrived, one from Slanos' division. He was covered in blood and his face badly bruised on one side, but he paid his injuries no heed. "Lance Ironheart!" He puffed, trying to catch his breath. A slender lad, he was dripping in sweat.

"Report," Isran demanded, breaking away from Tyir. Concern etched on his face, Sleeper walked over to the boy. It took him a while to recover his breath, before he looked.

"There was heavy fighting across all fronts," the messenger panted, breathing heavily as he leaned against Sleeper for support. "Fortescue's flank broke under weight of numbers, but they came up against our reserves and old General Forty held firm." He gave them a triumphant, yet exhausted smile. "The Keidan melted back into their forests and the Order gave pursuit, only for us to counterattack; I saw it all. Pittain was able to rally. Our army was able to punch through at the center, forcing them out. The day is ours, Lance Ironheart. The Keidan's been saved."

Armadis gave a snort at that remark, but Little Bird bowed his head in acknowledgment. Lance felt a wave of relief fill him.

It's not over yet, though.

As one, they stepped outside into the night. It was colder now, but at last the patchy fog was starting to clear. The horizon was now a hazy blue bleeding through the ebony, the newborn rays of dawn just beginning to peak through.

How long were we fighting?

The battlefield spread across the plain, the carnage evident. In the distance, smoke and flames smoldered, evidently from the remains of the Order's camp. Far to the left, Lance could make out a large throng of people, fleeing the battle like rats scurrying into the sewers.

Some of the flames had caught the tall pines flanking the death zone; some fighting was still going on in the center, a thin line of red cloaks still persisting in a blood-soaked sea. Even from this distance, Lance could see they were fighting to escape, not to kill. *We have truly won this day.*

Hundreds more men were marching in Lance's direction, carrying battle standards, the black and blue scorpion of Gollet. Just seeing it brought tears to Lance Ironheart's eyes. Their shouts were united:

"Ironheart! Ironheart! IRONHEART!"

Holding weapons of steel and stelwood into the air, his men were shouting to the heavens, both in the common voice and their own local dialects. A few ragged wings had started to pursue the routing enemy, but under the shouts of their officers began to return to the main host.

"We should pursue the Order," said one of the reserves, voice rough under his woolen hood. "Destroy what's left of them. In the Kahal they'll be out of our reach."

Isran had taken Lance's side, and it was he whom the man beseeched. "Why isn't Slanos giving pursuit! We have the battle won, we can . . ."

"No," Isran said. "Slanos is doing the right thing. It's been a long battle, we're exhausted. And who's to say the Order won't rally?" There was a flutter of movement over by the left mass of trees, both sides of dense forest encasing the Keidan stronghold in a serpentine coil of branches and leaves. "Looks like the Keidan are taking care of the stragglers for us."

Lance felt his knees weaken, but he managed to stop himself slumping with the relief. The messenger fell to his knees, Sleeper moving swiftly forward to catch him just in time. The man was so tired, he didn't even protest one of Tyir's men touching him. "Do you know the casualties?" Lance asked the messenger. Another soldier ran in with water for the wretched runner, and it was only after he took a well-deserved drink did he speak again, his breath coming in labored grunts.

"On our side? We're still figuring that out. I was in the center line with Slanos. I couldn't count more than twenty, maybe thirty dead? I'd wager Fortescue has suffered worse since he and Pittain took the brunt of the counterattacks, but we have no idea. Very light, I'd say. Less than a hundred."

It was better than Lance had expected. *I couldn't have asked a harder task of my men, yet once again, Gollet's legacy has remained unstained.* He was expecting at least twice the casualties, even if they had won. The messenger's legs gave way and the water-provider helped him out. The dip of his head at the young Scar was the coldest of courtesies, but it was one nonetheless. "You need rest," he said sagely. "I'll escort him to the medical tent immediately." Supporting the exhausted soldier on his shoulder, he inched away.

Lance felt almost light-headed. Isran pointed over to the east. "What was that, over there?" They squinted over at the edge; it was still dark, so all he could make out was movement, maybe a flash of fire. A torch. *Probably some of the Keidan.*

He pushed it out of his mind, and he and Tyir turned to face the High Keeper in a rare front of unity. He was looking around them all, with an inscrutable expression on his face.

We've upheld our end of the bargain.

"Well. That was a surprise. I was expecting most of you to die today, even if the end result was never in any doubt. I stood by and let you make your decisions, because an army must follow their own path without the interference from any outsiders, even when they are superior. But I am impressed. And that is very hard to do."

Tyir nodded. "So?"

Before any of them could reply, a plume of flames and rising black smoke fired high into the sky, not far away to the east. It was exactly where Isran had pointed out. The men standing around celebrating stopped dead, many pointing at the spectacle. Some were enthralled, others afraid. More drew their weapons.

"What is that?" Armadis frowned. Isran let out a yell, and his hand went for his sword. Something was happening. Everyone looked at each other; the

Ironhearts showing uncertainty, the two Keidan masters confused. It was their bewilderment which alarmed Lance most of all.

"Come on." Without another word, Armadis stalked away with a swish of his cloak. Little Bird followed, his face hollow and grim. Heart hammering in his chest, Lance led the others after them. What remained of the reserves picked up their weapons and followed Lance: with all the reinforcements during the battle, they now numbered less than one hundred. The air was even colder now, and in the distance something huge was stirring between the trees.

"What the fuck is that?" shouted a reserve spear.

"Whatever it is, it's coming straight for us!" That was an archer, green with fear. Isran blanched but he did not move.

"You know the drill!" Carver snarled, pointing his sword at the trees. "Wall of spears in front, archers behind!"

But even as they began to deploy, the pillar of fire faded, followed by the crack of oak roots snapping like brittle twigs. It was as though nature itself were trying to escape. A strange black mist was stealing over them too, the pillar its epicenter.

A group of Ironhearts on Pittain's wing had spotted the threat too and were quickly getting into formation whilst the archers reached for their quivers, but before they could do anything, they stopped in their tracks.

Lance watched half of them fall to the ground, the other half dropping their spears and running. Another writhed on the ground trying to get up, his face frozen in agony as he tried to stuff intestines back into the gaping hole that had appeared in his abdomen.

The men were fleeing. Their captains roaring at them to stand fast but a secondary lash of something stopped them cold, and more bodies littered the ground with gaping wounds.

"We have to help them!" Carver led their advance across the ground, Lance hurrying to keep up. Armadis and Little Bird too answered the call.

Ahead, Lance could see the true devastation to his men, bodies everywhere strewn like wreckage. Old Pittain, limping badly on one leg, was carried away by his sergeants. Whatever it was that had killed so many, it was getting closer.

Included in the reserves were a dozen of Tyir's men, looking very out of place in their ragged attire, but they took orders from Carver without question.

Scanning their faces, there was confusion and fear in every one. Sleeper and the two Scar bodyguards from the command tent had formed a defensive semicircle around Tyir, who drew his sword in readiness.

"What is that? What's going on?"

"Pull back!"

"Tyir? What's happening?" Sleeper demanded harshly. Tyir said nothing, his eyes wide watching the massacre. Pittain's line had completely broken. Lance couldn't look away from the sight as a shadow moved amongst them. The thing, whatever it was, was shrouded in black mist, but there was form to it, as if it had a body and was walking. Lance could hear the heavy thunder of every footstep. It was shaking as it got closer. It was less than a hundred feet away now, and gaining ground.

Most of the survivors had reached them, shouting encouragement to each other and reforming the line, but just as many were fleeing back to the command post. At least none were abandoning the field. Isran and Carver barked at them to stand ground, and two thirds eventually rallied. Lance took the front alongside his trusted generals. Tyir followed suit, as did his men. Darkness engulfed them and even with their torches, Lance could only just about make out the front line of his men. The mist, which stank of blood, flowed around them. Even the sound of the world seemed to die. "Stick together!" Lance held his sword higher. "Around me, men!"

Little Bird's dagger was shaking in his small hands. "High Keeper," he squeaked. "What's happening?"

His master did not reply but held his open palms outward, walking in front of Lance. They burst into flames brilliant white light, so blinding Lance had to shield his eyes. A moan of dismay from the men signaled that they could see the figure in the mist. It stood, fully formed, not moving, but watching with avid hunger in its eyes. There were three of them, burning beads that hated.

No god, on earth or Mora, could have consented to create this hell. Ten feet tall, clad in a full coat of glistening black armor which blended into its own body like a natural skin. Its crimson eyes glowed, three terrifying orbs of blood red hate. Lance struggled to move, but found himself paralyzed as he stared up at this monster. He had seen images of this creature before.

"It's a Messeah," Little Bird whispered. Then, almost a shriek, "A Messeah! A sentinel of the Mora Plane!"

A childhood nightmare. Its face was masked by a heavy black shroud. A cold, shrill cackle came from the creature, not from this world. How could it, when its very existence bred evil? The High Keeper stood rigid, his mouth open in shock as the huge creature advanced on him. For the first time, he was lost for words. Even worse, he appeared to be powerless.

No! If he dies, our cause here is lost. Something inside Lance broke. A reckless rage came over him. He charged in, ignoring Isran's shocked gasp as Carver

Jack bellowed the attack order.

"What are you craven cunts waiting for? Stop pissing your pants and KILL THAT THING!"

The twang of bows sounded behind, and men advanced with a burst of speed, overtaking Lance and charging headlong into the beast, their spears aimed at its legs. They were dwarfed by the Messeah. The arrows punched deep into its body, but the creature kept coming, its movement's jerky and labored.

Three more arrows took it in the shoulder, but still it kept coming, inexorable as an oncoming storm.

Four spearmen made the distance and took the first brave attempt, ramming their spear points at its legs.

Lance hung back, the cold in his chest freezing him to the spot. The creature's first swipe took off one head in a hail of blood. That did it for two of the remaining three brave souls, who tried to retreat, but a second swipe downed them both. The last man prodded a final couple of times in defiance, before the third attack killed him as well.

A horrendous, ear-splitting wail burst from the dark creature's ragged funnel of a mouth. Then Armadis was there hurtling in front of Lance, weaving in and launching a stream of flame at the Messeah.

The effort stopped it in its tracks, but only for a second; the creature's armor absorbed the deadly fire and after a few seconds the flames surrounding it dissipated.

With Armadis' horrified curses ringing in his ears, Lance spotted something around the monster's feet; a ring of flame and strange, black runes circling the blaze. *What is that?*

"BRING IT DOWN! BRING IT DOWN!" roared Carver. More arrows and crossbow quarrels hit it. One of the crossbow bolts bounced off, only to take an unlucky man in the throat. Then there was a flurry of movement from the left; and a dozen swordsmen came charging through the murk. The Messeah let out a rending sob of pain. Before Lance or Armadis could respond it was directly before them, a smattering of dead Ironhearts strewn across the ground after the creature's lightning fast assault.

"Die!" Armadis screeched, raising his hand, just as the Messeah conjured a glistening, silver weapon out of the air. A huge, two-handed greatsword appeared in its armored fist, swinging in an arc straight at the Keidan master, only missing as a blow from the shimmering wall of flame Armadis managed to summon kept it at bay.

Both man and Messeah were blown off their feet and thrown backwards. Another row of brave Ironhearts ran in to protect their leader.

Fools! Lance wanted to scream, but no sound came. He stumbled, managing to keep his feet. The Messeah advanced on him.

No! Quivering with an even darker fury than before, Lance turned to meet the foul shade. *I still have a purpose.*

With an effort that made every inch of his body scream in protest, Lance swung his sword, just in time to deflect the thrust from the Messeah aimed at Armadis' heart. The creature let out a petrifying screech as the two blades collided. Lance stared wide-eyed as his blade shattered.

A mailed fist swept in from the right pushing into his side, and Lance was thrown onto his back. As he stared into hateful red eyes there was a swish of a cloak, and somebody stood over him. *Tyir?*

Armadis had recovered, his eyes blazing, fire flowing from his palms. He advanced on the creature, flames enveloping it. The Messeah shuddered and threw its head back in a roar of pain, its maw open, revealing stumps of blackened rotting teeth. Something flew into its mouth; a tiny dart, and a boiling hiss issued from the wound.

The air was starting to clear around them, and Lance could see the dreadful carnage clearly, with dead Ironhearts everywhere. Then Sleeper and Tyir were there, pulling him up, Sleeper holding his blowdart to his lips and aiming at his target.

Armadis jumped forward, aiming a final spell into its chest. At last, it made its deadly mark.

With a great, shaking cry, the creature was breaking up, its body vibrating as it burst into flame. Lance was nearly blinded from the intensity of the light, and he looked down at the creature's feet. The ground began to crack, the ring of runes around its feet turning hot.

Within moments, the Messeah had vanished, the silence like thunder.

Tyir spat at the rapidly fading circle, his face a snarl of rage.

He saved my life. He and Sleeper.

Tyir turned to address him. "Are you alright?"

No. He grabbed tightly onto Tyir's shoulder. His vision was blurry, his legs buckled beneath him.

"Lance!" Isran and two of his men rushed to his aid, Isran gifting Tyir a nod of appreciation. Lance grunted in pain, even as the burning in his chest was easing. *I must have been out of my mind.*

"You alright?" Isran demanded, shaking him slightly.

"No." Lance repeated thickly. That was a Messeah. *How's this possible?*

Every part of his body ached. The darkness had lifted, leaving only the deep blue sky. The battlefield was wreaked with carnage. Body parts, scorched from an evil fire lay everywhere. Sobbing Ironhearts covered their faces, appalled at the scene while others rushed to their fallen. How many? Fifty? Sixty? He lost count of their corpses.

"I can hardly believe it. A living Messeah, before our eyes," Tyir whispered. He was unharmed, but his robes were ripped and muddy. He stared at the spot where the Messeah had vanished. The ground was charred black where the circle had appeared. A pungent smell of brimstone was in the air, as well as the copper stink of death.

"You saved my life." Armadis said as he approached Lance. "Your actions were foolish. What were you thinking, Ironheart?" His voice was ragged.

Lance wiped his forehead, glistening with sweat. All over the battlefield, the Ironhearts were combing the ground for their friends and comrades. Or what was left of them. A few were crying for help. Slanos was stumbling before them from the left, his brutish face flabby in grief.

"You were in trouble," Lance found himself saying. I couldn't just let you fight that thing on your own, could I?"

The High Keeper could only nod. "You have my thanks."

Lance regarded him in wonder. Did he detect a hint of respect, even gratitude?

"Can we get back to what just happened?" snarled Tyir. "They do not belong to this world. They guard the afterlife."

Armadis snorted. "You need to think on your beliefs, necromancer. The Mora isn't just some realm where only the dead dwell, ruled by a sentinel race of evil demons. Of course, dead from this living plane do join its depths, but I digress. It is a completely separate, living and breathing world, with a system which none of us can ever begin to understand, with rules we will never truly master. It is an infinite,

351

never-ending void where life begins again. The Messeahs are the same. They are vengeful spirits against life, for the Octane broke the Mora plane and shattered their hold, but it's not just a matter of black and white. They have their own roles, their own existence. There is no good or evil. Only shades of grey." The flash of anger faded. "But it does beggar belief. A Messeah walking our earth? It should be impossible."

Lance had a stirring memory then, from an offhand remark made by Brayson Toney only a couple of weeks before.

"Only a few days ago did I get a report from one of your scouts, Elric? They came across a village in the Kahal, Niehrin? Completely torn apart. Homes flattened to the ground, nothing but ash and rubble, and a few . . . body parts."

The evidence is staring us all in the face. It had to be the Messeah. Which means . . .

"It would seem the impossible has become truth," Tyir was saying. "Did you see its movements, the manner of its arrival? It was summoned. How? For the Order to do this, to actually summon a Messeah from the Torn World, it's just begging for destruction."

"Is that even possible?" Lance heard himself saying. "How do we know it was the Order?"

"I've heard of spells, strange rites, but they're old," Armadis replied. "Valian lore says that they experimented with the more powerful conjuring arts, but here in Harloph? There are old testaments of the lore, tomes and archives they brought from the west. We have access to most of it, but even we don't view it. Just like the Aegis Mora . . . although there is the copy in the Sepulcher. The Order would have been utter fools to discard all of their legacy. They're playing with something that's beyond them. This is utter madness! What could that fool Hinari be thinking? This changes everything."

"We took heavy losses today." Isran said. "We'll need time to prepare, to rebuild our forces. Armadis, you must help us."

Armadis looked deep into Lance's eyes. Finally, he nodded, unsmiling. "Yes. We have no choice."

"You sure, my lord?" Little Bird had hobbled over to them, his ashen face aghast at the unprecedented action his master was taking.

"No, I'm not. But they proved their worth, and they saved my life. The Circle must know what happened here. Until we know the truth, and the sole truth, we need allies."

Little Bird was unconvinced. "But we defeated it? You defeated it!"

"No." The lone word came out sharp and poisoned. "Not a single one of our mortal, living weapons could truly hurt it. My spells slowed it down, but could not wound it. Tyir's servant's foul poison did seem to trouble the creature, but it was the manner of its summoning which saved us. They cannot survive in a living realm for long, not without help."

"I noticed that," said Lance. "Its movements were odd, as if controlled, like a marionette." The thought of it scared him almost as much as the Messeah had. *If such a creature can be tethered, what power does the Order possess?* The lone demon had done more damage to his men than the Order's army had, thousands of mortal men.

"The only reason we weren't destroyed was because it's summoning had ended, some form of contract. I have no idea what's going on right now, but we must rise to meet it. Our eyes must remain open now." Armadis rolled back his sleeve, his hand outstretched to Lance. His flesh was taut and grey, pockmarked with livid scars. "The Circle needs to know immediately. The Keidan cannot stand apart any longer. I like it not, but it seems we have no choice. You proved me wrong. I, Armadis, High Keeper of the Keidan, accept this allegiance against our enemies."

"Will you consent then, to us gaining the Aegis Mora?" Tyir chimed in coldly. "It's the only way to stop all of this."

With a snort of mirthless laughter. Armadis extended his other hand to Tyir. "I'll approach the council. Gatekeeper, Trader. Altair and our Master Vorstren himself will all hear our call. They have to, I feel, after what happened today." The battle had changed Armadis' opinion of them completely. "I will do what I can. Scars of Tyir, Ironhearts of Lance. Let this triad mark our alliance today."

Their hands clasped together, the ring complete, as the sound of birdsong rang through the forest. Lance glanced up just in time to see a group of white ravens wheel across the sky. The easy goal had been achieved today, he thought. *But now, the true fight begins.*

CODEX

The Balian Empire – Dominant power on Harloph. Its war with the Selpvian Dominion of Klassos has brought it to its knees, forcing a military coup that conspires to unleash the Counterbalance.

The Selpvian Dominion – Largest power of Klassos. Five long years of war with its greatest rival Bawsor has bled both forces dry after the Dominion's alleged assassination of Empress Adriena.

Kingdom of Beiridge – A destroyed kingdom of Klassos that sided with the Empire during the first years of the war.

The Whisperers – Espionage organization in the Whisper Isles off the east coast of Harloph. Origin unknown.

The Pharos Order – Religious "survivors" of New Valia, founded after their namesake. Allied with the Empire. Made up of three major factions; the Sepulcher, Bawsor and the Kahal.

The Barta League – A series of neutral trading cities in the east of Harloph. Prior to the Great War, they enjoyed a lucrative and profitable alliance with both Bawsor and the Dominion.

Faxia – A mountainous tribal people in Western Harloph. Their trade is volcanic glass, unique to Harloph. A poor but barbaric land, Faxians have never been conquered by an invading power.

Voyava – The remains of New Valia, where old traces of Valian magic remain. Voyava is known for its religious prophets who can see into the world, called "Oracles". A pacifist people, but capable of mustering great power.

The Keidan – A religious, feared sect in Harloph, rumored to be the last pure Valian settlers. They take on acolytes for training, many of whom are converted to the faith of their goddess.

Uslor – Once part of the Bale Empire, it is now an independent power fraught with internal fighting and brutal barons.

Kahal – In the centre of Harloph, a rich and populous land torn by internal strife and the Order's violent occupation. Victim of several major wars, including the Voyavan prophet Telijin and the seat of Pharos priest Antoch Kramer.

Skyini – A multitude of clans living in relative comfort east of Yurn, sandwiched between Kahal and the Gaolian Mountains. Powerful and dangerous, they command a large professional army despite their tribal status, and have evaded servitude to Bawsor.

Vence – A protectorate of Bawsor, they enjoy relative autonomy, but keep up tax payments to the Empire in exchange for protection. Keeps a control over the old lands of the Empire where it was forced to withdraw from overextension. Depends heavily upon the Stewards of the South for military support.

The Harbonlands – A strip of territory hotly disputed between Bawsor, the Pharos Order and Kahal, a mesh of villages, towns and strongholds where fighting is rife for control of the rich lands.

The Keepers of Yurn – A Pharos financed organization that safe keeps the battered ruins of Sirquol, the last resting place of New Valia. Peaceful and religious designed to guard the legacy of Pharos, who saved the world during the Chaos

Tarantown – Pilgrim city, home to the heritage site where Harloph men and Valia signed the "Bloroc Pact" to defend themselves.

Irene – Poorest nation of Harloph and the birthplace of Tyir. Centuries of war and famine makes this a harsh place, with many tribes trying to emigrate north leading to much bloodshed with the Keepers, Kahal and Skyini.

The Dustons – Originally one of the Great Houses, they were exiled during the War of Mercer's Folly.

The Ironhearts – Originally a Beridgian mercenary company, they join Bawsor diplomat Lance Ironheart following the death of their leader Gollet Longspear.

Pyra – The "Bow and Sail", a small coastal nation to the far west of Klassos. The finest archers in the known world, made of the mystical stelwood tree.

The Thousand Scars – A mercenary organization founded by Tyir of Irene. Arch enemies of the Pharos Order.

Characters

The Aldmer Conspiracy
Bane Aldmer – De-facto Emperor of the Empire. Commander in Chief of the Imperial Army.

Carris Montague – Second in Command, Justiciar and Master of Law and Punishment.

Long Brandon – Keeper of Coin.

Hardenne – Childhood friend of Aldmer. Pacifist and realist. Chief Senator.

Petere Cordon – Head of the Imperial Office.

Pierad Cordon – Brother of Petere. Second-in-command of Imperial Office.

Mitori – Faxaen and Keeper of Swords.

Augustin Teminzar – Keeper of Ships.

Raphael Garro – Leader of the Pharos branch in Bawsor. Key to the "Counterbalance" conspiracy. Mentor of Bane Aldmer.

Valare
Lazarus – Jaal of the city. Ex-Pharos agent. Protector of Tyir.

Piez Vertigen – Official leader of Valare.

Tai Cassel – Master of the Keep Guard.

Tyir of Irene – Commander of the Thousand Scars, fugitive, alchemist, healer and necromancer. Highly respected by the populace for his talents, but secretly funds terrorism against the Pharos Order.

Tyrone Cessil – Exiled son of House of Cessil. Ex-scholar turned soldier.

Penor – Commander of the Mer Hammers Company. Mercenary.

Sil, Quinn and Loch – Ambassadors of the Pharos Order.

Oman – Friend of Tyrone.

Jeramine – Friend of Tyrone.

The Great Houses of the Balian Empire

House of Cessil – Stewards of the West. Power seat of Vern. Subordinate houses under Cessil: Deem, Fennick, Bywater, Hallem, Sandwater and Curn.

Nazir Cessil – Owner of the House of Cessil.
Adane Nesseton – Housecarl and protector of Nazir's household.
Vivian Cessil – Nazir's wife, matriarch of Vern.
Tomea Cessil – Tyrone's younger brother,
Keir Cessil – Heir to Vern. Tyrone's older brother.

House of Mance – Stewards of the North. Power Seat of Martown. Subordinate houses under Mance: Colby, Stanton, Bentvure, Montague, Teminzar, Ironheart and Grentia.

Arban Mance – Old Patriarch of the House of Mance.
Carr Mance – Arban's son.

House of Thendil – Stewards of the South. Safeguards the border between the Empire and the protectorate states of Vence and the Harbonlands. Their lands border the Kahal and Skyini. Power Seat of Manacul. Subordinate Houses under Thendil: Jarman, Roach, Anquee, Might, Throe, Naroon.

Gilbert Thendil – Steward of the House of Thendil.
Randyll Thendil – Front Sword of House of Thendil.

House of Bael – Stewards of the East. The House of Bael rules over the largest stretch of land in the Empire of the Great Houses, and as such commands the largest armies. Power Seat of Causco. Subordinate

Houses under Bael: Goslor, Lovell, Solsa, Keera, Hasting, Carel, Irina, Tallert, Wallace.

Valerie Bael – Matriarch of House of Bael.

The Pharos Order
Hinari Amos – Supreme Father of the Pharos Order, leader of the Sepulcher.
Raphael Garro – Leader of the Pharos branch in Bawsor. Key to the "Counterbalance" conspiracy. Mentor of Bane Aldmer.
Antoch Kramer – Leader of the Pharos branch in the Kahal.

The Thousand Scars
Horse – Pyran mercenary. Befriends Tyrone almost immediately. Close friend of Sleeper.
Sleeper – Ex-Jebatu cultist. Young and talented assassin and poisoner.
Ombrone – Irenian pirate.
Meira – A "walking dead". Technically dead and living.
One-Hundred-Jaques – Kahal rogue. Musician.
Rapier – First Soldier of the Keidan, defects to Tyir. Technically Undead due to his ties to the Stem. The most powerful of Tyir's swordsmen.
Jackal – Kahal mercenary. Brave and foul-mouthed, loves fighting.
Tounge-Kin – Uslorian prince gone rogue, a veteran of the civil war.
Iron Dog – Mentioned only by name. In the Kahal gathering forces. Looked on with scorn by the others for his tardiness.
Sybill of Bawsor – Balian born citizen, fled after a life of poverty and murder.

The Ironhearts
Lance Ironheart – Diplomat, wealthy businessman and reluctant leader of the Ironheart mercenary army
Isran Reus – First of the Triad who commanded the Ironhearts with Gollet Longspear.
Slanos Roach – Second of the Triad.
Fortescue – Third of the Triad.
Krause Volen – Youngest commander of the Ironhearts.
Combrey – Soldier and junior officer.
Iris – Young recruit from Harbonlands.
Brayson Toney – Leader of Tarantown.

The Keidan
Little Bird – Recruiter and spy for the Keidan.
Armadis – High Keeper of the Keidan.
The Eldar Circle – The elite members who run the Keidan's vast operations.
Vorstren – Nameless Eighty and Father of the Keidan.
Altair – Chieftess. Keen to destroy the Pharos Order. Leader of the growing revolt.
Soul – The "Trader" and recruiter.
Gatekeeper – The All-Seer and Oracle of the Keidan.

ABOUT THE AUTHOR

Michael R. Baker studied history at the University of Sunderland. He began writing the Counterbalance series after growing bored during a long bus ride. Michael is an avid video gamer, and writes an extensive blog about his favorite games. Alongside his passion for world building, writing and gaming, he also creates maps, bringing his own fantasy world, as well as other peoples', to cartographic life.

The Thousand Scars is Michael's first novel, and is the first of an epic fantasy series.

NORDLAND PUBLISHING
Follow the North Road.

nordlandpublishing.com
facebook.com/nordlandpublishing
nordlandpublishing.tumblr.com

NORDLAND

www.nordlandpublishing.com

Printed in Poland
by Amazon Fulfillment
Poland Sp. z o.o., Wrocław